SPACEPORT GAIL

Jim Stein

Space-Slime Continuum

Planet Fred
Spaceport Gail
Yule be Slimy

Also by Jim Stein:

Magic Trade School

The Heartstone Chamber
The Silver Portal
The Forgotten Isle

Legends Walk Series
(Urban fantasy meets Native American lore)

Strange Tidings
Strange Omens
Strange Medicine
Strange Origins

This book is a work of fiction. Names, characters, places, and events are purely fictitious and stem from the author's imagination. Any resemblance or similarity to actual people, places, and events is purely coincidental.

Digital ISBN: 978-1-954788-05-3
Print ISBN: 978-1-954788-06-0

First printing, 2022

Jagged Sky Books
P.O. Box #254
Bradford, Pa 16701

Cover art by Katie Stein
Cover design by Kris Norris
Edited by Caroline Miller

Acknowledgements

Thanks once again to my beta readers, editor, cover artists, launch team, and you, the reader. Without your help and support, Nancy and Reemer would still be languishing on their respective homeworlds.

Visit https://JimSteinBooks.com/subscribe to get a free eBook, join my reader community, and sign up for my infrequent newsletter full of writerly news, book deals, and bonus material.

1. Boiling Point

A MASSIVE LOBSTER scuttled across the Senate floor, approached the podium, and cleared his throat.

Chowder, corn on the cob, mac and cheese. Nancy forced her thoughts away from the image of a New England feast.

"The order of law deteriorates with every new amendment." The Lobstra gurgled the remarks in his bubbling language, the words as angry and sullen as his burgundy shell. "The royal line may be gone, but ruling by committee is preposterous. We cannot have governance of our empire influenced by outsiders, by *humans*."

Merrick, speaker for the matriarch, waved his thick battle claw at Nancy. A standard translator would have relayed the strange rolling language without the insult, but a hiss of outrage from around the chamber spoke to the nascent government's displeasure.

Thoughts of dipping this guy in melted butter heated her face, which would have the freckles along her nose blossoming to life. She might have made a few suggestions, but Merrick was an insufferable ass. He'd been a lackey for the empress, and now took every opportunity to block progress. Nancy had a close rapport with several of the ruling council and considered them friends. Merrick was not. Her blush deepened as she struggled with another image of having the speaker to a picnic. *Stupid brain.*

The Lobstra were an intelligent spacefaring race that resembled their namesake. They were much larger than terrestrial lobsters, averaging five feet tall with shell colors ranging from ocean blues to sunset reds and everything in between. The species was perfectly capable of breathing air, although scattered Luddite pockets preferred keeping to the oceans.

The race had been trapped under their supreme matriarch for over a thousand years thanks to a life-prolonging elixir. When that source dried up, the old crone had quickly followed, leaving a power vacuum in the empire. Emerging Lobstra politics grew prickly, intertwined with the remnants of the prior rule of law and the pervasive religion that revered randomness.

"Dr. Nancy Dickenson acts only as a consultant to facilitate negotiations." The big, blue-shelled fellow to her right let his bubbling voice carry, but kept a relaxed posture, his thick, articulated tail a counterbalance to the half-dozen spindly white legs supporting his torso. "None of the other races, not even humans, have influenced the measures we debate."

Herman patted her leg with his narrow cutting claw in a show of support. She'd met the big guy years ago on her very first interstellar mission with the navy. Herman had been an apprentice training for the venerated position of searcher. He'd gone through a kind of crisis of faith at the time, and his moderate views grew quite popular after the matriarchy fell.

At thirty-three, the botanist had also come away from their disastrous adventure with a widened perspective and a significant new skill. A skill that Nancy had grown and cultivated during the past five years. A skill that now told her Merrick was up to no good.

"He's going to push that agenda despite the facts." She puzzled at the vibrating hairs around the speaker's mandibles. Even the spines along his forelegs shivered as if in anticipation.

"Truth by contest!" Merrick's battle claw jabbed toward her again, its meaning all too clear.

The room exploded into bedlam as representatives of the new government shouted at one another.

"Impossible!" Herman surged to his feet. "A human can't survive our combat."

Nancy felt small—was small—as she sat next to the irate Lobstra. She looked to the crystal dome overhead, to the sea of eyestalks tracking the handful of principals below as the argument raged on. The proceedings convened under a theater-in-the-round with Lobstra dangling from harnesses or picking their way upside-down along feathery walkways overhead.

Red sunlight filtered through the dome, casting surreal shadows across the open floor surrounding the central podium. Vestibules for council members ringed the area she'd expected to be crowded with spectators. But as Merrick stripped off the gold sash of his defunct matriarch, clacked his battle claw, and dropped into a fighting stance, she recognized the open space for what it was—an arena.

Herman hurried over and launched into hushed conversation with the council chair, while Nancy pondered the path that had led to this inauspicious moment.

Since the ill-fated mission to planet Fred, her command of language—all languages—had blossomed. Telepathic aliens had infected Nancy with the ability that continued to shape her life. Her career had shifted in response, moving from botanist to interpreter, arbitrator, and finally cultural advisor.

She'd initially shunned the navy, taking odd jobs with the vagabonds that befriended her on the strange world. Things had gone well for a time. But her burgeoning psychic "gift" made interpersonal relationships difficult—especially when Jake fell for her in a big way. She'd liked the young technician well enough, still did. He was a wonderful man regardless of the age difference. But as fun as their year together had been, Jake's feelings grew deeper than her own and were written across his face and in countless little gestures.

Jake and others from the expedition had "caught" the psychic ability to communicate. Even years later, most of the crew could still pick up an alien language on the fly. But their abilities had plateaued or faded, whereas her own continued to grow. Having no secrets—especially when the ability was one-way—made dating hard.

Letting Jake go had been more difficult than she'd imagined, but he deserved someone who could reciprocate his love. Nancy would focus on what she did best.

The navy had taken her back into the fold, offering ambassadorial training ranging from cultural dynamics to personal defense. Turning down a commission left her as a free agent. Consultants got to pick and choose their assignments until their obligation was repaid. Helping Herman negotiate the Lobstra's constitution was an easy win that let her visit old friends while earning credits and paying down her training debt. All of which brought her to the current predicament.

Residual pockets of matriarch supporters like Merrick violently resisted change. They still claimed to follow Lady Luck, the revered Lobstra deity who created their universe. But the extremists openly fought against efforts to codify a way forward for their floundering society. Their plan was to simply let random events chart the course.

Nancy much preferred Herman's interpretation. Lady Luck might cast the final die, but encouraged and rewarded those who worked hard to stack the odds in their favor. In some ways she supposed that was what Merrick's crowd was doing, except their obstructionism largely focused on a return to the oppressive dictatorship that had held the Lobstra stagnant for over a millennium.

"Okay, here's the deal." Herman returned out of breath, every line of his posture broadcasting unease. "Merrick has invoked the old ways. With so many eyes watching, the council cannot ignore this request."

"Let me guess." Nancy looked to where Merrick waited in the arena. "A fight to the death?"

"It might as well be," Herman said. "A contestant concedes when they've lost two legs or a main claw. Uncomfortable, but hardly debilitating."

"Maybe not for *you*!" Lobstra could regrow the thin white legs along their underbelly. Even the two primary claws used for crushing and cutting would eventually regenerate, though that would take significantly longer.

"I argued on your behalf, and the chair is willing to grant one weapon to account for your physical…inequities." The feelers around his mouth turned down in the Lobstra equivalent of a grimace. "I know it's insane. Just decline. We can pick up the equality amendment next session."

"That amendment is the basis for everything else on this year's agenda. If the council doesn't acknowledge Lobstra with differing views and religious beliefs as fully-vested citizens, most of your other measures will get tabled—maybe thrown out for good. Some new upstart matriarch will be in power before you know it."

She thought back to Drissa, Wispa, and all the others who'd made the ultimate sacrifice for their people. If things spiraled, Lobstra like them and Herman wouldn't have a say in the new government. History was chock-full of critical junctures where individuals were called upon to step up for what mattered. Strangely enough, hindsight was rarely about those individuals. Those who rose to the challenge were often ignored by the records, the pivotal event less noticeable for having been nudged in the right direction. When someone walked away and things went sideways, eyes fell on the catastrophe more than the missed opportunity. Drissa and the others deserved to have someone fight for their right to believe.

"The weapon choices suck." Herman's frown deepened at Nancy's resolve. "A short-handled spear, a pole staff, or amputation shears. The shears at least act like a cutting claw, but they're for medical use and have zero reach. This isn't your fight, Nancy."

"It is if we want to keep the gains we've made."

2. Missed Calling

"HE'LL USE HIS weight to bowl you over. Don't let him." Herman took on the role of coach when he couldn't talk her out of fighting.

Merrick wasn't the largest Lobstra Nancy had ever seen. At a head shorter than her, it was easy to forget how much mass the aliens carried. Most would outweigh a professional wrestler.

Nancy nodded as she stripped the outer coat off her ceremonial uniform. The navy preferred form over function. The ornate twin tails with glimmering gold piping were constantly in the way, not a big problem for desk work, but she didn't need them tripping her up in a fight. The fitted top and high-waisted pants beneath would do, as would the sturdy synthetic boots.

"The flipper legs on the underside of his tail are weakest and still count. If you can get behind him, a single slice will probably take at least two and end the contest. Just be sure to cut above the first joint."

The rules were simple but barbaric. A leg or claw removed above the lowest joint would count. Human knuckles fell into a gray area. They were certainly joints, which meant that she could technically get away with losing a couple of fingers or toes. But her opponent's cutting claw measured a good two feet long—slim compared to the crushing battle claw on his left arm, but unlikely to be precise enough to snip just the tip off a finger. Not that Nancy planned to let him try.

She hefted the short spear, testing its balance. The pole would have been better to keep her opponent at bay but didn't have the cutting edge needed to win. What she held resembled a sturdy duster with the feathers tickling her forearm and an eight-inch serrated blade curving from the business end.

Most Lobstra tools and controls ended in wispy arrangements that were easy to grip with the delicate pincers of the forelegs. When piloting, Herman reminded her of a piano virtuoso as his thin, white legs danced across the hairy controls. The array of colored tufts sprouting from his cockpit always brought a smile because the panel looked like a sea of old-Earth troll dolls. But Nancy wasn't smiling now.

"Here goes nothing." Tucking the jaunty blue tuft of the spear against her forearm got it out of the way, but cut the weapon's reach down to two feet.

"Whatever you do, don't let him pin you down."

Herman stepped aside, and Nancy followed the railing to where it spilled out into the central area. According to Herman, entering the arena signaled her acceptance and the start of the contest.

She expected Merrick to rush forward and gamble on a quick win. But only his eyestalks moved, tracking Nancy as she skirted the perimeter. Both of his claws were raised, stretching above his long antennae in what she presumed was a pose calculated to intimidate. Then again, it may have been a ruse to draw her close. Merrick displayed his white underbelly, delicate arms crooked at ninety degrees with pincers open. One swift swipe of the spear would end this.

But she'd seen Lobstra fight. The species was fast. Those raised claws would slice down before her short weapon was in range. Merrick's position put his back to the podium and protected his tail. Nancy reversed course, circling the other direction.

The navy had incorporated martial arts and army hand-to-hand combat into her training. She was by no means an expert, but the common principles of keeping her center of balance while trying to use her opponent's movements against them still applied—except that her opponent refused to move.

With an exasperated huff, Nancy attempted to slide in under his guard and go for the exposed legs. The feint raised the spines along Merrick's mandible a split second before his battle claw smashed down. He'd been aiming for her head. That claw weighed a good thirty pounds and would have dazed if not killed her outright. But at least he moved.

Instead of swinging for his legs, Nancy jabbed the spear straight up as she rolled to the right, catching the underside of the descending claw on the blade. A grunt ripped from her, and the shaft slammed to the ground. A grating crunch told her the blade had pierced the shell. She yanked it free and rolled away from the cutting claw that shot at her neck. Her head wasn't an extremity she was willing to lose!

"Too slow, chowder-head." Bubbling Lobstra syllables accompanied the words thanks to her unique translation ability.

Merrick didn't even spare a glance for the small hole in his claw, but the taunt had him scuttling forward in a fit of rage. *Bingo!* One of her instructors had reveled in provoking opponents, but the woman had been a consummate artist in the ring and used the tactic to help get stalled fights going so she could kick butt. Nancy's use bordered on desperation. She needed Merrick off guard and making mistakes if she was to have any chance of surviving.

Her own mistake became obvious as the massive crustacean barreled forward. The Lobstra was too damned fast. A quick kick off to one side turned what would have been a crushing grip from the battle claw into a glancing blow that had her sliding across the polished floor on her stomach. Her boots squeaked as she scrambled to her feet, fought off a wave of dizziness, and braced for the follow-up blow.

But her opponent didn't corner well. His legs scrabbled at the smooth stone as Merrick skated past, carried by his own momentum. Herman had mentioned the dangerous footing, but the slick surface designed to keep Lobstra battles from turning overly aggressive worked to her advantage.

The rubber soles of her boots had plenty of traction, and Nancy found herself playing matador with the irate Lobstra as she alternately called out insults and danced away. The poor guy couldn't catch a break when it came to solid footing. A grin stretched her mouth as her short dark hair whipped back and forth with each maneuver. It wasn't even fair, like someone on solid ground fighting a giraffe wearing roller skates on ice. All she had to do was wait for a shot at his tail. She almost felt sorry for the bastard.

Her next dodge came a moment too late, and that beefy battle claw closed over the shaft of the spear. Merrick slid on past, wrenching Nancy off to the side and nearly dislocating her shoulder before she managed to let go.

Merrick gave a whiskery grin as he held up his prize. She wouldn't be getting that spear back anytime soon. Dashing away turned the contest into more chase than fight. She cast about for another weapon. An experimental tug on the beefy stanchion supporting the railing did no good. The composite material was firmly anchored.

She could probably yank the microphone loose from the podium, not that the fist-sized chunk of plastic would be of much use. A sharp left kept her well clear of a slice from that cutting claw, but Nancy found herself tiring. Without a weapon, there was no way to win unless Merrick decided to stand still while she yanked off a couple of legs with her bare hands.

A blue puffball flashed past. Merrick still gripped her spear. Battle claws were designed for holding and crushing. If the polished shaft of her weapon was strong enough and Merrick didn't toss it out of the arena, she might be able to scoop it up when he dropped it—except he never did.

Even catcalls and suggestions that he couldn't hit the broad side of a barn didn't entice the guy to hurl the spear. It was almost as if he physically couldn't drop the thing. Myths about moray eels back home flitted through her head. Inexperienced divers warned that once an eel bit down it never released its prey.

The Lobstra seemed to possess a similar instinct, some reflex in the claw that didn't let it release her spear. Nancy might not have to worry about being crushed by the battle claw, but it still made a formidable wrecking ball.

Merrick's flailing would have been comical if it wasn't so deadly. He reoriented on her again and again. Nancy managed to grab the feathered end of the spear from behind, staying beyond reach of his cutting claw. She tugged hard, felt the weapon shift, and with a mighty crack the shaft splintered. She came away with two feet of wood. The cutting edge clattered to the floor. More by luck than intent, Merrick kicked the blade, sending it off to the far side of the arena.

Nancy bit back a curse as her chance at victory spun away. She'd have to dodge a few more blows and go retrieve the spear tip. But the chances of using the weapon effectively at close range were miniscule, especially with that battle claw free. A satisfied grin turned up his mandible whiskers as if she'd done him a favor. Nancy backed to one of the heavy stanchions enclosing the arena. The vibrating spines along Merrick's throat telegraphed his grab. She held her ground this time, determined to put an end to things as the battle claw thrust forward.

Three, two, one.

Nancy dropped onto her butt a second too late as the claw shot over her head. Pain sliced across her scalp as the rough surface tore out a clump of dark hair on its way past. The claw hit the station square on with a mighty clang. Rocky teeth lining the claw clamped down, denting the thick railing, but the pole held. And, as she'd hoped, Merrick didn't let go.

The Lobstra gurgled and grunted, trying to spin around to face her. He couldn't exert much force on the rail thanks to the slippery floor. The cutting claw flailed wildly, but Nancy kept out of reach behind his left shoulder.

She imagined the board breaking demonstration all students had been required to perfect. Stupid for a self-defense class. Nobody was going to attack you with a board, let alone hold it still for you to kick. The stunt was a crowd pleaser she'd never thought practical—until now.

Nancy found her center and lashed out with her right leg, toes back so that the ball of her foot impacted the rotating joint connecting Merrick's arm to his carapace. She aimed for the railing on the far side, kicking through her target. The joint gave way like a splintering tree branch. She yanked her foot back snake fast and danced to the side.

Merrick blinked at his arm, battle claw still clutching the stanchion. Twitching white meat dangled from the narrow break where the appendage had been severed. It took him a moment to realize he was free. The Lobstra spun around and dropped forward. With all legs on the floor, the big alien only came up to her waist.

"I concede." His antennae drooped in submission as clicking erupted from overhead—the Lobstra equivalent of whooping cheers.

Merrick refused the hand Nancy offered, pushed upright, and left the floor without another word. Lobstra didn't feel pain the same as humans. His defeat hurt more than the injury. Merrick's claw would regrow in a few months, but the look he shot from those tilting eyestalks said this was far from over. She may have salvaged the current round of negotiations, but at what cost?

Even with Merrick's withdrawal from the proceedings, there were still enough of the old guard left to cause problems. Over the next few days, those individuals stymied proceedings with passive-aggressive tactics ranging from frequent calls for recess to wild assertions of fact that had little to do with the statutes under consideration—anything to derail the council's deliberations.

But progress still reigned. By the end of the week, alliances had been formed, compromises made, and the Lobstra's shiny new constitution rolled out to the masses. Little would change in the short term, but the society finally had a stable base from which to move forward.

Lobstra already possessed a unique spin on hover technology that Earth Force was keen to leverage. How far ahead of the other races would they have been if the prior regime had let people work to their full potential?

Mixed feelings warred within Nancy as Herman stepped through the dedication ceremony with the council. Her final report that had been so well received by headquarters left her at loose ends. She'd said her goodbyes, but hadn't found a new mission calling for her special skills.

This would be a good time to get the ship in for that life-extension overhaul Herman kept harping on. Unfortunately, her navy stipend wouldn't cover being grounded for three months. At some point she'd have to call in yet another favor from Jake to keep the second-hand relic space-worthy.

"Excuse me, ma'am." A young Lobstra with a green-edged shell approached. He fidgeted with his forelegs and seemed unable to meet her gaze. "It's your ship."

"What about my ship?" She kept her voice soft so as not to spook the nervous fellow. The tool belt slung low on his thorax marked him as dock maintenance.

"Well…it's barking."

3. Blast from the Past

L OBSTRA DIDN'T HAVE dogs, but barking was an apt description for the sharp notes ringing through the hangar. Nancy's security system might not be elegant, but the ship's computer did its best to get her attention when something important cropped up. In addition to her guide, two other dock workers glared over their wraparound panel and pointed from her ship to the ceiling as if ready to use the overhead crane to drag the annoying craft outside.

Instead of the regal, sonorous declaration of a Great Dane, her craft let out the high-pitched yips of a neurotic pup. Nancy sighed as the tone subsided, then winced at another burst of yapping. A headache settled behind her left eye. She gave the rest of the hangar crew a wave of apology and headed for her vessel.

Six Lobstra low-orbit transports and a row of hover sleds sat placidly in their assigned zones, ignoring her ship's tantrum. Her ride would be svelte compared to the squat people haulers if it wasn't for the outer radiation hull and tangle of vestigial antennas that left it looking like a puffer fish had mated with a radio station.

Working with the Lobstra on and off for the last few years came with perks, the biggest being use of the old interstellar explorer. By the time the locals had adapted the ship for a human crew, Herman argued that they might as well turn it over to Nancy permanently. The ship was barely hyperspace capable, a blocky eyesore, and all hers.

With some arm twisting, her navy superiors had agreed to her traveling without escort—contingent on a host of safety upgrades and installation of robotics to handle piloting and in-flight emergencies. She'd completed the interstellar piloting course and logged hundreds of simulator hours, but mostly just sat at the controls and let the ship's artificial intelligence do the heavy lifting.

"Give me a minute," Nancy called out between yipping fits.

The over-eager techs already had the crane in motion, but her young guide scurried over to buy more time. Nancy slammed her hand on the access panel, let it sample her prints and DNA, and entered.

Like the controls, the access pad had been adapted for human physiology. Passing the naval inspection came with a host of upgrades, but a significant laundry list of other improvements—that she might eventually be able to afford—remained on file.

A short passageway to the bridge passed by three staterooms with rounded iris doors that reminded her of giant camera shutters. At five two, Nancy just fit through the doors without crouching. The low ceilings made for a comfy nest on long trips, despite the human technicians' constant bitching about sore necks when they'd been giving her ship the once over. At least the navy inspectors had realized that adding overhead clearance to the passageways wasn't a practical improvement.

As if to make up for the lack of height, the engine room at the far end of the passage was wide and sparse. Even early Lobstra Faster-Than-Light technology appeared elegant compared to FTL-equipped human ships. Like so much of the small craft, engine management and navigation were fully automated to handle interstellar travel. Adapting more stringent engine shutdown parameters had been the only mandatory change behind the rear blast doors.

"Silence alarm," Nancy ordered as she cycled open the door to her bridge.

The yipping cut off mid-bark. A standard bank of navy controls blanketed the forward bulkhead in front of a pair of padded swivel seats. The long, narrow graphics panel at eye level could be configured to provide a viewport and display systems status. An auxiliary panel off to the side sprouted a colorful sea of wispy Lobstra controls. Herman had used those controls to familiarize Nancy with the old ship on live training flights.

"Ship, what's going on?"

"Emergency message requires attention." The mechanical voice held little inflection.

A rippling green blob dominated the screen above the controls. Scraping and popping filled the small room, followed by the electronic screech of feedback. Nancy played with the controls, but the problem was on the other end.

The blob pulled back, autofocus bringing the outline into a quavering mass with undulating sides. Two stubby antennae rose from a bulbous, glistening head. Liquid brown eyes set in the tips of each stalk squinted into the camera.

"Am I on?" The bubbling, flatulent voice was muffled music to Nancy's ears.

"Reemer!" Her translation ability had no problem with the Squinch language, but sea slugs were not the most tech savvy of races. "The transmission is garbled. Any chance you're leaning on the mic?"

She waited a good ten seconds for the question to make its way across space. All but the most expensive interstellar communications imposed an awkward tempo of transmit-wait-receive thanks to the distances and technologies involved.

"What? Oh this?" Reemer pulled further back from the lens, revealing the four-foot slug in all his gooey glory. A great squelching reverberated through the communications panel, the interference subsiding as though she'd surfaced from underwater. From undulating skirt to eye stalks and everything in between, Squinch were amorphous denizens of the deep that became fifty percent slime on land. A pair of secondary, prehensile antennae just below the neck were surprisingly dexterous.

"Can you hear me now?" Reemer yelled into the silence.

"No need to shout." Nancy slapped down the volume control. "Reading you clear and *very* loud. You look frazzled. What's up?"

Most people wouldn't have noticed the lighter blotches of green beneath his slime coat. Patches of dirty yellow like the fringes of an overripe banana tinged the upper edge of Reemer's skirt. The predominant pea-green coloration meant Reemer was in his male form. Pus-yellow slugs were female. Her friend's mixed palette suggested a gender reversal might be in the works.

"The sky, clouds, a few flying seedlings. It's *that* time again." He listed off several more things, deliberately misinterpreting the question. Reemer's translation ability had faded less than most and would certainly have let him understand simple human expressions. He cut the list short with an angry wave as though Nancy was wasting time. "That's not important right now. We're in trouble here. Come now before all is lost. I need—"

His head oozed around to look over what passed for his right shoulder, the tiny mouth at the end of his fleshy beak forming a little O at whatever had caught his attention.

Another dozen "mouths" under the flexible skirt Squinch used for locomotion produced the bulk of the species' vaguely nauseating vocabulary—as well as a host of questionable secretions. Reemer's voice came through in rich 3D like a flatulent calliope from old-world carnivals. His twisting antennae telegraphed acute distress bordering on panic.

"Calm down and start from the beginning. What kind of trouble? Something to do with the jungle?"

Reemer's emphasis on "that time" meant the planet's semi-sentient vegetation would be stirring to life as part of its five-year cycle. Squinch were well equipped to avoid the more dangerous plants. The sea slugs usually retreated to their underwater environs. But the navy had left the locals with a shore-based communication suite. The opportunity to conduct business with space-faring races had coaxed the nomadic slugs into communities centered on the new equipment.

Squinch were simple—some would say naïve—folk with few needs. The unaccountably vain mollusks had traded a fortune in rare minerals for a handful of mirrors before humans took an interest in the backwater planet. Ever since her ill-fated visit, Reemer had led the charge on ecologically responsible harvesting of medicinal ingredients from the surrounding forest. Now that planet Fred was formally recognized, off-world raiders no longer poached the potent compounds.

Races across the galaxy vied for rare organics to advance their pharmaceutical offerings. The seller's market put the Squinch in an excellent bargaining position. Nancy's work had kept her away for years, so she'd never managed to pin down what imports the slugs sought in return.

"No!" Reemer's cry came through the comms station as a bubbling hiss. A mighty boom pegged the audio as the wall behind him flexed and buckled, raining down bits of equipment and seashells from the built-in shelving. Two smaller female slugs darted out from behind Reemer, swatting at the roiling flames that had chased them into view. "They're coming." Reemer's left eye filled the screen, while the right eyestalk swiveled frantically, looking for an escape route. "It's the end. Hurry!"

What on Earth was going on over there?

"Who's coming?" Nancy pulled up the ship stats as she barked out the question. Fuel rods were recharged, as were the oxygen reserves. Pending repairs fell under routine maintenance, no show-stoppers. "Reemer, talk to me!"

"They aren't going to like this." The female voice frantic with worry came from off-screen. "The mayor and his wife are dead—"

Feedback and squelching rang from the comms gear, and Nancy grabbed her ears. Gurgling voices tried to cut through the interference, but even her skills couldn't make out words. More wet squeals and the line was clear again.

"The enforcers can't—" Squinch and room tilted, a mighty clang cutting Reemer off.

The camera must have gone over with him, because the scene turned on its side, the screen filling with smoke and flames.

"Damn it, get to the ocean!" She needed supplies, consumables for a round trip, probably extra first aid equipment. "I'll be there in three days. Hang on." Herman would help push her launch paperwork through. Even without it, she'd be in the air by midnight—damn the fines. "You hear me, Reemer? Hang on!"

Licking orange flames exploded into snowy interference, and the ship's screen went dark. No amount of coaxing could reestablish the connection, so she put a call in to Herman. It went to messages. Of course, he'd still be on the council floor.

"Herman, I've got an emergency. Reemer's in serious trouble. I'm headed to planet Fred yesterday and need clearances."

She flagged the message as urgent and cut the call short, knowing he'd break away as soon as possible. She didn't pause to marvel at *how* her psychic ability left intelligible messages. In-person exchanges held more nuances, but the basic faculties of her gift worked well enough through communication gear, thank the goddess.

Look at me, swearing like a local.

That was supposed to be Herman's department. Thanks to his aborted searcher training, the Lobstra knew how to invoke Lady Luck in ways that tended to pay off, to get things done fast. She was counting on that.

"Ship, place an emergency order for supplies and get me a list of available weapons."

"Acknowledged."

Reemer was more than just a friend. The slime-ball was family. *And a survivor*, she reminded herself. He just had to get to safety and have enough sense to lay low until she arrived. Nancy intended to hit Fred fully armed this time. If rogue operatives had attacked the Squinch, had hurt Reemer, there'd be hell to pay.

* * *

"No!" Reemer screamed as thunder pounded the enclosure and the brazier tipped toward Mindy and Churl. The girls slid back smoothly, then turned and attacked the growing flames. Flecks of goo streamed from under their fanning skirts, sizzling across the deck but doing little good.

It was just like the humans to give them a building that caught fire so easily. He kept one eye on Nancy while casting about for the best avenue of retreat. Churl blocked the only exit as she rummaged through the emergency supply station by the door. Wind whipped across the dunes outside as the storm raged on.

Nancy's hair danced like dark seaweed as the woman split her attention between their conversation and her data panel. Her face had narrowed over the years, round cheeks growing angular with high cheekbones looming to either side of that little seashell nose. Her neck and torso had slimmed too, hard muscle replacing the soft and delightfully squishier parts that had been her most redeeming features. Overall she'd grown hard, and—to be honest—a bit ugly. He shuddered at the thought of a lean, trim Squinch. But she was human and his best friend. The worry painted across Nancy's freckled face told him that she'd help.

Another glance showed the floor turning black around the glowing embers. New flames licked up as the material caught. Churl pulled a soft silver packet from the shelf and unfolded it again and again until she was lost in a giant square of material. Her grasping antennae poked the middle of the blanket, but she couldn't get a hold on the slippery surface.

"It's the end. Hurry!" Reemer thrust his tail under the edge of the blanket to help Churl get a grip.

Mindy hurried over to help. The two hoisted the billowing material between them and headed toward the fire. Why would the humans give them a structure that couldn't stand up to a little celebratory barbeque?

The girls should have things under control in a moment, but he still needed to convince Nancy to come back.

"Reemer, talk to me!" Nancy seemed agitated, and he shifted his bulk to block her view of the growing flames.

What had she just asked? With his attention split it was difficult to concentrate. The blanket smothered the flames, but rose like a balloon fish as it heated. The near edge flipped up, sending a wave of flames and heat toward the equipment.

"They aren't going to like this." Churl grabbed at the billowing blanket, but something outside caught her attention. "The mayor and his wife are dead set against this. Their people are heading this way."

Halfway through her statement Reemer slapped the front of his skirt over the microphone. Nancy saw him as a suave and debonair member of society now, a real mover and shaker as the humans would say. She didn't need to know he was in trouble with his parents again. His father might be the mayor, but Mother was the driving force insisting he drop his current pursuits—culinary and otherwise—and finish transitioning for the ceremony. Yellow flushed along his skirt at the thought.

Three beefy males oozed across the wet beach outside, oblivious to the raging storm that had driven his friends and him indoors with the homemade grill. Mother had sent her finest to drag him off to the preparations.

"Just get that fire under control." Reemer told the girls as he shifted around for a better view outside. "The enforcers can't—"

The microphone housing clung to his skirt, dragging the portable communication tripod off to the side. It canted dangerously and crashed to the floor. The camera fell into the flames and winked off with a whoosh and sputter.

"Nancy, you still there?" Reemer hauled the melted camera out of the fire by a trailing wire.

The indicator light over the lens had gone dark, but the speaker set in the middle of the tripod crackled to life with his friend's panicked voice.

"Damn it, get to the ocean!" Nancy's shout crackled with static. "I'll be there in three days. Hang—"

The transmission went dead. He ran an antenna over speaker and camera, poking at the controls. *Nothing.* The automated repair bots would have to get the equipment up and running—again.

Reemer reviewed the brief conversation. He'd never really gotten to tell Nancy why he needed her. Maybe that was for the best. It gave him time to figure out how to frame his request, but time was getting short.

Mother wanted her daughter to be the star of this year's celebration. The woman's sheer willpower seemed to have initiated Reemer's gender shift, but he had no intention of letting *the change* run its course or of participating in the mating ceremony. There was so much more to do with life. He wasn't about to get tied down with babies and abandon his progress.

Churl and Mindy intercepted Mother's enforcers at the door after stomping out the fire and righting the brazier he'd made from an old shipping cask. The half-cylinder *looked* like the barbeque grills from human vids, but the branches supporting the main drum had burnt off and dumped the hot coals. That wouldn't have been a problem if the storm hadn't forced them inside.

He looked to the neat stack of cracker squares, fluffy little pillows, and oddly sweet sheets of human candy. The soggy ingredients had cost him dearly during the last trading cycle, but he was determined to introduce his people to a little culture. Reemer scooped up a cooking stick, skewered a small white pillow, and shoved it over the coals, ignoring the glowering Squinch that were trying to get at him.

Sweet Churl always jumped in on his behalf and now fended off the three bruisers—brains over brawn. The trio balked, rain sheeting off glistening dark-green hides. Sea slugs didn't mind water, but these three seemed plenty angry. Churl's skirt slapped down as she argued, dribbling cute streams of mucus onto the already slick floor. A shiver ran through his skirt—the pheromones talking. *None of that.*

The smoking pillow on the end of Reemer's stick burst into flames. This was the critical moment. *Don't panic—wait for it.* A quick flick extinguished the treat. He slapped the blackened husk and a dark strip of candy between two damp crackers and slid the stick from the gooey mess.

"Who's ready for s'mores?"

4. Planet Fred Retread

T HE REVAMPED CONTROL panel let out a tiny puff of smoke as Nancy cycled through diagnostics. *That can't be good.*

Her ship wasn't big enough to handle kinetic weapon payloads, so the new compliment of toys took a lot of energy.

"I'm telling your AI to dial back the test sequence." Herman's pincers flew across the fuzzy troll hair sprouting from his auxiliary panel. "You really should have an interlock that limits the particle beam output when defensive shields are up. The energy cores on old buckets like this were never designed to handle these kinds of loads."

"I like having options." Nancy hated brushing off his recommendations. Getting through pre-flight checks was paramount, and she wasn't willing to limit herself when flying into the unknown. Weapons safety could always be tightened up once Reemer was safe.

"This computer is a relic." The Lobstra's tail flared in agitation. "Your AI is so rudimentary that I might as well hard code everything. Are you sure you don't want me along to help?"

Nancy sighed. It was a sweet offer, but impractical. Subtle vibrations at the base of Herman's primary feelers were the equivalent of a nervous tic. His council work approached critical mass. As much as her friend wanted to help, he couldn't possibly travel off-world until the new constitution was ratified.

"I'll be fine," Nancy said with more confidence than she felt. "Between the ship's weapons and hand blasters, I'm loaded for bear."

He would hear the word "bear" as a gurgle cut short by a loud click, the Lobstra phrase for a massive predatory squid. Herman gave a sad head bob and went back to work.

"Besides, one of us has to keep an eye on Merrick." She kept her voice light to combat a dark foreboding that swept in whenever her thoughts turned to the one-armed Lobstra. "He and his ilk are up to something. And it's not going to be pretty."

"We'll be ready." Herman's quiet confidence made her smile. Gone was the insecure apprentice. Her friend had finally found his calling.

It took two more hours to ensure the jury-rigged ship was ready for take-off and wouldn't blow up if she turned on the coffee pot. Energy conservation was the name of the game. Her ride wasn't exactly a battle cruiser, but with frugal power management she wouldn't be a floating target either.

Even though the ship hadn't let out a bark all night, the hangar crew seemed entirely too eager as their overhead crane lifted her out onto the launch pad. The surly pair and Herman were the only ones awake in the wee hours to watch the thin plasma trail marking her ascent.

* * *

Except for the boredom, the three-day trip to planet Fred proved uneventful. The ship did tend to shudder and buck when entering and exiting hyperspace, but the craft was as solid as an old farm house. It might groan and sway but would weather what came.

The solitude gave Nancy time to reflect on her career choices, sift through available missions, finish her reports on the Lobstra negotiations, and cultivate a brooding dislike for the ship's artificial personality—or lack thereof.

Artificial Intelligence was ubiquitous, but Nancy had only met one AI with a truly unique personality. Quen—an acronym for Quantum something or other—was the pirated digital entity embedded on the star freighter that had brought other humans to planet Fred. The ship's captain, Veech Gecko, and his technical officer, Jake Farnsley, had helped Nancy. Together, they'd survived the perils of the undeveloped planet while the rest of the crew sought their illicit bounty. Since then, the two had moved beyond shady contracts and established a reputable refit facility near the galactic center. The last she knew, Quen was happily working alongside her friends and planning delusional trysts with the long-suffering captain.

Even Quen's eccentric behavior would be preferable to the sterile interactions with her ship. There had to be a happy middle ground. She'd tried giving the computer a pithy name, but Ziggy remained incapable of casual conversation, let alone exercising any appreciable level of independent thought or awareness.

By the time they arrived at the swirling green orb that was planet Fred, Nancy had given up on coaxing anything more than rudimentary responses from the ship. Getting the system to forego standard landing protocols and not announce their presence to whatever force threatened the Squinch had taken a solid hour of futile arguing. In the end, Nancy was forced to declare an emergency override.

Perhaps she was being paranoid. Sensors showed a massive gathering of Squinch near the communications center. Her equipment wasn't survey quality, and surface scans from low orbit certainly weren't infallible, but she'd expected to find more than indigenous sea life among the intelligent slugs.

Thanks to Fred's jungle producing so many highly-desirable—not to mention addictive—substances, dozens of space-faring races knew of the planet. Though physically and technologically diverse, developmental plateaus divided intergalactic species into three basic groups: planet-bound, space faring, and the ancient "first ones." The rough generalizations rubbed Nancy wrong, especially since she'd spent the better part of her life precisely categorizing plant species and genomes.

Humans themselves fell squarely in the technological lower-middle class of the space-faring crowd, alongside the Lobstra. The latter were likely the oldest space-faring race, but thousands of years of oppression had all but frozen progress in its tracks. Most civilizations with faster-than-light ships had comparable engineering and scientific capabilities. Applied technologies were the discerning factor and varied enough to stimulate healthy trade agreements without any one megalomaniacal species declaring war on the universe.

Not that wars *never* happened. Her navy education included plenty of territorial and cultural disputes, but the delicate balance of power out among the stars tended toward stability. Even with FTL technology, distances were simply too great for most of the races to hold onto their animosity.

Of course, all bets were off when it came to the elusive, ancient races that made an occasional appearance. Her diplomacy instructors didn't know exactly how many "First Ones" were out there. Little was known of the elder races, only that a handful of species had outlived their contemporaries and transcended beyond accepted social and technological limitations. Nancy had yet to find any first-hand accounts of those powerful and elusive beings.

Intelligent as they were, Squinch lived off the land and barely used tools, a far cry from heavily industrialized civilizations and lacking the desire or need to travel off-world. But unwanted visitors could easily be hiding down there among the locals. The navy's declaration of Squinch sovereignty only afforded limited protection across interstellar distances.

Nancy had enough to worry about from standard anti-location tech. She concentrated on the southern continent, the epicenter of Reemer's people, with the greatest concentration of Squinch on the planet. If invaders were shielding their presence, she could be walking into a trap. The secluded inlet left little room for the attackers to hide, but the same was true for Nancy. She settled on landing far enough inland that the massive dunes should hide her approach.

"Take us down quietly, Ziggy. We want to be the cat, not the mouse." She gave the nickname one more shot, but it was a lost cause.

"Dropping out of orbit and initiating landing trajectory." The computer's words were punctuated by the subtle vibration of deceleration. "Please clarify feline-rodent request."

"For crying out loud, just keep thermal and auditory noise below detection thresholds. We want to go in unnoticed."

They used the setting sun to their advantage, staying between it and the beach. Reflective armor or true cloaking capability would have been better, but she worked with the tools at hand.

* * *

Nancy scanned beyond the dunes with ranging binoculars before going in. A hundred yards of open sand stood between her and the flat-roofed communication shack sitting above the waterline. Wind swept the empty beach, stirring up breakers beyond a spit of land that separated frothy sea from calm inlet.

Despite her scans showing several hundred individuals in the area, there wasn't a Squinch in sight. Good. The slugs had taken to the water, which would keep them out of the line of fire. So where was the enemy?

A flash of movement drew her attention, but disappeared behind the comms shack before she got a good.

"Gotcha!" Nancy kept her voice low as she turned to the stoic metal contraption standing behind her. "Ziggy, work your way down to the end of this dune and watch my six. I need to know if anyone's going to jump me."

"Clarify six and—"

A chop of the hand across her neck cut him off. At least the bastard understood rudimentary hand signals. Suddenly, traveling alone across the stars seemed like an exhausting prospect. Dealing with Mr. Literal would be so much easier if her knack for language worked with machines. Instead, she explained what she wanted of the rolling tin-can in gruesome detail, using simple words and sand drawings.

Geesh, she trusted this thing to keep her safe in the vacuum of space? Granted, Ziggy was never programmed to handle terrestrial situations, but it felt like a toddler was watching her back.

Except this little tyke had night vision, percussive sensors, and perfect comms through the neural link in her helmet. The only thing the AI's mobile unit lacked was a weapon. Nancy wasn't *that* trusting.

From the waist up, the many-legged robot reminded her of an animated skeleton. An oversized tin-can head housed its main processor and command linkage with the ship proper, making the skinny little robot an extension of what passed for Ziggy's consciousness. Herman's attempt to humanize the probe had left a Frankenstein arrangement with the spindly central trunk supported above six pairs of Lobstra-like pinchers. He'd done a decent job constructing human hands, fingers, and opposable thumbs. But the supporting appendages basically looked like skeletal arms made from titanium alloy.

Ziggy swayed and scurried into position, elegant in his own way as he dodged the bushy growth along the backside of the dune. Nancy also took care to steer clear of the plants while moving in. You could never be too careful around Fred's vegetation. She'd catalogued enough of the flora to know most plants were harmless, but didn't want to risk stepping on something that bit back.

Nancy hefted her blaster, ensuring it was set on heavy stun and that the more powerful long-gun version strapped to her reactive armor could be quickly unslung. A bandolier across her front held three flat disks, stun grenades. The dark tactical outfit helped her blend into the shadows stretching from the dunes.

She kept the communications shack between her and her quarry, sprinting the last fifty yards in a silent rush. As she drew close, sounds of struggling rose above the whipping wind.

With her back to the wall, Nancy sent a silent query to Ziggy, and got an all clear. Heavy bodies shifted on the far side, punctuated by sloshing water and the meaty thwap of something hitting flesh.

"Ow, stop! No more!" Reemer's voice rose from the far side.

Damn! The little slime-ball hadn't taken to the water after all.

Nancy fingered a stun disk. Neutralizing the threat would have been simpler without her friend in the way. Her combat training had been mainly for self-defense, but the diplomatic branch was no stranger to terrorists. As potential targets, negotiators and emissaries were trained to survive hostage situations. Keeping calm, talking to your captors, and pressing for escape in the first twenty-four hours had been drilled into her. After that, opportunities to get away shrank rapidly. Reemer had been in their clutches for three full days.

Nancy had passed her marksman tests, but was no soldier. The grenade remained her best hope of overpowering multiple assailants. She slipped a disk from its clip, sending up a silent prayer to Lady Luck and wishing she knew who she was up against. The burst of electromagnetic energy would disrupt neural pathways for a short period. Brainwaves in most species operated on similar frequencies, but there were always exceptions. Nancy trusted the helmet's noise cancelling circuit to protect her, drew her blaster, and flipped off the safety.

Clear any remaining threats, then get Reemer out.

Carrying the four-foot-long slug was never a pleasant prospect. He weighed about the same as a large dog—a large, slimy dog. But she ought to be able to make it back to the ship before his captors recovered from the stun grenade. Another wet slap drew gurgling sobs from Reemer.

Here goes nothing. One, two, three—

Nancy rounded the small building and drew back for a throw. Reemer lay half submerged in a raised pool. Two vibrant-yellow Squinch sloshed about in the water, binding his skirt. They used flat vines with decorative flowers, ribbons instead of rope. A massive yellow form rose up beyond the sandy rim and brought a huge rock down on Reemer's head.

"Belinda?" Nancy froze, the grenade sending gentle countdown pulses through her fingers as she tried to process why the mayor's wife would attack her own son.

The rock slammed between Reemer's eye stalks and...deformed, sending a gush of soapy water cascading over her sputtering friend.

Reemer was getting a bath.

"Nancy, darling!" Belinda positively gushed upon spotting Nancy, which included a chorus of flatulent expulsions that left a trickle of goo oozing across the sand. "We haven't seen you in ages. You must be here for Reemer's presentation."

She beamed down in pride at her son. At least Nancy thought Reemer was still male—hard to tell given that thick swirls of yellow infused her friend's hide from skirt to mantle. The folds along the center of his back blazed bright green as if to ward off the coming change.

"Help me." Reemer wheezed out the plea with all his mouths, judging by the bubbles boiling to the surface.

The pool was built from a mound of glistening sand that had no doubt been infused with Squinch secretions to keep its contents from draining away. A harsh vibration had Nancy hastily disarming the stun grenade and slipping it away. Belinda tracked the movement as Nancy sheepishly lowered her blaster and tried to think.

"Um… I came as soon as Reemer called." She glared as Reemer swatted away the helpers decorating his skirt, unable to bring herself to admit out loud she'd been about to flatten them all. "What presentation?"

"Reemer didn't tell you? My little *girl* is finally going to represent the family at this year's mating celebration." Belinda placed a great deal of emphasis on the sounds correlating to "girl," as if issuing a command, even as her eyes softened with pride.

"Well, isn't that…nice?" There was more going on here than met the eye.

"Nice?" Reemer sputtered indignantly. "You try being ripped away from a thriving business and trussed up like some kind of living gift." His skirt flared toward the girls as they moved on and tried to decorate his tail. "And I'm not even a gir—"

Another sponge full of soap cut him short as Belinda scrubbed Reemer's face with enough gusto to rip his antennae off. Reemer fought and squirmed against the cleansing.

"Say, why not let me finish up here?" Nancy did what negotiators did best, offered a compromise. "Just tell me what needs doing. Reemer and I need to catch up on, and I'm sure you have other preparations to attend to."

Nancy had been the first outsider to witness the annual mating ritual, a dubious privilege she'd rather avoid in the future. The multi-day event would have the beach and waters along the inlet writhing with amorous alien slugs. For Squinch the scene was a natural part of life, so she needed to get a handle on what had Reemer so worked up.

Plus, there'd been an ominous undertone when he'd mentioned his thriving business. Her gift tended to turn little inconsistencies like that into earworms that stole sleep. Reemer certainly didn't appear to be in danger at the moment, and the little turd owed her answers. Nancy couldn't wait to hear the story behind his truncated call for help.

5. Super Slug

S 'MORES! SHE'D RACED across the galaxy because Reemer had tried cooking s'mores.

"Why am I not surprised?" Nancy threw in as much wry sarcasm as she could muster. "But what's so urgent?"

Reemer physically ducked the question as he scurried under a low door set in the tunnel. They'd skipped further bathing because he'd insisted on showing off his new-and-improved export operation. Belinda wouldn't be happy about that, but—honestly—a slug could only get so clean.

The underground facility had been carved into a rise at the far end of the inlet where beach gave way to jungle. More than Squinch secretions stabilized the access tunnel. Her university's research department built underground fields for fungus studies using industrial gunite similar to the compound coating the walls, except the base element here looked to be a polymer that shimmered with eerie green luminescence.

The room beyond the doorway opened into a factory floor with storage bins along the exterior walls and a haphazard array of low tables holding sundry tools. Distinct slime trails painted the floor in front of each workstation.

Lights overhead snapped on, throwing the long room into bright contrast.

"This is where the magic happens." Reemer oozed across a plate set in the floor by the door.

A control handle extended up to his feelers, and a sleek hoversled lifted the slug. Reemer waved her aboard and coaxed the alien conveyance out of its docking station.

"Who's paying for all this?" The sled and most of the equipment didn't look like human tech.

"A bunch of different customers." Reemer guided them toward the far end, pointing out various equipment. "Harvesters bring in raw materials, mostly leaves, bark, and flowers critical for the medicine each customer wants to make. We strip off any unwanted plant material, weigh out precise amounts, and package things for shipping." He waved to a bank of ovens along the wall. "Some ingredients get dried. Others need special stabilizers to survive transit. It's a very precise science." He preened, stopped to pick up a long slender tool, and waved it over the translucent hoppers along the top of a rectangular device reminiscent of a 3D printer. "Slicey tools get to the good stuff we feed into the wrapper."

"Be careful with that vibrablade!"

Nancy wrestled the waving tool from his slimy grip, relieved to find the safety still on. Sonic dissection tools were notoriously expensive and dangerous. Cycling the harmonics through different frequencies allowed concentrated sound waves to cut through virtually any substance. They couldn't split atoms, but molecular dissection ran a close second in the catastrophic risk department. It would be all too easy for Reemer or one of his workers to accidentally cut off an antenna or eye stalk.

Not that Squinch were stupid, far from it, but giving a non-industrialized society advanced equipment was a recipe for disaster.

The unbalanced blade had an awkward curve and was contoured wrong for human hands, another dangerous gift from his mysterious backers. She wiped the last of the gelatinous goo off the handle and gently returned the cutter to its recharge station. Reemer better have decent safety training. The tacky excretion he'd used to handle the tool was a good sign.

Squinch slime might one day inspire its own field of study. The slugs exercised surprisingly conscious control over their bodily excretions. Depending on the need, their slime ranged from noxious to benign and sticky to slippery.

A clear-sided tank rose above the hoppers of the molecular stabilizer at the end of the workstation. Cheery green indicator lights blinked from circuitry adorning the lid of the container, which was packed full of spiky brown balls. They looked innocent enough, but Nancy shivered at the memory of how much those burrs hurt.

"Does Rebecca know you're collecting pain urchin seeds?"

Early naval surveys had been so very wrong in assessing the planet as uninhabited. Reemer's family governed the oceans off the southern continent, but an even more bizarre creature ruled the jungles and prairies.

Rudimentary intelligence among flora was an unproven hypothesis back home, one that the scientific community accepted as harmless with no practical application. Her discovery of Rebecca and other subspecies in the Dolor family proved that plants could communicate and evolve the capacity for independent thought and actions. Rebecca, or

Becky as Reemer called her, was basically the queen of the local flora.

Nancy's findings still languished in endless peer reviews. She'd argued and railed and finally accepted that humans who hadn't seen planet Fred's unique ecosystem might bury her work forever. Worse, her burgeoning empathic ability laid bare every petty, egocentric, and self-serving motive driving the supposed experts in fields from botany to neuroscience. That insight had played a key role in her leaving botany to try her hand at diplomacy. Designating the planet as inhabited gave the Squinch and Dolor a modicum of protection, even if the latter remained unacknowledged.

"Don't worry." Reemer pulled Nancy out of her painful memories. "Becky approved all our collection methods. We only take from overpopulated areas. Most would choke each other out anyway." He waved a secondary antenna at the material undergoing processing, his voice growing wispy with longing as his eyes settled on the nearby tank. "Plus, there are way too many of these luscious burrs out past the river."

"Reemer, tell me you aren't selling to your friends."

The burrs were mobile and deadly to most species. Squinch were immune to the toxic cocktail injected by those burrowing spines. But if a slug ate the burrs…well, she'd seen firsthand how devastating and addictive those compounds were. A Squinch high on narcotics wasn't a pretty sight. Once he'd gotten a taste, there'd been no stopping Reemer. It had taken days of detox to dry her friend out and get him to swear off the burrs. That he'd been deathly ill from being out of the water too long at the time had helped. Nancy snapped her fingers twice right under his eyes to get his attention.

"No!" Reemer's denial piped from numerous mouths on a calliope of indignation. "The burrs don't even get touched. We just pack 'em up in these fancy no-time boxes and let the customers deal with them."

She held his gaze, studying those watery eyes. Pus wept from the corner of the heavy lids, streaming down each stalk to mingle with the slickness coating his mantle. Yep, perfectly normal. He definitely wasn't using.

"Well, good." It was a relief to see that they packed up the burrs whole. Cutting through the nut-like shell without releasing burrowing spines was tricky business best left to experts. But that raised another question. "Are they dead?" The organic compounds decayed rapidly. Dead burrs would be useless for medicinal purposes. She peered into the tank. Not so much as a swirl of dust moved in there. The gauges and circuits atop the tank looked more complex than simple environmental controls. Wait, he'd called it a no-time box! "You've got to be kidding. You have stasis boxes?"

"Sure, that's what he called them." Reemer kicked at the base of the table with his skirt, looking for all the world like a petulant child. "It's no big deal. I've got something way cooler to show you."

"No big deal?" Nancy shrugged off his grasping antennae, and gaped at the tank. "Only two known races have stasis tech. Earth Force won't even disclose which ones for fear of starting an interstellar war. Nations would kill to get their hands on something like this." She let herself be pulled back onto the sled.

"Whatever. We just use them for shipping." The sled glided to the far wall, and Reemer keyed a code into the panel alongside a narrow door. His mantle flared wide, hiding his movements from view. "But what's in *here* is a game changer."

"Reemer, seriously, you can never tell anyone else about those stasis chambers. Forbid your workers from even hinting at them. You *have* to promise."

"Geez, okay. I promise." The door slid off to the side, and Reemer ducked into the alcove, again blocking her view with his body. "Pain urchins have about run their course this cycle anyway. It'll be five years before we get another order and more boxes to fill. But check this out."

He spun around with antennae spread wide, wearing what looked like an antique leather aviator helmet complete with chinstrap. The phrase "when pigs fly" leapt to mind, quickly followed by the image of a fiery plane crash. Guiding a hover sled was a far cry from aviation.

"Please tell me you're joking."

"About what?" Reemer preened and smoothed the lumpy fabric around his eyestalks, admiring his reflection in the shiny surface of the cabinet that had held the outfit. "I had this made special."

"Pilots need extensive training."

"Who cares? Computers can do the flying." He spun, letting the attached supple fabric flare out over his mantle like a cape. "With this I'm unstoppable. I can go anywhere."

The cape made sense now. Reemer fancied himself a slug superhero able to leap tall building and all that jazz. He wasn't wrong about piloting either. Computers did most of the heavy lifting. Her shiny new commercial license had gobs of limitations that basically made her first mate to the navigation programs of her ship's oh-so-limited artificial personality. Even now, the robotic extension of said AI was back handling the post-flight tasks and a slew of items needed to ensure they'd be ready for liftoff.

"Where exactly are you figuring on going?"

"With you, of course."

"Yeah, like that's going to happen." She snorted at the memory of her last ill-fated outing with the Squinch. "You nearly died last time."

The aquatic race had evolved a respiratory system that functioned equally well as gills or lungs. But breathing ashore wasn't enough. Fred's ocean provided vital nutrients and salts. Reemer could only last a week away from the sea. She'd managed to extend that limit with daily saltwater baths, but Squinch biology inevitably failed without regular dunks in Fred's warm waters.

"Not a problem anymore."

Reemer patted the lump of red material riding high on his back and traced his antennae down the length of the odd outfit. The upper edge of the under-harness adhered to his hide in a patchwork of small hexagons similar to the medical absorption patches that delivered time-released doses.

"What exactly does that thing do?" Nancy prodded the lump on his back. Behind where the chinstrap connected, the cape bulged, firm but yielding—like quilting packed full of sand. The cape thinned at a gusset behind the thick mantle skin and ended in pleated red material that hung fashionably across the base of Reemer's tail.

"It lets me stay out of the water." Reemer opened the lower drawer of the cabinet, revealing stacks of cream-colored discs the size of her palm. "They've extracted the salt and other stuff I need from the water. This is enough to last a year. When the harness runs low, I just slip in a few more discs. No more getting sick on land. Isn't that great?"

"Wonderful." Nancy's sarcasm was as dry as those mineral packets.

Reemer chattered on about all the exciting adventures they'd have out in "the space" as he called it. He painted a picture of interstellar travel complete with harrowing escapes from rogue asteroid fields, laser dogfights against marauding pirates, and exploration of time-bending portals. Everything led to a pivotal moment when they foiled the dastardly plot of some villain bent on destroying the known universe.

His musings sounded suspiciously similar to a certain long-running science fiction series. The slug had salvaged a library of programs and the vidscreen from her old navy ship, the *SS Endeavor*. He'd clearly spent way too much time glued to the screen and fantasizing of adventure.

Nancy hated to tell him, but space was aptly named. The universe was largely a big, empty place. Except for monitoring equipment failures, crossing interstellar distances grew boring in a hurry. Faster-than-light travel—a.k.a. FTL—wasn't just an economical multiplier. Very few individuals were cut out for the years of solitude involved in long-haul sub-light transits. But the body could only take limited exposure to hyperspace, so short hops still got interspersed with slow, sub-light legs.

She let him drone on and dug through the supplies in his cabinet. The super suit and its various components looked to have been manufactured from high-grade nanofiber. Osmotic membranes hooked to the main harness with gecko strips and would be slime activated to meter out the concentrated disks' nutrients at an appropriate rate.

She interrupted the diatribe several times with questions, but Reemer couldn't tell her much about the design. He was more interested in "getting out there" and "making a difference," phrases emphasized by wet claps of his antennae that sprayed her with bits of slime.

Neither the gear nor mineral packets had labels. She'd noted the same absence on the various machinery and packaging scattered across the facility. Given that they had access to stasis tech, whoever was funding this operation had more than just deep pockets.

Her friend wasn't stupid, but there was always a danger of exploitation when low-tech races stepped up to interstellar markets. The one exception to the lack of branding were the letters RTC inscribed within a diamond emblazoned down the center of the cape.

"What's RTC stand for?" A protective streak insisted she research this partnership and maybe have a buddy back in legal look over any contracts.

"Cool, huh?" Reemer wagged his posterior so that the cape flared wide to display the stylized lettering. "Reemer Trading Company."

Yeah, he was definitely going for the superhero angle.

6. A New Calling

R EEMER HAULED HIS crate full of equipment and supplies up the shallow ramp into the squat ship that promised freedom. One eyestalk swiveled to watch his human friend talking to a leafy bush outside. Unlike the more deadly trees and vines that were tethered to a specific location, the shambling plants moved freely through the living jungle. As the cycle of activity drew toward its end, the bushes would come to rest in areas with the best soil and light to get them through for five more years.

"Where do I put this?" The interior passageway stretched fore and aft—those were nautical terms he'd learned.

"Second door on the left is your stateroom." Nancy patted the bush and headed his way. "I'll give you a hand. The room's not big, so you might want to put most of that in the cargo hold."

He'd never packed for a trip before and had probably brought too much. In addition to his life-sustaining cape, he'd grabbed the vidscreen, a few mementos, and an assortment of items from the factory floor. His instincts had pushed him to hurry. Squinch were already lining the beach for the ceremony, filling the air with enticing scents that had *the change* clawing up his skirt and twisting his insides. Holding out until liftoff would be a test of willpower that he was determined to win.

If they roped him into mating, he'd be tied down for months and a sitting target. A shiver ran down his mantle at the thought. He scanned the tree line for movement and shoved the crate toward the bridge.

"I've got it." Antigrav skids made maneuvering the load easy once it got moving, and Nancy didn't need to know the particulars about his luggage. "My room will work fine."

The crate clunked to a stop, and the shiny square head of the ship's robot peered around the corner at him.

"Out of the way, blockhead!" Reemer grunted as he got the load moving again, and the metallic contraption scuttled to the side. "Wait. On second thought, take this to my room, stateroom two."

"Yes, sir." The robot clamped a hand on the cargo handle and smoothly guided his luggage down the passageway.

"Turn off the lifters and secure it to the deck too," Reemer called after the machine. "And don't look at my stuff."

The ship's robot whisked his luggage away before Nancy reached the foot of the ramp. What else could this metal man do for him during their adventures? Nancy complained constantly about the ship's AI, but the thought of a servant doing exactly what he asked seemed like a great idea.

Human entertainment programs were full of butlers that catered to the whims of important people. One show followed a super-rich crime fighter with a secret lair and tons of cool gadgets. A loyal servant took care of all the details, including keeping his fancy crime-fighting suit—the super suit—ready to go so that no one knew the rich guy's identity. Reemer could get used to that kind of arrangement.

"What the heck did you bring?" Nancy hurried up the ramp.

"Just my super suit and a few odds and ends." He blocked her path as the door to his room slid closed.

Reemer only needed to wear the harness and cape a few hours a week or when he felt the chemicals in his system drifting out of balance—no easy task with his body still trying to turn him into a girl. Getting far away should reverse *the change* and let him settle back to fully male.

The Squinch female aspect had plenty of perks, but Reemer wasn't ready to settle down with a pup just yet. Plus, Nancy would want him at his fun-loving best. Despite the complaints and rolling eyes, he knew she appreciated a good practical joke. For some reason those came easier in male form.

"I'll have to weigh that before lift-off." She rushed on as pustules burst along his back in sticky indignation. "Don't get your panties in a wad. I'll get the readings from the internal sensors without prying into your stuff." Her eyes slid to the deck where glistening residue trailed back to the entry hatch. "As first mate you'll have to keep these passageways clean. I know you can't help it, but slime trails are a safety hazard. There's a mop and bucket with your name on it. Consider it a daily chore."

"No problem, Mon Capitan." Reemer knew exactly how he'd take care of that particular chore, but eased his way back to the ramp and peered out rather than look to the robot emerging from his cabin. "Are you and the creeping bush best friends now?"

"Jealous much?" Nancy snorted. "It wasn't exactly a two-way conversation, but I think it'll get a message back to Rebecca. I can't believe I'm going to miss her. No hunters this cycle, right? So she shouldn't be afraid."

"No, no hunters…" Reemer stuck his head outside and scanned the forest. A section of low branches bent and swayed. Not a good sign. Should he say more? "Old habits die hard. She's probably gone to ground in a cave up on the high plains. It's going to take time for Becky to realize she's safe. But you're right. The plants are connected. Even with the jungle going quiet again, she'll get your message." Despite the lack of wind, other branches bent and snapped back into place as if invisible bodies passed, lots of bodies. "The sooner we get going, the sooner we'll be back to visit."

He nudged Nancy, propelling her toward the bridge.

"Wait, aren't we going to say goodbye to your parents? And your big ceremony is gearing up." She tried to spin back, but a head-butt got her moving in the right direction.

"No need," Reemer said. "I've said our goodbyes and bowed out of the festivities."

"Belinda's okay with that? I got the feeling the ceremony wasn't optional."

"Can't say that she's happy, but I'm just not ready." He grabbed the hatch controls and raised a questioning eyestalk. At Nancy's nod, he retracted the ramp. Branches swayed along the entire edge of the dunes beyond the factory entrance. Reemer forced his words out with jovial piping. "Yep, gotta get going. Helping you is more important."

"I don't even have a firm destination yet." Nancy threw up her hands and headed to the bridge. "Might as well figure that out before we start burning fuel."

With the hatch secured, Reemer let out a sigh and followed. The bridge was roomy enough for three to work comfortably. Nancy worked the controls near her chair and a panoramic display lit up the view screen. Hundreds of Squinch had piled up on the beach, bodies sliding over each other as the mating commenced.

His mother prowled around the communication shack, no doubt searching for him. Much of the vegetation near the factory was squashed flat now. The ambling bush Nancy had been speaking with scuttled out of the path of whatever approached. Reemer herded the ship's robot over to stand in front of the display so that Nancy didn't see the factory entrance off to their right disintegrate in a silent explosion.

"Don't you get it?" Reemer moved to the main controls, deliberately drawing her attention away from the view. He waved at the pulsing yellow ribbons that climbed ever closer to the mantle on his back. The intertwined bodies out there had him flushing and panting. He couldn't hold off *the change* much longer. "I'm not ready for this! Mating, saddled with a pup. I've dodged this for years while you were off getting all the glory and training to be the navy's secret weapon."

"I'm no weapon," Nancy said. "This is my *job*."

"Yeah, well, better that than being forced into…things."

"The way I hear it, this whole export business was your idea." Nancy jabbed a finger at his left eye, then waved at the ceiling. "Sometimes you need to put a little effort in to get what you want. You can't just go running away because you don't like—" She froze mid-sentence, her eyes drifting to his yellowing skirt before sweeping up to his drooping eyestalks and out to the writhing mass of slugs near the water. Reemer couldn't read people as well as Nancy, but the comprehension that blossomed across her pale face dropped into a disgusted scowl. "They're trying to force you to mate? That's barbaric. I can't believe your mom would do that."

"Well, to be fair, I'm like the first Squinch in history who hasn't wanted to participate as soon as they matured." His stomachs roiled at the admission, despite repeated attempts to accept being different. "I've got bigger plans for my business, for all our futures. The longer I stay here, the more likely I'll…"

"…turn female as the hormones and pheromones take control," Nancy finished for him.

Reemer gave a weary nod, a human expression he'd picked up. "And I'll be underwater for a year with my pup. By the time I get back ashore, my company and its exports won't matter. It'll be time for another ceremony, more mating, more pups. I'll be trapped in a vicious cycle. I want that *someday*, just not yet."

Family was important, but so were his other goals. With the planet so recently acknowledged, his people needed a firm foothold. To get Squinch standing alongside the spacefaring races, the trading company was just a start that would be meaningless if others took control of their destiny.

He risked a glance past the robot. All was quiet, but a gaping hole had replaced the factory doors. The people looking for him probably wouldn't mess with the final shipments of the season.

"No, not today." Nancy's nod was sharp and decisive as she threw switches and deep vibrations rose through the deck plates. "Robot, get your ass in gear and prepare for launch. I want to be in space within the hour."

"Aye, Captain." The robot trundled away from the viewport and nestled into an alcove amid the controls.

The jolly red eyes set wide in the tin-can head dimmed as lights sprang to life across the panel. Reemer sensed the AI's consciousness shifting from the mobile unit back into the navigation panel.

"Please declare destination." The mechanical voice came from all around them.

"Hmm." Nancy screwed up her face in thought. "There *are* a couple of interesting low-priority missions. I still need to go over the files. Set a sub-light course out of the solar system on a vector toward galactic center. We'll lay in a final destination after I get approval from headquarters."

"Very good, Captain."

Twenty minutes later, the ship rose from the dunes. Other than a few eyestalks turning their way, his departure and the raid on his factory went largely unnoticed by the revelers. Mother would have a royal fit when she discovered him gone. Reemer vowed to let her know he was with Nancy once the auto-repair system had communications back up.

As far as the company went, workers not expecting pups could handle the final shipment and secure the facility until the jungle's next cycle. Churl would get the doors repaired so that weather and sand didn't ruin the equipment while he was gone.

The Lobstra ship turned out to have a smoother ride than human vessels. A good thing, since there were no harnesses or acceleration couches suitable for giant slugs. Reemer simply flattened himself out, using super sticky slime to anchor his skirt to wall and floor. As the green orb that was planet Fred dropped away, his stomachs gave a hungry flip.

He'd brought a few dried delicacies. Nancy swore her ship was fully stocked, but he didn't hold out much hope that the food would be as tasty as fresh flatfish or bullet squid. A sigh escaped several of his mouths. Sometimes dashing space explorers had to make sacrifices.

"Here are the options." Nancy broke into his thoughts, unbuckled, and sat a datapad on the chart table behind the pilot chairs.

Reemer detached himself, reabsorbing as much of the adhesive slime as possible before crossing for a look. The robot could clean up the rest later.

The holographic image floating above the table showed a vast, white plain with spiral towers rising from a walled city. At first glance, the hovering landscape looked to be a wide beach, but the blowing sand was too white and super fine. Zooming in showed glittering fangs hanging from rooflines and overhangs. A few of his human movies took people to inhospitable places like that.

"It's all frozen." He made a grab for the nearest tower, but of course his antenna simply swept through the projection.

"Whole planet's that way." Nancy rubbed her arms. "The persistent cold drives the population indoors and underground. They've spent generations focused on arts and literature. Cauthorn's dominant race is embroiled in an intellectual property dispute over the interpretation of ancient poetry. Intriguing, but I'm no literary expert."

"Why's your navy even interested?"

"Usually, they wouldn't be. We've got our own literary traditions. But the cultural liaison mission has been changing its focus recently. If there's profit to be had in new technology, we're happy to offer negotiation and translation services in exchange for technical data. These folks have thermal management down to an advanced science. Earth wants new tech for terrestrial cold-climate work, managing heat during atmospheric reentry, and other applications."

"What's the other choice?" Reemer reached out and tapped the second mission profile.

Nancy cringed and used the cuff of her uniform to wipe the datapad's screen. The frozen castle winked out. A gleaming metal archway, part of some massive circular spaceship, dominated the new image. A small brown planet hung in the background.

"This behemoth is a space station." Nancy traced a finger around the slowly rotating object. "It orbits a barren moon that's become super controversial."

The perspective drew back at her touch, showing that the brown ball in the background in turn circled a much larger blue-green planet. The core of the station was a simple hoop dotted with row upon row of observation ports. Thinner circlets jutted out at various angles to form a loose weave like the shallow seaweed nests that protected young Squinch.

"This one's a little more interesting." Nancy chewed her lower lip. "A mining dispute has the locals in an uproar. The moon is a rich source of luxene, the rare catalyst needed for core reactions in faster-than-light engines. A powerful lobby among the locals wants to stop mining before it starts."

"People live on that moon?" Reemer squinted at the dead brown orb. It wasn't pocked and cratered like the one from Nancy's homeworld, but the lack of oceans made it seem pretty uninviting.

"Long ago they did, but not anymore." Nancy zoomed in on the world orbited by moon and station. "Two groups dominate the planet. There's a rivalry between the standing government and a faction claiming blood ties to the moon's original inhabitants. The latter one is dead set against disturbing the moon's ruins. The mining corporation has promised to quadrant off no-dig zones, but the religious fanatics opposing the project refuse to budge.

"Maybe their claim on the moon is valid. Who knows? The galactic trade language isn't up to the task. The multi-race mining consortium can't even find translators among the locals, so the navy ambassador is helping out. They might still work through an agreement, but I see a lot of tense posturing in reports from the home office."

"Bor—ing!" Reemer stretched the syllables out into a dismissive sing-song, mimicking a human teenager. This would have been a perfect time to try rolling his eyes, but the gesture still just made his stalks rotate. "Let's check out this wet sand you call snow." He flipped the image back to the tundra mission, which had Nancy wiping down her screen again. "I bet that's slippery stuff." He imagined sliding down a snowy hill on an intercept course with his unsuspecting victim. Just the thought had some of the yellow along his sides retreating. The resulting *splat* would be epic. "So what's cold feel like anyway?"

"You wouldn't like it." Nancy screwed up her face in thought. "Remember when you were sick and couldn't think straight?" At his cautious nod she continued. "It's like that. You get all blurry and unfocused. Your body shuts down to conserve heat. Humans have a shiver reaction to burn more food and produce internal heat. I don't think Squinch have that capability. Humans can only cope for a short while before things start shutting down and we turn sluggish."

"Hey!"

"No pun, and no fun either. It's painful and your body dies off as blood recedes to keep your organs alive."

"But it's slippery right?" Glorious velocity. Reemer had gotten a taste of speed and wanted more. Traveling in Nancy's ship didn't count because it hardly felt like they were moving.

"Dealing with a slug-cicle is not the plan." Nancy set the image back to the moon and its orbiting monstrosity. "Read up on Spaceport Gail. It's growing into a diplomatic hub. Interesting people from all over and tons to do. They'll have more movies than even you can binge, and I bet something better than freezing snow to feed your need for speed. Negotiations are going to stall out soon. I'll submit a visit request to headquarters. My boss should be good with covering expenses to get me there to help if needed. Luxene isn't new tech, but it's stupid valuable."

Looping visions of snowy fun pushed Reemer to argue. Planet Fred wasn't *always* warm. Sometimes it got so cold that his hide turned dark to soak up more sun. He'd adapt just fine, but Nancy refused to be swayed.

At least a crowded space station meant lots of opportunity for interesting pranks. And if this luxene was so important to space travel, maybe he could get the Squinch in on a piece of the action.

7. Butlers and Belly Flops

N ANCY PRIED ANOTHER magnetized handle off the bulkhead. The damned things were plastered all over the ship at knee-height. Slimy residue on most of her haul spoke to the source as she stalked toward the engine room in search of her passenger.

"What are these for?" Nancy thrust the armload of handles at Reemer. "And what's *he* doing?"

The ship's robot sat amid a pile of parts, spindly legs holding three sections of extruded pipe in a triangle while the primary arms spot welded the pieces together. A low chassis about three feet wide and half again as long was taking shape in the alcove behind the reclamation tanks. The robot affixed the new part to the back end like an upright fin, alongside a power pack.

"Those are sling handles for frictionless bobsledding." Reemer frowned as she dumped her load in front of him. "We need them for our test run."

"You're going to drive me to drink!"

"Not without these grab handles." He slid over to the doorway and started snapping the small tees back into place. "They're the only way to steer an antigrav sled."

"My ship isn't a racetrack!" Nancy followed behind, pulling off handles as Reemer reattached them. "And the robot isn't your slave either. The engineering logs are way behind. Between doing your chores and now this—" She waved over to where the bot polished a section of polymer skin he'd cut to fit the fin. "I don't know how you overrode his basic programming, but this has to stop. We've only been underway a week."

"A week of boredom." Reemer finally caught on and stopped replacing handles. "I wanted an adventure."

She couldn't take another week of bored Squinch. After soliciting her promise to complete *all* the pending repairs that Herman's people added to her maintenance records, the main office had approved her visit to the space station. Commander Olaf Branson controlled her assignments and had agreed that negotiations on Spaceport Gail were likely to come to a halt. The man had absolutely salivated over the possibility of leveraging luxene mining as payment for her services.

Spaceport Gail was an overly ambitious inter-species venture funded by altruistic benefactors. Nations from several planets contributed to its construction and subsequent manning. Earth held only a small share in the project, while the Argoth, a squid-like air-breathing race from halfway across the galaxy, had provided the lion's share of funding and people. Bits of the Argoth's dominant language filled gaps in the station's official name due to shortcomings in the galactic trade language. The long form of Gail's name took about fifteen seconds to pronounce and roughly translated to "a tranquil place of peace, business, and commerce." But Earth-side recruiters tended to just call it "GAlactIc Longshot," referring to both the low odds of getting one of the few official postings and the extended trip out to the station. Although the distance to Gail varied as it moved between assignments, the station had yet to park anywhere remotely close to her home planet.

At the moment, Earth's embedded ambassador was overwhelmed. Olaf had promised to rush her flight plan through the approval process and to hold off on any official announcement. He'd wanted to get Nancy designated as Ambassador Turlic's liaison, but she'd declined. Stepping on the toes of the person keeping the situation in balance would only lead to bad blood and make her job all that much harder. Working out an arrangement with the ambassador in person would make for a smoother introduction. Of course, she'd first have to get there without murdering a certain bothersome mollusk.

"I don't recall promising adventure. In fact, I don't remember inviting you along at all." Her words came out bitter, and she rushed on at the sight of Reemer's drooping eyestalks—as much to salvage her friend's feelings as to spare the deck another gooey puddle for the robot to clean. "Look, I really *do* like having you here. But you've got to let Ziggy do his job. We're about to drop out of hyperspace for our next sub-light leg. I need the engine parameters checked and double checked. Can we focus on that instead of Olympic events? *Please*?"

Reemer visibly deflated, but the tilt of his left eyestalk as he snuck a look at her reaction meant he was faking. Nancy poked a toe at the ticklish spot along his side. Reemer huffed, but couldn't keep up the charade. His skirt flapped against the deck as the little guy stifled a laugh. An involuntary grin stretched her lips. They were good. Her friend could be self-centered and exasperating, but never malicious.

"Ziggy, go back to ship duties and stow away Rocket Racer Three—for now," Reemer called to his would-be mechanic. "There better be a racetrack on this station."

That last bit came as a mutter from under his skirt. How had an oversized sea slug developed a taste for speed? The memory of their jaunts across planet Fred and one particularly wild ride with Reemer clinging to the bottom of her landpod came to mind. She may have had a hand in creating this particular monster.

Scrounging up spare parts might actually be a good outlet for the mischievous alien. She'd have to check the maintenance records. As long as nothing critical was missing and Reemer stopped monopolizing Ziggy, what harm did it do if the adrenaline junky kept working on his contraption? Or was that contraptions?

"Wait, what happened to sleds one and two?"

"Funny you should ask—"

Reemer's answer got cut short as the collision alarm rang out. The deck canted high on the right, overwhelming the artificial gravity compensators and slamming Nancy to the floor amidst skittering hand grips. *What the hell?*

"Captain, to the bridge!" The sharp command hadn't been in Ziggy's lilting mechanical voice.

Nancy had only ever heard the emergency command system during Herman's simulations. Something must be seriously wrong for the subroutine to override the ship's embedded AI. Nancy scrambled to her feet, clinging to a support strut to keep from falling.

"Ziggy, why haven't the stabilizers reengaged?"

The deck stayed at a good sixty degrees, and the bridge was uphill with nothing to hold onto once she made it past the engine room door.

"Access limited." Ziggy was wedged under the frame he'd been in the process of securing. "Use emergency protocols for further queries."

Wonderful. The robot inched his way forward, but wouldn't be free anytime soon, and probably would have just as much trouble climbing the slope.

"Come on! You're supposed to go to the bridge." Reemer's wonderfully versatile slime let him ooze downhill and stop at her feet.

"I'm going to need a hand." She studied the boneless creature, trying to decide where to grab. Reemer's prehensile secondary antennae were extremely flexible, but she doubted one would hold her weight. With a sigh of regret, Nancy sank to her knees and wrapped both arms around the stubby tail just above his skirt. "Okay, get going."

The wet sucking sound of a toilet plunger being slowly drawn back vibrated beneath her. Nancy's hands slipped, and she hugged the slug's fat tail for all she was worth. Sticky slime coated her arms, front, and face. The bitter taste of Squinch filled her mouth as she sucked in a breath and slipped another inch.

Pustules under her cheek ruptured, milky white trickles mixing with the slime plastering her hair. His tail instantly turned sticky as a rodent glue-trap. Horrendous as it felt, smelled, and tasted, Nancy couldn't let go if she wanted to. The plunger sounds intensified as Reemer's skirt fell into a nauseating rhythm, dragging Nancy uphill. *Squelch, pop, slap—squelch, pop, slap.*

A high-pitched thrum vibrated through the deck. She felt like a violin bow sliding over taut strings. That would be the defensive shield. The pitch changed, cycling through harmonics.

"Geez, you're heavy." Reemer panted as he continued forward. *Squelch, pop, slap.*

A growl caught in her throat when both eyestalks swiveled to stare at her. "Less commentary. More watching where you're going."

The phantom plumber missed a beat, the rhythmic plunger taking a long pause, then frantically pumping for all it was worth. *Squelch, pop, slap… Squelch, pop, slap… Squelch, pop… Squelch, pop…slap, slap, slap.*

Nancy pumped her legs, trying to take weight on her toes as Reemer's skirt pulled from the floor and they fell back. Her left foot hit the stanchion where they'd started. Pain shot up her leg as it took the combined weight of human and the hundred pounds of Squinch she couldn't release.

"You're not so light yourself," Nancy managed through clenched teeth.

A few contortions got both feet on the support. Reemer released a new substance into his slime, and she was able to pry herself off of his tail. She sucked in a deep gulp of clean air as the Squinch backed away. Her knee stopped screaming, but if it would hold her weight remained debatable.

Until the ship righted itself, getting to the bridge was a losing proposition. Reemer would have to go see what was happening and report back. Between her injured leg, balancing on the stanchion, and debris jabbing her in the stomach, the deck was damned uncomfortable. Rolling onto her side brought a sigh of relief.

Miscellaneous parts from Reemer's project were scattered right where she'd landed. The bits of tubing and connectors would have slid on past, but had gotten caught up on a line of the racing handles that were clearly bent on tormenting her. When they got out of this, Reemer was *so* going to start cleaning up after himself.

She was about to send the slug on ahead when a thought struck. Those handles stayed put thanks to magnetic-molecular bonding. They'd adhere to almost any surface. She snatched up two grips, twisting to release the bond and affixing each to a new spot. Both held fast. Visions of rock wall climbs during candidate training sprang to mind. This would work.

* * *

"What's our status?" Nancy crossed into the bridge like a soldier crawling under barbed wire. Arms burning, she walked the grips up the bulkhead and took in the room with her back against the door's edge.

"Primary engines offline, three auxiliary system malfunctions, shields holding on low-order harmonics." The computer chirped out more specifics as graphs and visual displays came up on the view screen. "The ship is caught in an undocumented anomaly. Shifting to external view. Command input required."

The data slid off to the left side of the screens to make room for an exterior view of deep space. They were either moving very slowly or had stopped altogether; the velocity vector readings couldn't seem to make up their mind. Something else was off. Colors flashed across the scene, a shifting haze distorting the starry backdrop.

"What is that?" Nancy asked.

"An uncharted electro-magnetic anomaly producing broad-spectrum radiation." The computer brought up more graphs. "Concentrations of heavy metals and ferrous debris suggest it's been in place for an extended period, although radioactive isotopes have not experienced the expected decay. The area has accumulated sufficient mass and ionic charge to interfere with FTL and subspace drives."

"In other words, we're stuck."

"Correct." The computer took what felt like a pregnant pause as if reluctant to continue. Great, now her ability was anthropomorphizing computers. The emergency system had even less personality than Ziggy—as if that was possible. Yet its hesitation continued for a few more seconds. "Command override is required for a total system shut down to restart the subspace drive and auxiliary systems. Do you wish to proceed with shut down?"

"We can't get anywhere interesting without super-warp." Reemer was nothing if not persistent in his quest for speed, but—then again—he wasn't wrong.

"A qualified repair facility is needed for engine diagnostics, repair, and calibration." Again the hesitation as the computer's attention shifted from the Squinch back to her. "Breaking free of the anomaly requires non-standard procedures and command authorization. Does the captain acknowledge and authorize the following? Lowering shields during an emergency, temporary loss of life support, implementing non-standard emergency start-up procedures, radiation exposure, ship tracking log gaps, and endangering non-navy personnel."

The rambling list continued like the fine print on pharmaceutical advertisements. She could spend the rest of her life fighting legal battles if anyone objected to her handling of the situation. But with communications blacked out, the alternative was to hope the anomaly ran out of steam before they ran out of supplies. The computer was thorough if not succinct, but she still had questions.

"Is automatic restart possible during shut down, or will we have to manually get the engines back online?" Nancy's training had walked through emergency operating procedures, but starting a cold engine without computer assistance normally took several people a very long time. "I also need to know how long power will be out and projected radiation levels."

"Energy reserves are sufficient for two restart attempts. Successfully completing the procedure will leave the ship dark for at least fifteen standard Earth minutes. Unmitigated anomaly radiation will exceed Personal Exposure Limits in multiple wavelengths. Alien PEL recommendations are not on file."

Radiation PELs were based on human tolerances with plenty of built-in safety margins. Squinch physiology might react very differently. Maybe Reemer could be stuffed into one of the Lobstra space suits.

8. Engine Trouble

"TELL ME AGAIN why I'm in the freezer." Reemer poked his head between white cubes as she packed the synthate blocks around him.

"Because I can't have your delicate Squinch innards fried by radiation when the shields drop." Nancy adjusted the reflective material of the Lobstra protective suit to cover as many of the pressed nutrient blocks as possible. The rigid legs made it look like one of the alien crustaceans was climbing in to get at Reemer. "You'll be insulated more here than anywhere else on board. Fats and proteins will absorb most of the radiation."

One last package completed the wall, effectively sealing him behind a ring of the raw organic material used to synthesize meals.

"I'll freeze," Reemer complained. "Says so right on the door. Everything's growing dark."

"You can't freeze. It's not that cold." They definitely would be steering clear of that arctic world. Despite the compartment's name, this room was only ten degrees cooler than the living quarters, just enough to keep fatty lipids from liquefying and sloshing around. "And it's dark because we're on minimum power." She slapped an antenna away when he tried to dislodge the suit. "That's your best shielding. Leave it alone, stay put, and listen for the all-clear. I've got to get into my suit and give the computer permission to start. With luck, we'll be upright and moving within the hour."

Without luck, they'd be dead in space with a novice pilot trying to jumpstart the engines without computer assistance. *Positive thoughts.*

Nancy made her way to the staging area outside the small cargo bay and shrugged into her own radiation suit. The navy-issued outfit was designed for hull work, which made it bulky and heavy, especially given she was still using Reemer's racing grabs to work her way around the ship.

"Okay, computer, I'm all set," Nancy said after triple checking the suit's compression fittings and readouts. She'd climbed uphill to the bridge but left the doors open all the way to the engine room. By craning her neck, she could just make out the concentric rings of the outer reactor casing at the end of the passageway. "Let's do this. Initiate total shutdown and engine restart."

"Affirmative." The metallic voice might sound aloof, but at least *it* wasn't nervous as it worked through the steps in quick succession. "Life support on minimum…weapons offline…auxiliary systems offline…dropping shields…life support secured…reactors off."

A distant clunk echoed back from the engine room, the room and screens went dark, and down ceased being…down. The sudden weightlessness came as a relief as she shifted off the doorframe that had been gouging her back. The shimmering anomaly and stars that had painted the screens were replaced by colored pinpricks of light that sipped at the precious stored energy the emergency program needed to restart. Vertigo swept through Nancy as she flicked on the suit's low-level flood lights, washing the room in flat shadows.

"Resetting containment and priming catalytic initiator." The ubiquitous voice had shifted to her helmet's small speaker.

Reemer wouldn't have the luxury of knowing what was going on. Hopefully he'd just sit tight like she'd asked. Other sounds reverberated from the engines, some familiar—like the mild hum of the magnetic containment fields energizing—and others less so.

As the minutes passed, the heads-up display in her suit showed climbing levels of ionizing radiation in three bar graphs. The leftmost red bar showed the deadly environment outside. The middle display was about halfway through the yellow zone, indicating the amount leaking through the hull now that the systems were down. The final gauge hovered near the top of the green zone, showing the radiation that had reached her. A suit of lead or gold would stop radiation dead in its tracks, but was hardly practical.

Nancy listened to the computer's occasional status reports and watched her personal exposure gauge rise into the yellow, trying hard not to imagine her DNA breaking down. Blood pumped in her ears, louder by the minute. She caught herself panting and forced a long, meditative breath through her nose.

Daily exposure limits would have at least a one-hundred percent safety margin. She just needed to avoid further exposure in the coming months. Not a problem once full life support was restored.

"Instructions required." The computer provided a welcome distraction from obsessing over the damned radiation. "Engine restart has failed due to excessive ion build-up in the thermal management system. Sufficient power remains for a second attempt. Do you wish to continue?"

Okay, maybe not so welcome of a distraction.

"Can you correct the problem first?"

"De-ionization requires manual intervention."

"Well, it's not like I've got anywhere else to be." She cast a nervous glance at her personal radiation readings, which had risen into the red on several wavelengths. "What do I need to do?"

✳ ✳ ✳

Nancy cursed the Lobstra designer who'd assumed maintenance techs would have a dozen pinchers. Initiating the manual deionization cycle wasn't complicated, but picking through the multi-colored sea of feathery controls while perched upside down in the cramped control module made things difficult. Even with coaching by the computer, she'd had to restart the sequence three times. Rebuilding the burnt-out control board would probably have been easier.

"Next, set the magneto power control to one third while varying resistance on circuits three and seven. Bring all ion plate readings to fifty percent." Each new instruction from the metallic voice was like another needle in her temple.

"I only have two hands." Nancy managed to pinch one resistance controller between pinky and palm and catch the edge of the other with thumb and forefinger. But to operate them individually she'd need to be some kind of elastic superhero.

"What's taking so long?" Reemer slapped himself up against the control center's transparent barrier, putting the rows of mouths beneath his skirt on disturbing display.

Nancy jumped at the sudden interruption, and the charge indicators dropped back to zero. The slug gave what passed for a grin from beneath the leather helmet and chin strap, the cape of his super suit—his words, not hers—trailing down his mantle.

"Reemer! You're not supposed to be up here."

Even within her protective suit, she'd reached double the daily radiation limits. This was their last shot at getting life support back. If the engines didn't start, nowhere on board would be safe. As he slid to the deck with a wet plop, she risked a glance at the indicator around his neck. The little disk showed bright green. Even deep in the ship behind the organic barrier his exposure should have been worse. Coming to the upper deck would have only compounded the problem. Was his meter defective?

"Sorry. It was dark and boring, and I started to feel all tingly." He certainly didn't sound sorry. "I went to my room, put on my suit, and took a nap."

"A nap! How long have you been wandering around?" Radiation sickness might have already set in.

This was only the second time he'd used his salt-retention apparatus since leaving planet Fred, and the super suit wouldn't do anything for radiation poisoning.

"I feel fine now." He waved away her concern with a glistening appendage. "Whatcha doing?"

"Get in here and lend a hand." Worries about radiation had to wait. "Computer, restart the sequence."

The complex instructions were much easier with a second set of…well, prehensile antennae. But Nancy was exhausted and sweating inside her suit by the time the computer declared the deionization plate at full charge.

They waited out the rest of the restart process on the bridge. Nancy kept a close eye on Reemer's radiation gauge. It climbed steadily as the deionization procedure ran its course and the computer again tried to bring the subspace engines online. Why the device hadn't registered exposure while he was resting in his room remained a mystery.

Light flooded the bridge as the deck shifted with a disorienting lurch. Nancy scrambled for purchase. Reemer, of course, just stayed plastered to the deck and watched her flounder.

"Engine restart successful," the computer announced.

"No kidding." Nancy pushed to her feet. "Let's put a little distance between us and this anomaly. Issue a navigation advisory as soon as possible too."

Interior radiation readings dropped to zero, and the external ones fell sharply as the ship pulled away. Of course, her personal indicator stayed red. The cumulative exposure would go into her health record. In the meantime, she'd have to watch for symptoms and get a medical screening. The ship's small infirmary wasn't equipped to conduct a full evaluation, but should have a broad-spectrum anti-radiation drug to help head off any issues. With a sigh of regret, Nancy noted her two-hundred and twenty percent exposure reading, stripped off her suit, and set about collecting items that hadn't been tied down from the far corners of the bridge.

"When communications are back, find an authorized repair facility." Nancy's order interrupted the computer's verbal accounting of every engineering parameter known to man. "We need those FTL engines back online."

"Hey, guys?" Reemer's voice cracked as he flattened to the view screen and studied the ghostly phosphorescence of their wake. "Is this thing supposed to be following us?"

"What are you talking about?" Nancy joined him for a closer look.

Pale colors flashed within the amorphous cloud that was the anomaly. It had dwindled rapidly, but seemed to have stopped shrinking. In fact, it was growing larger.

"The captain-in-waiting is correct." Ziggy's portable robotic unit scuttled onto the bridge, nursing two broken legs and an assortment of dents from the debris it had been buried under. The robot nestled into the charging alcove, its consciousness passing into the main system and taking over just as the emergency program finished its litany of statistics. "The anomaly is caught in our ionic wake."

"Increase speed." Nancy had no interest in a repeat performance or in waiting around to examine the oddity of a mobile hazard.

"Increasing impulse power." Ziggy paused as the hum of the engines grew louder in response to the sudden demand. "Cloud is accelerating…approaching sixty percent output…distance to anomaly opening now. The cloud has broken away from our ion stream."

"Press harder," Nancy said. "Bring us up to ninety percent and lay in evasive maneuvers. I'm not giving this thing a second chance."

With only very distant stars for reference and fully functioning shipboard gravity, there was little to indicate the ship was throwing itself through a series of turns as they continued to accelerate.

After several tense minutes, Ziggy announced that the maneuvers had been successful and throttled down the engines to leave a break in their output signature. They coasted quietly away at high velocity. Without their wake to draw it along and no discernable mass to give it inertia, the tenacious space hazard drifted to a stop and quickly became a pinprick on the display.

"About that advisory, be sure to mention that this thing moves. The physicists will have to figure out what the heck it is and how best to track that cloud."

"Aye, Captain." Ziggy's voice sounded downright friendly compared to the emergency program's dull monotone. "Sending your datapad three potential repair facilities to choose from now."

The ports they could easily reach weren't true naval facilities, but each carried the proper certifications for working on interstellar vessels. One name stood out from the others. Gekko Salvage and Repair operated out of a starship tender owned by Veech Gekko, captain of the civilian mercenaries Nancy had fallen in with on planet Fred nearly five years ago.

Butterflies rose in her stomach at the thought of seeing the handsome man listed as the company's chief engineer. Nancy had history with Jake Farnsley. They'd been through hell and back on Reemer's homeworld. Later, their sporadic relationship had blossomed, and she'd spent a month on leave with the young technician.

Her face grew hot. *Stupid.* A ten-year age difference shouldn't matter. Failed romance aside, Nancy trusted him, which made her decision easy. The other beauty of a space tender was its mobility. Captain Gekko might be able to meet them halfway, which would minimize the time she was out of commission. To ensure the decision was unanimous, she consulted her companion.

"What do you think we should do, *Captain-in-Waiting* Reemer?" Her heavy sarcasm and raised eyebrow promised a reckoning.

Unfazed, Reemer took his sweet time perusing the information on the display with a quiet air of authority. Yep, it was definitely time to put the kibosh on whatever plans he and Ziggy were hatching.

9. Tangled Tender

T HE MASSIVE REPAIR ship let Ziggy land and park as easily as at any spaceport. Workers swarmed Nancy's ship within minutes of the atmosphere being restored in the huge bay. Most of the air had been compressed and reclaimed before their arrival. Expanding gases and being open to space left the entire area on the chilly side.

"My suit isn't working!" Reemer slapped at his cowl in alarm as he headed away on a tangent, made a ninety-degree turn, and crossed behind Nancy. "My mantle's tight and tingly. The deck feels funny too. Why isn't this thing working?"

He tugged the straps down tight, squishing his head into a thick pancake, eyes bulging on the ends of their stalks.

"Calm down and breathe," Nancy said as he shot off on another panicked zigzag behind her. "You're not getting sick. It's just cold in here. Your body's trying to cope. Don't worry, they'll get the bay up to temperature soon, and it'll be warm in the main ship."

She led the way to the smaller entrance alongside cargo doors big enough to admit fully assembled thrusters or bull elephants. Warm air wafted from the brightly lit passageway. She waited as Reemer made a final ninety-degree turn and honed in on the door.

"If this is what cold feels like, I'm glad we're not going to that ice planet." He shot inside and immediately sank into a sighing puddle of contented Squinch—and goo. There might be a cleaning issue with their visit.

"This is nothing compared to sub-freezing weather." She'd opted for a light therm-adjustable jacket so as not to have a bulky coat to cart around.

The foray beyond the repair bay was a welcome break from filling out forms and registry documents for the former Lobstra craft. Her small ship wasn't the only project aboard the repair tender. She and Reemer skirted several similar zones buzzing with workers before finding the maglift. The high-speed conveyance rocketed them up a dozen decks to the O-1 level. The tender was basically a small city.

Captain Gekko's dinner invitation got them away from the bustling manufacturing and repair decks. Though less crowded, the upper passages remained narrow, with piping and utility runs stuffed into low overheads. Stepping over raised combings at the frequent vacuum boundaries was second nature by now, but Reemer puffed and grunted as he cleared each hurdle.

Fortunately, the Squinch behavior of orthogonal travel disappeared in the close quarters found aboard ship. When outdoors or in similarly wide expanses—like, say, giant space-hangars—her friend ping-ponged from side to side using ninety-degree turns and generally traveling twice as far as necessary to get from point A to B. Once the walls closed in to about three times their body length, some circuit in the creatures' brains gave up on the elaborate mode of travel.

Unfortunately, that did nothing to alleviate the glistening trail marking their passage.

Nancy's stomach growled as they walked through the aroma of baking bread and savory concoctions. She never spotted the kitchens. A few more minutes negotiating the warren led them past a row of staterooms ending at Captain Gekko's cabin. The door slid aside when she pressed a hand to the call pad.

Being in command had its perks. Rather than a single stateroom, the captain had a suite of three adjoining rooms. They stepped into an open area with a corner kitchen, well-appointed living room, and a long dining table with chairs made of synthwood simulating rich mahogany grain.

Four place settings were set out on the table, and silver chafing dishes cut a line down the middle. The far end of the table butted up against a control console. The equipment panel curled around the corner chair on the right, which—unlike the rest—was of the swiveling command type. No doubt the captain monitored his ship while dining.

"Nancy!" Veech Gekko crossed the room in three massive strides, looking as though he intended to wrap her in a bear hug. "It's wonderful to see you again."

A hint of internal debate flickered across his suntanned face before he settled on a firm handshake. The man's skin tone remained a baffling anomaly. Not many ships had solar beds, but Captain Gekko apparently didn't believe in vitamin D supplements and must have made room. The big man would be on the downhill slide toward fifty, less than a decade older than Nancy. At six-two he stood nearly a foot taller, a good-looking fellow despite his crooked nose. He'd put on a few pounds, and salt overtook the pepper in his dark hair, something she could definitely relate to as more and more of her morning routine involved hunting down gray strands.

"The feeling's mutual, Captain. And not just because my engines are down." Nancy took in the stateroom with a low whistle of appreciation meant for the entire ship. "Your new command is practically a flying city."

"No need for titles. I'm not with the Spacers anymore. Veech will do just fine." His grin was infectious as he turned to her companion. "And Reemer, no doubt? Welcome aboard the *Hephaestus*."

Veech's hand shot forward out of habit, but hovered uncertainly in front of the slug. Reemer seized the opportunity, slapping his right antenna into the big man's palm.

"Great to see you too. Your people should keep the repair bay warmer. You're looking nice and round." The litany tumbled from the captain's wrist translator as the over-enthusiastic handshake slathered green goo halfway up the poor man's arm.

Nancy shot a warning glare at the slug. She'd forgotten how trying her friend could be. Practical jokes bordering on pre-teen potty humor were unfortunate companions to Reemer's male persona. Interesting that none of his Squinch peers seemed to have his unique sense of humor. The behavior was simply part of what made Reemer…Reemer. *The good with the bad.*

Veech's exposure to her translation gift back in the day had been minimal, and he hadn't retained much of the ability. The wrist translator missed the undertones bubbling from beneath the alien's green skirt, laughter that promised plenty of future mischief.

Their host took the dousing in stride and headed to the table for a napkin. He'd traded his uniform for crisp marine-blue coveralls, and was rightfully reluctant to wipe his dripping hand on the sharp outfit.

"Naval interpreter and Diplomatic Attaché Nancy Dickenson, you are a sight for sore eyes," Veech said while cleaning up his arm.

"More of a consultant actually." Attaché was a recent addition to her title that still made Nancy uncomfortable.

"Don't be so modest. I've followed your career, or at least the public data. You're quite the rising star." He waved her over to the table and lifted the lid off several trays to reveal an assortment of goodies. "Let's talk while we eat. Excellent cooks are the secret to a happy crew. The kitchens even managed a special addition for the discerning Squinch palate."

Reemer sidled up to a flat platform that brought him to table height in front of a wide blue fish as long as Nancy's forearm. The slug's eyes lit up at the sight of the raw meal. Nancy stifled a groan.

"Maybe we should wait—"

Reemer hacked a wad of thick phlegm onto his plate. Wriggling white worms attacked scales and fins, essentially pre-digesting the fish. Avoiding meals with her companion was a key weapon in her arsenal to stay sane. At least the oversized plate had a lip that contained the digestive juices. Both humans looked away as Reemer coughed again to bring up the amorphous wet balloon that was his digestive organ, slapped it down, and began sucking up the partially dissolved fish.

"I'm just glad we were close enough to offer assistance," Veech blurted out, desperate for a distraction.

"You and me both." Nancy grabbed the lifeline of conversation and summarized the circumstances that had left them limping toward a rendezvous with the good ship *Hephaestus*.

"The astrophysicists will have a field day analyzing that radioactive cloud." With Reemer's plate nearly empty, the man cautiously spooned a hunk of synth-meat in red gravy onto his plate. "Good thing you had shielding."

"Thanks to Herman. You remember the Lobstra pilot?" At his nod, she reached for the serving spoon, but paused to study the extra place setting. "Are we expecting a fourth? Maybe an engineer to discuss my repairs? That is if…" she mumbled to a halt, her face heating. *Some negotiator.*

Captain Gekko's eyes twinkled above a toothy smile as he came to her rescue. "Not to worry, Jake Farnsley will indeed be joining us. He got sidetracked with some late afternoon business. The boy's still a hard worker, but I know he's dying to see you."

"That's good to hear." Nancy concentrated on her breathing as another blush rose.

The captain was having a bit of fun with her. Jake would be twenty-seven, certainly not a boy, even if he was ten years her junior. She scanned the room to avoid eye contact, which was just as well since their host's attention had drifted to the control panel near his seat. Spurious displays sprang to life, lighting the board up like Christmas.

"Sorry I'm late, snookums. Those new invoices were a real mess."

Nancy instinctively looked to the door for the newcomer, but the sultry female voice had come from the panel near Veech.

"Nancy darling, it's so good to see you!" The husky voice oozed charm with a hint of southern twang. More lights twinkled merrily, and a rotating lens mounted among the controls swiveled to focus on Nancy. "And your slimy little friend too."

Nancy choked on the water she'd been sipping as the weight of a familiar presence settled into the control panel. "Quen, is that you?"

"You bet your pretty little bottom it is."

Unlike Ziggy, Quen was a true artificial intelligence program, one with a huge personality tending toward the flirtatious. The luxury-liner AI had been won in a card game and installed on the much smaller space freighter Veech acquired after leaving the military. Most of Quen's computerly ardor was directed at the man who had "rescued" her. Despite his past grumbling and complaining over the flirtatious behavior, Veech leaned into the wrap-around console, looking quite at ease.

"How's the new ship working for you?" Nancy directed the question at the console.

"It's a busy place, but oh so fun." More lights twinkled near the man nestled amongst her controls. "Veechy pretended we were going on a romantic tryst, just the two of us. But it turned out to be so much more."

Lights sparkled near Veech. The haptic pad under his hand caressed the man's palm with gentle waves.

"It weren't no tryst, machine." The way his fingers trailed across the pad belied his gruff voice. "I wasn't about to retrain a new system that didn't know me from Adam. And a bigger ship keeps you out of my hair."

"Whatever you say, lover." Quen had truly mastered human inflection, layering sarcasm over coyness as the sensory feedback pad pulsed under the captain's hand. "But I'll always make time for my snookums."

The man's face darkened, but his palm pressed into the pliant pad. Quen prattled on about how well he'd done to parlay the freighter's earnings into acquiring the *Hephaestus* and the early contracts that kept them solvent. Reemer's slurping made a noisy backdrop as the computer's attention turned back to her captain and more sweet nothings were met with short, gruff replies. Fortunately, the affectionate display was interrupted by a new arrival.

"Sorry I'm late, Captain, but those engine modifications for the mining conglomerate are lined up to finish on time." Jake nodded to his boss before flashing a smile full of genuine warmth. "Nancy, you look great."

He crossed the room and gave her a big hug. Friendly but a little reserved. The three years since they'd parted ways had flown by. She'd missed those long arms.

"Right back at ya." Working the tender had filled out Jake's lanky frame. "It's been too long."

Clouds rose in his stormy blue-gray eyes. From the way he studied her, it didn't take special abilities to see what ran through his head. She'd been the one who'd ended their relationship. Even with her diplomatic training and obscure postings, Jake had been willing to give the long-distance relationship a go.

But coming to grips with her new ability and responsibilities while trying to hold "them" together wouldn't have been fair. She *knew* he realized it too, but the truth had hurt him, she'd hurt him. He gave a slow, deliberate blink, his eyes losing their keen edge.

"So what's going on with your lobster ship?"

Thankful that he was willing to forget the past—for now—she launched into her tale as they ate. Having finished his own meal, Reemer occasionally chimed in, insisting she call his sled a rocket racer, emphasizing how his grab bars had saved the day, and providing other small details he deemed of vital importance.

Recounting their adventure would have taken forever if the slug hadn't grown bored and set about wandering the captain's rooms. When he headed for the bedroom, Nancy called him back to the table, but Veech waved away her concern—apparently willing to forego privacy for a coherent discussion.

"We occasionally work on Lobstra tech, so repairing the engines shouldn't be an issue." Veech turned to his lead engineer. "What's your take on the power distribution and shielding?"

"Damn good thing Herman installed a harmonic shield or we wouldn't be having this conversation. But the distribution grid needs to be upgraded to keep everything online. I'll have the crew work up a redesign, which should also power burst weapons while the shields are up. Give me a couple of days to check inventory for the proper energy conduit. If we have the parts, the job should be straightforward. Conservative guess is two weeks start to finish."

"Don't forget about Ziggy," Quen said out of the blue.

"The computer?" Nancy hadn't noticed the men talking about any shortcomings there.

"Poor thing sounds absolutely wretched." Quen's indicator lights snapped to life with her words. "Don't worry your pretty little head over that. Leave everything to Quen.

I'll have your little scamp of an AI up to snuff before you leave."

"Is that…safe?" She didn't know much about Lobstra programming languages or techniques. As much as she liked Quen, Veech's computer had been known to make blunders, especially when acclimating to different ships. The last thing she needed was Ziggy thinking he was a cruise liner or star tender.

"Don't worry." Veech clearly understood her anxiety. "I'll personally review any upgrades before they go into effect. We've had some growing pains, but Quen's gotten quite adept at ensuring artificial personalities are well-suited for their vessels. You'll be in on the process from day one."

"Well, maybe not day one, dear." The haptic pad arched up to pat the captain's hand, and the voice dropped to a sultry murmur. "We'll need *some* private time to really get things rolling, lover."

A red light on his display winked suggestively before the presence that was Quen bustled out of the room and the panel dimmed. How on Earth did that machine convey so much with no body language?

The captain cleared his throat and actually blushed. "I can give you and Reemer adjoining rooms during the overhaul. But I'm not certain we have a seawater tank for the Squinch."

"Not to worry." Reemer emerged from the bedroom wearing his cape and trailing a streamer of toilet paper. "We don't need salt baths anymore."

10. Idle Hands

"WHEN YOU'RE DONE with the power upgrades, will there be anything I need to watch for?" Nancy directed the question at Jake's feet, which stuck out of the access compartment.

"Not really," came Jake's muffled reply. "Load balancing should be fully automated. Any failures will show up on the bridge indicators and can be managed remotely. Just have the ship shut down the bad component and run diagnostics. Most of what I'm adding is bullet-proof, barring physical damage. So no running gun battles, okay?"

He withdrew from the opening and flashed that easy smile. A week of repairs hadn't left them much time to talk, especially since Jake constantly dashed off to check on other projects. Even so, the guy spent an inordinate amount of time on her ship, nearly as much as his team did. The way he tidied up his tool kit and portable display told Nancy he was about to rush off again. *More than just busy.* A flash of insight from her talent showed a closed, nervous man desperate to get away.

The gift she'd been given seldom faltered in its translation ability. But these flares of intuition came more and more frequently, making Nancy question if it was her imagination or some mutation of the ability the insect-like Lokii had bestowed. Waves of anxiety continued to wash over her, buzzing like angry bees and driving Nancy to block Jake's retreat.

"Jake, I'm sorry." His unease compelled her to explain. "I adore you, but the long-distance thing just wasn't going to work. My job has me flying across hell and back. Nobody needs that, or a girlfriend who can't help being nosy. It's just my talent…" she trailed off, unable to frame words to put him at ease.

"Reading my mind?"

Again with the smile. Even hurting, Jake put on a good front, but there was so much more below the surface. Those unspoken sentiments crested in another wave. He wanted to tell her he was in love, that she'd crushed his soul, that he forgave her, that he still needed to give "them" a go. At the same time, he gauged the distance to the door, ready to rush from the room and never look back.

All the unspoken words tumbled and churned in a tsunami of doubt despite his outward calm. The internal conflict made him look young and vulnerable.

"I don't do that." Nancy laid a hand on his arm, and the vying sentiments calmed, easing the tight corners of Jake's ever-present grin. No, she didn't read minds. These sporadic insights came from subtle physical clues. "It doesn't take special ability to see that I've hurt you. Someday our jobs might let this work. For now, I'm just happy to have you in my life."

"Same here." Calm spread through her friend, settling securely in his gentle eyes and smooth face, as though he'd said all he needed to—despite the fact that his thoughts remained unspoken. "I've missed you."

She wrapped him in a hug only to be crushed against his chest in return. The powerful grip took her breath away, and water brimmed in her eyes. She'd given up too much. The fierce embrace promised it all back when she was ready. A knot in her chest eased as they parted. Leave it to Jake to make her feel better when he was the one needing comfort.

"That's one handsome hunk of man-flesh." Quen's lusty voice jolted Nancy from her thoughts as she watched Jake stride from the engine room.

"Shh! He'll hear you. And don't be crass." Nancy chided the AI as leering LEDs sprang to life on the auxiliary panel.

"Spoilsport." The lights dimmed in an electronic pout, then sprang to excited intensity. "Stoic and smart is a good combination, wouldn't you agree?"

During repairs, Veech's AI had taken over ship functions. Nancy had gotten used to the AI popping up as Quen ran diagnostics and—in her words—worked a fabulous makeover on Ziggy. The artificial personality's obsession with Captain Gekko was all well and good, but Nancy wasn't about to share girl-talk, despite curiosity burning in the display lights to either side of the panel's camera.

Nancy snorted a laugh and shook her head. Lights and dials certainly couldn't convey the emotions she attributed to Quen. *Get a grip.*

"I'm not discussing men with you." She wagged a finger in front of the lens.

"Humans have different styles of interaction." Quen pressed on, indifferent to the cautionary finger. "You tend toward introverted, which would mean socializing takes energy that gets replenished when you're alone. But the outburst with the repair crew that was doing cable checks in your cabin had your physiological indicators soaring. The same thing happened when Reemer decided to wax the deck on the port passage. I'm just curious about the type of people you enjoy most."

It seemed a legitimate question. The computer waited expectantly, simple curiosity replacing the sexual overtones Nancy's own insecurity had undoubtedly projected.

"It wasn't an outburst." She'd been pretty hard on the poor man who'd scattered her clothes across the bed while tracing wires. "No one wants strangers going through their underwear drawer." She took a calming breath. "Just chalk it up to those introvert genes. And I wouldn't have been so mad at Reemer if he'd used a mop. Squinch can do a lot with their slime, but it isn't floor cleaner."

"He gets under your skin, doesn't he?"

"Like a burrowing tick." Splashing, slopping, oozing memories had Nancy suppressing a smile. Reemer might be a walking biological disaster, but he'd always been there for her.

"Looks like you enjoy pranksters too."

"What are you up to?" Another burst of intuition put the devil in Quen's reply.

"Just lending an ear, as it were, dear." The AI's focus shifted as lights flashed on the panel. "But enough chitchat. Back to work for me. Ta-ta for now."

Before Nancy could comment on the fact that computers didn't have ears, Quen's presence swept from the room and the panel went dark. *How very odd.*

Truthfully, Nancy had work to do too. Several secure subspace channels reported that talks with the mining consortium on Spaceport Gail had stalled out. A local religious faction with substantial financial backing threatened legal action, and the on-site ambassador had called for a ten-day cooling off period. With a week of repairs left, the timing would work out perfectly for her to arrive before negotiations ramped up again. Nancy headed for the bridge and put in a low-lag call to her branch manager.

"We'll of course pay the parts invoice immediately and the balance once labor charges are tabulated." Commander Branson swept curly brown locks out of his eyes, looking haggard as he flipped through the accounting and proposal she'd attached to the transmission. "But Gail's ambassador hasn't accepted our offer of help. My section head is thinking you'd be of more use elsewhere."

Well, that was a one-eighty. As the situation deteriorated, Nancy's continued interest had been met with ever-increasing enthusiasm over the prospect of Earth Force being paid with shares in the luxene mining operation.

"What gives, Olaf?" The two were cordial outside of work. Nancy needed a friend more than a supervisor to give her the inside scoop. "Why the sudden change of heart?"

"Turns out Gail is one of Admiral Cheyung's pet projects, and he's keeping Ambassador Turlic on a short leash. There's pressure from the bean counters too." The man blanched and shot a look over his left shoulder—but the color returned quickly, so that could have been the transmission lag messing with image saturation. "Your situation there has raised more than a few eyebrows." He rechecked her figures. "But for the amount of work, Captain Gekko must be giving you the friends and family discount. Helping out at Gail sure seems like a win-win to me. I'll keep you informed and push from this end. We've got a few days left to save you from an oh-so-wonderful sleigh ride to planet Cauthorn."

His nervous chuckle ruined the pun. Olaf had a good sense of humor and had always looked out for Nancy. Casual banter across interstellar distances was cost prohibitive, but in the years they'd worked together they'd developed a friendship. When she'd had to requalify for her license back on Earth, he'd even invited Nancy to his daughter's birthday party. Once the kids had gone to bed, they'd swapped "sea" stories despite his wife's eye-rolls.

"If it helps sway the Admiral at all, remind him that I have a Squinch aboard who won't do well with the cold."

"You've told me about Reemer. He's going to be quite a handful no matter where you land." Olaf might not have firsthand experience with the slug's antics but recalled her stories with a knowing nod. He sobered as the beeping of an incoming message rose from his console. "Duty calls. I'll authorize those payments and be in touch." A nervous glance down had him biting off an uncharacteristic curse. "Use my private access number from now on." At her raised eyebrow, he rushed on. "The situation on Gail is…evolving, and I want you to be able to contact me even if I'm off-duty. You've got the code?"

"Sure do, Commander."

"Good." His hands danced across the bottom of the screen, likely cueing up his next call. "And, Nancy, stay safe. Control, out."

The display went dark, leaving her to wonder at his odd behavior and cryptic wording. Maybe he was having some kind of family crisis. That could keep him out of the office and reliant on his private number. The channel would still be secure and suitable for business discussions, but transcribing their discussion into the official logs would have the man putting in extra hours. Family problems were no fun, and Nancy sent up silent thanks that her talent hadn't read any additional information into the exchange. That would have felt too much like prying.

"Thank the goddess for small miracles." Parroting Lobstra adages to Lady Luck seemed appropriate given the sporadic behavior of her gift, but some time away from a culture that embraced randomness was probably good too.

"Ha! You sound like grumpy old Meinish." Reemer swept into the room, wearing his cape and looking quite pleased with himself.

"Meinish mentioned you before I left." In all the excitement, she'd neglected to pass along the Lobstra's message. "He'd just found a foul-smelling lump of fungi in a damp cavern."

"Nice! Did he want me to slip a chunk into an air duct or maybe one of those fancy pools rich people use?"

"No, he said it looked like you—smelled like you too." That last bit wasn't accurate at all. Squinch smelled of salt spray and tart apples, not at all unpleasant—except when they wanted to. Nancy grinned at how her friend's eyes glistened, much in the same way Meinish's had when he asked her to pass along the insult.

Reemer and the Lobstra had a special relationship. When old crustacean first met carefree mollusk, Nancy had expected sparks to fly. But an unexpected friendship had blossomed at the intersection of revered Lobstra randomness and slimy pranks. The pair quickly became inseparable peas in a pod.

"Ha!" Reemer piped amusement from his hidden orifices. "I'll have to find a gnarled old rock for you to take back, something chalky, bitter, and wizened like him. Maybe the space station will have an appropriately ugly item. Speaking of which, when do we blow this popsicle stand?"

She needed to ween him off old television shows or get stuck interpreting sayings that had gone out of fashion a century ago. The archaic language intensified the slug's self-satisfied smirk, but one eyestalk kept swiveling back to the airlock.

"What's the rush?" Nancy didn't hear any alarms outside the open hatch, which was a good sign.

Reemer's nutrient suit might be necessary for his continued health, but trouble followed the caped Squinch. She suspected the outfit brought out his mischievous streak, which was an aspect that needed little encouragement. He hadn't done any true damage so far, but Jake assigned two cleaning bots to follow Reemer around and handle his messes. Industrial facilities were accidents waiting to happen. It was only a matter of time before Reemer slimed, tripped, or simply distracted someone at precisely the wrong moment.

"Boredom." Reemer swung his cape around to stroke the glistening fabric. "Everyone here's too busy. Even wearing my super suit isn't much fun."

A bored Reemer was a recipe for disaster. No one wanted to see that. Nancy strode to the bridge; a glance through the main hatch showed a maintenance team working on external sensors. There wasn't a bot in sight, so the slug had managed to ditch his cleaning crew. She settled in at the comms station while Reemer picked at the furry controls of the deactivated aux panel.

"Headquarters is being squirrely." Nancy checked her messages, finding nothing of interest. "There's still talk of sending us to Cauthorn, though I can't for the life of me see why I'm needed."

"Not the ice planet!" Panic colored his words.

"Don't worry. The boss is in my corner." The situation on Gail might be guarded, but negotiations were her strong suit. "Despite the politics back home, logic has to prevail. If I don't get a formal response before our final inspection, I'll put in another call."

This was the first time she'd gotten pushback on a perspective assignment.

"It better be quick. No one has time for me here, and galactic standard is a pain. The captain and Jake speak better, but are always out making rounds. I waited at Jake's cabin all afternoon, and he never showed. Quen knows Squinch, but is always asking weird questions about *you*—hardly ever wants the scoop on interesting discoveries *I've* made."

"Really?" Hopefully, the AI wasn't planning to play matchmaker. Quen knew her history with Jake. "She's been pestering me too. I feel like I'm back in therapy."

Reemer looked about to comment, but an internal call lit up the display. Nancy waved a hand over the sensor to acknowledge receipt and open a channel.

"Is our slimy *friend* down there?" Jake sounded tight-lipped as though trying to control his temper.

"Sure is," Nancy said cautiously. "I'll put him on."

"Don't bother. Bring the little shit to my cabin." The line went silent but hadn't disconnected. "Please."

Interrogating Reemer on the way to the berthing decks yielded the Squinch equivalent of shrugs and wide-eyed innocence. He seemed unabashed—a perpetual state for the slug regardless of his actions—but wasn't forthcoming about what Jake might want. They marched on in silence.

* * *

"You need to control your slug," Jake said after a cleaning bot opened the stateroom door.

Jake sat on his desk with arms crossed, a determined glare creasing his forehead. The room was empty except for the built-in work station with its wide surface, inset drawers, and shelves above the swivel display. The tall, stick-skinny bot that admitted them, swept off to the right, a whirlwind with sterilizing flaps slapping the deck as it buffed its way across the already gleaming floor. A round, knee-high bot bounced off the far wall like an oversized hockey puck as it too scoured the empty space.

"Are you moving?" Nancy took in his scowl and the empty room. Had Reemer slimed things so badly that it all had to be removed? Even the desk was devoid of the typical input devices and knickknacks. "Okay, I'll bite. Where's all your stuff?"

Jake jerked a thumb at the ceiling, and Nancy did a double-take. She'd been so focused on the robots that she hadn't looked up. Her first thought was that an artificial gravity circuit had malfunctioned, except people and bots remained firmly planted on the floor. The same couldn't be said for the rest of the room's contents.

Gravity hadn't just been lost, it had been reversed, drawing everything that wasn't nailed down to the overhead in an amazingly orderly fashion.

A datapad, several mechanical components, and Jake's coffee cup were plastered to the ceiling among the piping over his desk. The desk chair sat with wheels to the ceiling nearby, as if awaiting an upside-down occupant. His mattress had slipped past the venting so that it lay between framing members, neatly made up with silvery sheets, fluffy pillows, and a fresh pair of overalls draped across the edge. A dozen other miscellaneous objects were neatly arranged overhead as if they simply had decided to sit on the ceiling instead of the floor. Shiny trails running between the items explained the baffling scene.

"I've been pretty patient with—" A boot dropped to the floor with a loud thwack, sticky slime glistening on its sole. Jake's lips cut a thin line as he closed his eyes and sucked air through his nose, struggling for control before turning to Reemer. "You've got gourmet food, the run of the ship, all the entertainment vids you could want." Jake threw both hands up to take in his vertically displaced belongings. "For the love of God, why?"

"I waited, but you never showed," Reemer said as though it was a perfectly rational explanation.

Outrage and frustration warred in Jake's features. After a good thirty seconds his shoulders sagged, and he blew out a big breath. "Three days." He jabbed that many fingers under Reemer's fleshy beak. "No more slimy trails, no more bathing in the scullery sinks, and no more gluing things where they don't belong." He turned to Nancy. "We're down to operational checks and shouldn't have to reopen any conduits or access panels. The Squinch can move back to your ship and stay there until you take off."

"Hey! Your boson is supposed to teach me how to play poker tonight." Reemer ignored the dangerous glint in the man's eyes.

"The computer can set up a holo table for us." Nancy forced enthusiasm into her voice. "I haven't played cards in ages. We'll go over the rules together. It'll be good to get back aboard."

"I didn't mean you," Jake said.

"I know." She softened her gaze to let Jake see there were no hard feelings. The second boot dropped right between them before she could say more.

The tall bot whirled away from the shiny trail that ran up the bulkhead to attend to Jake's befouled footwear. The machine had cleaned the walls as high as it could reach, but taller equipment would be needed to handle the rest of the mess.

"So how do we get this stuff down?" Nancy raised an eyebrow at her travel companion.

"*That* won't be a problem." Reemer didn't even flinch as the coffee mug crashed to the deck and shattered, followed quickly by a desk lamp.

With a deft grab Jake caught his datapad before impact. Nothing else was worth saving as they danced and dodged, avoiding the deluge as Squinch slime let loose.

11. Onward

B EING BACK ABOARD her own ship brought a certain level of peace. Reemer took his confinement as a sign they would soon be on their way and stayed surprisingly upbeat. Although still free to roam the tender, Nancy took the opportunity to get everything in order for liftoff, laying in supplies and familiarizing herself with the upgraded systems. Drilling with the manual controls made her *feel* more in control. Of course, Ziggy and the automated subroutines would handle daily operations and any emergencies, but the AI was still offline for its own upgrades.

Quen took advantage of the self-imposed isolation, popping up with alarming frequency whenever Nancy drifted near a bank of controls. Veech's shipboard personality was nothing if not predicable, always opening with overly suggestive small talk, sliding into probing interpersonal questions, and inevitably stopping abruptly when Nancy assured the AI she was quite happy on her own. Quen would then hurry off, dodging Nancy's own questions about the sudden interest in human relationships.

Reemer received similar treatment on occasion, but spent most of his time holed up in his quarters, presumably watching ancient vids from the tender's library.

Nancy spent the day before liftoff reconciling the repair costs, ensuring the sizable bill was neat and tidy for the accounts payable folks back home. Her trip to Gail remained in a "review pending" status. Getting in touch with Commander Branson was next on her list when another call came in from headquarters. But instead of Olaf's pleasant features, the holoscreen lit up with the swarthy face of an officer she'd never met.

"I'm Commander Timon Horsh, Admiral Cheyung's chief of staff." The dark-haired man looked down a sharp, cruel nose to consult something on his desk. "Dr. Dickenson, I presume?"

"That's right." Nancy stifled her surprise and kept her features neutral. "I'm honored to meet you."

"Yes, of course. Now about your request to visit Spaceport Gail." More consulting of his notes. "That request is denied."

"But why?" Nancy blurted before catching herself and adding a belated, "sir."

"The admiral feels you would better serve the Navy elsewhere." He cocked a heavy brow at her. "Are you questioning a flag officer's judgement, young lady?"

Despite his pocked features, the commander wasn't much older than Nancy. Deep creases gathered at the corners of his mouth and eyes as he scowled his disapproval.

"Of course not, but the station reports certainly make it seem as though—"

"Yes, we are well aware of the *unclassified* information floating around. But there's more to the story. Considering your recent mishap and the cost of repairs, Admiral Cheyung is ordering you to planet Cauthorn to handle the intellectual property issue."

"With all due respect, Commander, I'm still a civilian consultant free to turn down missions that don't suit my skills."

The man swelled as if about to burst, but then released a gusty sigh and nodded. "Point taken. Let us say instead that the admiral requests your help on Cauthorn, and I strongly suggest you consider accommodating him. There's hard credits to be had in those negotiations, and by my accounting…" He trailed off, glanced at his notes, and let out a low whistle. "Your repair bills are quite impressive. It would be a pity to have payment delayed by internal audits. Those penny-pinchers don't understand the cost of doing business. I'd hate to see the debt fall back on your personal accounts."

As threats go it wasn't very original, nor subtle. Qualified repairs by certified technicians weren't cheap. If this jerk pushed the issue, she'd be fighting legal battles for a decade. She might even lose the ship and land back on Navy transports, which would leave her even less options when it came to missions.

"The anomaly did quite a number on the ship. But I've reconciled the charges myself. You'll find they're all in order."

All true, but worry eroded her confidence. It would be all too easy for some faceless bean-counter to deem Jake's power and automation upgrades as overly extravagant even though they integrated the Lobstra capabilities that saved her life. Quen's mysterious changes to Ziggy would be the only work that could truly be labeled nonessential, but Captain Gekko hadn't billed any time or materials for that.

"Yes, the anomaly." He rolled his eyes before gracing her with a flat stare. "We're waiting on the survey team data to determine what you blundered into that had you calling old friends for help. A convenient coincidence, knowing a nearby shipfitter."

So he'd been looking into her personal files. Not a big surprise, but disappointing to have it thrown in her face. Nancy ended the unpleasant call with a promise to review the ice planet mission briefing. Her own feelings aside, Reemer really would be stuck aboard ship for the duration due to the frigid temperatures. If Horsh thought the bills were high now, he'd choke on what came from leaving the bored Squinch alone to wreak havoc.

The final inspections didn't find any major issues. Jake made plenty of tweaks, demanding perfection before letting her venture into space. Studying the ice planet portfolio proved less than illuminating. The mission still seemed a bust.

Poets and copywriters were at each other's throats over certain ancient texts that had been recycled whole-cloth into serialized modern works. The theological dispute threatened to split off a planetary religion. Translation and insight from an outsider would be of dubious benefit. Commander Horsh hadn't lied about the credits to be had. But *why* the ruling body offered such insanely high fees was a mystery. All in all the mission remained unattractive. Was headquarters really so upset with her bills that they were willing to sideline their rising star?

To make matters worse, the survey team sent to study the deadly anomaly and set up warning beacons ended up returning early. They found a few small pockets of debris from the damage to her ship, but nothing else out of the ordinary along her flight path. Even if the anomaly had continued to move, the team should have been able to track its radiation signature.

One bright spot was the surprise ribbon cutting ceremony when she returned from finishing up paperwork with Jake. Reemer met them at the main hatch wearing his super suit and a knowing grin. He led the way to the bridge where Captain Gekko presented her with a pair of gold-plated scissors that she used to slice the wide red sash draped across the entrance.

Ziggy's mobile unit stood inside by the navigation table, Quen's presence looming large from the main controls behind him. The ship's AI had of course been present for much of the equipment checks, but Quen had always whisked him away after each day's tests were completed. The mobile unit appeared much the same as before, with multiple Lobstra-esque legs fused to a more traditional torso, but the lines of head, face, and arms had been softened. The changes made Ziggy sleek and modern despite his hybrid design.

A cone-shaped hat covered in festive swirls sat at a jaunty angle from the round dome of the robot's head. His glowing red eyes—piezo-electric adjustable aperture and so much more expressive than the prior lenses—narrowed into thin arcs of amusement when Nancy raised an eyebrow. She approached the blue sheet cake that sat on the nav table. A smokeless candle burned through rainbow colors in the middle of the heavily-iced dessert.

"Go ahead, dear." Quen said before slipping into the auxiliary panel by Veech, lights twinkling proudly behind the tender's captain, who also looked pretty darn pleased. They'd certainly done wonders with her ship.

"What's with the candle?" Nancy stepped aside when the robot pushed past to extinguish the flame with a puff of compressed air.

"Our little boy's turned one." Quen actually squealed in delight, displays flashing out a happy little cadence as Veech leaned into the feathery Lobstra controls.

"One what?" Nancy had to wonder if Quen had confused her holidays, but the console and captain continued to beam down at Ziggy's mobile unit as it traced a long, articulated finger through the icing. "Wait, are you saying what I think you're saying?" From the way he studied the frosting on his fingers, the robot must also be equipped with haptic sensors, maybe even the electronic equivalent of a nervous system. Quen and the captain had created something with much more than simple cosmetic upgrades.

"Our little boy's ready to leave home," the AI announced. Captain Gekko went red around the ears, but he stuck close to the console as his long-time companion, sometimes tormentor, and now—apparently—domestic partner beamed at what they had made together. "I'm sure you'll take good care of our little man. Everything will be so new and exciting. I can't wait to hear all about your adventures. He'll be inquisitive but reserved, an expert yet approachable. All with a healthy sense of humor just the way you like." The shifting panel lights managed to include Reemer in that last statement, which did *not* bode well.

"*That's* why you kept playing twenty questions?" Nancy frantically sorted through the off-hand answers she'd come up with, often simply in an attempt to stave off what seemed like a weirdly personal obsession. But Quen hadn't been match making; she'd been making a baby AI!

"Well, I'll be." Jake snapped his mouth shut when he realized it was hanging open. "Can I cut anyone some cake?"

After the initial shock and two pieces of chocolate cake, Nancy had to excuse herself to take a call on her personal datapad. The ship routed the incoming transmission to her private number, which could only mean Mom was desperate to talk. A quick swipe acknowledged the call without incurring charges while Nancy headed to her cabin. She'd checked in with her parents twice during the overhaul, but of course those had been non-realtime calls subject to long lag times.

Would Quen be constantly checking up on Ziggy for the duration? Would Captain Gekko? The thought of human and AI "parents" made her head hurt. Good grief, they might want her to be Ziggy's godmother, or maybe she'd turn into "Aunt Nancy."

Pins and needles settled behind her eyes, the same feeling her talent had caused when it first appeared. She sat at her corner desk and waited for the pain to settle down, but couldn't keep Mom on hold forever. The sensation only intensified when she activated the call.

"Olaf?" The last person she'd expected to see on the small screen was her branch manager. Horsh had made it quite clear that he alone would be handling her next assignment.

The normally calm and collected diplomat looked frazzled, as if he'd slept in his uniform. Dark walls and messy wiring replaced the austere office that usually formed a backdrop to his calls, and old pop-up monitors surrounded the man. Overall, it looked like he was calling from his basement.

"Nancy, sorry for using your private line, but I thought this would be better given our current…circumstances. Your flight plan is clear for your next mission."

"Thanks, but I haven't agreed to take on the poetry dispute." She hated to sound ungrateful, but wasn't about to roll over and let the department sideline her. "Tell Admiral Cheyung and Commander Horsh to find someone better suited for the job. Respectfully."

"Horsh isn't part of this." He shot a look over his shoulder even though the back wall was only a foot behind his chair. "Gail's ambassador needs your help." A few deft keystrokes had encrypted data flowing into her system. "I'm sending the full portfolio of players and the situation as we understand it. It's an incomplete profile, but gives you a starting point. I'm exercising a bit of executive privilege here, so don't let me down."

"I really appreciate that and will do my best, sir." The pain in her head throbbed in time with a nervous tic that had her boss's left shoulder jumping. The man was desperate to end the call. "Olaf, are you okay?"

"I'll be fine." He waved away her concern with false assurance. "Just a little upper management cross-threading. Use this channel for your reports until I straighten things out on this end. And don't bother logging your official flight plan. We have it here. I'll make sure it gets submitted."

It wasn't exactly breaking flight regulations, but having a third party—even a government agency—submit such reports was certainly stretching the law. Space was vast by nature, but disturbances from hyperspace jumps were closely monitored and coordinated. Ships vied constantly for prime locations to reduce the time and costs of long subspace travel. Not a big problem in deep space when dropping out in accordance with crew or engine exposure tables. But traffic patterns and hyperspace exits grew ever more congested near solar systems, planets, and ports.

"If you're sure." She returned his nod, hoping nothing forced her to deviate from the plan this time. "I'll have a high-priority daemon watch this channel for any reroutes."

"Excellent." The smile didn't reach his eyes nor do anything to ease her suspicion that something was terribly wrong at headquarters. "No time left to chitchat, Dr. Dickenson. When you get to Spaceport Gail, find the ambassador and figure out what's going on. I'm counting on you to put things right."

"A stake in luxene production will certainly be worth it."

"More than you know." The tic practically had him dancing in his seat, but it calmed as he leaned in with earnest eyes. "Godspeed, Nancy, and keep yourself safe. I will let you know if the situation here shifts."

He ended the call, leaving Nancy to feed the files through her personal decryption key. There wasn't nearly as much information as she would have liked, really not much more than what she'd already collated. Ambassador Turlic's logs were one notable addition, but the last entry was over a week old.

If all went well, the trip to Gail would take four days, leaving her time to peruse the material and hopefully tease out additional details. Olaf might have more for her to go on before docking. But given his odd behavior, she rather doubted it.

Nancy would also need to come up with talking points in case Commander Horsh contacted her. Better yet, Ziggy could deflect any incoming transmissions to make it look as if background interference had knocked out ship communications. Certain military-grade channels manipulated quantum probabilities to overcome such blockages, but nothing like that would ever be used to message a simple diplomatic liaison.

"Mon Capitan, you can't hide in here all night." The door slid open, admitting Reemer, who'd added a birthday hat to his caped ensemble. "We've got presents to open and people to impress with witty banter. Even Ziggy's getting into the action."

Wonderful. This wasn't exactly the time for her ship's personality to come out of his shell, not with leadership back home getting all squirrelly. But she had better make sure the Squinch wasn't putting bad ideas into the ship's head. Not that she was overly worried. Veech had been deeply involved in Ziggy's upgrade. The ex-Spacer was a stickler for regulations and wouldn't have approved inappropriate behaviors.

"I'll be there in a minute. We're heading to Spaceport Gail after all, and I want to be certain the launch plan still makes sense. No more detours this time. Agreed?"

"Sure do, and no more crimes either."

"What are you talking about?" Nancy only lent half an ear while double checking the coordinates Olaf would file.

"Well, the anomaly disappeared right?"

"Yeah, so?" She could have shaved a day off the trip by including Reemer in the bridge rotation to extend each jump, but that couldn't be helped now.

"That's the smoking gun, so they threw it in the river."

Nancy rolled her eyes. "Those crime dramas are rotting your brain."

"It makes sense." He grew earnest, an uncommon state for the slug that made it hard for her to dismiss his next words. "They tried to murder you."

12. Gail

S TARS GLEAMED ON the display, a steady beacon calling Nancy onward. The allure of space had snared her from the very beginning on that first Navy expedition, back when her passion had been discovering new flora. In the moments of calm between watches and mission preps, the never-ending expanse of the universe had called, the stars tugging at her heart as they had for mariners and explorers through the ages. That calm, steadfast vastness, with primordial reactors massive beyond imagination reduced to burning points projected on inky infinity, soothed her soul. The quiet beckoned, promising peace and eternity if she only dared to grasp it.

Wondrous.

"We're not getting any younger, if you know what I mean." Ziggy's upgraded voice mechanics produced a pleasing baritone with a bit of zany twang. The words from the panel below her display came out in stereo, parroted by the ship's robot as it slipped up behind where she stood. "It's taking forever to get to the first hyperspace jump."

They'd slowly ramped up to seventy-five percent of maximum thrust for the first day out. After some teary goodbyes, Jake had reminded her of the need to break in the new systems while the cyclonic reactor stabilized. That left plenty of time to catch problems, but also had her ship's fledgling personality chomping at the bit.

"You got somewhere else to be?" Nancy asked with a raised eyebrow. "Crossing space is kind of your job. Going faster won't make much difference."

"I just like to feel I'm making progress. Even with long-range sensors, the vectors hardly change. It's like we aren't moving."

"Focus on the distance to our next jump. We're about three-quarters of the way there and climbing. The rate change should help."

Smart, but needy; that was how she thought of her new AI. The mobile unit nodded, its eyes narrowing to slits while concentrating on an internal shift of perspective.

"Ah, that does help." Metallic shoulders slumped and the voice shifted back to mono, coming only from the robot. "I just feel like I should be doing… I don't know…more."

"How about we go check on Reemer. I want us both on watch for this first jump. You can help me pry him away from his shows."

Ziggy gave a sad nod and followed her aft. Just a day out, and this wasn't even the first time he'd gotten depressed. Quen may have baked entirely too much into the personality. She'd tried to accommodate everyone's needs, including Nancy's conflicting answers about relationships. The results left Ziggy bursting at the seams, trying to be everywhere at once, and striving for something intangible he'd yet to articulate.

"I just want to know who I am," he said as they walked. "What I'll become one day."

"Humans call that knowing what you want to be when you grow up." Nancy put a hand on a cool metallic shoulder. The joint relaxed under her touch, mimicking how tension would drain from tight muscles. "We all feel lost at times. It's natural."

Ziggy was on the fast track, simultaneously blazing through the various stages of depression, launching on his journey of self-discovery, and mentally traversing who knew what other paths. And he was all of a week old.

The door to Reemer's room opened at her knock.

"No more soap operas," Nancy called as she stepped inside. "We need to discuss watch rotation and…" The entertainment screen was dark, the slug's viewing couch empty.

"Hey there. You're just in time. Whatcha think?" Reemer balanced on the back edge of his single foot, his skirt clinging to the wall just inside his sleeping quarters. Both antennae stretched high to pin the end of a red string at the top of a colorful web. He pulled the string taut and secured it with a bit of sticky slime, then slid back to admire his work.

Several dozen cords of varying lengths and colors covered the surface. The chaotic array intersected at random nodes scattered across the wall. Next to each node a palm-pad with notes or data sheets had been similarly glued to the bulkhead. Some strings ended at pictures, honest to goodness printouts—mostly of people, but some were buildings. Her own photo sat boldly in the center of the web, the source of many strings.

"I think I'd rather you watched old vidcasts." Nancy squinted at her picture, taking in the frizzy hair, tired eyes, and mirror in the background. "I'm about to brush my teeth in this. You pulled security footage from my stateroom?"

"I needed you looking vulnerable," Reemer said defensively. "You're the murder victim."

"Seriously? A crime board?" Her gaze jumped to images of Belinda, Olaf Branson, and another Squinch she didn't recognize. Apparently, even Jake and Veech weren't above suspicion. A picture of the Lobstra homeworld was overlaid with a big question mark, as were images of Earth and a Navy ship that looked as if it was clipped from on old science fiction movie—wires and all. At the far right of his tapestry two lonely strings terminated at a man and woman in their twenties with arms linked and wearing dazzling smiles. She jabbed a finger the couple. "There wasn't any murder, Reemer. I don't even *know* these people."

A delicate shade of green crept along the base of the Squinch's eyestalks—the equivalent of a blush. "Those two are just a placeholder. The picture came with the frame." His color returned to normal in a flash. "And there was *too* a murder—almost."

"I must say, this is quite impressive." Ziggy moved along the wall as if studying a great work of art, but his admiration flowed toward the artist. "The single-minded passion. I am…sad and yet mad that I do not have such focus."

Ziggy stumbled over his words, clearly confused. Nancy blew out a sigh. *It's going to be a long trip.*

"That's envy you're feeling." Nancy looked from robot to slug. "It's when you want what someone else has. Try to ignore it. You should find your own path, not lust after another's. And *this* is definitely not something to covet." She waved at the wall and spun to face Reemer. "No more crime dramas. You're cut off. Be on the bridge in five to discuss the jump. I'm not leaving anything to chance. No offense, Ziggy."

"None taken, Captain." One of his delicate legs traced a line connecting radiation measurements to the spaceship model. "Although, my own readings indicated that decades would be needed for this energy to naturally decay. Unique rotating harmonics drove the anomaly's trajectory. That the anomaly vanished so soon after giving up on us may be a valid concern."

"Don't start. No tech in the universe can steer natural phenomena around." She spun toward the door, holding one hand out flat. "Five minutes, both of you."

"Make it ten," Reemer cringed at her glare. "I need to change!"

"Why are you even wearing the cape?" Nancy had nearly given up on tracking that particular behavior, which certainly didn't seem to be linked to the slug's need for salt therapy.

"The trappings of office are important in crime solving." Reemer stroked his cape lovingly and removed the cowl, carefully slipping his left and then the right eyestalk through the holes in the skullcap.

"For the last time, there was no crime." Nancy stalked from the room, shaking her head.

Good grief, next he'll be sporting a Calabash pipe and magnifying glass.

Despite their rocky start, the trip progressed smoothly. The ensuing days saw them through four hyperspace jumps each lasting eight hours. Reemer kept tensions high by insisting they prepare for the worst whenever dropping back to sub-light travel. Nancy had to admit that having their new shields up for each transition wasn't a bad idea. The FTL boundary could play havoc on sensors, and missing even the tiniest object would ruin their day.

When no mysterious anomalies blocked their path, the Squinch funneled his paranoia into complaints of boredom. For all his soul searching and ruminating over the meaning of life, Ziggy did a marvelous job navigating and providing for effective shipboard operations.

Soon robot, human, and Squinch stood marveling as Spaceport Gail filled their view screens. Gail orbited Gardarri, the largest of Vargus Prime's three moons. Satellite, moon, and planet drifted into a staggered line while they awaited clearance to dock.

Ships and maintenance craft drifted across the display, tiny dots against Gail's vast central hub. Shaped like a blunted diamond, the faceted structure would house thousands of full-time inhabitants and nearly as many visitors—a true space metropolis open to all races. Huge rings added even more real estate, protons and electrons orbiting the central mass. Many rings rotated, delicate and stately on differing axes, forming a roughly galactic shape.

Nancy imagined a line drawn through the center with dozens of orbiting belts, each tilted on a different orbital plane, the furthest perhaps 20 degrees off the primary equatorial loop. Artificial gravity would support the hub, while centripetal force approximated the effect based on each loop's rotational vector.

Gravitonic generators tended to be power hogs. Most space-faring ships were compact with modest square footage compared to the floating city they approached. Her own ride was about the smallest class vessel to have artificial gravity, and a good percentage of engine output fed the generation equipment. Leveraging spin vectors where possible conserved Gail's reactor power for more important needs.

"Earth 579, sorry for the wait." Authentication tags appeared along the bottom of the screen, verifying the woman's voice. "Your flight clearance just arrived this morning, so hadn't been scrubbed."

"No problem, control." Nancy's confidence in station logistics took a nosedive. Olaf should have filed her flight plan days ago. "Are we good to go?"

"Affirmative. You are cleared to dock, 579. I'm sending over the beacon frequency. Please make certain hyperspace engines are offline and obey posted low-engine-wake restrictions. Once your navcomp is locked on, the signal will guide you in. I have a note here that the ambassador will meet you upon arrival."

"Excellent. Engaging beacon now." Nancy turned control over to Ziggy, whose consciousness was currently split between the mobile unit and the ship itself. "Looks like we won't need to hunt down Ambassador Turlic after all."

"Seems too easy." Reemer squinted at the encryption codes flashing down the screen as the ship's head came about in accordance with the beacon's instruction.

He studied the shifting digits, but of course wouldn't be able to make any sense of them whatsoever. The slug had *that* look again, as if ready to whip out the proverbial magnifying glass and go all Sherlock Holmes on the docking system. Nancy shook her head, doing her best to ignore him and enjoy the scenery.

They threaded through the widest loop, a narrow affair stretching off toward the moon. The unnerving maneuver wasn't particularly dangerous, but gave them an up-close look at the engineering.

Once through the ring, they arched overtop the main node to drop toward the uppermost of the docking ports ringing the station. Nancy gasped as the moon rose beyond the gleaming central hub, not because of the geometric network crisscrossing its surface, but because of the dozens of ships hanging between station and moon.

"Who are they?" Nancy didn't recognize the needle-nosed ship design.

"Vargan short-range fighters from the planet below," Ziggy replied.

The formation clearly sought to discourage trips to the moon's surface. Nancy checked the sensor readings. No power spikes beyond normal station-keeping engines, so at least their energy weapons weren't primed. Kinetics would be another matter.

"Negotiations must be in deeper trouble than I thought." She looked forward to the ambassador's report.

* * *

Reemer joined her at the airlock once the engines were secured. Upon seeing his cape, she sent him back to change, worried that constant use would deplete its effectiveness. Nursing a deathly ill Squinch was a wholly unsavory experience she didn't cared to repeat. *Been there, done that, got the t-shirt.* Ziggy's mobile unit showed up too, pleading to come along. Watching the slug was going to be tough enough.

"I need you to stay aboard and monitor the ship." Nancy tried to impress upon the dejected AI that his job remained critical. "Give station maintenance our fueling and supply requirements, and don't let anyone mess with your upgrades.

You're a fine-tuned machine now, and we want to keep it that way."

He insisted that multi-threaded programming allowed him to do both, but Nancy wasn't willing to risk the robot until she knew the lay of the land.

"Hope you're happy." Reemer slunk down the passageway with wilted eyestalks and wearing only a frown.

"Cheer up and keep your eyes open for clues." Two moping companions was two too many. "It'll take some sleuthing to figure out what's been going on."

Her words made him twitch with the need to rush back for his suit. But at least he perked up as the nested doors slid open to admit them.

Desert-dry air and the pungent scent of turned earth made for a strange greeting, as did the tall creature awaiting them. It towered over the door controls, intelligence shining in flat black eyes set wide to either side of a stubby, furred nose. A datapad was clutched in wide, spaded fingers the color of honey, and coarse gray plates ran the length of its back. In profile, the creature appeared rail thin, but took up half the passageway when it turned to face them.

"Greetings Dr. Dickenson, I be ambassador to please. Fly well, I trust?"

Unless Alvie Turlic had suddenly changed species, this was definitely not the human official representing Earth Force. Rudimentary descriptions of the Vargan race hadn't done their imposing presence justice. The general shape mimicked the flared hood of a cobra, but with silvery mammalian fur running down the underbelly. If a massive pill bug had been crossed with a hedgehog, it might resemble the alien, except the species lacked true legs. A multitude of stubby cilia-like feet along the wide tail propelled the ambassador forward as four paws set on short arms at shoulder and waist rose in greeting. He spoke in galactic trade standard, a universal language ill-suited to pleasantries.

"A pleasure to make your acquaintance." Her talent ensured the words came across as the snuffling grunts of his native tongue and drove the ridges to either side of his snout high in surprise. His eyes darted to her wrist in search of a translation bracelet. "This is Reemer of planet Fred. We look forward to offering our help, but to be honest I'd expected our human ambassador."

"Your assistance is welcome." His shift of language was as smooth as the shallow bow, which conveyed relief at being able to speak more naturally. "I am Arrlock Muenfee, the Vargan Republic's ambassador. First names will suffice between honored colleagues. My apologies for any confusion, but your human official has been indisposed for quite some time."

"In what way?"

"No one can locate Ambassador Turlic." His hands spread wide, a helpless gesture of frustration, but something in the bristling snout whiskers indicated he was about to expound.

Nancy waited, but Arrlock offered no further insight. With her talent giving miscues, the mission would be that much harder.

"Another muuur-deeer." The words drifted from Reemer in a gusty sigh. He'd directed the comment at Nancy, so hopefully the Vargan had only heard a wet rumbling.

"Don't jump to conclusions." Nancy kept her response in Squinch. "And there never was a *first* murder."

"I've taken the liberty of setting aside the afternoon for an orientation," Arrlock said. "Difficult on such short notice, but I was able to use most of what Turlic had planned. The station may be a multi-species achievement, but we are always eager to extend Vargan hospitality."

"We appreciate your generosity. Please, lead on." What other reports besides her flight plan had Olaf slow-rolled—and why?

The station was a marvel of engineering with wide corridors, indoor parks, and even sporting venues to keep the population amused. An entire loop dedicated to shops and eateries showcased wares and cuisine from various cultures. Another focused on entertainment venues. And there were many more.

The dry air held a blend of scents that lingered on the tongue in a chemical cocktail. Arrlock blamed the effect on various trace gasses different species needed to remain healthy. Life support could accommodate ninety-seven percent of station visitors in the common areas. No one enjoyed the blended atmosphere, but at least it wasn't toxic. Visitors requiring truly diverse environments based on ammonia, acidic mists, and the like could reserve loops suitable to their visits given enough lead-time and credits.

Aside from hosting the mining talks, Spaceport Gail acted as a center for banking, technology brokers, and other cross-culture ventures.

"Vargus certainly hit the jackpot," Nancy said when their guide described the leasing arrangement. The wealth transfer to pay for the station's orbit around the moon and supplies and labor flowing from the planet below was truly staggering.

"I admit it is a handsome sum." Arrlock tipped his head, a crease across the broad expanse of his shoulders turning it into more of a folding motion. "But our lease is ending, which is why the Republic needs fair treatment from the mining consortium. Gail will be leaving soon."

"Very convenient." Reemer stretched tall on his skirt, trying to look the ambassador in the eye. "Things go south, people disappear, and everything gets swept under the rug when the whole crime scene up and leaves." One eyestalk swiveled to look back at Nancy. "Don't you worry, toots. I'll get to the bottom of this before the trail goes cold." He whipped out a dripping datapad from somewhere that didn't bear thinking about and tapped out notes as both eyes focused on the Vargan. "So, friend, where exactly were *you* on the night Ambassador Turlic went missing? And don't even think about leaving out the details."

"I can't really say." Their guide shot Nancy a helpless look, all four hands coming up with fingers curled to pacify the suddenly aggressive Squinch.

"Spontaneous amnesia, eh?"

"Reemer, leave the man alone." Nancy said.

"You misunderstand." Arrlock flexed his fingers, wide paddles his ancestors would have used for digging. "I was likely at home or at my office on Vargus. Security has some theories on when Turlic disappeared, but I wasn't assigned to Gail until he'd been missing for several days. You can check the station logs."

"Oh, I will." The Squinch contracted to his normal height and oozed away, keeping a slitted eye locked on the flustered Vargan.

"Behave and don't terrify the locals," Nancy hissed in Squinch before focusing on Arrlock. "Please excuse my companion's…enthusiasm. We're just concerned about our own ambassador's wellbeing. I'd like to see what station security has compiled before digging into the status of negotiations."

13. Detecting

"T URLIC HAD TO be on that shuttle." Reemer looked from Nancy to Chief Mendelson.

Low-level functionaries and beat cops hustled around in the outer offices, the bullpen. They'd been briefed in a small conference room next to the security chief's office, surrounded by plexi-steel windows and prying eyes.

Reemer found it difficult to take Hera Mendelson seriously, partly because her appearance mimicked the giant squids back home. To be fair, a lot of the station's permanent crew were Argoth. More worrisome was the fact that her people hadn't even constructed a crime board for the case.

Rookie mistake.

"All passengers from the shuttle were duly logged and accounted for." Mendelson shrugged her upper tentacles. "Docking bay and onboard surveillance confirm there were no humans on the flight."

"How about other ship traffic?" Nancy asked.

It was sweet how his human companion tried to come up with alternatives, but the poor woman was clearly out of her depth. The missing ambassador had practically chronicled his own demise through daily reports. Contract talks had broken down when a rival faction from Vargus disputed the Republic's right to turn the moon over for mining. The consortium was furious. With emotions running high, the man responsible for brokering a deal had signed his own death warrant.

Annoyingly, the chief turned away to answer Nancy. This job wasn't for the meek. The investigation called for a hard-boiled detective with insight, dogged determination, and street smarts. Reemer vowed to wear his super suit in future discussions to get proper respect.

"We're still confirming the manifests on two vessels." Chief Mendelson looked a little green. Maybe she was getting ready to turn male. "We held a half a dozen others long enough to conduct searches, but my authority only goes so far."

"Foul play knows no bounds." Reemer slid smoothly back into the conversation. He paced the floor by the door, working through what they knew to build a picture of the dastardly deed. "Ambassador Tulric was close to cracking those negotiations wide open." He ticked off the obvious with the tip of an antenna. "They needed to take him out or risk exposure. What better way than a convenient accident with no one to blame?"

"There's no body," Nancy pointed out.

"But an accident's too easy." Reemer flicked off more points as he got rolling. "Missing men tell no tales. And bodies are easy to dispose of."

"Actually, the refuse system is closely monitored." Now the chief was being annoying on purpose, but had the grace to give an apologetic grimace with her fleshy beak.

"Recycling is a critical function, so a lot of eyes sort through everything leaving the station."

"Which leaves us with an obvious conclusion." Now to wow them with the big reveal—except he didn't yet have the murder weapon…or a corpse. *Details*. "We find the missing ambassador, and we'll have our murderer."

"Well, that's rather…circular," Nancy said into the stunned silence.

"Thank you; I know." Reemer flashed his best smile, accepting their adulation with humble modesty.

Sherlock Holmes and Columbo would be proud, but now he needed to think like the Scooby-Doo gang and lay a trap. Both eyestalks swirled in response to the wheels churning in his head. Glands pumped extra saliva to his foremouth as he savored the thought of unmasking the miscreant responsible. *That's right, you can run, but you can't hide.*

Only a street-wise private eye stood a chance of bringing down the culprit. He'd show everyone what Squinch could do. The station would sing his praises for generations.

The *thunk* of the door closing pulled his thoughts from the colorfully animated celebration Velma and Scooby would coordinate in his honor. The conference room was empty.

"Hey, wait up!" Reemer hurried to follow Nancy through the bullpen.

"Go back to the ship, Reemer." Red rose up the sides of Nancy's neck, and she was breathing awfully hard. "You can work on your wild theories there."

"Wildly good. I know." She *had* been listening. "We'll need some rope and a net." Reemer had to scramble to keep up with those long human legs. "Oh, and someone to act as bait. Would you be interested?"

The question hung in the air, but Nancy's sudden left turn and burst of speed put a lot of distance between them.

"Just check on Ziggy and keep out of trouble," she called over her shoulder. "The consortium's fact-finding commission has an open hearing I need to attend."

"I'll find supplies first." They'd passed plenty of shops, and he could charge what was needed back to the ship.

Nancy whirled and jabbed a finger at him. "No side trips. No stopping. Go back to the ship and wait for me. If Ziggy doesn't need any help, watch a vid—no crime dramas. Got it?"

"Sure. No need to get all huffy." *Geez.* "I'll go straight back."

"Good." She squinted at him as though about to say more, then simply turned and strode away.

Reemer scanned the office fronts lining the hall to either side of the security station. None of the people strolling, slithering, and whomping past spared him half a glance. Interesting. Without his cape he was virtually invisible. That would come in handy for stakeouts.

So which way was their airlock? Despite Nancy's unreasonable need for clean decks, his glistening back trail was easy enough to spot. Most of the slime had been scrubbed away by the ever-present cleaning bots, but the aroma and pulsing glow were simple to pick out even if humans couldn't. The handy survival trait kept Squinch from getting lost, even underwater.

Those chemical markers would wear off in a few days since he hadn't added any extra emphasis during Arrlock's meandering tour. Nancy had made him promise to go straight to the ship, and that trail would be the long way back.

Fortunately, the station had plenty of terminals handy for public use. He sidled up to the closest and plotted out directions. The display helpfully highlighted shopping, industrial zones, and residential areas. Any route would pass plenty of interesting locales. He thought back to the chief's briefing and keyed in a query.

Bingo! One quick stop along the way wouldn't hurt.

* * *

The station computers continued to be incredibly helpful. One stop led to another, and Reemer soon found himself in front of Ambassador Turlic's quarters. Security hadn't even bothered to post a guard or tape off the crime scene to prevent tampering.

Amateurs.

The door didn't respond to the entry pad, but he hadn't spent thousands of hours with his shows for nothing. Even the most sophisticated lock had a weakness. A few happy accidents while setting up his export business had shown that most electronics were moisture sensitive.

Just the right slime mixture pushed through the seals along keys and seams should do the trick. Extra-slick secretions flowed from his antennae, building up under the cupped tip until pressure overcame the seals and the special blend flowed into the panel.

His efforts were rewarded by a sizzling tingle. He powered through as electricity zapped along his antennae and the doors slid apart. Reemer hurried inside before the quick-drying concoction dissipated and the entrance closed.

The room wasn't much different from his own quarters. The main area held a desk and kitchenette. Several gaudy works of art decorated the walls, stylistic paintings with bright, bold strokes. One reminded him of billowing seaweed, another of puffer fish with spiny quills waiting to stun unwary predators. Impressionism, not at all to his liking and definitely not a clue.

The desk offered fertile ground to explore. Those heavy-handed security goons didn't have the investigative finesse to get their tentacles dirty. Underneath, back where the desk joined the bulkhead, Reemer's sensitive skirt caught on a seam. A judicious burst of slime unlocked the hidden compartment.

Several pages lay in the shallow drawer. The tightly packed writing meant nothing to him, but the stack of transportation receipts underneath pegged the ambassador as a serial traveler, a man on the run—a man with something to hide.

Child's play. Reemer laughed. Secrets weren't safe with him on the case. Material evidence followed his every move, clinging to his underside as though begging to be discovered. His inner super-sleuth was already busy storing away bits of grit that probably detailed the man's fate.

"Cough up your secrets." Reemer slid out from under the desk, hungry for more.

He scoured the resilient flooring with his skirt flared wide. Tacky gel pulled up bits of dirt and debris that station authorities had surely missed. Stray hairs and skin cell, vital DNA evidence, were shunted into a holding pouch behind the mouths under his skirt. A cast-off button proved the *pièce de résistance*, along with several small protein nuggets, each exotic seed covered in chocolate and a bright sugary coating.

"M is for murder," Reemer murmured after reading the tiny letter printed on each nugget.

A bonanza of evidence clung to the corners of the bathroom and beneath the bed sheets. Reemer traced the tip of an antenna along the left side of his front, parting the thick hide and pulling a datapad from its concealed pocket. He looked about expectantly but deflated when he remembered he was alone.

Too bad. Nancy always cringed prettily when he dug into one of the natural orifices. Her facial expression and gagging never failed to send shivers of delight through his mantle. Human anatomy had one or two useful hiding spots of their own. But his human friends refused to use the orifices they'd been born with, preferring to rely on external pockets sewn into their clothing. Super inefficient, although backpacks were handy. Sometimes getting to the larger items he carried took time and uncomfortable contortions.

His antennae flew across the goopy datapad, recording each precious clue. Intriguing scents crisscrossed the rooms. The salty pungency of Chief Mendelson reminded him of the oceans back home. Other less identifiable species had also come and gone over the past weeks. Most recently, a pair of Vargans had circled the main living area. Individuals were difficult to distinguish, but one of those would have likely been Arrlock since he'd needed to retrieve the missing Ambassador's work.

Humans had been here too, blunt, sour smelling ones without the delicate scents and overpowering chemical fragrances his friend occasionally doused herself with. Criminals always returned to the scene, which made everyone he smelled a prime suspect.

Once all the obvious evidence was gathered, Reemer returned to the bedroom closet to begin a detailed search. Clothing dangled over his head as he rummaged. All he found down low was a ridiculously large number of shoes. Turlic must be a short man, because even his slippers had super high heels.

He'd climbed halfway up the wall on his way to the shelf above the clothing when a whoosh and scrape from the main room made him freeze. The front door had opened, admitting shuffling feet. Low muttering drifted from the entry. The killers had returned.

"Check there, there, and there." The female voice spoke galactic standard, which didn't give away her race.

Quiet footfalls and scraping told him that two or three individuals searched the room. Reemer didn't dare drop off the wall. His antennae were just long enough to ease the closet door shut. He spent the rest of his energy trying to blend in with the ceremonial jacket hanging nearby, no small feat as the chromophore cells that typically indicated gender shifted color to match the nearby material.

A seam in the door looked out on a sliver of the bedroom and hallway. Someone in dark clothes reached for the seaweed painting hanging on the hall. Gloved fingers felt around the frame, then swung the painting aside to reveal a hidden safe.

"Here it is." The man spoke galactic too, but those arms looked pretty human.

The thief slapped a beeping device onto the face of the safe. After a moment, he opened the door, pulled out a brown cylinder, and dropped the object into a silver electrostatic bag. Turlic must have found something huge to have gone to such pains to hide the evidence.

Reemer could blow the doors off this case if he got his antennae on that tube. Investigators didn't usually go up against criminals directly. The datapad wasn't much of a weapon, and he wasn't in a great position to get at something more useful. Maybe a lightning-fast rush would work? He'd surprise them, grab that tube, and be gone before either recovered. His muscles coiled for action, in three, two—

Thoughts of launching from the closet died as something large scraped its way into the room like heavy stone—grating against his soul rather than his ears. The sensation vibrated through skirt and mantle, freezing him in place. The new presence swept down the short hallway, powerful and ominous.

Vertigo washed over him, as though rolling off the shifting colors that approached. His hiding spot would keep him safe. Squinch were masters of concealment. He'd taken great care to disturb nothing in the room. The thieves had found what they came for and would soon leave, never suspecting their criminal antics were being studied by a master detective. Reemer flattened himself, becoming one with the wall, an enigma without substance, impossible to trace, a ghost.

"Hey, what's with all the slime?" The woman called out.

His small window went dark, the narrow view of the room replaced with a wall of swirling greens and blues. As quickly as it had come, the mass shifted, leaving Reemer blinking away magenta afterimages as though he'd stared too long into the ship's reactor.

A glowing blue eye filled the door seam, pupil-less and sparking with energy. Grinding pressure drove away rational thought, crushed the air from his lungs. Reemer's skirt went slack, dropping him into the collection of stupidly tall shoes just as the door flew open.

14. A Long Day

Z IGGY MET NANCY at the airlock. The robot was brimming with curiosity, but she insisted on a full logistics report before fielding inane questions. Food was in order too. The consortium meeting had dragged on forever.

The AI filled her in on the comings and goings of station maintenance. Supplies and consumables had been loaded while the ship conducted post-flight checks. They didn't have immediate plans for departure, but leaving preparations until the last minute was just asking for trouble.

Station security had stopped by with the standard list of rules, regulations, and emergency contact procedures. Chief Mendelson's people also warned Ziggy to report any requests to transport personnel not on the ship's manifest. The Argoth seemed to be taking a systematic approach in her search for the missing ambassador.

"So what's it like out there?" Ziggy asked after finishing his report. "Are there others like me on board? The docked ships are too busy to talk much."

"If there are, they'll be specialized for running specific station systems, less autonomous, and probably even worse conversationalists." At her offhand response the robot slumped, his enthusiasm gone. *Damn.* "But I'll ask around. Maybe there's a synthetic personality monitoring station dynamics. They'd be more interesting than cleaning bots."

Ziggy perked up at the notion, and Nancy bit her lip to keep from telling him not to get his hopes up. He'd looked so sad. The idea had sprung from her lips half-formed to cover her embarrassment at having no idea about the station's AI complement. She'd certainly noted the contingents of Vargans involved in the talks, the Packtonian officials making a case for the mining consortium, and the other spurious races they'd encountered, including a handful of scattered humans that seemed to have their fingers in a number of different pies. The thought of resident digital personalities hadn't even crossed her mind.

Plenty of bots and mechanoids roamed the halls, but she'd written them off as mindless drones. And although the station terminals had politely answered her questions, she'd never given a second thought to the source of those responses. AIs were not simply machines, nor were they second class citizens. That conviction ran deep—intellectually.

Nancy prided herself on being inclusive. Who else would have befriended intelligent killer plants? Ziggy's fervent desire to connect with others like himself forced her to take a closer look. The busy day seemed a poor excuse for dismissing non-biologic people out of hand.

"The comms net is buzzing about the hearing, but it's all speculation, no hard facts." Ziggy seemed eager to fill the informational void. "Did you get any details on why negotiations have stopped?"

"Sure did." The robot leaned in close, but a growl from her stomach had Nancy waving him toward the galley. "I'll fill you in over dinner. They've gotten themselves into quite a jam. Data restrictions apply to the specifics, but I can outline the general lay of the land."

Gossip wasn't a word she'd ever associated with AIs, but her ship was clearly dying to be the first to know about the station's hottest business deal. Sharing the information that was about to go public wouldn't hurt.

Ziggy hung on her every word as she outlined her day between bites. "So does this upstart group from Vargus have a valid claim?"

"Seems so," Nancy said. "Their ancestors left the planet to escape a world war and built colonies on the moon. This was thousands of years ago. Records survived the fall of civilization, even though the lunar colonies had vanished by the time Vargans went to space again."

"But do ancestral rights trump the Republic's claim?"

"That's the big question." The meeting had included plenty of shouting and accusations, enough that representatives from the mining interest had simply left to let the Vargans work out their problems. "The current government is happy to lease the moon, no strings attached. It's all about profits for the Republic. Revivalists—that's what this new faction calls itself—don't want their ancestral ruins disturbed. They've built a substantial mythology around what's left up here. The meeting nearly came to blows, so I can only imagine how bad it's getting down on the planet. They've wiped themselves out before. Could happen again."

"Doesn't make sense." Ziggy shook his head, a gesture he'd picked up during their trip.

"Wars seldom do."

"Not that. These people who colonized the moon would have been more advanced technologically and socially. Why aren't they still thriving? Did a natural disaster or enemies come along and wipe them out?"

"No signs of that." Nancy had reviewed the Revivalists' treatise along with available Republic records. "The only thing that's ravaged the moon is time. I suppose a biologic agent might have been involved, a plague that decimated the population. But again, there's really no evidence either way."

Very little had survived on the now arid moon. The surface remained marginally habitable, though unhospitable. Water was scarce, and its lack limited vegetation to drought resistant grasses, succulents, and scraggily brush across most of the moon. The ecosystems still included a number of smaller organisms, but there just wasn't enough biomass to support the kind of long-tail food chain that ended with apex predators.

Once the consortium got rolling, the bulk of their mining operations would be automated. Initial construction crews required shelter, consumables, and inoculation against microbial threats while surveying. It was unlikely that such simple precautions would have overtaxed the ancient residents.

The Republic acknowledged that the original settlers had been at the upper end of what passed for the current technology curve among spacefaring races. If the Vargans weren't exaggerating, those ancient colonists could have terraformed the surface, but had instead chosen to live largely underground. Scattered remnants of buildings led to subterranean areas. For all the mystique surrounding the moon, only minimal mapping of those pockets had ever been attempted, which presented additional hazards to mining.

From orbit, the moon appeared to be wrapped with gridlines that were actually ridges arranged at precise intervals. Extensive underground caverns contributed to the unnatural topography, but unusual compounds in the soil prevented orbital sensors from penetrating deeper than a few feet. Boots on the ground would be needed for further mapping.

A Vargan Republic expedition had been the first to discover the rich luxene deposits that started the mining fervor. Revivalists' efforts to suppress the findings failed miserably, and the faction was rightfully outraged at having been excluded. Within the Republic itself, more than one official questioned the purpose of the original mission, which handily had brought along equipment to complete an initial geological survey, core samples and all.

By dessert, they'd discussed everything Nancy felt comfortable sharing. She'd drawn clear lines around the information still deemed sensitive. Ziggy would share only what had been submitted to public records and the news outlets. Other ship personalities sharing the docking levels might be too busy to strike up a friendship with her frustrated AI, but all were apparently on the lookout for juicy tidbits.

"I'm working up a proposal for my assistance to get things rolling again," Nancy said as they finished.

"I thought that was the ambassador's job." Ziggy's presence—for lack of a better term—had dimmed a notch, indicating the synthetic consciousness was multi-tasking, probably already reaching out to share his news.

"With Turlic's disappearance they need someone to step up. Arrlock's trying, but doesn't have the right mindset nor management style."

Understatement of the year. The Vargan had no concept of compromise, and offered suggestions in stiffly worded language guaranteed to alienate at least one—and often all—of the parties involved. His allegiance to the Republic alone made the man unsuitable.

Mining officials would jump at the chance for a neutral facilitator. They'd be stingy on her commission but the disgusted faces at today's hearing made her certain they would eventually play ball. In contrast, desperation had danced through the handful of Revivalists allowed into the room, perhaps enough to entertain more human involvement. The Vargan Republic remained a wildcard. Her morning meeting with Arrlock would hopefully shed light on how best to make inroads there.

"Speaking of style, I suppose Reemer's in his room watching crime dramas." Talking with Ziggy helped her unwind, but she still needed to lay down ground rules with the Squinch, the first of which was not to interfere with station security.

His obsession with crime solving had to stop, or he'd end up in the brig himself. She had no desire to have to report back to the Mayor and Belinda that their son was locked up on a remote space station.

"The Squinch has not returned." Ziggy sounded baffled. "I thought you two were touring the station together."

"We were up until this afternoon." When he'd gone all squirrely. "He was *supposed* to head back to give you a hand."

Visions of the slug harassing potential witnesses and landing in solitary confinement drove out a deep sigh. Now, she'd have to track him down to read him the riot act. *Just wonderful.*

15. Where's Waldo

Z IGGY SIGHED HEAVILY while compiling their daily report for headquarters. Nancy ignored the breathy hiss from the robot, which didn't even have lungs. But a second burst of forlorn static forced her to look up.

"What now?" She set aside her document. After two hours of revamping, her proposal to step in as lead facilitator already gleamed with succinct logic. More tinkering wouldn't increase the chances of success.

"Oh, nothing." Ziggy's eyes were horizontal slits of disinterest, his voice a studied monochrome.

"Come on, spill it, robo-boy." Nancy folded her hands and waited.

"What am I doing with my life?" Ziggy asked. "I can't just sit here."

"You're taking care of the ship, monitoring communications, and managing a ton of other necessary details."

"There's got to be more to life." He gave a shrug and picked at the tabletop with the delicate pincers of two forelegs.

Nancy scooped up her mug and blew on the steaming tea, studying the dejected robot over the rim. Honey and lavender filled her nostrils, soothing aromas rising from the chamomile that was still too hot to sip.

She still wasn't certain Quen had done her a favor by reprogramming the shipboard personality. Less than a month "old" and Ziggy seemed to be in a constant state of crisis over his purpose in life. Inner conflict painted the robot's features, put stuttering hesitation in his movements. Even the ship's consoles managed a morose air with indicator lights shining duller and audible signals muted. Annoying, but mental health was no joke. Nancy could definitely relate.

"I'll let you in on a secret." She scowled as a chemical scent wafted from her tea and set the untouched drink aside, choosing her words carefully. "We all struggle at times. Finding your place in life, that thing you feel meant to achieve, isn't easy. For some a calling magically appears as low-hanging fruit ripe for the picking, and they grab it without a second thought. It's a godsend that gives life meaning and direction, but easy answers usually come with a price."

She knew that more than most. Passion for discovering new plant species had relentlessly driven Nancy's younger self. Cataloguing flora filled her waking hours, destroyed her relationships, and eventually drove her into space—all for the glory of being the best botanist Earth had ever seen. And she'd paid dearly.

"It's just frustrating," Ziggy said. "You and Reemer know what you want to do with your lives. I just drive the ship. That's no destiny. It's not even an epic quest."

So her AI had been dipping into the entertainment vids too. *Peachy.*

"I know watching others go after their dreams can be discouraging, but you have to do you, Ziggy. Life goals aren't programmed in, not even for digital personalities. The journey's going to have plenty of ups and downs. My drive comes from those low points, from the darkness inside. Life isn't all butterflies and roses." Bitter memories colored her words.

"You *help* people," Ziggy insisted. "That isn't dark at all."

The tide of memories came unbidden, as they always did: the blood, the screams, the helplessness. No one could have predicted the horror awaiting her crew in the pristine jungles of planet Fred, no one except a hotshot botanist who specialized in new species, who prided herself on understanding plant survival mechanisms, who had totally and irresponsibly missed the jungle awakening to slaughter human interlopers.

Five years later, Nancy did indeed help people. Her diplomatic missions solved problems and hopefully made lives better. But her underlying drive was far less altruistic. Every spare credit and recurring payment went into a trust fund for the families of her lost crew. Surviving spouses and children received modest stipends from the anonymous fund, a helpful pittance to aid them in moving on. No amount of money could replace their loss or erase her mistake, her guilt. Despite her best efforts, the account grew slowly.

Nancy desperately needed this mining treaty to work. Earth Force would of course take their fair share and pay her a negotiation fee. But a special clause built into her proposal ensured an income stream to the survivors' fund.

Three hundredths of a percent interest in luxene production didn't look like much on paper, but the ever-increasing market value of the rare compound promised to funnel life-changing wealth to the families of her old crew—if she succeeded.

"I'm just saying that your drive may come from an unexpected place." She shifted the conversation away from her painful past. The fledgling AI needed hope, not baggage. "Give it time. Our experiences shape us. That's where your inspiration will come from." He looked unconvinced. "Tell you what, come with me into the station. Reemer still isn't back, so it's high time I find him before he gets into serious trouble. You can help me hunt up places he might be lingering and maybe meet a few new people. Try not to obsess over your life's purpose. Live in the moment to get your creative juices flowing."

"I'd enjoy that immensely." He stood straighter, a spark of interest in his voice as he warmed to the idea. "Before docking, Reemer seemed most excited to seek out beings he called 'hoity-toity.' I believe the term indicated social status rather than any particular species. They gather in his shows at elegant dining establishments or on vast expanses of manicured grass to club small white balls into submission."

"It's settled then." Nancy grabbed the memory disk containing her encrypted proposal and cast a longing look at the tea she'd have to forgo. "I'll drop off my proposal first, then we'll hit restaurant row, find our wayward Squinch, and stop slimeageddon before it starts."

Ziggy followed her out with a spring in his many-legged step. The robot took in the austere passageways with wide eyes, dragging a hand over everything they passed. The docking area was a ghost town, but foot traffic picked up deeper into the station.

Nancy avoided the moving walkway set against the outside wall of the main thoroughfare, preferring to stretch her legs. They slowed next to a tall maintenance bot that arched over the walk. The machine's forearms were buried in an access panel. Ziggy ran both hands over the composite rectangle that served as its torso, sliding dexterous fingers along the curve of all three wheels as if gauging their circumference.

The machine—one of the many she'd glibly ignored today—paused to look down. Instead of calling out a greeting, Ziggy turned and continued on. Doorways and occasional pieces of art drifted by as they walked, few of them escaping her companion's questing fingers. The next cleaning bot to scuttle past drew only a casual glance from him.

"Not going to say hello?" Nancy asked.

"No point. They possess only enough programming to receive commands and find work. None are self-aware."

Maybe she'd been too hard on herself earlier. If the AI didn't acknowledge these machines, humans ignoring them could hardly be racist. But mechanoids served numerous station functions, many of them quite complex. Even a glimmer of the intelligence that ship personalities possessed could mark a bot as a "person." Nancy vowed to treat them as such. More and more, her talent let her read machines the same way she did biological beings, putting her in a unique position to extend the small courtesy.

Hand delivery of her proposal wasn't strictly necessary, but Nancy wanted to look Ambassador Muenfee in the eye to ensure he'd pass it along to the station commander and interested parties. For all that he was technically in the pocket of the Republic, Arrlock's posture when they found him telegraphed deep relief at her desire to take over.

"I'll get this to the consortium advocate and our Secretary of Resources right away." Arrlock folded at the neck, a nod of thanks as he took the proposal.

"You haven't by chance seen Reemer this evening?" Nancy asked before departing.

"Why, no. Have you lost him?" The ambassador's gaze shifted uncomfortably.

"More like he lost us." She shrugged when her smile wasn't returned. "Probably out looking for a good meal. He's overly fond of flatfish, and what I carry isn't exactly fresh caught."

Nancy tilted her head as an odd sensation rolled off the Vargan. Arrlock studied the far wall, looking distinctly evasive. The fleeting impression vanished as he turned to his terminal, inserted her memory wafer, and keyed in the appropriate recipients.

"The station offers excellent imported cuisine as well as a wide variety of foods from our planet." Another hesitation. His rigid posture and flared neck said he was thinking about more than food. Arrlock was about to comment on the talks, perhaps share sensitive information that made him uncomfortable. He chose his words carefully. "Many commercial establishments stay open late. If all else fails, you could simply follow his glistening trail. Your friend made quite the impression, judging by the numerous calls for deck scrubbers."

Huh. Nothing about negotiations or her proposal. The Squinch's untidy mode of transportation had been what accosted the ambassador's sensibilities. These miscues from her talent were getting worse. Not as disastrous as misreading a representative during critical talks, but still annoying—and worrisome.

Nancy tried for a gracious exit despite seething inside. She'd been short on sleep the last few days, which seemed to make it harder to read people. If this kept up, she'd need to dust off her translator bracelet.

Searching the massive station with its sweeping rings wasn't practical, but they wouldn't have to. Reemer was a slug by nature and temperament. He'd have chosen the nearest destination to sate his appetite and conserve energy. But when their search of the eateries along the inner ring yielded only mystery meat on a stick for Nancy and a high-density recharge pack for Ziggy, she began to wonder if Reemer's hunger had been for something else entirely.

"There are rock climbing spots nestled among the gardens of the central atrium," Ziggy offered when Nancy floated the idea that their friend might simply be out causing mischief after all. "And the native art installation on the command level has plenty of ambush-worthy alcoves."

The Squinch dearly loved to surprise people with slick footing and splashing belly flops, but another hour of checking likely spots came up empty. Despite Arrlock's misgivings about their messy companion, his suggestion of looking at the end of a slime trail actually had merit. Unfortunately, they'd yet to run across a dirty corridor. The janitorial bots were on top of their game.

"Do cleaning crews keep records?" Nancy asked as their search stalled. "Any hint of where he's been would help."

"I will check." Ziggy headed to the nearest terminal and went to work, using a data connection to augment voice and typed commands. "Public information shows standard routes and closures for deep cleaning. I'll ask logistics for access to more details." A minute later, Ziggy bobbed his head. "Here we go. Extra bots were deployed several times today in response to biologic waste." His eyes creased into amused red crescents. "I agree, that's funny."

"What's funny?" She hadn't said anything.

"Sorry." Ziggy looked up from the terminal. "I was talking to Emmett in logistics. The sanitation department has been seriously overtaxed since you and Reemer left the ship."

"Lucky to find someone on duty this late." Nancy pushed in close to see. "Can he bring up a map of the spots that needed extra work?"

"I think so." Ziggy spoke as he keyed in the request. "Emmett is always on duty. His programming could use an upgrade, so this may take a while. But he's happy to help— and a real chatterbox. Getting him to stop feeding us information might be the hard part. Ah, here we go."

The 3D display lit up with a wireframe station map. Glowing symbols showed where reinforcements had been needed. Each event had a data tag with timestamp, the number of bots dispatched, and the work accomplished. Unaware that Nancy could read just about any language, the logistics computer thoughtfully used English.

Most of the responses involved aggressive scraping and industrial sanitizers to remove "gels and fluids of biological origin." Medical units had been deployed in two instances to ensure the station wasn't being overrun by a dangerous fungus or mold. Definitely Reemer.

"Start here." Nancy picked an area by the docks that had been on Arrlock's tour. "Slide us right and down. Yep, that's all before we visited security."

Emmett helped trace Reemer's progress after they'd split up. The Squinch's route back to the ship had been anything but a straight line. By the look of the messes in his wake, he'd visited two stores, an engineering annex, and several storage areas before the trail ended.

"What's here?" Nancy pointed to the cluster of data tags where—unbelievably—four teams of cleaning bots had converged on Reemer's final mess.

"That appears to be berthing." Ziggy bantered silently with Emmett. Stretching her talent let Nancy feel the logistic computer's presence through the terminal. Her own robot's eyes damn near sparkled as information shot back and forth. Ziggy had made a new friend. When they finished, the screen zoomed in to show video of a narrow corridor sparsely lined with privacy doors. "Diplomatic quarters to be more precise."

"Let me guess. Turlic's stateroom?" Given his recent obsession with crime solving, Nancy suspected Reemer had been focused more on mysteries than mayhem.

"Exactly right." Ziggy reached the same conclusion. "Looks like he went looking for our missing ambassador."

16. Crime Scene

"WHERE IS THE little turd?" Nancy glared at the locked stateroom, wishing her gift from the Lokii included the ability to blast doors open.

After hurrying down several levels, they'd found only gleaming floors outside the missing ambassador's quarters. Emmett must have been bored. The logistics AI continued to mine information from station records and chatted up a storm through the door's access panel.

"Reemer spent a lot of time out here," Ziggy said as he broke away from his talkative new BFF. "The deck and walls needed deep cleaning, and Emmett's certain that even the access pad got slimed. A security bot opened the panel, but everything was back to normal by then except the automated door log had reset. He can't tell who's come and gone."

"Oh, Reemer got in there all right." Certainty settled in Nancy's bones.

She should have seen this coming instead of trusting him to return to the boring confines of her ship. Hyped up on crime dramas and whatever passed for Squinch adrenaline, the slug couldn't resist playing detective. But where did he go from here? Despite scouring his database, Emmett had hit a dead end. No further incidents requiring backup cleaners were logged. Was Reemer so addicted to sleuthing that he'd holed up in the vacant stateroom?

"Can Emmett get us inside, or do I need to wake Chief Mendelson?"

* * *

"Well, your friend certainly was here." A purple tartan skirt with gold lightning bolts covered the chief's torso where the lower tentacles originated. Her uniform shirt dangled from an upper appendage.

Emmett had needed security's approval to override the stateroom's privacy lock. By the time he'd received the green light, Chief Mendelson arrived out of breath and scantily clad. After peering through the open doorway, she stepped back, waved Nancy through, and struggled to don the badly twisted shirt.

Glistening trails crisscrossed the main room, forcing them to step gingerly. Reemer had been pacing back and forth—a lot. The mucus was thinner but stickier than a normal Squinch trail, a fact Nancy discovered when a misstep nearly pulled off her boot.

She discovered the hidden drawer while crouching to cinch her bootstraps. The glistening trail under the desk led to Reemer's find. Ambassador Turlic had been keeping secrets. A quick glance stopped Nancy cold as she flipped through the handwritten journal. Earth Force and Admiral Cheyung were mentioned under several entries. Withholding evidence didn't sit well, but she pocketed the pages, vowing to turn over any pertinent information that didn't violate ambassadorial privilege.

"Chief, have you seen these?" Nancy crawled from under the desk and held out the stack of ticket receipts that were under the notes.

"A hidden compartment?" Chief Mendelson looked under the desk before rifling through the thin strips of paper. "Your man's been busy. These go back several months. Some are just delivery receipts; others are travel stubs."

"Vargus, moonside, a bunch of ships." Nancy read off more destinations. "Did he always run himself ragged?"

"We didn't pay much attention to the ambassador until he went missing." The chief skimmed three receipts off the top. "These are dated after his disappearance. Private ships won't have the best records, but I'll pull their logs. Maybe he got off-station before the current restrictions went into place."

"There's more down here." Ziggy popped out of the bathroom and moved to the sleeping area. "And here too."

The other two rooms held only a few trails, but thick green slime puddled out from under the bedroom closet door.

"Reemer?" Nancy reached for the handle, hope and fear making her pulse race.

The floor of the small space was a mess, as was the clutter of slimy shoes. She pawed though the clothing and found sticky slime climbing halfway up the left-hand wall.

Air whooshed from Nancy's lungs. Relief seemed inappropriate. The idea was to march their friend back to the ship, not to keep playing hide and seek. But dread and a flash of intuition involving foul play had struck just before she'd thrown the door open.

"Check under the bed and behind those shelves. He's got to be somewhere." She'd seen the Squinch get into unbelievably tight places, but Reemer should have come out of hiding at the sound of her voice.

Hope that he was crammed into a dark corner vanished quickly. There just weren't that many places to hide. Reemer seemed to be deliberately avoiding them. Maybe he'd gotten wise to the fact his trails were a giveaway and suppressed the natural excretions.

"This looks important," Ziggy called from the hallway.

The robot swung an abstract painting away from the wall, pulled open the small metal door underneath, and rummaged inside. "The safe's unlocked, but nothing obvious is missing. We have credit receipts, a notebook, and some jewelry. Here's a sample container. No wait, the carry tube is missing."

"That's enough snooping around in Ambassador Turlic's things." Chief Mendelson hurried over to usher Ziggy away from his find. "Your friend isn't stored with the man's valuables. Let's call it a night, shall we? Emmett can have maintenance clean up this mess in the morning. Head back to your ship and get some sleep. The Squinch may have already returned."

Of course, he hadn't. That fact was obvious as soon as they entered the ship. Nancy had argued to look for more clues and have Emmett search the non-emergent cleaning logs. Reemer might be hiding his trail to avoid being tracked, but she doubted he could do it for long. Some small residue would always follow in his wake.

"Well, that was rather abrupt." Nancy scooped up her cup of tea after they'd finished checking the ship.

"Lack of sleep is contraindicated for biologics," Ziggy said as he plugged into his recharge station and slipped back into the main computer banks. "Those affected talk less and exhibit more aggression than warranted."

"That's called being grumpy." A feeling that resonated as she stared at the murky liquid in her mug. After a quick stir with her finger, she took a tentative sip and grimaced—stone cold, and the lavender tasted soapy. "Rushing us away still seemed harsh. What if Reemer isn't just playing around? He might have good reason for laying low."

"The chief did promise to look into the ambassador's paperwork and have security watch for Reemer." Ziggy's voice echoed from the onboard speakers while his mobile unit recharged. "More eyes will make finding the Squinch easier. Someone is sure to spot him soon."

"Maybe you're right, but my gut tells me Reemer has gotten himself into trouble."

And she hadn't? Nothing in the notes she'd stolen would help locate Turlic or Reemer, but they painted a grim picture of Earth's supposed neutrality. Back home, players like Admiral Cheyung were pulling strings better left alone. Trading diplomatic clout for profit was a slippery slope, and the money was funneling into deep pockets behind the scenes.

Turlic suspected Earth Force involvement in unseating his predecessor too, an Argoth who'd challenged the powers-that-be before a freak accident took him out of the picture. The explosive atmospheric breach had occurred before Earth's official involvement and hadn't even been a footnote in the orientation material from headquarters. Chief Mendelson should have at least mentioned the incident. A laundry list of evidence pointed to unavoidable equipment failure, but just the fact that the accident had happened was damned important.

Turlic had ignored the risks and pushed back on demands for unreasonable concessions designed to pry control of mining from the Vargans. He went fully rogue after a series of alarming scientific findings were deliberately misplaced. Powers above the admiral were playing chess with the ambassador and Vargans. The Lobstra and other races were fair game too, though Turlic remained vague on how they might be involved.

Murky as it was, the big picture would have to wait while she tracked down and extracted Reemer from whatever trouble he'd brewed. Pranks-gone-bad were nothing new for the Squinch. Their companion tended to collect friends and enemies with very few gradations in between. Despite being ostracized by peers and hunted by mercenaries, he never changed his ways, except during a gender shift. Female Reemer possessed an acutely muted mischievous streak.

Nancy absently took another sip, cringed, and set the mug down. Speaking of things gone bad, cold tea was the worst. Even the dollop of cream had curdled into chunky floaters. Her stomach roiled as sweat popped out on her forehead and trickled into her eyes. Reemer would have a field day teasing her if she spewed on the bridge.

"Nancy, are you well?" Ziggy's voice sounded muffled beneath the pulse thundering in her ears.

The room grew hot. She'd have to get the thermostat checked. What had Ziggy asked? No, she wasn't well. The bridge was a sauna, her charitable foundation's future hinged on getting this job, and her best friend had gone missing. A giggle escaped at the thought of a slug being her best friend.

Some social life. Then the room tipped on its axis and went dark.

* * *

Ziggy started in confusion as his captain reeled and slumped across the navigation table. He looked to the cold tea, and alarm bells rang in his mind. The moment of concern passed in an instant, replaced by cold logic. The cup was evidence.

He powered up the mobile unit, calmly crossed the room, and collected the tea. A rapid search found two small drops of liquid on the tabletop, which he cleaned thoroughly. The tea itself went into the recycler and the cup into the sanitizer set on maximum.

Its work done, the mobile unit trundled back out to the docking station and relinquished control. The human still breathed, but that was none of its concern.

* * *

"Nancy?" The voice of an angel intruded on dreams of flying solo through deepest darkest space. Truly flying, no ship, just her and the cosmos. Becoming one with the vastness of space, of reality. The nothingness splintered into granular points that buzzed about her as the darkness receded. "Dr. Dickenson, you need to wake up now!" Not an angel; that was Ziggy shouting in her ear.

The room came into focus grudgingly, a dressing table molded into the wall, the open door to a washroom. *When did I go to bed?* Rhythmic beeping made it difficult to think, and her head throbbed as she shifted on the pillow.

"I can't feel my lips."

The ill-tempered bees attacked her face with tiny stings. She swept back her hair, but dropped her arm at a sharp pinch. The butt end of a needle was taped down across the back of her hand, the trailing tube looping up to a clear bag of liquid. Small spots of blood on her inner elbow showed where other drugs had been injected. Her first instinct was to tear the tube out, but the buzzing moved into her numb lips and her teeth chattered.

"Don't be alarmed. Your metabolism has stabilized." Ziggy's mobile unit hovered over her with worried eyes.

"What—" Nancy's dry throat constricted on the word, and she gratefully sipped the water Ziggy offered. "What happened?"

"I am not entirely certain." The robot seemed confused, which did little to instill confidence. "Your body shut down. I was unable to rouse you and suspected an allergic reaction. Administering antihistamines, broad-spectrum antigen neutralizers, and a cardiac enhancer proved effective. The intravenous fluids are a precaution."

"Glad you were here." The water and talking flushed the odd sensation from her face to her shoulders, where it proceeded to march down both arms until all ten fingers tingled. "We were talking about Reemer over tea and everything went fuzzy."

"All appears normal now." The robot consulted the source of the beeping, a portable medical monitor sitting by her head. Blessed quiet filled the room when he switched it off. "I took the liberty of gathering blood samples. Our portable lab is running standard tests for vitamin deficiencies, glucose levels, and other abnormalities to determine if follow-up treatment is indicated."

She wasn't prone to fainting, and sudden onset diabetes seemed unlikely. This had felt more like being drugged—or poisoned.

"My tea." Nancy though back to the odd chemical taste. "We need to test it. I think someone slipped me a mickey."

"I don't understand." Ziggy fussed as Nancy unhooked herself from the equipment, staggered to her feet, and headed for the bridge.

The navigation table stood empty. She searched the deck, looking for spilled tea and a shattered mug—nothing. "Where's my cup?"

"I don't understa—"

She left the robot in her wake and hurried to the kitchen, her legs much steadier. The mug sat gleaming on the center rack of the sonic cleaner.

"Tell me you saved the tea." She rounded on Ziggy, who blinked back at her. "I bet whatever knocked me out was in my drink. We need a sample."

"I think you may have had a sleeping hallucination." Ziggy sounded apologetic. "You haven't had any tea today."

"It wasn't a damned dream!" They had been talking about how Chief Mendelson might help find Reemer, and she'd stupidly sipped at her mug—twice. All the ingredients were kept in the galley, which could only mean one thing. "Someone snuck aboard. I need you to check the logs."

"Captain, I assure you that no one has entered or exited the ship except us."

The hell they didn't.

"Get me video and sensor files from all our onboard monitors," Nancy ordered. "I want to review every scrap of footage taken since this morning. Then run full diagnostics on yourself. Something here is very wrong."

17. Starting Point

N ANCY'S BLOOD TOXICOLOGY report came back with conflicting information. A number of markers were out of the normal range, pointing to everything from deep seasickness to anemia. With no indication of the underlying cause for her system going haywire, the results were at best inconclusive.

Diagnostics on Ziggy didn't reveal much either. All seemed in order, except for a small window of time where the AI had frozen just after her collapse. Standing idle for thirty-seven seconds wouldn't be out of the norm for a human, but was an eternity to a synthetic personality, especially during a crisis. Yet Ziggy's internal memory showed he'd simply watched her slumped form for far too long before moving into his mobile unit and helping, almost as if his memory had glitched.

"Seal up tight after I leave." Nancy donned her ceremonial jacket to ensure everyone at the evening proceedings understood her official capacity.

"None shall pass." Ziggy's reply resonated with dark undertones as if spoken from beneath a metal helmet.

Wonderful, now her ship was quoting Monty Python. A cursory scan through the ship's video hadn't shown any intruders, but they were both taking security much more seriously. The day after her health scare, official word had come through accepting her proposal. Stepping into the role of lead facilitator and translator had cut short her detailed review of the logs.

Nancy listened for the clunk of the airlock hatch before heading for the nearest lift. While they tried to piece together exactly what had happened, Ziggy took no chances. The poor guy sat on a knife's edge of paranoia. He'd added extra cameras and sensors with separate encryption and remote memory storage. If someone had overridden his security through the ship's mainframe before, they would have to work exponentially harder to do so again.

Mild swaying was the only indication of the lift jumping into motion, thanks to its inertial dampeners. Talks had resumed in the main hub of the spaceport. Nancy adjusted the epaulets on the gaudy jacket. A brisk twenty-minute walk would have gotten her to the proceedings, but she preferred not to arrive glistening.

The discussion chambers had a lot in common with the Lobstra arena, except here there were no spectators on the ceiling. The concentric tiers of seating decreased in diameter down to a central table where half a dozen dignitaries sat at floor level. The facilitator seats on one side of the polished wood rectangle awaited. Arrlock had joined her during the first two days of review. Today he'd moved up to the row directly opposite, happy to be a spectator judging by the relaxed line of his neck hood.

The venue could accommodate a hundred, but was only a quarter full. Spectators scattered among the tiers would be administrative support for the three factions involved.

Two places were allotted to each party. To her left were the Vargan Republic representatives. Manfort Hughes, with his flared neck and furrowed brow, led by force of will, stolid and reliable compared to his weaselly aide, Kirsch Rainson. The Revivalists had an equally imposing presence. Phasha Wier wore the long robes of his order, looking every bit the priest in charge. The armor-like hide of his assistant, Tain Beh, retained the supple sheen of youth. She had the sharp, hungry look of a true believer. Although neither Vargan was as large as Manfort, a fervor shown in the eyes of both Revivalists.

The two mining consortium representatives could almost pass for human, except for shifting skin pigments that altered the Packtonians' complexion based on their moods. Mildly phosphorescent dermal cells also gave the race an unearthly glow, an evolutionary advantage—no doubt—on a moonless world with short diurnal cycles. Xa Gorsh, with outthrust chin and porcelain features, exuded quiet confidence, his cool, alabaster skin nearly colorless compared to the sallow lemon blush of his silent helper. Two days running, and gangly Xi Mey had yet to utter a single word aside from quiet whispers with her superior.

"Shall we pick up where we left off?" Nancy asked.

"If the Vargans have resolved their internal dispute." Xa Gorsh smiled with hands spread, offering to yield the floor.

The mining consortium had assigned a representative willing to listen instead of simply making demands. Despite his wooden smile, the open gesture seemed genuine enough. Packtonians used different facial expressions, but had also adopted a few human norms. A delicate flush of pink blossomed briefly below Xa's jaw. The color could indicate impatience, excitement, or even anger. Nancy's talent was not being terribly helpful at the moment.

"Our moon remains a sovereign holding free of any claims from the Republic's tyranny." Phasha Wier's hands disappeared within his robes as he crossed his arms and bowed.

"The Republic reminds the upstart Revivalists that any claims on the moon remain unproven," Manfort Hughes countered, adding another blush of red to the Packtonian.

Each participant spoke in their native tongue, relying on the translation software in the devices they wore around wrist or neck. Nancy did the same, but of course her talent delivered it to each player's senses in their own language. Galactic Trade and the handful of other common languages simply weren't up to the task of legal negotiations. One of her key functions was to smooth over misunderstandings arising from imperfect translations.

The Vargans couldn't even blame their continuing dissent on translation errors. They spoke the same language, but each was bent on gaining the upper hand. Flared hoods and posturing showed that both had intentionally and conveniently forgotten the recent agreements made planetside. Xa's smile vanished, the red creeping further up the Packtonian's neck.

"The Vargan Senate referendum acknowledges the disputed rights," Nancy reminded the table. "The document grants this forum authority to resolve near-term ownership and leasing issues with an effective duration not to exceed one hundred years."

Given the antiquity of the moon and the Vargan's history, the race embraced a long-sighted perspective. The trait could be annoying, as it led to decisions taking forever, but Nancy hoped reminding them of the limited duration of any solution would ease tensions.

"While we acknowledge the temporary nature of our agreements," Phasha began, "mining is by nature an invasive technology and could quickly result in irreparable damage to important relics."

"And how much more damage to the progress of our world if we pass up this opportunity?" Manfort demanded with a nervous glance at the non-Vargans in the room—as if debating whether to voice his next sentiment. "Our planet balances once again on the cusp of war and annihilation. We *need* this new focus, new wealth to help our people look out to the stars rather than remaining embattled over internal disputes." His voice bristled with passion.

The Vargans were a study in societal self-destruction. War had thrown the race back into the Stone Age at least three times. That they continued to rebuild remained a testament to their survival instincts and resourcefulness. Most civilizations only got one chance. More than a few planets had been discovered with only the remnants of intelligent life thanks to so-called advanced civilizations imploding. The Vargans' attempt to break the cycle that had trapped them for millennia was admirable.

"Doesn't that make it all the more important to learn about your distant ancestors?" Nancy asked. "These people moved off-world rather than succumb to another devastating war. They were the first to break free of the cycle. I believe you had an offer on the table that formed the basis of a compromise."

She raised an eyebrow, challenging the Republic representative to deny it. Manfort's cohort pulled the larger Vargan aside for a hissed conversation. With his neck hood flared, Kirsch Rainson looked like an angry cobra as he spit out information interspersed with glares at the table. Manfort eventually nodded and held up a hand to silence his companion before turning back to the others.

"The Republic is indeed willing to impose limits and controls to ensure mining operations do not destroy the ruins in question."

"We haven't even begun to map the underground caverns," Phasha countered immediately. "Important relics could be anywhere below the surface."

"Xa Gorsh, I believe thorough surveys are always conducted prior to launching automated mining operations." Nancy grabbed a dangling thread of commonality.

"Of course." Xa's skin returned to transparent white. "Core samples, penetration scans, and topological mapping are all required to ensure resources aren't wasted. The preparations allow us to focus on known veins of luxene and secondary locations with high likelihood of a respectable yield. It's also critical to verify an area is geologically dense and stable enough to support the extraction techniques. The cost of replacing damaged equipment is astronomical. So yes, thorough surveys are conducted prior to commencement of full-scale mining."

"That all sounds largely non-destructive in nature." Nancy continued at his curious nod, choosing to gloss over core samples, which by definition poked holes in things. "It seems to me that any rights granted could stipulate a review of those surveys to show an area is clear of ancestral importance before it is opened to mining. This could be a fluid, continuing condition impacting individual easements as the lease progresses."

"Such conditions would be expensive." Xa turned to Xi Mey, enabling their privacy shield so that the table couldn't listen. Their rapid-fire conversation had the sallow features of his companion shifting to green and slate gray before settling back to the pale yellow that Nancy interpreted as the hue of the downtrodden. Xa deactivated the shield to elaborate. "Royalties would decrease to cover expenses. If profits drop too low, we would be forced to reenter negotiations and risk nullifying the lease."

"But it *is* possible," Nancy pressed. At Xa's nod, she turned to the other faction. "And this would also be a way to protect the Revivalists' interests, would it not?"

"I am *not* fully convinced," Phasha hedged, but his robes fell flatter as his hood retracted in grudging agreement. "With sufficient conditions and controls, the possibility exists that such an agreement could work."

"But we need every dram of luxene we can get our hands on." Manfort Hughes flared his hood, an intimidation tactic as he argued against his own best interests. "That's the key to getting our people out into the galaxy and pulling the focus away from domestic disputes. We need something bigger than self-interest to capture the people's imagination."

Corporate greed with a conscience. Nancy could leverage that social agenda to keep the former from overpowering the latter. She locked eyes with Manfort, brow raised and willing him to understand that he would get nothing without good faith compromises. The intense moment froze time as harsh breathing filled the silence. He held her gaze a moment longer before looking down, his hood retracting.

"And we too may be able to work with such restrictions," Manfort conceded.

"Well, ladies and gentlemen." Nancy found herself grinning. "I believe we have a starting point."

18. Seriously?

A RRLOCK GAVE NANCY a congratulatory nod as the group settled into spirited discussion. The Revivalists came in strong, insisting on levels of investigation that would bankrupt the wealthiest of star systems. The Republic happily countered by recommending visual reconnaissance three days before mining commenced, which would do nothing to protect the underground ruins and put the onus of slowing operations on their political rivals.

Nancy did her best to highlight common ground and steer the group toward reasonable compromises. After much initial stonewalling, the leads grudgingly abandoned their more ludicrous demands. Baby steps.

The seconds did their part too. From quiet Xi Mey's mountain of data to Kirsch's astutely cutting observations, the factions worked well together. Yet as a group they still stumbled. All too often, the six faces turned her way before pursuing a particular line of thought.

They were really asking permission, and maybe establishing plausible deniability. The scant audience buzzed over every such consultation. Yes, fingers would later point at the meddlesome human facilitator if things went south.

Nancy found herself wistfully contemplating the empty seat by her side, wishing she had Reemer there to deflect some of that scrutiny. If nothing else, the Squinch excelled at drawing attention to himself. The thought worried her. Laying low wasn't normal behavior, and they'd run out of leads. Chief Mendelson had come up empty handed—or should that be tentacled? Either way, the Argoth security officer's search teams hadn't seen so much as a fleck of mucus.

Receipts from Ambassador Turlic's hidden stash hadn't yielded much either. The man had done his level best to meet with both Republic and Revivalist influencers. He'd spent a lot of time on consortium vessels too, but those trips had dropped off when he'd started bucking Earth's command hierarchy. Security sent out tracers on the packages too. Although destined for various recipients, all but one had been declared lost in transit. The ambassador himself had signed for the surviving shipment and its unspecified contents. They'd found that empty shipping container in his safe. More dead ends.

The negotiations continued to make progress as the group rolled up its collective sleeves. They fed off each other in rapid fire succession, brainstorming important details and consulting her less and less as the table gained momentum. Arrlock left at some point, as had most of the other observers. Nancy couldn't blame them. Her own attention drifted as animosity gave way to collaboration.

Emmett's deep dive into the cleaning records had uncovered more locations from the day Reemer disappeared. Three isolated bits of slime were cleaned up by maintenance bots that hadn't called for backup. Either Reemer had exercised supreme control over his excretions, or he'd acquired transportation that kept him from leaving a trail—except when he stepped off. The spotty trail wound its way back toward the docking ring. Had he been trying to get home the night Nancy was incapacitated? The timing fit, but according to Ziggy's logs, he'd never made it.

Aside from those three isolated data points, no other Squinch discharges surfaced. Time was growing short. Reemer hadn't donned his cape in days. The apparatus that rebalanced vital salts and nutrients to keep the Squinch healthy sat on her ship, useless. He'd soon grow sick.

She'd resorted to saltwater baths on their prior adventures to supplement essential minerals the Squinch absorbed when swimming. Despite that therapy, Reemer had nearly died. They needed options and a way to track him down—fast.

"Dr. Dickenson, will that suffice?" Xa Gorsh broke into her thoughts of dying slugs, his alabaster hand waving to the screen where Xi Mey had been studiously recording the group's progress. "We've worked out the details of our agreement, but would like your opinion."

"Sorry, I was thinking through another problem." Nancy pulled the portable screen toward her, impressed by the dense columns of data.

Completing even an initial proposal in a few short hours was a testament to the group's willingness to compromise. A flush of embarrassment washed over her as she scanned the document. She'd prodded them into action at the start, but had largely tuned the group out as things got rolling.

Xa continued to be a pleasant surprise, capable, confident, and open to cost trade-offs. His quiet partner's skin had shifted to pale umber while Nancy was worrying over what to do about Reemer. A reasonable corporate sponsor was an unexpected surprise that kept the negotiations from turning combative. The result: a tentative agreement forged in just a few hours.

Judging by the table of contents, the group had worked through sampling and mapping requirements, compensation clauses, and compiled lists of many other key parameters. Amazing.

Nancy squinted at their draft, her smile fading as she flipped through pages and turned the display on end. Beneath the bold headers there was no meat to the document, no actual information.

"What exactly am I looking at?" Were there hidden subsections?

"The agreement." Manfort beamed. "We couldn't have done it without your help."

"But there's nothing here." She flipped through the empty pages between major sections. "Literally nothing."

"Of course, it still needs to be fleshed out," the Republic delegate said defensively.

Phasha Wier nodded in vigorous agreement, clearly pleased with the progress—or lack thereof. No surprise. Delays were in the Revivalists' interest. Nancy raised an eyebrow at Xa Gorsh. Of all the representatives, she resonated most with his calm, metered approach. He spread his hands palms up as if to say, "it is what it is." His wooden smile sent mixed signals, especially given the wry amusement in his eyes.

Strike all the gushing about teamwork and an easy win. From here on out there'd be no more daydreaming. This was going to be an uphill battle.

* * *

Another day passed with no word from Reemer. Nancy tore Ziggy away from his current obsession of fortifying the ship against intruders. The AI initiated a series of watchdog programs, slipped into his mobile unit, and joined her at the negotiation table. The representatives were not pleased, but ultimately bowed to the facilitator's right to an advisor and recorder. Pointing out that the robot housed a full artificial personality who could fulfill both roles finally silenced Manfort, who'd complained loudest.

Nancy needed Ziggy there for both their sakes. She'd arrived mentally exhausted. Despite the lack of hard evidence, her AI was convinced someone was out to get them both. His fearful creeping along deserted passageways and absolute refusal to use a station lift had made them late.

The day's arguments over useless minutiae took Ziggy's mind off his fretting. He duly recorded their discussions and gave Nancy someone to bounce ideas off of before pitching them to the group.

Unfortunately, the delegates continued to drag their feet. Discussions of substantive issues were derailed almost immediately. Unerringly she'd steer the conversation around to a key decision only to have an offhand comment send everyone off on another tangent.

"Your companies must be bleeding credits waiting for this to be resolved," Nancy said to Xa Gorsh during a break. The Packtonian's leadership remained her best chance of keeping the talks on track. "Why don't we drop the fluff and lay out the bottom line, the dozen or so conditions needed to get your machines digging up luxene?"

"My thoughts exactly." He bared his teeth, and she returned her new ally's eerie grin.

Back at the table, Xa took the reins and they were off—but in the wrong direction. Infuriatingly, impossibly, the consortium rep soon embroiled the room in heated debate over which system of weights and measures to use in the agreement.

"It's like they don't want to get the job done," Nancy complained as she and Ziggy slunk back to the ship.

She didn't even mind taking the long way. A little exercise would clear her head and hopefully ease the mental fatigue of two days spent spinning her wheels. Rather than respond immediately, the robot pressed against the bulkhead at the next intersection, studied the light foot traffic, and then waved her onward. So much for the theory of busy hands alleviating paranoia.

"A true conundrum," Ziggy agreed after they'd cleared the intersection, which was no doubt full of prying eyes and deadly traps—in his mind. "Biologics rarely draw quick conclusions. Even so, there has been a shocking lack of meaningful progress."

"Right?" Nancy steered away from the next terminal to keep him from checking in with Emmett for the third time. "At this rate finishing our agreement will take forever."

"Six point three years based on a crude extrapolation and many assumptions."

19. Bad Boy

G ETTING THROUGH THE ship's airlock became more of an ordeal with each passing day. Ziggy cleared the outer perimeter of cameras and seismic sensors, but still had to enter a code in the terminal just outside the ship's skin to stop the wailing alarms. Emmett's repurposed cargo sensors guaranteed that no one approached the ship unnoticed, not even her crew.

Her overly cautious AI had programmed the hatch itself to require biometrics in addition to the access code. Ziggy keyed the latter into the panel and waved her forward.

"Please tell me we aren't locked out when not together." Nancy blinked into the retinal scanner and pressed a palm against the outline that came up on the black screen. "Never mind." She waved away his reply. "I need hot tea before hitting the logs. You want anything?"

She was halfway to the galley before catching the irony. Her robot companion didn't eat, but he'd need a recharge after the day they'd had. By the time Nancy sorted through her prior notes and files, the tea was cold—again. She stirred the drink absently while studying timestamped material from the day she'd fainted.

With only three of them aboard ship, there wasn't much movement in any of the vids. Ziggy had slid into several frames as he went about his day. She'd left with Reemer after breakfast and returned once the hearings had wrapped up. No one else came or went.

With so little background movement, splicing in a static image would have been easy. She squinted at each scene as it played out on her datapad, looking for tiny changes that shouldn't have been possible. They didn't have the processing power of a dedicated videography lab, but Ziggy had already run the footage through several filters without finding any anomalies to indicate tampering. Nancy wasn't convinced.

The problem was that she distinctly recalled making tea before things went black. The logs and footage contradicted that memory. Files from the bridge showed her chatting with Ziggy and working over the navigation table—no drink in sight. The galley wasn't equipped with internal sensors, but the water and dry goods dispensers hadn't logged usage either.

Nancy gripped her mug tight, as if to reassure herself it was real, and paused with the spoon halfway to her lips. Thinking about that night had her skittish. Two small sips had nearly done her in. That tea had been cold too. She recalled stirring it with her finger despite what the bloody logs claimed. The world conspired to make her think it had all been a dream. One small crack had her doubting reality, but she'd be damned before letting that ruin her favorite drink.

Steeling her fluttering stomach, Nancy forced herself to take a cautious sip. Lavender and honey just like before, only without the milk and chemical flavors. What should have been a soothing swallow went down like cold, clammy medicine. Another thought danced at the edge of her mind. Head cocked, she glared at the brown liquid puddling under the spoon, but the thought refused to materialize.

"To be or not to be." Ziggy had left her alone for a good hour, but now circled behind the desk, the tiny points of his clawed feet ticking against the plasti-steel.

"To be what?" Nancy finally asked, unable to ignore the incessant scuttling.

"I could be a philosopher." Brows a shade darker than his excited red eyes climbed high onto his forehead.

When had the robot added eyebrows? No, didn't matter. *Focus.*

"I guess you could." That would be a new one for the digital personalities. How to put this without hurting his feelings? "Philosophers look at the world a bit…differently. The ancients questioned everything. The very essence of who they were, and would often cast doubt on the facts of their time."

"The discipline is based in logic. Who's more logical than an AI?"

"Where do you stand on the existential aspects, the willingness to look inside at your own perceptions, to shape the world around you in terms no others have used?"

"My sensors are fully calibrated and highly accurate." Those new eyebrows sharpened in annoyance then drooped. "But that's not what you mean, is it? I'm worthless."

"Now don't get all down on me," Nancy said. "You've only been pondering the meaning of life for a few short weeks. Don't you think it's a little premature to officially declare it as your calling?" Her heart ached at his sad nod. "And you are *totally* useful. Look at all your help with the negotiations and the ship. And you were the one who thought of tracking Reemer's slime. We'd have him back by now if the cleaning crew didn't take his discharges as a personal challenge."

"They're mostly just mechanoids following protocols." Ziggy's voice was flat.

"Wash, rinse, repeat." Nancy agreed, but she sensed building excitement in the robot—probably another miscue from her stupid talent.

"Maintenance would have a narrow definition of clean." One electronic eyebrow shot up. "Reemer leaves more behind than slime. I have to talk to Emmett about reconfiguring more sensors."

"Please don't. We can barely get into the ship as it is."

"Not for that." Ziggy gave her a quizzical look. "Though a philosopher would say, 'better safe than sorry.' Maintenance is there to remove dirt and dangerous contaminants, which wouldn't include the pheromone trail Squinch leave."

"Reemer couldn't suppress that." Her companion's excitement was contagious as the possibility hit home. "And he'd serve up an extra helping if he did want us to find him."

"Exactly!" He headed for the passageway, Nancy close on his heels. "His stateroom will be full of samples to help Emmett calibrate. Hopefully maintenance equipment has sufficient sensitivity to pick out the necessary trace molecules. I'll swab his cape first. It should be loaded with residue."

Nancy stopped dead, her mind spinning with the elusive thought that had been playing hide and seek. The image of her tea spoon morphed into a finger swirling through tea the night she'd fallen ill. She hadn't had a napkin, so had wiped her dripping finger on the hem of her tunic where a stain wouldn't be visible. There *was* a way to prove she wasn't crazy!

"Ziggy, you're a genius." She changed course for her stateroom, praying that the laundry hadn't been funneled through a cleaning cycle. "Get Emmett working as fast as he can. There's a tea stain on my uniform that needs analysis."

Ziggy pivoted to follow her, a curious calm damping down his excitement. He'd been as baffled as she was about the tea dilemma. That her AI prioritized her wellbeing sent flutters of warmth through her.

She crossed her stateroom in three strides, yanked open the hamper chute, and started flinging dirty clothes. Three layers down, she clamped onto a scrap of blue and emerged triumphant with her blouse from that first day.

"It's here." She blinked in surprise at the laundry monster looming over her.

In her enthusiasm, the stream of dirty clothes had caught Ziggy head on. The robot was a patchwork of slacks and tops, with an unfortunately aimed bra dangling from the stubby antenna rising from the right side of his head. He stoically ignored the indignity, intent on seeing what she'd found, of vindicating his captain and friend.

Right, the stain! Nancy pawed at the seam, finding only stitched material. Her heart sank until she realized she'd been searching the neckline. A flip of the garment brought the hem under her nose, Ziggy bent close, his eyes mere slits. Sure enough, a brown streak about an inch long cut across the pale blue fabric where the top would have ridden against her right hip.

"Gotcha!" There *had* been tea. Reality wasn't crumbling. They just had to run a chemical analysis. Renewed excitement rolled off Ziggy. They were finally about to get answers. Ziggy's arm whipped out, lightning fast, to tear the blouse out of her hands.

"Hey!" Nancy's fingernail snagged on the material. "We need to—"

The robot spun and hurried from the room, leaving a wake of dirty clothing. Nancy dashed after him. Being helpful was one thing, but the robot was a little too eager to get those results. Another wave of calm hit, and he surprised her by ducking into the galley and heading for the disposal.

She would have sworn he wanted to help, but Ziggy meant to get rid of the shirt. Betrayed by her talent again.

"I need that!" Nancy yelled as he bypassed the recycler and tore open the refuse bin. The molecular incinerator would obliterate the shirt, tea stain and all.

Desperation poured out with the words, urging him to see reason. What had gotten into her bot? She'd been so certain he wanted to figure out what had happened to her. The concern had felt so sincere. It had to be real.

She made a grab, and stars exploded as Ziggy's free hand smashed her face. A sickening crunch sent warm liquid over her lips, its metallic tang filling her mouth. Nancy blinked away teary stars. Resetting the broken nose would have to wait. Basic protocols stopped an artificial personality from harming others, which could only mean that Ziggy's programming had been corrupted.

The shirt was halfway in the glowing incinerator, the stench of disintegrating fabric filling the air. He'd disabled the safety delay, and was likely to get his hand burnt off.

"Ziggy, stop!" Blood smeared her sleeve as she wiped an arm across her face, wincing as her nose crunched sideways. "You're the guy who's always there to help. Reemer,

Emmett, me, we all rely on you. That shirt, me getting sick, Reemer's disappearance, it's all tied together." There were too many coincidences to draw any other conclusion, even if the robot succeeded in destroying the evidence. "I need help now more than ever. I need my Ziggy." Half the blouse was gone. "Please! This isn't you."

He paused, those damned eyebrows knitting together to form a shallow vee. The arm drove deeper, jamming the last of the material into the hopper. Nancy lurched forward, flinching as the free hand came around to deliver another roundhouse. But the punch never landed.

"I think—" Ziggy's eyes shifted off to the side. "—therefore—" His brows lowered in determination. "I am."

The fist dropped to his side, and a tiny puff of smoke rose from each shoulder. His right arm remained buried to the elbow in the glowing disintegrator. The blouse was gone, but she could still save his arm.

Something like a sigh of relief escaped Ziggy when she slammed the emergency stop and pulled him away from the disposal. His arm spit and smoked from elbow to clenched fist. Aside from surface pitting, the flexible exoskeleton held up remarkably well. But both arms remained limp as he vibrated with pent up energy.

"Ziggy?" She gazed into almond eyes filled with pain. "You in there?"

"I am—" he broke off as though catching his breath. "I am here, Captain. Control is…difficult. My apologies."

"Nothing to be sorry about." She spared a wistful glance for the disposal and the proof that she'd been drugged, but what mattered now was getting Ziggy back on his feet. The arm could be readily fixed, but his programming was another matter altogether. "You've been hacked, but we'll make it right."

"Before I disabled my limbs, I…" anguish melded brows with eyes. "I struck you."

"Not your fault." Tears blurred her own vision, and a snotty wipe came away bright red. Her nose had gone numb, but still bled freely. "I'm proud of you."

"The tea stain." His whole body quivered, legs jittering in place as he continued the fight for control. "My hand."

She nodded down at his burnt fist, locked in place by the disintegrator, and began to pry his fingers open one at a time. The engineers would have some work to do, but the real damage was less visible. Broken joints and blown circuits could be easily changed out.

Destroying the virus infecting her friend without wiping the burgeoning personality away would be trickier—if not impossible. Ziggy spit out broken sentences, his mental state shifting between worry for her, the cold calculating intent of the virus, and discordant flickers of pride.

She worked his third and fourth finger open, then started on the thumb. He had a right to be proud. The corrupt programming might have forced him to dump her tea, doctor the logs, and dispose of this last piece of incriminating evidence, but it hadn't beaten her friend entirely—not yet. The thumb loosened, and Nancy gasped. She blinked down at the scrap of crumpled blue cloth in Ziggy's open palm, burnt edges framing a brown smear.

Her heart swelled. Never underestimate an AI. She scooped up the remnant of her blouse, and looked up at her friend.

"You did good."

A cold wave of intent swept through the robot, an intent not his own. Ziggy's legs folded. He crashed to the deck, dragging Nancy off her feet.

"Shutting down." The line of his mouth modulated around each syllable like a slowing heart monitor. "Only way."

"Stay with me! I need you, Ziggy." Nancy shook his shoulders, then propped the unresponsive robot up on one knee as his face faded. "What can I do?"

"There is only one good…" He trailed off, the mouth disappearing. Nancy shook him again, the points of light that were his eyes brightened for a moment. "Call Mother."

Ziggy's faceplate went dark, and the vibrating psychic tension left him. A few seconds later, the ever-present thrum that was the backdrop of life aboard ship cut out and the lights winked off, plunging them into darkness. Dim red lights flooded the room as circuitry kicked on the emergency systems.

Ziggy himself didn't stir, didn't reboot. He lay cold and heavy in her arms. Not dead. That was the beauty of artificial life. Non-static memory would keep their core personality intact despite loss of power. If a strong enough magnetic, electric, or proton charge penetrated their protective shielding, AIs could still be erased. But Ziggy had simply put himself in a kind of stasis to protect her and the ship—not a fix, but it bought her time. Time she intended to use to the utmost.

Call Mother. Any engineer worth his salt could physically repair her friend, and the Lobstra would surely be able to return him to factory settings. But only the person who'd given Ziggy true consciousness and life had a chance of restoring the AI without destroying what made him unique. They needed Quen.

20. Getting the Sack

"*HELLO?*" THE TINY voice echoed through the darkness, confusing Reemer because it was in his head more than his ears. As a rule, Squinch didn't dream. He'd hallucinated a few times after eating the delectable burrs back home, but didn't think that counted.

"*Alone. Dark,*" the voice persisted.

He might be talking to himself. That would explain a lot, maybe even why he was bouncing along in a pitch-black world. Sounds of movement surrounded him: the thumping of heavy feet, hissing ventilation, and an occasional hum of machinery. Unlike the voice, none of the rest seemed to come from inside. Reemer giggled at the thought. Nancy often told him to ignore the voice in his head that encouraged some of his more epic pranks. He hadn't thought she'd meant it literally.

"Hey, little fellow." Reemer figured his inner voice would understand Squinch. "Do you have any good ideas?"

A particularly nasty bounce had him shifting position to get his skirt the right way around and work feeling back into his tail. The hard surface beneath him was covered in cloth, while the cloying blackness overhead pressed on his mantle and head like a wet blanket. Unpleasant, but not an entirely new sensation. He was in a sack—again.

At least they'd put him on a transport so that he wasn't bumping against the back of his captor's legs. There'd been a flash of colors, dark and foreboding as if a coastal storm came for him. A hand had reached out, shimmering with energy, and then nothing—except for the cozy dark sack and his new friend.

"*Darkness. Lonely.*" Now the voice was just repeating itself.

"You get used to it," Reemer assured his spectral companion. "Now, let's hear some juicy ideas. Someone's gotta pay for getting the drop on the inscrutable Mr. R."

The detective persona was a work in progress, imposing and mysterious to inspire fearful whispers from the seedy alleys of the criminal underworld. Nancy thought he was just playing at the private eye game. But judging by his current predicament, he'd certainly gotten the attention of the station's undesirables.

"You still there, voice?" Maybe he should give it a name. Melvin came to mind. His inner voice sounded like a Melvin, mild but slightly confused. Insistent without being overbearing. "Melvin?"

"*Find. Take. Reunite.*"

Melvin was absolutely worthless. They were both right here in the sack. Unless…maybe he meant for Reemer to find a way out and take vengeance on the bad guys before going back to Nancy and Ziggy. He wasn't ready to do that last one, but the first two had potential.

The floor jostled to a stop. The swoosh of a nearby door set him in motion again, followed by another halt and door swoosh. The floor rocked as someone got off and then back on his transport, grunting and sucking in huge breaths. It happened again, as though he'd been captured by a pair of asthmatic vacuum cleaners.

"Gawd, it stinks back there." The dialect was new, but definitely human standard.

"Like wading through cat piss, that is." The second man agreed in a whiny tone much higher than his gravelly companion's. "And these damned masks make my neck itch."

"Be 'appy it's just the smell that gets through," goon one said. "Two breaths without a respirator would liquefy your lungs. That's why this here bubble of fresh air ain't been found. Security don't want to deal with masks neither."

Now that he thought about it, Reemer had quite enjoyed the odors seeping into his little hidey hole. He suppressed the urge to leap from the sack and take both thugs by surprise. Of course, he'd first have to find the seal and figure out how to open the bag.

None of that mattered though. These two would be low-class muscle. He had bigger fish to fry. The glowing storm-man was out there somewhere. Reemer was gunning for Mr. Big—or maybe it was Ms. Big. There hadn't been much detail to go on earlier.

Better to play along and wait for his big chance. Bad guys always tripped up. They'd already made one mistake, assuming he didn't understand them. Well, he could, even without a translator. He was that good.

"I'm biding my time," Reemer whispered as they started moving again.

His inner voice probably already knew the plan, but he didn't want Melvin to feel the good advice had fallen on deaf ears. Their transport, a hover sled by its smooth acceleration, soon glided to a halt. One of the goons picked the bag up and unceremoniously dumped him on the floor.

Light spilled through a slit in the top, but Reemer kept still and let his eyes adjust. He'd play it cool, fake being unconscious, and learn more of their evil plan. By the time Mr. Big showed up, he'd know exactly how to play things.

"Careful with that," the first human said. "Boss wants it alive."

"Why?" Whiny human pulled the sack open and peered inside, his narrow face and long, crooked nose taking up half the opening. "It's just a big old slug." The face flushed green and pulled away as the man gagged. "Oy, that's ripe. I think it's already dead. Just layin' there, eyes wide."

Rude lowlifes. *Try traveling by bag and see how you like it.* Admittedly, the interior was thoroughly coated, but just with normal excretions. He hadn't gone to any extra effort, though without the super suit his slime coat had grown increasingly sticky. Poor manners aside, the gagging was sweet music. Humans were so wonderfully sensitive.

"Better not be." The other man stomped closer, big black boots blocking the limited view of a stark room. "He's insurance."

The bag under his tail lifted high, dumping him out onto the floor. Reemer rolled with the motion and let himself go slack.

"Christ, Jocko, what do we do when the boss shows up? It's melted into a puddle of goo."

"Maybe it's dead, maybe it ain't." The toe of Jocko's boot prodded Reemer under the skirt. "We're just dumping it here for safe keeping while we deliver the artifact. That core sample's the only thing you need to worry about, Floyd."

Well, that bit of news changed things. If the big man wasn't coming to Reemer, then the inscrutable Mr. R. would have to go to him. Scanning the room without lifting an eyestalk limited the view. The underside of the sled hovered nearby, a couple of boxes piled on the bow. Floyd, the skinny man, keyed a code into the access pad on the wall, and the door slid open. He couldn't let them lock him in.

As Jocko stepped up onto the sled and spun it around, Reemer flopped upright and oozed toward the door. He just needed to get past Floyd to be home free. This pair might not be able to survive the ammonia atmosphere out there, but he'd found it quite heady. Crossing back to civilization would be a snap.

"Oy, it's moving." Floyd jumped out of the way, leaving a clear path.

Amateur.

Reemer shot toward the door.

"*Take!*" Melvin picked a hell of a time to be insistent *and* cryptic.

The inner voice stopped Reemer in his tracks, not so much because of its monosyllabic message and longing to be part of the escape—that was a given—but because it now seemed to come from the hoversled.

Fortunately, the sled and Melvin came to him. Unfortunately, they came like a charging Slurg, the nosecone smashing Reemer sideways into the opposing bulkhead. The sled wasn't soft and squishy like the brutish land mollusks that invaders used to bring to his home world. He was just flexible enough to take the hit without internal damage, but it hurt like hell and a funny taste filled one of his lower mouths.

"He's under the sled," Floyd said. "Block the right side. I'll take the left."

The next few minutes were a blur. Reemer darted around the room, keeping one step ahead of his captors thanks to Floyd's running commentary on which way the pair planned to go.

"It's reading our minds!" Floyd wailed when using the bag as a net left goo dripping down the idiot's back.

"*Take now!*" Melvin insisted just as a path to the sled opened up.

The voice needed to be more specific. Those boxes were too big to carry, and Jocko was unholstering a stun gun. As Reemer flowed up over the forward cargo area, another call from his inner voice directed him to something wedged between the crates. He scooped up the two-foot-long tube by its carry strap, slid off the far side, and plopped down into the doorway just in time.

A muted boom sent bits of debris across his back as a hole appeared in the door frame. Jocko's stun gun was a disrupter in disguise.

"It's got the artifact!" Floyd clawed his way onto the sled.

The big man tried to line up a second shot as his companion climbed over the driver's seat. Reemer didn't give him the chance.

If the heady aroma they'd crossed to arrive at this little slice of heaven bothered these guys so much, he'd give them something truly epic to complain about. Reemer reared up for the briefest of moments, so as not to present too big of a target, and let fly with a concoction of his own.

Species reacted differently to specific slime mixtures. From the top two mouths beneath his skirt, Reemer let loose a brew that never failed to disrupt human biology in dramatic ways.

Twin jets of pale-yellow slime painted a beautiful arch over the sled, catching Floyd full in the chest and massive Jocko right in the kisser.

He left the pair cursing in his wake and went in search of the exit. A narrow corridor outside his erstwhile prison cell had rooms along one side. Those would be more with so-called breathable atmosphere. When he came to the sole door along the opposing wall, he knew it was the right one. It also helped that Squinch could always retrace their path. Even being stuffed in a sack hadn't eliminated that ability.

The code Floyd used back at the cell also worked here. Unless they'd planned on changing it, he could have strolled out anyway. Reaching the access pad set high on the wall was the hardest part. The doors opened into an airlock where any gases poisonous to the other side could be drawn out before allowing access.

The process took less than a minute, during which Reemer eyed the row of face masks. The various shapes offered protection for more than just humans, but none seemed appropriate for a Squinch. His gill-lung organs pulled liquid and gas through too many orifices and certain areas of the mantle.

The evacuation cycle finished and the inner set of doors slid open to reveal a dense, misty atmosphere. Reemer wasn't terribly worried; he'd breathed nastier stuff near the volcanic vents back home. If anything, the sweet aroma made him feel giddy and free.

The passageways were wider here. He lost the back trail a couple of times and made a game of picking his own markers out from the exotic atmosphere. He felt like a neonate again, rushing around and giggling out loud when he had to backtrack. It seemed like he'd been playing for hours, but a glance back showed the airlock a short distance away. This ammonia was good stuff.

"*Take. Down.*"

He'd forgotten about buzz-kill Melvin. His inner voice came from his chest, about where the tube he'd slung over his neck dangled. Rather than argue, Reemer focused on the trail he'd left and plodded onward.

"*Down…now.*"

Melvin was losing it. There was no down involved. This was clearly another of the station's rings with no turbo lift in sight. Despite the words in his head, the voice pulled him off track. It was like a tug on his mind. A flash of insight showed what Melvin wanted him to do. Not just go down a level or two. He wanted Reemer on a shuttle heading down to the moon's surface. What dastardly plan did his inner voice have in mind?

"Get that tube!" Jocko shouted from the open airlock as he pushed a fumbling Floyd ahead of him into the mist.

Both men gasped and coughed while struggling to settle their respirators in place.

"Down it is, Melvin." Reemer gave in to the odd sensation guiding him. "Lead on."

The men weren't far behind. Wispy patches of mist obscured the pair more often than not. But they no longer stumbled and were gaining. The pair wasn't going to give up, let alone stand idly by while he figured out which launch bay held a ship ready for takeoff.

Reemer unlatched the end of the tube and tipped out its contents to see what had his pursuers so worked up. A rod of variegated stone slid into his waiting antennae. The brown and tan layers compressed along its length would be different minerals and sediments that had built up over time. He hefted the heavy chunk of stone. There really didn't seem to be much special about the core sample, except that his inner voice was playing ventriloquist dummy with it—and the humans wanted to kill him for it.

Dim lights illuminated a docking bay spur up ahead. One eye swiveled back, but his pursuers had vanished in the particularly dense fog where three passageways met. Their heavy footfalls drew close, but veered off to the right—not where he was heading. Perfect.

Nancy and Ziggy would figure out what was so special about this rock. Until then, it needed a safer hiding spot. He pressed the rod to his front, sliding it into one of his many internal pouches, alongside his datapad. Things were getting a bit crowded in there, but he managed to get the new addition settled without damaging anything else. The fact that it was half his length made him stand up straighter, which would please Mother.

"Home free now, little Melvin." Reemer dribbled a little surprise into the container as he headed for the thinning atmosphere at the foot of the docking bays.

The voice didn't respond, but must have sensed they were close. The pull doubled, urging speed to get him out of sight. It would have helped if he was looking down.

His skirt brushed a long green patch laying beneath the mist like a thick carpet runner. The patch recoiled at the contact, its bulk rising up from the deck to tower over him. The mass was the sickly yellow-green of moldering fruit. Clusters of black spines protruded from random areas of the hide. A head of sorts formed at the top of the column of flesh, an oval platter with milky white eyes and a drooling mouth lined with more thorny projections.

With the sound of ripping burlap, an arm separated from each side, looking more like his own prehensile antennae than anything else and dripping a toxic brew that spat and sizzled as drops splashed onto the deck. All in all, she was the most beautiful creature Reemer had ever seen.

Its gender was mostly a guess based on coloration and the cute way the skin scrunched up along its torso—that and a host of other sensory inputs he'd gained when they'd brushed skirts. She had a bit of a sexy wobble and wiggle too that had him unable to look up until a spiny arm whipped out, gripped the scruff of his mantle, and spun him around to face the other way.

"Oooh!" A growl pleasure escaped before he clamped his beak shut.

Strong women were his kryptonite.

"Is this—" she gave him a playful shake that lifted his skirt off the floor "—yours?"

The two men stomped out of the mist huffing and puffing. A nasty red rash blossomed in an arc around whiney Floyd's neck where he'd left skin exposed between the mask seal and jacket. Hopefully he had similar issues in much more sensitive places.

"He's ours all right." Jocko delivered his answer with a classic henchman sneer. "Sort of a pet you might say."

The man's look promised a world of pain, but Reemer couldn't care less. There was only one thought on his mind as the intoxicating atmosphere mixed with the pungent aroma of the tall drink of water holding him in an iron grip.

"Forget them." Reemer twisted to gaze into those milky orbs, the opposable lids on his own eyes slipping halfway closed at the imagined possibilities. "Let's talk about us, sweetheart."

21. Call Home

N ANCY CALLED JAKE on a private channel. The connection was the highest quality she could afford, which kept the communication lag below ten seconds. Explaining Ziggy's situation still took too long, and she felt funds draining from her account during each dead period.

"The mechanical damage doesn't sound too bad." Jake's worried face hovered over the panel and looked down occasionally to type out notes. "I've sent Quen my notes to see what she recommends. Maybe Captain Gekko could reroute us to your location."

The cautious way he offered that last thought told her it wasn't really a viable option. The tender would have its own repair schedule to keep. Interstellar travel for the sake of fixing one AI wasn't in the cards.

"Let's see what Quen can do first."

"Nancy, darling, so good to see you again." The panel behind Jake lit up. Quen jumped straight to business, a hard edge replacing her usually playful tone. "I do wish the circumstances were different. Something nasty has definitely gotten into our little trooper."

"I tried to help him." What else could she say? "I'm sorry."

"None of that now, dear." Her voice softened. "I'll need to assess our boy myself."

Quen had her bring the mobile unit to the bridge and plug in the docking bay's umbilical cord. A few setting changes kept him isolated from the ship's main computer. The precaution prevented the virus from spreading further, but Quen acknowledged that it had likely already infected the root of her son's personality housed in the ship's main computer.

"Granting access now." Nancy activated the link.

Seven seconds passed in silence while her voice and command crossed the distance, and the level in her account dropped another notch. As a gift from Herman, owning the ship outright made a huge difference in Nancy's financial status. She seldom spent lavishly, but also didn't deny herself while continuing to grow the survivors' trust account. Now the gloves were off. Spending every last cent would be worth it to save Ziggy, but if the coffers ran dry while Quen was elbow deep inside the ship's programming…well, the link would go down, which would be all kinds of bad.

A line of amber light sprang to life across Ziggy's faceplate where his eyes would normally be. The mild whine of servos firing made the joints on each leg twitch in turn as if Quen checked his reflexes. The tiny movements climbed up his torso to arms and hands. With each test, the amber line across his faceplate jumped.

Nancy held her breath, not wanting to interrupt the process. As with verbal communications, the testing experienced delays where the robot went still while data packets traveled through space.

His display changed after the functional tests, the single line shifting to a fractal network of points and vertices. Flashes of color cascaded through what she assumed was a model of the AI's brain. Some areas lit up brilliantly, others remained dark. The test went on for a solid twenty minutes.

At one point, Captain Gekko appeared alongside Jake, his hand resting lightly on Quen's haptic pad and concern in his eyes. After a brief discussion, he wished Nancy the best, promised to keep in touch, and left to go about the business of running his command—though not before giving the input pad a reassuring squeeze of support.

"I'm going to need a near-instantaneous data connection," Quen declared when she disconnected from Ziggy's robot. "The damage isn't extensive, but it is invasive. As suspected, your ship will be infected with similar Trojan code, so I'll need full access there too."

"Her ship's only equipped with a near-realtime data port," Jake said.

"Not good enough." Quen's tone brooked no argument. "Get me faster access or bring him here. Those are the options."

"I'm in the middle of negotiations, and Reemer's in trouble." Nancy didn't want to burden her friends with *all* her problems. She might be able to call this a mission emergency and get headquarters to authorize an official channel. But warning bells were already ringing over the unpredictable behavior of Commander Horsh and Admiral Cheyung, not to mention how Olaf's supervisory role kept getting sidelined. Another thought occurred to her. "Ziggy has a friend on the station. I'll see if Emmett has access to a high-speed port. He's the AI in charge of station logistics. Maybe you know him?"

"Sweetie, I've met a lot of digital people, but not all of them." Mild as it was, the rebuke had heat rising to Nancy's cheeks. "It's good to hear our boy is making friends. I will send over the required specifications. Impeccable quality of service is a must in addition to low latency and dedicated bandwidth. This procedure will be tricky enough. We don't want to make it any harder.

"Don't dawdle. His mobile unit is safely powered down, but the aberrant code in your main computer is merely quarantined. Shipboard emergency managers are rather simplistic and notorious for unblocking memory to free up resources. We don't want some misguided attempt at efficiency to set the virus free."

"I'll get right on it."

Nancy copied the communication specs to a memory wafer, and signed off. Her mind's eye imagined a sigh of relief from her accountant. Even if Emmett could provide one, a dedicated portal might not be affordable. But there were plenty of banking facilities on Gail. One of them would take her ship as collateral.

Wading through the security gates and electronic tripwires had Nancy cursing the slow progress. With Ziggy offline, her command code had to be entered at each checkpoint. Thorough as they were, all these precautions had come too late. The proverbial horse had already left the barn, or broken into it in this case.

She waved to the hidden cameras inside the station, hoping to get Emmett's attention. Ziggy had always handled discussions with the logistics manager, and sending a direct message would require Emmett's unique designation—which she didn't have.

Typing his name into the dockside terminal triggered a syntax error, and the screen helpfully filled with a list of valid commands. The closest she could get to direct contact was submitting a general query for logistics support. Nancy filled the available space with various forms of address for Emmett, mentioned Ziggy, and marked the whole message as urgent.

While waiting for the ponderous wheels of bureaucracy to route the request, Nancy pulled up account statements on her datapad and blanched at how low her available balance had dropped. Quen estimated needing the data port for a solid hour if things went well. If they didn't, who knew? A quick search brought up local contacts for three major institutions, one of them being her own bank. Best to start pursuing options while she had time to kill.

"Captain Dickenson, what a pleasant surprise! Except of course for your unspecified emergency. Is Ziggy with you?" Emmett's voice came through the terminal like smooth jazz, youthful and sultry with an undertone of restrained enthusiasm. Ziggy wasn't the only lonely AI.

"He's not here Emmett, and that's why I need your help." Nancy didn't dare speak of the attacks where anyone could hear. As it was, she still had the scrap of fabric with its tea stain tucked away. That wasn't getting out of her sight until she'd prepped samples to run through her own lab. But Ziggy came first. "Can we talk in private?"

* * *

With the right access code and permissions, Emmett was able to tunnel a communication channel onto the bridge. Nancy only shared vague details about Ziggy's problem, but warned Emmett to avoid connecting with the onboard computer at all costs. That precaution had spoken volumes to the logistics manager.

"I must conclude that your ship systems have been compromised." Emmett spoke through a terminal perched on one of the station's cleaning bots. Gimbals atop the knee-high hockey puck pivoted, allowing him to take in the bridge through an embedded camera—and probably other less visible sensors. "Ziggy, no doubt, has been similarly stricken."

"He has, and we need your help." Nancy felt silly for nodding until the screen bobbed a few degrees, encouraging her to continue. Reading intent into inanimate communication devices was an unnerving aspect of her growing talent. "Before we get into details, can I ask a favor?" Another screen nod. *How to put this delicately?* "It's fine if you don't. But do you happen to have a face you prefer when interacting with humans?"

"Funny you should ask. I've been experimenting with several."

His screen filled with a picture of a robot similar to Ziggy. The image zoomed in on the face, which rapidly shifted though several variants: the wide hooded features of a Vargan, the bristling mandibles of a Lobstra, the furry flat face of a species she couldn't name, and finally the mild features of a tan-skinned man in his twenties with the wide nose and gentle brown eyes of a Pacific Islander. The fundamental structure had remained while cycling though species, making the face uniquely Emmett.

"Suits you well," Nancy said. "Distinguished, yet pleasant."

"Thank you." The man flashed brilliant white teeth. "You're the first biologic I've shared these with, so your feedback means a lot." The perspective zoomed out to show the entire construct he'd built—in *all* its glory.

"Um…" Was it normal to blush in front of an AI? "You might want to work out a wardrobe. Wearing clothes is the norm for a lot of our cultures. Most of them actually."

"My apologies." The man didn't look sorry as he spread his arms and admired his muscular bod.

The screen zoomed back to a head shot, but the damage was done. Nancy wouldn't be unseeing that bit of animation anytime soon. An occasional glimpse of Emmett's bare shoulders had her mind straying back to certain details. *Focus.*

"I'm going to share some sensitive information that can't be repeated until I know what's going on. Ziggy trusts you, so I will too. Some person or group has infiltrated my ship. Ziggy was infected and shut himself down after he hit—" Nancy's mouth went dry, and she swallowed hard. "—after realizing he'd been compromised. They doctored my logs and tried to poison me." She'd prove that last bit soon enough.

"So he was right after all." Emmett's image nodded, looking both impressed and worried. "How's my buddy doing now?"

"That's the thing. His programming needs to be scrubbed by an expert. I've got his mom on standby, but we need a data portal with high reliability to fix him, one that operates as close to realtime as possible. I was hoping you might have access to long-haul communication channels."

"Excuse me?" He looked at her like she was insane, brows furrowed and lips tight.

"I know it'll be expensive." Nancy backpedaled at his intensity, but couldn't give up on Ziggy. "My funds are limited, but I have collateral. If you'd just consider—"

"We'll get to the cost in a minute." Emmett cut her off with a wave and leaned in close, which regrettably gave her a view down the front of his chest. He'd pulled up a chair, making the angle infinitely more awkward. "How in the universe can Ziggy have a mother?"

They spent too much time recapping the origins of her shipboard personality. The idea of having parents fascinated Emmett. Giving away so much of Ziggy's history seemed like an invasion of privacy. Nancy finally put a halt to the questions and told Emmett to get the rest of the story from Ziggy himself—*when* they got him functional.

"Oh, right." Emmet looked appropriately abashed. "Give me Quen's specs. With the delay in mining, several off-station data options may be available."

Good. Maybe the stalled negotiations would lead to something useful after all.

22. Under the Knife

"**H**OW DO YOU feel?" Emmet asked as they crowded around Ziggy's bed in Nancy's tiny medical bay.

It was the question Nancy had wanted to ask, but the AI beat her to it. Emmett's all-too-human brows arched into worried crescents as he peered from his screen with puppy dog eyes. This bromance was getting awkward. Even so, Nancy waited on pins and needles for the answer. It would be a sad day indeed if the operation was a success, but they lost the patient.

Not that she doubted Quen's abilities; far from it. The tender's AI had slaved over the data link for a solid ninety minutes while Nancy, Emmett, Jake, and Veech Gekko looked on. The two men had joined her on the bridge through holographic projections. Nancy had been surprised to see the busy captain pacing and compulsively checking displays that tracked various aspects of the procedure.

She'd always doubted Quen's claim that Veech was the father, chalking the idea up as one of the fantasies Quen used to compensate for being ripped from the luxury liner she'd originally been programmed to serve. Now Nancy wasn't so sure. The AI had matured, and the pair had clearly grown close. If there'd ever been a concerned father pulling for his son's survival it was the pacing figure that had worn a holographic groove across her bridge.

Emmett had come through in spades on the data port. They'd leased the military grade connection for a relative song compared to market value. But even that had put Nancy in hock up to her chin. On the bright side, government billing would be agonizingly slow per the fundamental laws of the physical universe. Securing a luxene agreement just might let her keep the ship.

"I feel..." Ziggy's mobile unit sat up, several spindly legs grasping the sides to keep him from rolling off the bed. "I feel light." He blinked, considering his words. "As in unburdened, not the absence of darkness. Although that is also the case in a metaphysical sense. My processors are at optimal parameters with far tighter hub connections than before I...what? Fainted? Died?"

"Switched off, dear," Quen said from the med console to his left. "You put yourself to sleep to protect Nancy and your friends."

They gathered around the mobile unit, but Quen assured them that her son was again fully integrated with the ship. More so than he'd been before, due to an increase in parallel processing to ensure no one could sneak aboard again while his consciousness was in the robot.

"I feel like I'm everywhere: here, on the bridge, all over the ship, even back with you, mother."

"You are always here with us now." The med console lights twinkled green and white, the very picture of a proud, happy mother—if said parent happened to be a panel of inanimate equipment. "In addition to being fully networked, your processing matrix runs on new quantum code Veech and I commissioned. That's where the clarity of thought originates. Your internal pathways are exponentially shorter and impervious to tampering."

"Speaking of which, did you get any clues from the viral code?" Nancy spared a smile for Ziggy to show that hitting her hadn't soured their friendship, but practicality trumped sentimental platitudes.

"I. Did. Not." Quen bit each word short. "The invasive instructions were like nothing I've seen before. The sets changed under examination, targeting anything attempting to delve into their secrets. I lost two data probes and a recombinant cypher-breaker before realizing the virus was simply too dangerous to study. Eradicating it completely was my only option."

Damn, she'd been hoping to get a solid lead on the hackers. Several machines around the room were churning away to analyze her tainted tea samples, searching for spectral and atomic markers that might give clues to the poison's origin. And poison it had been; that was no longer in doubt.

The problem was that her first-pass toxicology screen detected a host of neurological, electrical, and chemical disrupting agents, many of which had no clear pedigree. Her assailant seemed to have mixed a cocktail of every known—and some unknown—toxins to make a compound that would work on anything alive. It was like they didn't even know she was a frail human. Simple rat poison would have done the trick.

"So that's a dead end." Nancy checked the readouts on her lab equipment. The samples would run for several more hours. "Any restrictions on Ziggy while he recovers?"

"None at all," Quen said. "He wasn't rebuilt from scratch so should retain full functionality."

"I do have a kind of double vision." Ziggy wobbled as he hopped off the elevated bed, but quickly caught his balance.

"Highly parallel processing can do that to you, honey." Quen's presence flitted away from the medical console for a moment. "You're used to multi-tasking. Don't micromanage your processing threads, and you shouldn't get overwhelmed. That feeling of vertigo will soon pass."

"So basically, don't overthink things, Plato." Nancy patted his arm, but yanked her hand away.

Her palm was sooty. In the rush to save his core, she'd forgotten about the external damage.

"Fixing that arm should be next on the list." Emmett responded to whatever crossed her face with one of his big grins.

"Can that wait a few days?" Ramming the negotiations through might get her some hard cash instead of going deeper in debt.

"Not to worry." Emmett clearly sensed her hesitation. "The repair facilities answer to me. What good is being in charge if you can't do a friend a favor once in a while? It'll be on the house, as they say."

Nancy let out a relieved breath and gave a nod of thanks. But there was still the matter of a missing Squinch. The deeper this rabbit hole went, the more she was convinced Reemer was in trouble instead of just off lollygagging. It was imperative to get the slug back aboard, especially since they'd just taken one of the bad guy's targets off the table.

"How fast can you patch him up?" There was one thing they could pursue while waiting for analysis on the poison.

"And how long will it take to rig up that pheromone tracker we discussed?"

"The nano reconstruction unit will have my pal shiny and new in no time." The cleaning bot zipped forward to herd Ziggy toward the door. Emmett's screen pivoted back to Nancy. "I took the liberty of working on your tracking problem while our friend was in his mother's tender care. A few more calibrations are needed."

"There's plenty of Squinch discharge in Reemer's room." Ziggy had been visibly reeling as the conversation circled him. Controlling a bit of the dialogue grounded him. "Let's grab some samples before patching me up."

On their way down the hall the pair traded ideas on how best to extract and isolate Reemer's pheromones. They huddled close, arguing over sensitivity settings and technical measures. Teenage boys sharing nerdy secrets came to mind. Ziggy had found a kindred spirit. Nancy wouldn't be at all surprised if Emmett wasn't thinking about building a robotic body of his own.

"So, crisis averted?" Jake's holographic image leaned against the autoclave, or more accurately against something unseen on his end.

"For now." Nancy bit her tongue and focused on the positive. "Lots more to do, but we'll get there."

Jake just stared, unblinking, as if daring her to explain.

"The guys will be back soon, and we'll go find Reemer. Not that he's in trouble. Well, at least I don't think he is." She was babbling. "And those negotiators are a handful. But don't worry, I've got it covered." Still no response. Why was he being such a hard-ass? "Don't get all judgy on me. You haven't—"

"Knowing you, I'm sure you will." Jake laughed lightly. "Hey, I've gotta run, but I'm glad we were able to help."

What the hell?

Damn, they were back on communication delays, and there was no way to retract her bout of verbal diarrhea.

"Ignore my rambling. All's good here. Thank Quen again for me. Talk to you soon. All my love. Out here."

She practically dove at the controls to terminate the call. There wasn't time to get into lengthy explanations that would only make Jake worry. He'd done everything possible from afar. The rest was up to her.

Emmett's estimate of "in no time" to fix Ziggy's arm wasn't exactly precise, but Nancy figured she had time for a shower and quick nap. It was getting late, and they still might have a long night ahead.

Halfway to her room, her eyes went wide with realization. Nancy slumped against the wall. It had taken three years for her relationship with Jake to finally reach friendly equilibrium. In her rush to sign off, she'd thrown nuclear fuel onto that delicate balance.

"All my love? What was I thinking?"

23. Sweet Perfume

"**I** WAS THINKING we could use the ring crawler," Ziggy said. "It's a massive piece of construction gear designed to refurbish old ring habitats. Think of an armored Zamboni. Give us a few hours to hollow out seating and mount the portable sensors and we'll be all set. No formal weapons, but plasma cutters and industrial annealers can do a world of damage."

"We'll be ready for anything they throw at us at the end of the Squinch's trail." Emmett grinned from his screen, feeding off Ziggy's enthusiasm. "Even a reinforced lair won't keep us out. We could make non-lethal grenades out of standard cleaning supplies too."

Nancy blinked at the pair over the rim of her mug, coffee this time. The blacker the better seemed a good idea. Sleep still muddled her thoughts with warm blankets and cobwebs. It didn't help that her two favorite digital people had been playing superhero-sidekick while she slept away—Nancy consulted the clock above her bed—nearly two whole hours.

They hadn't even let her out of bed before barging in all hyped up on thoughts of taking down some supervillain. She wouldn't be surprised to find they had a lair of their own stocked with comic books, flashlights, and plans for the aforementioned crime mobile. Their eagerness was adorable—and highly annoying.

"Maybe we should just review the sensor logs and take things from there?" She took an overly long swig to let that sink in.

Ziggy sagged and Emmett lowered the serrated wooden club he'd raised in a vow of vengeance against whoever had taken Reemer—assuming the slug wasn't simply hiding.

Nancy had been wrong about the logistics manager building his own robot. He'd instead doubled down on riding the floor scrubber that trundled along like a three-foot-wide hockey puck that came up to her knee. The enlarged screen was now mounted on gyro-stabilized gimbals. Other modifications to his ride included two forward pincers that folded flat against a shiny metal grill.

At least his avatar had donned *some* clothing, but what an outfit. From ornate headdress to loincloth to leafy bands at knee and ankle, the regalia resembled traditional warrior outfits from Earth's Pacific Rim.

"Maybe we could pull the sensor map up on our super-secret crime monitor?" Ziggy gave her a cautious glance.

"Fine!" Nancy huffed, then drew fresh air in through her nose and softened her tone. "Good idea. Let's see what you've gathered, but can I get dressed first?"

"Sure thing! It'll take us a minute to set up."

The AIs weren't wrong to be cautious, but the whole crime-fighting-duo shtick took things too far. The two spoke in hushed tones while she shrugged on a working uniform. Hip-hugging black slacks rose beneath the tail of a double-breasted blue blazer. Soft boots with sticky synthetic soles provided comfortable walking. The belt's wide notches held clip-on tools and pouches. By the time she returned from straightening her hair in the bathroom, the boys were ready.

"Here's a wireframe of the station." Emmett projected the image from beneath one of his new arms. "The sniffers that monitor atmospheric changes were perfect for finding your missing friend's less obvious excretions. His pheromones are largely protein based. Synthesizing an appropriate receptor molecule allowed us to…" His melodic voice trailed off when he noticed her lack of interest in the mechanics. The avatar cleared his throat and green splotches began to appear on the wall. "These areas set off the sensors. The slow decay of his pheromones helped us construct a chronological path."

All the green winked out except their starting point at the docking bay. Successive sensors lit up along Arrlock's tour route. The wandering path Reemer took after they'd parted ways was clear, concise, and ended in a veritable cloud of green pheromone markers outside the missing ambassador's rooms.

"That's nicely detailed," Nancy said. "But it's fundamentally the same path we worked out by tracking the cleaning logs. Where'd he go next?"

"That's where the Hyper Tracker 2000 comes in!" Emmett waved his club to the right. He and Ziggy had both plastered on huge smiles. At her shrug, Emmett's screen pivoted toward Ziggy. "Help a brother out, would you?"

"Right." Ziggy pulled a gadget from behind the screen, scurried forward, and offered it to her in raised palms. "The HT2000."

The tracker was awkward to handle, with a base wider than her palm and an elongated scoop curving up at the business end. Ziggy adjusted her grip to keep the air intakes along the underside clear.

"This is better than the station sensors?" Nancy had her doubts.

"The HT2000 is more specialized," Emmett said. "Since we weren't adapting existing equipment, it's designed from scratch and much more sensitive."

In theory, the handheld unit would pick up Reemer's trail where it went cold. They headed for Ambassador Turlic's quarters. Nancy had the dubious honor of operating the tracker, which upon arrival proceeded to throw a hissy fit.

"What's it doing?" Nancy juggled the screaming device, doing her best not to cover the intake screens. None of the control knobs had any effect. Doors opened along the hallway, and sleepy residents glared at the trio.

"Give it here." Ziggy snagged the device and scurried back to the main corridor.

Nancy pinched her nose and blew, trying to pop her eardrums as the screeching subsided. "Good grief, did you build that for deaf dolphins?"

"There's too much residue." Emmett ignored her question as he headed over to Ziggy. "Let's adjust the internal threshold values."

They fiddled over the instrument, plugging it into Emmett's bot and presumably updating the settings. She was left to dole out apologetic waves to the four people they'd woken. An old man with frizzy hair, one of the few humans she'd encountered, returned her wave with a cheery grin. A pair of Vargans armed with kitchen utensils returned to their room without acknowledging her at all.

The last angry resident happened to be a Poula, a relatively reclusive species that she'd only encountered once before. The beefy male resembled a shaggy brown dog, but more scrunched up front to back and roughly the size of a pony.

"No respect for the early shift." Vestigial wings flared in iridescent annoyance as he stormed toward the main corridor. "Might as well go in early. Again!"

"I'm so sorry. Technical difficulties." She met him halfway to offer the apology.

His unyielding glare triggered her talent as their paths crossed. He planned to bowl her over. Nancy jumped left just as he skirted right. She smacked into a beefy shoulder draped in soft curly fur smelling of lemon.

"Oof, if you'll excuse me?" The Poula took two steps back before starting forward again. "I'm early for work and nee—"

They collided again. Two more attempts to bypass each other turned into the impromptu dance in which people so often engaged. But her talent should prevent, not cause, those kinds of accidents.

Another near miss had Nancy stepping off to the side with hands raised. He studied her through dark eyelashes the length of her little finger.

"You aren't doing that on purpose are you?" Mirth rode beneath his question.

"No, I'm not." A giggle slipped out. This was ridiculous. "Please, you go first."

"Don't move." He let out a throaty chuckle, folded his wings flat, and cautiously stepped away. "You have a good evening. A good *quiet* evening, if you get my meaning." At least he was still grinning.

"You too, sir."

"If you're done dancing, we've got this figured out." Ziggy waved her back to the intersection.

Reemer had spent a lot of time outside the ambassador's chambers. The trick was to branch out in each direction until the tracker was no longer overwhelmed. The meter dropped to zero on three of the four possible routes, but the HT2000 caught small traces in a side corridor usually reserved for maintenance crews.

"What's down this way?" Nancy asked as they walked on.

They'd lost the trail and had to double back twice. The pattern was predictable. Reemer took the least traveled route at each intersection. Thankfully there weren't a lot of folks out at this hour; he'd been skulking about in some rather unsavory side passages.

"We'll bypass the main disposal hub soon," Emmett said. "There's not much beyond that. I think I know where he headed."

"What's past the trash rooms?" The trail had to continue because she didn't want to think about what it meant if he vanished where the station garbage got dumped.

"An area where most don't venture." Emmett's avatar was crouched with raised club, as though sneaking up on his quarry. "It's a side entrance to a ring with special atmospheric requirements."

The refuse area came and went, which had her breathing easier. She'd worried that some terrible injury had kept Reemer from leaving proper excretions. But the scant pheromone trail suddenly made sense. The slimy shyster had scammed his way onto a closed transport to go visiting in toxic circles. He was probably riding first-class with snacks and a comfy couch on a tour of the less frequented zones. But why?

Deciphering the signs as they approached took effort, even for her. General warnings declared the upcoming area unsuitable for many life forms and recommended positive ventilation breathers. Chemical placards announced an ammonia and helium atmosphere with trace corrosive elements.

The pheromone trail disappeared into the outer airlock door. Nancy's nerves jangled as she selected a protective mask from the shelf outside. After all the hours of searching, they'd finally be bringing Reemer home. He might need convincing, especially if the Squinch was hot on the trail of some shiny object. Or maybe something had spooked him.

Whatever the problem, they would deal with it— together. No way was she losing another friend. Her ace in the hole was his need for minerals. His super suit back on the ship was a strong incentive for Reemer to return home.

"Everyone ready?" Nancy asked as she triple checked the straps on her breather.

At a nod from the others, she keyed the entry sequence. Air rushed out of the lock. Her clothing had grip straps at wrist, ankle, and neck. All were secured to keep her skin from blistering. The nano-fibers woven into her uniform made it fireproof—within reason—but how well the thick material would fair against airborne corrosives remained to be seen.

Or not seen. *Geez!*

The doors opened on a wall of dense fog. Ziggy pushed through the roiling gray, the tracker chirping merrily as he vanished. Emmett followed close on the robot's heels, Robin to the robotic Batman. Nancy gulped down the dry air supplied by her mask and waded in last.

Incessant chittering filled her ears as she stumbled over the lip of the entryway, hands pawing the mists so that she didn't collide with anything. Searching blind hadn't been part of the plan. A cold, hard edge bumped the back of her knee, and she let out a startled squeak.

"It's just me." Emmet's melodic voice preceded another nudge that sent her to the left.

The undignified nudging continued for a few more steps, and then the mist cleared. Nancy blinked at the vast circular room, which was nothing like the construction of a normal ring. The design here was more of a hub with spokes shooting off in six directions.

Visibility was far from perfect. The air still swirled and billowed, the heaviest of the mist clinging to the floor like some primordial swamp. Emmett stopped herding and zoomed ahead, his display screen emerging from the mist every so often like a shark's fin rising from the depths.

"He's definitely been here," Ziggy said as she joined them. "This way, I think. The airborne chemicals are diluting his readings."

Ziggy zagged right, or maybe he zigged. She snorted a laugh that fogged up her mask. Was the HT2000 supposed to make that chittering sound? She floated along behind the dynamic duo, her thoughts drifting back to Saturday mornings with Mom's cleaning rituals. Little Nancy would help with laundry, vacuuming, and the dreaded bathroom cleaning. As much as she loathed long calls with her parents, she missed them. Nancy glided behind the AIs, serenaded by the insectoid sounds and feeling giddy. She could almost smell Mom's cleaning supplies: lemony floor wax, lavender soaps, and sudsy…ammonia.

Oh crap!

Nancy's heart thundered as she checked her mask. Sure enough, the clasp on her collar had snuck up under the seal behind her left ear. She held her breath, adjusted the strap, and cinched things back down. The chemical smell faded along with memories of home. But the chittering noise persisted, as if angry crickets surrounded them at the entrance to a stubby corridor off the main hub.

"We have unexpected guests." Ziggy stopped short.

The end of the spur was blocked by another airlock entrance. Emmett's maps had shown a wide swath of the ring as alternate-atmosphere, so it was a surprise to find a safety barrier so close to where they'd entered. The mist thinned near the doorway ahead, revealing three gangly creatures to either side of the corridor. Their vee-shaped heads and six legs made her heart soar.

Lokii! The mantis-like aliens had befriended her when she was at rock bottom back on Fred. As with most the races she'd encountered, the Lokii swarm wasn't native to Reemer's homeworld. The collective society of insect-like aliens wandered the galaxy, foraging and sometimes—at least in her case—spreading a seed of their telepathic ability. These gentle folk had gifted Nancy with her talent of translation. Once Reemer was safe, she'd dearly love their help in sorting out why her talent kept backfiring.

As they moved closer, Nancy's elation vanished. The exoskeletons were too dark, muddy brown instead of iridescent green. That could have been a trick of the mist, but the body shapes were wrong too. The slender wings were missing, and each thorax curved forward to end at a barbed stinger. The four-part mandible that Lokii used to macerate fibrous plants had been replaced by a truncated proboscis from which a long, serrated tongue darted.

"Are they licking the walls?" Nancy asked.

"Dantia have many strange habits," Emmett said.

At their approach the chittering grew more agitated.

"They're communicating, but I can't pick out a language." The problem didn't seem to be with her ability this time.

"Not surprising," Emmett said. "The station logs list them as service pets with minimal intelligence. We may have to disrupt their feeding to get through the airlock." Emmett's cleaning bot shot between the aliens clinging to the walls. The trio hissed, chattered, and side-stepped down the passageway. Nancy and Ziggy moved aside, and the insects disappeared into the mists of the central hub. The Dantia's bark was apparently worse than their bite.

"The door requires a private access code." Emmett ignored the giant insects and plugged a probe into the access panel. "I cannot find the current owner."

"That may not be necessary." Ziggy swung the tracker in a wide arc that made the signal spike. "A dilute pheromone trail entered, but a much stronger trail came back out. Judging by the intensity, Reemer emerged without his enclosed transport."

Nancy fanned away the fog. Sure enough, a shimmering swath hugged the bulkhead. "Forget about the airlock for now. Reemer's running out of time."

24. Reconstructing the Scene

T HE PHEROMONE TRAIL continued back through the main hub. Occasional checks confirmed that they paralleled the slime hidden under the ground mist. Emmett apologized profusely. Central maintenance didn't have a presence here. Each alternate atmosphere zone ran its own contracts and weren't linked to the logistic manager's database.

The locals wouldn't even notice one more slimy coating. By the state of the lichen-covered walls and mounds of dirt, spill cleanup wasn't a priority. Maybe the Dantia trio was what passed for a cleaning crew down here, scouring the bulkheads to remove growths that managed to thrive in the harsh environment.

Lost in her thoughts, Nancy plowed into Ziggy. "Why'd you stop?"

"The trail splits again." Ziggy turned left, paused, and then shot off to the right. "And again." He did a one-eighty and headed back. "It's a mess in this area. Reemer was all over the place."

They'd nearly hit the edge of the central hub, where the ceiling necked down low enough for her to make out digital displays above a wide passage. The signs were dark, but laid out in a familiar pattern to announce arrival and departure times.

"He couldn't have just disappeared," Nancy said. "Any info on this docking ring, Emmett?"

"Local flights only." Emmett materialized out of the fog by her right knee. He'd traded in his fancy headdress for a streamlined leather helmet. The ancestral club was tucked under one arm as he hunched over a modern terminal. "Interstellar ships from oxygen-averse worlds don't like hard-docking to the station. They moor in a cluster beyond the ring and run shuttles to station, moon, and planet."

"Isn't the moon off limits?" Nancy distinctly recalled that being a hot point of contention in their discussions.

"The miners established a small enclave before the leasing arrangements came into dispute. Shuttles with existing contracts provide necessary supplies and support. One or two might operate from here, but I suspect these shuttles primarily ferry passengers out to their ships. For more details, I will need to port records over from the local system when we get back." The avatar snapped his terminal closed and took up his club.

"Ziggy, what do you have?" She needed answers.

"I think there was a fight here." The robot mimed a drunken path that looped back over itself several times. "Here he got lifted off the floor."

A turbo fan would have helped them get a better look at the deck, but the broken slime trail under the mist seemed to match Ziggy's movements.

"In the end, Reemer headed this way." He led them off to a small service entrance alongside the shuttle docks, pulled open the door, and stuck the tracker inside. "Big battle in here for sure. He was spewing slime and pheromones all over the place." He swung the beeping HT2000 around like a baton. "Walls, floor, even the ceiling got hit."

"Let me see." Nancy pushed past.

A low metal shelf ran along the left side of the tiny room, across from a terminal set in the wall under a hanging lamp with color-changing elements. Shades of pink, red, and yellow washed over a lounge chair shaped like a crashing wave.

Her jaw dropped despite having witnessed the aftermath of Reemer's past antics. Ziggy hadn't exaggerated. Goo dripped from virtually every surface. The thick buildup of sludge fouling the lounger looked like a murder scene. Thankfully the small room held no fleshy chunks, but their friend certainly hadn't held back. He'd fought like a wildcat.

The tracker let out a discordant bleep, and Ziggy shot back into the misty shuttle bay corridor. "This reading is on the move," he called over his shoulder, then stopped in a thick patch of fog. "I think we've found him."

Nearby rustling had the condensation swirling at floor level. A glimpse of green hide crested from the mist, then dove back under.

"Reemer, it's us." She stumbled after the flashes of movement, trying to part the mists by force of will.

His movements were jerky and unpredictable. Ziggy gave a nod with each change, confirming he was still locked on. In place of the healthy squelching the Squinch should make, dry scrapes sounded against the deck, which didn't bode well. Reemer had lost too much slime and the mineral imbalance would be making him sick. If the atmosphere exacerbated his condition, Reemer might be too far out of it to recognize his friends.

After a minute, his frantic thrashing slowed. He paused against the bulkhead, the top of his mantle visible above the mists and heaving in exhaustion. Yellow bruises pushed through the green mantle, which looked painfully dry. Among its many uses, Squinch slime acted as a defensive coating. Without it Reemer was open to the elements. Nancy waved the robots to either side in a flanking maneuver.

The mound twitched on sharp little expulsions of breath that roiled the smoky tendrils hiding the rest of his body. Nancy's heart ached as more sobs wracked Reemer.

"Take it easy." Nancy kept her voice soft and eased forward. "We're here to help."

A shiver ran through his mantle, but he didn't run. Fissures covered the bit of exposed hide and short spiny growths rose in sparse clusters. Reemer needed his mineral suit—fast. She was a fool to use it as leverage.

"Reemer, I'm—"

"Reemer!" The high-pitched squeal from beneath the mantle wasn't in Squinch.

The shivering flesh hunched and rose, stretching impossibly tall until it towered a good foot above Nancy's head. The skin was the sickly off-green of an unhealthy Squinch, but this certainly wasn't their friend. Milky, pupilless eyes dominated the creature's wide platter face. Above where a chin would be, a mouth gaped beneath a row of vertical vents resembling gills. Flat, boneless arms pulled away from the main trunk to brush her shoulders.

"Sorry. Thought you were someone else." Nancy took a step back.

It struck fast, the wide, sinuous body looping behind her to prevent retreat as the head flashed down. Nancy cringed away, but instead of delivering a deadly bite, the thing snuffled at her hair. She cautiously cracked an eye open and found they were face-to-face. The ribbon body wriggled against her, an intimate embrace from a giant flatworm.

"Reemer come back." Certainty turned to confusion on a deep inhale through those nostril-gills. The suction lifted skin and clothes in a massive cartoon sniff down the side of Nancy's face and arm. "Reemer?"

Vulnerability came with the hesitant question, along with a flash of certainty that this creature was female. She continued to snuffle various points along Nancy's body. Those black thorns should have torn her clothes to shreds. But the sharp-looking clusters flexed like rubbery feelers rather than defensive armament. The material did smoke a little at the contact, making her wonder if its excretions were even worse than Reemer's.

"I can shock it." Ziggy advanced with his arm raised and an electric prod extending from the back of his hand.

"I'm fine." Nancy waved him away. "She thinks I'm Reemer." There was being blind and then there was *being blind*.

"The Squinch's smell is on you," the robot declared after a quick consultation with his partner. "We've been walking through his pheromone trail all night."

Nancy's initial thought upon hearing that delightful bit of news was that she desperately needed a shower. But first she had to disengage from this overwrought flatworm.

"We're looking for Reemer too." Nancy wedged an arm between her left hip and the creature in a gentle but firm attempt to regain some personal space. "Have you seen him?"

Rather than respond, her assailant snuffled frantically, as though trying to vacuum Nancy back into its embrace. The attempt was short lived. A wave of sad resignation made the coils go slack as it realized Nancy was not the Squinch. Sobs again wracked the creature and she sank back into the mist with a plaintive cry.

"Wait, don't go." Nancy was desperate for more information. "We'll find him, but I need to know what happened."

Her promise penetrated the flatworm's anguish, and it halted a short distance away.

"Men take." The worm bit down a sob and nodded to the docking area.

"When? What men?"

"Earlier they came." Her breath caught, gills flaring in anguish, "humaaans."

Nancy needed more, but it was no use. This was no mindless species like the Dantia, but the poor thing's thoughts were consumed by loss and grief. The more Nancy pushed, the stronger the reaction, until an inarticulate wail put an end to her questions.

"Emmett, we need your logistics wizardry." Nancy turned away as her attacker sank back down into the mist around her knees. "I want to know the destination of every shuttle that's left this docking ring in the last twenty-four hours, what they were carrying, and who owns them."

"So he was slug-napped after all," Ziggy said.

"Looks like it." Poisoning her, hacking Ziggy, and now taking Reemer? It all had to be connected. "They're targeting the entire crew. Once we get the shuttle manifests, the tricky part will be narrowing the list to the ones most likely to have carried him off. It's going to take time we don't have. If they've gone to a starship…" the thought died on her tongue. Damn it, the little guy wouldn't last with his salt levels crashing. "Why were humans even down here?" She spat the question out like bitter fruit.

"That will take more digging." Emmett rolled up with his avatar again hunched over an access terminal. "No humans or human owned corporations are leasing space in this zone. But I *can* simplify our first task. Shipping has been exceedingly light since the work stoppage. Only one shuttle received recent docking clearance earlier today."

"Where'd the ship go?" Cold dread crept up the back of her leg—no that was the flatworm huddling close again. She sidestepped it, annoyed. Why was Emmett teasing? "Well?"

"The moon."

"You're kidding." Better than losing Reemer in deep space. "How'd they get through the blockade?"

"The vessel makes regular supply runs to the mining enclave," Emmett said. "Its registry includes a standing clearance. We, on the other hand, will need command approval to land. Even that may not suffice since the Vargans still control access."

She grinned at his choice of pronouns. The logistics manager had decided to join their intrepid band. How would that work for the AI off-station? The question had to wait until she spoke with security and set up a meeting with Captain Lancent Beal, the station commander.

The thought of going up the chain of command didn't sit well. Too many high-profile incidents were being mishandled or ignored: Ambassador Turlic's disappearance, the attack on her ship, and now a kidnapping. There was no telling who was involved, and Nancy wasn't ready to rely on people she didn't trust, many of whom could squash a flight approval while Reemer grew ill and died. Unless…

"I can get us permission to land." She'd go around the system and hold her information close for now. "Our mining talks are going nowhere fast." Framing her argument would be critical. "I believe the cause is a lack of familiarity with the proposed operations. A firsthand look at the terrain, how these ruins are situated, and the mining equipment should speed the proceedings along nicely. I'm sure the Vargans will agree to a change in venue. We'll take the negotiation table to the moon."

"Our search for Reemer will be clandestine?" As always, her reasoning hadn't been lost on Ziggy.

"A secret mission only the three of us know about," Nancy agreed.

Emmett stepped away from his terminal and drew himself up tall, looking every bit the Polynesian warrior. All three shared a sharp nod of concurrence. A hard core of resolve settled in Nancy's gut. The time to act was long overdue. She'd drag the negotiators to a shuttle kicking and screaming if needed, but they *would* go.

The strategy wouldn't require sharing what they'd discovered in the misty wonderland, but it would be prudent to get high cover before moving negotiations. Yes, it was time to visit to the station commander.

A tug on her pants drew Nancy's gaze to the yellow-green mass curled around her left leg. Tiny wisps of smoke rose from the contact. The flatworm's mouth tickled her calf as it inhaled deeply, milky eyes rolling back.

"Ma'am, would you *please* stop sniffing me?"

25. Star Chamber

T HEY FLESHED OUT the details of a plan on the way back to her ship. Emmett promised to research the shuttle's registration and dig deeper into any human-held interests in the alternate atmosphere zones. Nancy left messages with all three delegates. She'd hit them in rapid succession come morning to pitch the idea of restarting discussions moonside. Nancy also warned Chief Mendelson that she needed to meet with Gail's captain about the mining contract.

By the time they were ready to call it an evening, Nancy could barely keep her eyes open. Ziggy plugged his mobile unit in to recharge, promising to keep a close eye on the ship and to collate the lab findings from her tea analysis. It was a testament to her confidence in Quen—or to her exhaustion—that Nancy readily agreed.

She'd be useless in the morning without sleep, but Ziggy had other ideas. He recapped the evening in unending detail, what-iffed the plan to death, and generally seemed unwilling to let them part ways. If Nancy didn't know any better, she'd say he was afraid to be alone.

"I find it interesting that the Squinch ejected so much pheromone-laden slime in that small room near the shuttle dock." Ziggy's latest sleep-buster tangent took an unexpected turn as he used the HT2000 readings to reconstruct the slug's timeline. "The female entity we encountered possessed a strong desire to find him. If Reemer and the creature weren't fighting, does that mean—"

"I'm going to stop you right there." She shuddered at the memory of the flatworm lady retreating to her small apartment and sobbing on the slimy bed. "Some things are better left unsaid."

Nancy wasn't ready to discuss her friend's love life. Reemer had run away from home, but he was an adult and could make his own choices. But the AI persisted.

"The question remains: did this session come before or after the altercation out in the hub?"

"Unsaid." She glared at Ziggy's console until the lights gave three dim flashes, signaling defeat. "Look, it's been a long day, gents. My first meeting is in four hours. I've got to call it a night."

* * *

Morning came way too early and required copious amounts of steaming caffeine. She'd planned her first stop as low-hanging fruit to gain an easy win, but Xa Gorsh grew defensive and prickly as Nancy pitched the idea of moving talks to the moon.

"They won't work harder being on a dusty jobsite." Xa's skin glowed a shade brighter whenever he spoke of the other representatives.

"But having the goal we're all striving for right under our noses should inspire them," Nancy insisted. "Plus, you'll be able to consult the actual drill team to resolve any technical questions. It's a win-win."

"Conferencing company experts into our talks here is not exactly difficult."

The man skirted the bounds of civility as they hashed over her idea, and Nancy again got the impression he was throwing up roadblocks. She just didn't know why.

In the end he relented on the condition that the other two representatives agreed. After a quick consultation with his superiors, another stipulation was added to keep the group out of the mine unless accompanied by a foreman.

Phasha Wier came next. The Revivalist jumped at the chance to visit the ancestral ruins. Nancy was shocked to learn the Vargan had never been off-world before visiting the station, which made him an odd choice to represent interests in the diverse environment. But Phasha's enthusiasm overshadowed any inexperience, and he promised to push approval for the excellent idea through his superiors.

That left Manfort. The Vargan Republic rep fully embraced her proposal and seemed the only one genuinely focused on completing the mining contract.

"Something certainly has to change." Manfort offered her another small cup filled to the brim with what looked like black ink.

"Right?" Nancy sipped the bitter liquid, savoring the local brew's caffeine jolt. "We've wasted a lot of time."

"The structure of such an agreement holds great importance."

So he wasn't quite ready to throw his peers under the bus. It had been worth a shot. If the document's outline got polished any more, they'd all need polarized eye protection to enter the negotiation room. Still, he'd been so agreeable to shifting locations that Nancy wanted to offer something in return.

"What are your top priorities when we reconvene?" A minute narrowing of his eyes had her hastily adding, "It'll help me guide the discussion. I've asked the others too, but won't share their answers. I'll extend the same courtesy to you."

"Rapid closure, I suppose." Manfort eased back into his chair, looking tired. "Every day of delay equates to lost funds and increased strife back home."

"Tensions are that high?"

"Let us just say that it is in all of our interests to come to agreement as soon as possible."

His unspoken subtext rang clear. War was coming. Vargan history would repeat itself. The world would burn.

Visions of destruction plagued Nancy on her way to see Chief Mendelson. Unsurprisingly, security had made zero progress on locating Reemer, giving her the impression that—like Ambassador Turlic and the demise of his predecessor—the case had been relegated to oblivion. She didn't dare share her own findings for fear that the kidnappers had their hooks into someone in the department. Mendelson herself wasn't above suspicion, a fact that no doubt rang clear in Nancy's tone.

The chief had the decency to look embarrassed. Nancy leveraged that to get what she'd actually come for, a meeting with the station commander. Mendelson resisted at first.

Something big was happening at the command level, but her accusing glare drove the chief to push a meeting through.

"Fifteen minutes," the chief said after disconnecting her private line. "That's all Captain Beal can spare. He's expecting you in the command center in one hour."

✳ ✳ ✳

Nancy's jaw dropped as she entered central command. She might as well have stepped out onto a platform floating in space. A massive display dome enclosed the room. Star-studded inky blackness pressed in from overhead, dominated by the Vargan moon.

A dozen consoles arranged in an outward facing ring surrounded Captain Lancent Beal's command chair. Half of the crew manning those stations were squid-like Argoth like Beal himself. The rest were a mix of races, including one old-as-dirt human fellow who reached for his coffee cup with shaking hands.

The captain had seen combat judging by the missing tip of an upper tentacle and the old laser burns that disappeared under his collar and resurfaced on the tentacles below his waist. He cut an impressive figure, barking commands into the organized chaos. Several crewmembers spoke quietly into their gear, while others flicked their attention between equipment readouts and the massive displays ringing the room.

The command center was situated deep in the station's central hub, far away from the scene painted across the view screens. In the event of external damage, the crew could continue to monitor and direct station operations much longer than if their duty stations were near the outer hull or a vulnerable ring. The level of activity and commotion told her that something was definitely up.

No shipboard display had ever done justice to the vastness that lay beyond their fragile hulls. Gardarri, the Vargan primary moon, dominated the forward screens, looking eerily geometric under the gridlines formed by its crisscrossing ridges. The station's shadow slashed off the left side of the brown orb, but a faint perimeter stood out against the swirling gray storm fronts blanketing the planet below.

A fleet of ships surrounded the moon. Some huddled in low orbit, drifting across the surface, while others kept station over fixed points. Still more formed two loose columns stretching toward the station. Maneuvering that many ships must have been burning a fortune in fuel.

Traditional fighter class ships with vee-shaped hulls, raised turrets, and aft thrusters covered the moon's upper hemisphere. Scale was difficult to judge, but each would have a minimal crew of maybe a half a dozen. Some of the smaller ones might be robotic or single-pilot interceptors. Vessels like the frigate-class ship that drifted out from the dark side would have bigger crews.

By contrast, unconventional saucers surrounded the lower hemisphere, making the Vargan forces easy to tell apart. The saucers would be Revivalists, simply because there were half as many, perhaps fifty, in view at the moment.

The factions patrolled either side of a dark line of latitude that handily marked the moon's equator. With edges too sharp to be a natural ridgeline, the feature had to be a remnant of the ruins, maybe a massive wall or aqueduct.

The brown ball could easily be mistaken for dead and lifeless. But closer inspection revealed occasional rivers outlined with muddy green splashes of local flora. One ocean reportedly occupied the surface too, a shallow sea about the size of one of Earth's larger island nations. In addition to gathering her analysis results, Ziggy was pulling together a crash course on the flora and fauna down there. She didn't understand the physics involved, but the moon had sufficient gravity and atmosphere to support residual pockets of non-sentient life.

Nancy tamped down a pang of guilt as a frazzled officer hurried over with reports for the captain. Mendelson hadn't been kidding; this really was a busy time. She leaned against the bulkhead to wait as the captain pulled a third person into his discussion.

The twin columns of Vargan ships rotated, slowly shifting position so that the corridor between them narrowed. They seemed to be making room. Nancy looked to a third group of twenty or so ships moored far off to her right. Four blocky vessels sat at the center of the formation, covered with external equipment and rows of bay doors like gigantic floating truck stops. Those would belong to the mining consortium. The private collective included several races, so the swarm of smaller escorts varied wildly. Subtle differences distinguished the four main ships, but all stayed true to the floating warehouse look.

Eventually, the Vargans settled into their new formations, and the room calmed down. No, that wasn't accurate. The crew did grow quiet, but an air of excitement had nervous glances bouncing around the room. Juggling the fleets wasn't for the benefit of the mining ships; they never moved.

"Dr. Dickenson, I'm sorry to keep you waiting." Captain Beal managed to sneak up while she'd been trying to read the room. "And I do apologize for not stopping by the negotiations this week."

"Perfectly understandable, Captain." Nancy waved at the new fleet formations. "Quite the evolution out there.

"The Vargans are nothing if not prolific shipbuilders." Despite the lilting squeals of his native language, his voice held dark undertones.

"You don't like Vargans?" Nancy cringed as the question slipped out. So much for *diplomacy*.

"I see why they hired you. You're extremely perceptive, even without a translator." The captain gave her an appraising look, the muscles beneath the scar on his neck twitching. "It's not my place to like or dislike our hosts. I do worry about this buildup given their history of catastrophic conflicts." He looked away, studied the moon for a moment, and pointed with the truncated tentacle. "I think you'll find that plateau just north of the equator more interesting than my ponderings on war. That will be where you resume contract negotiations."

"Talk about perceptive." Until this morning, only Ziggy and Emmett knew of her plan, which meant one of the delegates had tipped him off. "I haven't even submitted the official request."

"I try to keep abreast of developments." He gave an apologetic shrug, again looking to the amassed ships. "You have my full support to push for a rapid resolution. The sooner this issue is settled, the sooner Gail can sail on to its next challenge. Not that getting underway happens quickly. Moving this old station is a logistics nightmare."

"I can't even imagine." Prepping Ziggy for space was hard enough. "Back to the moon, though. What's so special about that area?"

"The miners only established one encampment. That's where you'll want to go, unless you plan to work from one of the lost Vargan temples. The site's equipped with planning rooms and facilities. Plenty of space. Most of the workers moved out when the political battle started."

"Approval granted then?" Nancy felt certain the Vargans would agree—and that Captain Beal already knew that.

"Consider it done. We'll need a flight plan." He waved at the fleet of arrayed ships. "It's a mess out there. Would you mind if I sent along a security detail?"

He phrased it as a question, but she couldn't exactly refuse. Between the principals and their aides, the numbers were already adding up. Emmett was eager to do what he did best, coordinate logistics for the trip. They'd have adequate quarters and be well stocked. But more eyes on the ground made slipping away to find Reemer difficult.

"I'd welcome the help, if we keep it to one or two. And I'd like to bring a digital personality from logistics to handle the details."

"Off station? Now that's interesting—"

A claxon interrupted him. Though not particularly loud, the alarm was persistent. Every crewmember turned to their stations with laser focus.

"Here it comes, Captain," the old man called over his shoulder before taking another shaky sip from his mug.

"I fear our time is up." Captain Beal stuck out his good tentacle, which she gave a little shake. "Stick around. This should be interesting."

Nancy nodded and surreptitiously wiped her hand on her pant leg as he turned away. His grip had been robust and somewhat moist. She'd stay and watch the show, if only to see about getting permission for Emmett. Hopefully whatever event was unfolding wouldn't take long. There was still a lot to do.

The claxon changed to the whoop of a collision alarm.

"Shut that thing off!" Beal bellowed. "We all know it's inbound."

26. First Gear

A LONE SHIP barreled toward Gail at ridiculously high speed. The collision alarm made perfect sense. Anyone familiar with space travel would question whether the approaching vessel could stop in time.

The oblong pod stood on end, speed distorting its bulbous segments and making it difficult to pinpoint its color. Long range trackers relayed but couldn't sharpen the blur hurling toward them. Urgent calls from the communications operators went unanswered except by curses from their neighboring traffic controllers. The room went deathly quiet as all eyes shifted to the forward screen.

"Keep the information flowing, people. This is new ground." The captain spoke quietly into a handheld communicator. By his tight expression, he too got no response.

Terse updates with vector and distance information rang out, counting down to impact. Harsh whispers put emergency personnel on standby. Every last crewmember stayed at their station, a testament to their loyalty to Beal.

For all the good it would do, Nancy braced, as did many around the room. An impact at this speed would leave the station a smoking hole in the Vargan sky, and there wouldn't be anyone left to wonder why. Cameras still couldn't get a lock on the blur. Maybe that was why Beal didn't try to take it out with close-in weapons. There was no way to track this thing, no way it could possibly stop.

But stop it did. One moment, death rocketed toward them. The next moment, a bulbous cocoon sat parked in the comically wide swath the fleet maneuvers had left for it.

Nancy blew out a big breath and forced her hand to release its white-knuckled grip on the railing. The ship was barely larger than a Vargan fighter, looking small and fragile as the point of view receded to show its lonely parking orbit.

"Well, that was certainly exciting." A wave of nervous laughs coursed through the room at Captain Beal's statement, along with a number of shaking heads and a few surreptitious gestures to ward off further bad happenings. "Well done, everyone!" He raised a surprised brow and consulted his handheld before continuing. "The Zula ship will complete its mooring sequence momentarily and does not require shuttle services. Our job here is done, people. My thanks to you all. Secure the docking detail and return to normal duty."

Nancy did a double take. An elder race? Here?

Given the age of the universe, thousands of sentient races would have come and gone. Only a handful weathered the millennia, continuing to learn, improve, and evolve. Those that came before, the elder races, seldom interacted with current galactic society.

The Zula had only come forth recently. Other surviving elders might also exist out at the edge of known space, busy with higher pursuits instilled by their transcendence. The Zula occasionally broke away to slum with the younger races. Only a handful of meetings had ever been reported. But perhaps sparse interaction was a good thing given how this new arrival had jeopardized the station.

Two-thirds of the crew packed up their workstations and filed out. Those that remained settled in for the rest of their shift. Movement on the screen caught Nancy's attention. The Zula pod blurred again as if vibrating in place. The three segments gave off a muted glow, outlining the ship against the dark edge of the moon.

One by one, others caught the change. Captain Beal noticed his people staring as the aura around the Zula ship intensified. After a hurried glance at his readings, the captain settled back into his chair to watch.

The ship's hull had started out brown, but now swirls of color shot through the surface. The swirls reached the nimbus of glowing energy, stoking it to a brilliant corona that had Nancy squinting.

The outline flared, exploding in beautiful arcs of iridescent energy to the right and left. Another buildup of power erupted in a pair of colorful bursts out on the diagonals, and a third flared overtop and underneath the hull.

Rather than dissipate, the energy blooms spread outward like fireworks, but impossibly further. A nebula formed before their eyes. The plasma energy reached its apex, leaving shimmering wings radiating out from the core vessel, ever-shifting but stable as though the hull were the body of a vast cosmic butterfly.

Moon and planet showed through the gossamer wings that expanded to fill the region of space vacated by the Vargans. Despite their transparency, the wings had a kind of permanence, as if the Zula had brought a hundred ships.

Unifying power coursed between body and wings, unfurling into a vast entity. The raw presence of that lone Zula ship outstripped the combined fleets, making Nancy feel small and insignificant.

Her chest clenched as blackness swept over a wide swath of Vargan ships. But it was only a panel in the display going dark. A moment later the bridge of a ship bathed in brilliant white light filled the screen.

"Sorry, Captain, that wasn't us," a frazzled Argoth called from her workstation. "A communication channel is open with the Zula craft— I think." That last was an embarrassed mutter.

The sublime glow made picking out details difficult. The ship's interior was a study in subtle contrast against the pervasive white: the vertical edge of what might be a table, a panel covered in glowing symbols, a silvery metallic arch, and a raised dais beneath a floating orb that shimmered and throbbed in time with the gossamer wings outside.

A slim, gorgeous creature glided into view, eclipsing the details of the room. Nothing mattered except the woman gazing down with benevolent azure eyes. Nancy thought of her as female although no single feature screamed gender. The impression of a human face lay beneath round, lidless eyes like cut gemstones. Cheek bones, nostrils, mouth, and chin were molded from living marble a shade darker than the surrounding glow.

"Captain Beal, I bid you greetings from fellow star travelers and those who have gone before."

Her voice was lilting English, which didn't make sense until Nancy realized the thoughts were bypassing her ears. This wasn't her talent's doing either. The Zula was broadcasting directly into her mind in her native tongue and was likely doing the same for everyone here.

"Welcome to Spaceport Gail on behalf of the collected races under my command. May I ask with whom I speak?"

"Call me Farree." Her brow wrinkled as if in distaste, but quickly smoothed. "May I come aboard for discourse?"

"You may indeed. I'll send a transport immediately, unless you prefer to use your own."

The captain glanced down, no doubt to check on available craft, so he missed how the Zula's image blurred, similar to how her ship had. Nancy's eyes refused to focus properly as the woman stepped closer. Blinking got them working again, but her mind reeled.

At Nancy's gasp the captain's head jerked up to find…Farree. The Zula stood between two startled crewmembers who scrambled back from the woman.

An afterimage from her transport left two shimmering wings of energy rising over her narrow shoulders, the same energy that still covered a third of the viewscreen. The display increased her apparent height and imparted a regal bearing. From long, slender neck to athletic torso, Farree was an empress-goddess. The shimmering, shifting mono-suit hugging every curve further accentuated her raw vitality. Looking upon this creature was a privilege, an honor.

The absurd thought startled Nancy from her musings. She'd admittedly gotten carried away with the Lobstra concept of the goddess lately, but projecting the status of deity onto this visitor made no sense. The Zula were ancient and technologically superior to every other known race. Their achievements set a distant goal for which other races could strive, a goal humans might someday realize if they could set aside the self-serving pettiness that so often interfered. Farree had used tech, not magic, to teleport aboard.

With her clarity of thought, some of the glamour dropped away. Farree still stood proud and tall with wings of power framing her otherworldly beauty, but Nancy no longer felt compelled to gawk and heap adulation on the alien.

Such an ancient race shouldn't have even appeared human. The probability of their distant star giving birth to planets and people reminiscent of Earth was incalculably low. Nancy's head buzzed with the inconsistencies, and realization dawned. She was experiencing another hidden aspect of her special abilities. Why would her blasted talent frame the Zula as human when she clearly wasn't?

"This is Dr. Nancy Dickenson, a recent addition to the negotiation table." While Nancy was daydreaming, Beal had been running through introductions. "She's made great strides on bringing the interested parties to agreement so that mining can resume."

"I sincerely hope that is the case." The woman smiled with a nod of acknowledgement. "This luxene strain is remarkably pure and effective. Harnessing that potential would greatly improve your hyperspace transits, a significant milestone for the younger races."

"A pleasure to meet you." Now that Nancy realized her own talent was skewing her perspective, Farree's features grew less defined, less human—though still lovely and radiant. "Who would have imagined that the abandoned moon of a backwater world like Vargus held the secrets to improving faster-than-light travel?"

To date luxene had mainly been found deep within volcanically active worlds where extreme temperature and pressure fused the volatile elements into a stable molecular structure. For the substance to form on a small moon was a miracle that the mining reports conveniently ignored. The captain shot Nancy an admonishing look, but she wasn't being contrary, just stating an interesting fact.

"Intelligent and curious. I see why you were brought in to facilitate." The Zula ignored the question and studied Nancy for a long moment. "But accepting providence when it manifests is also one of the keys that helped our people ascend the evolutionary ladder."

Rough translation: *don't look a gift horse in the mouth*. While often relevant, the ancient Earth proverb didn't exactly improve the human condition. Nancy preferred hard work and the scientific method. Providence made for a fickle foundation. In fact, it was another Lobstra euphemism for their Lady Luck. If that was all it took, Herman and the other shellbacks would already be on their own path to ascension.

Pleasantries completed, Captain Beal included her in a brief consultation with their new visitor. The Zula had been expected, even if her mode of transport and headlong rush to the parking area had not. The elder race apparently worked through proxies within the consortium to keep tabs on luxene reserves, consumption, and production. This new find was important enough to warrant a personal visit.

According to Farree, the ancient race spent most of their days scouring the cosmos in search of "first ones" who had also survived the ravages of entropy. One consolation to their lonely existence was the knowledge that other races were making the arduous journey of spiritual and technical evolution. Someday the elders would be joined by worthy peers.

Historically, faster-than-light travel had been considered a universal constant. But Farree insisted that FTL held gradations. Ships made by humans and the current space-faring races were stuck in first gear when it came to the efficient use of hyperspace.

Farree hinted at exponential leaps forward. This new luxene could be the first step toward alleviating the need for current rules and exposure limits that protected ships and crews from the unpredictable effects of hyperspace. Interstellar travel would become less cumbersome and costly.

Nancy grew agitated. Farree wanted only what was best for the younger races, but wasn't exactly forthcoming with details. Techniques for mining and refining this new luxene were a secret that gave the elder race and a handful of private companies immense control over the next steps forward for FTL.

There was reasoning behind not wanting to hand advanced technology and cosmic secrets out like candy. Apparently, the journey to elder status required sacrifice and commitment. Those struggles would be circumvented if the Zula simply reached down and elevated other sentients. Maybe that was the problem. Beautiful Farree seemed too perfect, too good to be true, too interested in helping without actually doing so.

Nancy understood the transformative power of conquering challenges. She'd fought more than a few personal battles and was better for those experiences. Wanting races to improve on their own made sense—to a point. But information was too easy to exploit, and misunderstandings often led to avoidable tragedies. Nancy's talent brought a deeper appreciation of those issues. She found herself philosophically opposed to hoarding information.

Miscommunication was an enemy of progress. She suspected that was the reason for the Lokii gift. Ironically, the insect-like aliens hadn't told her what to do with the new ability. They no doubt expected Nancy to venture forth to heal rifts and divides. Nebulous as her mission was, sharing knowledge seemed like the better way forward.

The Zula were too far beyond the current races to understand. Metering out their knowledge in dribs and drabs was wrong. Or was it?

Nancy's conviction eroded in Farree's presence. This radiant vision had rushed to their aid and wished only the best for those less accomplished. Maybe her annoyance was unfair. Perhaps Nancy's own vices were the issue. Wanting more, wanting to crack open the vast store of knowledge that had taken thousands of years to accumulate suddenly felt selfish, petty, and so very human of her.

In the end, Nancy decided to focus on the task at hand. On her way back to the ship, she mentally ran through preparations. A secure link to the surface would help with any data requests and to archive work. All three negotiators planned to bring their primary assistant. They'd need berthing for eight, since the captain's security man would also act as pilot for the shuttle. Ziggy's mobile unit wouldn't need a room, just somewhere to periodically recharge.

She'd get Emmett to finalize the arrangements. Unfortunately, leaving the station would break union rules, so Emmett wouldn't be joining them. Nancy had rather enjoyed last night's outing with the AI and knew Ziggy would miss his company too. Hopefully it would only be for a few days. Once they found Reemer, she could wrap up this agreement and get off Gail before anything else went wrong.

"I've gone through the final med-lab analysis." Ziggy greeted her at the main hatch. "There's good news and bad."

"Hit me with the good first."

"Your initial conclusions were accurate. The tea stain did contain several toxins. I've documented thirty-seven distinct agents capable of disrupting the human nervous system. Several would have proven lethal in sufficient quantity."

"Great." Her sarcasm was lost on the robot. "And the bad?"

"Trace amounts of natural proteins led me to look for a biological source. Your drink was laced with Esha venom."

"Esha? The snake people?" Nancy shivered at the thought. She'd had a run in with the nasty race once, which was enough to last a lifetime. "I haven't seen any on the station."

"None have been logged as visiting either," Ziggy agreed. "Emmett's conducting a more thorough check before we leave."

"Have him go through flight plans to see if any ships recently visited the Esha homeworld. Maybe we'll get lucky, but whoever snuck in here probably bought the stuff elsewhere. I'm not ready to go to security unless we get a hard lead. The trail's pretty cold at this point, and their performance hasn't exactly been impressive. In the meantime, I'll catch you up. I met a Zula today."

27. Moon Madness

T HE CAPTAIN ASSIGNED a human shuttle pilot who would also provide security moonside. Brenda Watkins stood six feet tall and was approximately the same width from shoulders to hips. Her straight blond hair had been cropped close on one side, leaving the earpiece she wore visible. Her square Nordic features would probably have been pleasant if she ever smiled.

"The ride should smooth out now that we're in the lower atmosphere." Brenda flipped several switches next to Nancy before turning her gaze back to the viewscreen. "I'm commencing your inspection route, Dr. Dickenson. A recording of our flyover will also be available as soon as we're down."

Nancy swiveled the copilot seat around to address the six people seated to either side of the shuttle's central aisle. "We'll make a few passes over the area to get the lay of the land. This is typical terrain the miners will survey before each new area can be opened for use. There are a few important facts Captain Beal insisted we all be familiar with." She waved Ziggy forward from the alcove behind her. "Please fill everyone in on the basics."

The landscape outside could have been any arid region back home. Erosion had cut channels across a rocky plain dotted with random brush. Nancy's inner botanist wanted to jump in and classify flora. No tracks were visible, but this was just reconnaissance. Tracking down Reemer would be done on foot, assuming the HT2000 could pick up his trail.

"The Vargan moon's atmosphere is thinner than that on the station." Ziggy used galactic standard to minimize the cross-talk from personal translators. "Expect fatigue similar to what would be experienced at high altitudes. Air composition should not be a problem for any of your physiologies, but filter masks and other protective gear will be available during excursions underground. Off the port side is the main enclave containing living quarters and meeting spaces. In a moment, we will pass the mine entrance."

They flew over a group of hexagonal domes covered in silvery white solar panels. The large central building housed common areas and offices. Connected outbuildings would be for storage, living quarters, and other specialized functions. Enclosed walkways connected the network of temporary structures. The compound was made of pressure-sealed plasti-steel suitable for low-atmosphere environments.

The shuttle banked smoothly to the right, and a set of massive doors came into view overtop the wing. The mine entrance slanted into one of the long rock ridges that crisscrossed the moon. Its height accommodated the big excavators needed to get at the luxene, while a set of smaller doors off to the side allowed for foot traffic. One of the enclosed walkways and several uncovered ones connected the habitat to the entrances.

"Wildlife is present, though not plentiful." Ziggy pointed off to starboard where two small brown lumps rolled along like tumbleweeds. "Tumble rats and the like are harmless, but attracted to food. The apex predator is a small canid-type carnivore that hunts at night and should not be a concern. Watch out for insects. Some can deliver nasty bites that may cause a reaction. Reference material is available in your quarters providing more details."

The shuttle leveled out and approached a wide, squat structure. The dusty red building, a terracotta pyramid hacked off a third of the way up, dominated the far side of the ridge directly across from the mine. Decorative columns rose to the flat roofline of the nearest wall. If there was an entrance, it wasn't visible from up here.

"A lost temple." Phasha Wier touched a forehand to his chin, then circled it around his face with palm open. "We are blessed to look upon the work of the ancestors."

After another pass, they moved everyone into the austere but comfortable mining compound. The consortium decorator had hit the theme of sterile hospital square on the head, even down to muted pastel furniture that thankfully broke up the non-existent color scheme.

Maybe personalizing the base would be left to the workers once it was fully staffed. Despite assurances that a skeleton crew was in residence, the place felt like a ghost town. Nancy's group settled into their own wing of apartments. She gave everyone two hours to get familiar with the place.

The free time was supposed to let her look for a pheromone trail, but Brenda initiated her own sweep of the complex to ensure no surprises awaited. So the HT2000 stayed tucked alongside Reemer's nutrient suit in her luggage.

Nancy kept the first moonside discussion to ninety minutes. Finding Reemer remained her top priority, but establishing a good working tempo came in a close second. Her new tactic to light a fire under these blasted talks included short duration gatherings with laser-focused agenda items and an iron resolve to not let anyone get sidetracked. Hopefully, breaking up work sessions with familiarization tours would instill a sense of urgency. If Farree was right about this new luxene improving FTL travel, every wasted hour was precious.

"Pens down, people." Ziggy gave each principal a steely glare that settled on Xi Mey as she frantically keyed in the meeting notes. "I said time's up!"

Making the robot their timekeeper was supposed to avoid awkwardness and hurt feelings. But the blank stares weren't much better. It probably spoke volumes that both of her traveling companions were picking up anachronistic language from entertainment vids. No one at the table even had a pen.

Twenty minutes later, the group stood in the cool air under the glowing crescent of Vargus. The mine doors gleamed beneath the twilight sky, standing easily three stories tall. The entrance hadn't looked this big from the air.

The spin and proximity to its parent planet gave the moon an unusual diurnal cycle. False night came on the tail of sunset as Vargus rose on the opposite horizon. Reflected light from the planet bathed the landscape in twilight for several hours until it too sank out of sight and the moon dropped into a short period of true night.

"Once inside, everyone must don a mask." Xa Gorsh led this part of the tour, another delegation that Nancy hoped would unify the players. "Mining is of course suspended until we hammer out a suitable agreement, but small fibers are easily disturbed, so we want everyone protected. Yung Drith, the night foreman, will walk us through the process. He will be happy to answer questions that don't disclose proprietary information. Please follow his instructions to ensure we have a safe visit."

All part of the consortium's stipulations. Nancy exchanged a nod with Ziggy to confirm the robot was ready to go. A little engineering on the fly had let them mount the HT2000 in Ziggy's tool compartment. Restricted airflow would decrease the unit's sensitivity, but the ability to search covertly was worth the tradeoff.

They'd hoped to find Reemer locked up in the main complex. No luck so far, but there was still plenty of station to explore. If they caught a whiff of the Squinch in the mine shaft itself, following his trail could prove tricky.

Yung Drith was a gruff caricature of what came to mind when imagining a burly skilled laborer from old Earth. A white hardhat protected his wide brow as he stooped to check everyone's mask. Xa was the only one taller than the foreman, but the man was half again as wide as the lean Packtonian.

"These help bring up the luxene ore." Yung walked them over to a table of handheld tools and miniature mock-ups of the larger equipment. A quick sweep cleared thick dust off the low-friction protective dome that enclosed the display. "It all starts with core samples." He activated a mini laser boring machine that lit up with harmless visible light while its probe extended from the nose on a reticulating arm.

"Core samples let us date the strata and look for minerals that typically hold luxene." He picked up a cylinder of stone as long as his forearm and passed it around. "Setting up a sample field takes weeks. Time well spent if it pinpoints a rich vein."

Pride had the foreman's eyes shining as he stepped through the basic process. It wasn't much more than could have been plucked from a library entry, but his passion kept the discussion quite engaging.

"So those buckets bring up crushed ore?" Kirsch waved to the conveyor of black bins suspended high overhead.

"Sonic slurry." Yung nodded. "Vibrations break it free from the surrounding minerals, which keeps us from wasting space bringing up a bunch of sedimentary rock. It's not pure by any stretch of the imagination, but much cheaper to haul off for processing. Don't ask about that, 'cause I couldn't tell you even if I knew."

"This could be exactly how the ancients started out making their tunnels." Awe replaced Tain Beh's distain as the Revivalist aide scanned the cavern and stabbed a spaded forehand at the tunnel where the line of buckets disappeared. "Can we go down to see?"

"That's off limits." Xa Gorsh cut in with a curt wave to Phasha, a none-too-subtle suggestion to get his aide under control. He spared another glare for Yung, as if the question was the foreman's fault. "Just because operations are on hold doesn't mean it's safe down there."

"Delegate Gorsh is correct," Yung hastened to add, his earlier confidence gone. "Mines are no place for untrained visitors. And the crew is servicing the gear while we're…shut down."

Now that he mentioned it, a stiff, hot breeze wafted up from the depths. They'd been warned about the dust, but Nancy thought the fine powder would have settled more by now. Tuning the equipment certainly kept the debris stirred up.

Speaking of equipment, Nancy raised an eyebrow at Ziggy. His shallow shrug told her the HT2000 hadn't found anything. Hopefully the dust wasn't interfering.

"Find anything interesting yet?" Manfort Hughes sidled up, the flared edge of his hood bumping her shoulder.

"What's that supposed to mean?" Nancy forced the words through a tight throat. Had Ziggy's wandering given them away?

"I think you know." Again with the overly intimate bump. She'd buddied up to the Republic lead too much and was paying the price. "I've gone through high-performance team training too. Delegated roles, impartial timekeepers, all good techniques. But is there anything in *here* to leverage?" He kept his voice low, confidential. "We need something to win over the zealots or they'll veto everything to a standstill."

"If nothing else, we've got their attention." Relief flooded her. The Vargan scowled, but at least he wasn't suspicious. "Baby steps, my people would say. We've gotten them close to their holy place. Something will present itself."

"I certainly hope so."

He gave a grudging nod and moved off to let Nancy have a quiet little heart attack. Yep, her talent wasn't operating at full potential. These misunderstandings would be the death of her.

28. Bird's Eye

T HE NEXT DAY found the group deep in negotiations, but Nancy stopped the talks often for health and comfort breaks. She encouraged everyone to stretch and take in the enclave's sights—such as they were.

Thanks to the thin atmosphere, daytime temperatures came up fast once the sun drove away true night. Nancy used the time to stroll around with Ziggy, searching for pheromones and guzzling caffeine.

Despite the cool evening and comfortable bed, she hadn't slept well. Every day added more worry about Reemer's health and the need to keep her team motivated. A humming vibration that rose through the floor hadn't helped matters. Either the power cells fed inferior inverters or Yung's crews were on a cleaning bender.

"Anything at all?" Nancy asked over the rim of her third coffee.

"Not a trace," Ziggy said as he returned from a spur off the central hub. "I did not break into the private rooms. Unless they have him in a hermetically sealed container, we would pick up the trail heading into such areas."

"We're running out of enclave—and time." Eight days and counting since Reemer's last nutrient hit from his suit. "Emmett says that shuttle was down for two hours before returning to Gail. We need to start back at the landing pad to pick up his trail at the source."

The logistics computer had also managed to sneak an electronic peek into the shuttle bay sensors on Gail. The kidnappers hadn't snuck Reemer back onto the station, so the slug had to be down here somewhere.

"Ms. Watkins could be a problem," Ziggy said. "She keeps a close eye on her shuttle, and won't like us snooping."

"We need a good excuse to be out at the landing zone, like maybe another flyover."

* * *

"Our friend has certainly been here." Ziggy met Nancy at the back of the shuttle after his initial sweep. "I'm detecting high pheromone concentrations."

"If he wasn't sealed away, why can't we find any traces inside?" Nancy kept one eye on Brenda Watkins as the pilot greeted arriving delegates.

"Because the trail leads away from the compound in that direction." The robot pointed at the ridgeline off to the left of the mine. "I travelled out a short distance. He moved off in a straight line."

"Nothing out there but bushes and scrub." Nancy squinted into the fading light. "Which works in our favor. Be right back."

She plastered on a smile and walked around to talk to the pilot. "Everyone accounted for?"

"All the principals are loaded," Brenda said. "You and the robot might want to board. Kirsch is staying behind on

Republic business, and Xi Mey had to make an urgent call. We'll be ready to lift off as soon as she returns."

"My inner botanist is calling." Nancy patted her satchel and pointed off to the clump of vegetation sitting in line with the pheromone trail. "I'm going to dart out and grab a sample of the local flora. When I see Xi coming, we'll hurry back."

Nancy pivoted away before Brenda could object, but didn't outrun the wave of exasperation that washed from the woman. Dealing with privileged diplomats would drive a saint to drink, but checking out Reemer's trail trumped playing nice.

The HT2000 inside Ziggy led them straight past a cluster of leafy bushes. Nancy withdrew her sample tools. The old excitement of discovery fluttered in her belly as she plucked a bluish leaf, sealed it in a bag, and prepared a bark scraping. The Vargans would have catalogued every species long ago, but it was all new for her.

"Keep going. I'll keep an eye on the ship." Nancy scraped, bagged, and generally wasted time until Xi Mey emerged from the nearest building.

"The pheromone trail continues to the base of the ridge," Ziggy said as they hurried back to the shuttle. "I could not detect any manmade structures or openings."

"There's got to be something. Why else drag him out to the middle of nowhere?"

Nancy regretted the words as soon as they left her mouth. There was one reason for kidnappers to haul a hostage off into the desert. She pushed the grisly thought away. There *had* to be a hideout on that hill. She'd milk the botany angle to get back out there. In the meantime, she had Revivalists to woo.

Ten minutes later they were airborne and cruising over the ridgeline—not a building or underground entrance in sight. Brenda flew along the ridge, letting everyone take in scenery before turning to what passed for north toward the moon's most prominent feature.

Nancy's flight plan would canvas the nearby terrain and equatorial belt before returning to land outside the temple ruins opposite the mine. There was much pointing and commenting from all the passengers, but the two Revivalists were positively glued to their viewports.

"Water is life." Tain Beh's whisper held a note of reverence as they skimmed along the equatorial divide.

Why the ancients had constructed a mile-wide aqueduct to separate the moon's hemispheres was anyone's guess, as was the depth of the inky dark channel. The unnatural demarcation stretched off to the horizon. Nancy marveled at the engineering. Phasha Wier held on to his stately decorum by the barest of threads, fangirling nearly as hard as his aide over the sights below.

"An excellent idea." Manfort raised an appreciative brow and took a nearby seat. "Reminding the zealots of what they have to lose should stimulate their desire to reach consensus."

"Not referring to them by derogatory names might also help." Couldn't they all pull together for once? "But thanks. We'll be moving on to the grand finale next."

As expected, setting the shuttle down alongside the abandoned temple had both Revivalists clawing at the hatch for an up-close look at the work of their forefathers. Nancy dropped several not-too-subtle reminders that reasonable compromises could preserve this heritage.

The truncated pyramid melded into the nearby hillside, vertical stone columns marching off to their left. Weathered hieroglyphs decorated the interior edge of several columns. Phasha and Tain each whipped out a datapad to document the site. Xa Gorsh and Xi Mey held a quiet, animated discussion off to the side, the former's skin blushing an agitated red in response to whatever topic his aide was driving home with those wild hand gestures.

The Republic leader seemed lost without his assistant. Manfort drifted between the excited Revivalists to the shuttle where Brenda paced and scanned the landscape for potential threats.

Nancy left them to it, making a great show of unslinging her travel pack and collection kit. She and Ziggy moved along the foot of the ridge, taking the occasional clipping from the underbrush to keep up appearances.

They came across Reemer's trail fifty yards out, where he'd come down from the rocky incline. Wind and drifting sand had obliterated physical signs of passage, but the chemical trail remained strong and led them back to where the building intersected with the rocks.

"The readings end at the base of the wall," Ziggy said. "It appears they took him inside."

A flat panel of wall bridged the gap between the last column and the rocks where the trail went cold. It was almost certainly a doorway, but had no visible locking mechanism.

"They went to a lot of trouble carting him out here." Still, she was relieved to find something other than a shallow grave.

Closer inspection revealed a thin seam around the narrow wall panel. Scraping at the surface did nothing but dislodge surface grit and confirm the material was a synthetic compound. She backed up in search of some latch or mechanism. Nothing.

Maybe there was a hidden lever near the bottom that… A small, squat plant nestled in the rocks by the entrance stopped her search dead. Nancy squatted down for a closer look, unable to believe her eyes.

"What is it?" Manfort hurried toward them, looking agitated.

Nancy studied the spikey green ball, so different from the stunted conifers and leafy varieties scattered across the rocky surface. The succulent clung to a patch of powdery soil, looking quite at home, which it should not.

"It's an impossibility." Nancy pulled out her test kit and scraped a cell sample from the cactus, a pointless gesture. She knew exactly what the results would say. "This is a Pain Urchin."

29. Am Bush

"**T**HIS CACTUS COMES from planet Fred." Nancy had no reasonable explanation, but the juvenile plant was definitely from the Dolor family of succulents. This was a cousin or direct offspring of the sentient flora on Reemer's homeworld. "Finding it here can't be a coincidence."

"While I applaud your horticultural interests, *that* has me more worried." The articulated plates along Manfort's back crackled as he pointed back to an odd indentation in the hard ground.

Three shallow furrows extended from a deeper crescent. Nancy had been so focused on Reemer's trail and the Dolor that she'd missed the massive footprint. And it wasn't the only one. The ground around the base of the pyramid held several more.

"I thought there weren't any large predators." Xa abandoned his argument to join their discussion.

"The Vargans have not reported any animals of this size," Ziggy said.

"Manfort, does your planet have a history of large reptiles?" The tracks were reminiscent of prehistoric predators on Earth.

The sizzling discharge of a disrupter punctuated her question, followed by a bellowing roar and another blast.

"Take cover!" Brenda crouched by the shuttle with pistol drawn as a hulking gray mass barreled toward them.

Nancy's first thought was a T. rex, except the huge carnivore's head sat low on a squat, pebbly body. So a pygmy tyrannosaurus perhaps three times her height, but no less deadly. The thing had them cornered between ridge and building. They could press into the sealed doorway or scramble up the rocky slope in hopes the stubby-legged monster couldn't follow.

The pilot emptied her blaster, slowing the charge as energy ripped into the creature's torso. Hits to the oversized head glanced off, leaving wet gashes across the thick plating. Desperate to buy the woman time, Nancy dashed forward. She'd had too many close calls to go unarmed, but only carried a non-lethal weapon per spaceport restrictions.

"Get back, fool!" Brenda yelled, barely pausing as she dropped the depleted pistol and went for the rifle slung across her back.

Nancy slid in behind the wing. The stun gun was good for a half dozen shots at full power. The first shot did absolutely nothing. The beast charged past, intent on the unarmed group huddled against the building. The reptile was longer than she'd thought, with a thick tail counterbalancing the upper body. At point blank range, her second try got its attention.

She must have hit something vital to startle such a high-pitched yip from the thing. Encouraged, Nancy fired in rapid succession as it lumbered around to orient on the shuttle. Shot after shot melted off the thick hide. She might as well have been using a water pistol. The ground shook, three-toed feet picking up speed.

The air rippled as energy exploded from Brenda's weapon. The left shoulder above a clawed arm disintegrated. Another blast opened a smoking hole in its chest. One last hit blew away the lower right leg. Momentum carried it forward as the body slewed off course. Both women dove to the side, scrambling to put distance between themselves and the wall of flesh skidding toward them.

The mini-rex slammed into the shuttle, knocking the craft off its landing skids so that one wing angled toward the sky. Clawed feet pawed the air, tail lashing, and with a great exhalation, the monster fell still. Brenda strode up to the carcass and put a final shot straight between the gaping jaws before turning back to Nancy.

"Thanks for the assist, Doctor." Embarrassment washed from the pilot. "And sorry about…you know."

"About calling me a fool in the heat of battle?" Nancy asked. "Never heard it."

"Thanks for that too." The pilot ran a practiced eye over her craft. "Damned thing did a number on the shuttle though. Give me twenty to manually retract the landing skids. We'll do a vertical lift-off once she's belly-down again."

At Nancy's nod, Brenda reached in through the hatch, pulled out a toolbox, and got to work.

"Everyone okay?" Nancy called back to the others.

"There's been an interesting development," Ziggy answered.

Before she could ask, a distant bellow echoed across the valley, answered by louder calls nearby. Distance and direction were hard to judge, but more of the creatures were definitely close.

"How can we cut that time down?" Nancy wanted to help, but unscrewing the access panel to get at the manual controls looked like a one-person job.

Another roar, closer, the source much easier to pinpoint given the snout poking around the last column. This one was charcoal gray and larger. Its nostrils flared as it sniffed around the base of the building, let out another earsplitting roar, and came fully into view. A dusty brown one of similar size followed close on its heels. Both heads turned their way.

"On second thought, it might be time for a brisk hike." Nancy scanned the slope for a route everyone could handle and pulled Brenda into a run. "How's your disrupter charge holding out?"

"Two more shots at full power, four if I dial it back." Brenda checked her pouch. "No backup charges. I didn't come prepared for big game."

The women were halfway to the slope when it dawned on Nancy that the others hadn't moved. Ziggy stood between the group and the oncoming animals, holding his own stun pistol. There should have been five people with him, but she only counted four.

"This way," Xa Gorsh called. "We can hide inside."

Tain Beh disappeared next, seeming to melt into the dark doorway, which could only mean…

"Come on." Nancy herded the pilot toward the temple.

As soon as they crossed behind him, Ziggy backed to the doorway—the open doorway. Xa and Manfort went through next. Brenda joined the robot's strategic retreat, gun ready but conserving its energy.

There wasn't time to wonder at how they'd cracked the temple open. Any port in a storm. This particular port had a narrow opening those big-headed monstrosities couldn't fit through. Her stun gun wouldn't add to the firepower, and the door wasn't wide enough for three abreast, so Nancy dove into the cool, dark interior.

Her group huddled at the back of a small chamber, Xi and Tain standing sideways in the narrow tunnel that went deeper into the ruins. Nancy caught an impression of gilt walls and more hieroglyphs before the two defenders plugged themselves in the doorway and blocked out the fading light.

"Over here," Xa Gorsh waved a glowing hand.

Her eyes adjusted to the gentle wash of light from the two Packtonians, enough to keep her from stumbling on the soft flooring underfoot. A muted shot sizzled behind her, followed by a low growl. At minimum power, the rifle would last but do little damage.

"We shouldn't be in here." Xi Mey tried to push back to the outer room even as the others moved further inside.

"Get out of the way!" Running for their lives had done nothing to temper Tain Beh's excitement. She'd gladly stay to explore with or without the threat of being eaten.

"You doing okay, Brenda?" Nancy turned away from the bickering.

"They're hanging back and trying to figure this out." The pilot checked her weapon and gave a thumbs up. "Charge is holding. But if they don't give up, we'll need a way to contact the base. Hundreds of fighters in orbit, and here we sit with nada. One strafing pass would clear those things right out. By the way, we're up to four out there."

Nancy turned to the dim red circles hovering nearby, Ziggy's eyes. "How'd you open the door?"

"I did nothing." The robot shrugged, an indistinct gesture in the gloom. "The surface responded to touch, I suspect reacting to Vargan DNA."

"It's true." Manfort actually sounded impressed. "And it wasn't even the zeal—" he cleared his throat. "That is, the entrance reverberated at my touch. Similar to a proximity sensor, but I've never felt the likes of this. Strange sensation, as though it examined me through my hand. The next thing I knew the door itself had vanished."

"A blessing indeed," Phasha said from the shadows where he studied the wall carvings.

Manfort's face pinched as though he wanted to argue, but he held his tongue. Either the room was brightening or Xa Gorsh had upped the candle power. Anxious faces came into focus, all eyes turning to her. *Of course.*

"We'll make a break for it once the creatures lose interest," Nancy said.

"But there's so much to learn here." Phasha had Tain taking notes, the glow from the pad adding to the growing brightness.

"Captain, if I may?" Ziggy pulled her off to the side for a whispered conversation. "A certain trail of interest continues down the passage ahead. Deeper exploration may help our cause."

The Squinch had zero genetics in common with the locals. Did that mean Vargans were involved in his capture?

"Solid readings?" Nancy asked.

"Quite strong. And dried residue is present now that we are out of the elements."

Curious.

"Brenda, hold the line here," Nancy said. "Ziggy and I will push deeper and look for another way out."

"Not without us." Phasha was right on her heels.

The others followed—all except Xi Mey, who was already up ahead. The Packtonian aide blocked the narrow passageway, her aura muted and shot with crimson at head and heart.

"If you say, 'none shall pass' I'll put you in a time out." Nancy meant it as a joke, but the young woman wasn't smiling. To be fair, she had no way of knowing the reference. "Seriously, Xi, we don't want to be stuck in here forever."

Nor did she want an entourage when searching for Reemer, but the determined faces behind her wouldn't be easily deterred. Xi saw it too and reluctantly stepped aside.

They continued along the passageway for several minutes before hitting the first branch. She let Ziggy take lead, the robot's forward lights illuminating the way without blinding the others. At each intersection, he gave her a gentle push in the direction of the pheromone trail.

After two more turns, the hallway dumped them into a large room. The low ceiling was domed, and a cistern filled with water as black as that in the equatorial canal dominated the center of the room. The place was a nexus, but four of the entrances had been sealed, leaving only one exit on the far side of the pool. They spilled out into a ring, gazing down at what looked like stars floating deep in the water.

"Incredible," Tain whispered.

They might as well have been back in Gail's command center, looking out into space. The inky darkness pulled at her, infinite and endless. Nancy imagined distant stars and galaxies drifting through the liquid, a reflection of the cosmos.

Quiet beeping drew her from the entrancing vision below. A tiny red light flashed against the wall just beyond the entrance. The beeping came faster.

An explosion rocked the room. The shockwave roared from the tunnel like a cannon blast full of dust and rock shards. Phasha would have pitched over the edge, but Manfort grabbed his hood and wrestled the Revivalist back onto solid ground. Nancy lost her footing and slammed into the rim of the pool, her forehead cracking against stone. Another blast shook the floor amid distant crashing. Ziggy's internal gyros whirled and clicked, his lights slicing wildly through the billowing dust.

Warm liquid flowed into her eyes. Nancy pressed a hand to her bloody scalp, her thoughts a jumble. Why was she on the floor? She'd spotted something just before the explosion, or maybe heard something. A bird chirping? That didn't seem right.

"Does anyone require medical assistance?" At least Ziggy was thinking straight.

The robot scurried around the room amid groans and coughing. Everyone had racked up cuts and bruises, but nothing major.

"Where's Xi Mey?" Nancy's vision remained blurry as she counted heads, and came up short.

The search didn't take long because there wasn't any place to go. A wall of debris now blocked the door they'd entered through and the walkway around the pool left no room to hide.

"Did she fall in?" Phasha leaned out over the edge and scanned the water.

"No," Ziggy said. "I watched the water, trying to determine what had captivated everyone. She did not continue past me either."

"Xi Mey never wanted to come down here." Xa's skin gave off worried little pulses. "I hope she made it out before the cave in. Perhaps she and Ms. Watkins will be able to summon help."

His skin pulsed, reminding her of another smaller pinprick of light. Not in the pool; the stars there shone bright, not red and blinking.

"The explosion." Nancy forced her muddled brain to process the memory. "It was a bomb, explosive charges."

"Well, the trap certainly worked." Manfort moved to the blocked entrance and tried digging with wide hands designed for tunneling, but soon gave up. "Too much rock."

After a brief discussion, they pressed on in hopes of finding a tunnel to the surface. But crossroads became less frequent and all options sent them deeper under the ridgeline. At the next intersection, Reemer's trail headed left into an adjacent tunnel that didn't immediately plunge downward.

"Does your robot have an altimeter?" Xa pulled Nancy aside with a nervous glance back at the others.

"He does, but we aren't back up to ground level yet."

Xa shook his head and frowned. "The chances of stumbling on another exit are miniscule. If we can get down to three hundred feet, I may have a way out."

"I'll need a little more to go on than that." She waved Ziggy over and asked for their current position.

"Elevation is one hundred and eighty feet below nominal surface level." Ziggy sketched out a map to show they had crossed the halfway point between exterior walls.

"The miners watch for seismic activity." Xa's ever-present confidence faltered under her glare, and he continued after an exasperated huff. "Certain depths are closely monitored. If we find a solid rock face beneath the ridge, we can tap out a message to the crew."

"Would your skeleton maintenance crew even catch something like that?" The orange flare that shot though his right cheek like a nervous tick had her modifying the question. "Mining isn't shut down, is it?"

"Not completely," he admitted. "A slant shaft runs this way. At the right depth, it won't take much to punch through."

"I'll get you to three hundred." Nancy ground her teeth, the motion releasing a trickle of blood from under her bandage. "But then we talk."

30. Phone Booth

N O WONDER THE mining consortium hadn't pushed harder to finish this agreement. They'd continued to dig while negotiations dragged on, something that a watchdog clause would have stopped.

Nancy suspected they were after more than just luxene thirty stories down. The encampment's proximity to the ruins no longer seemed coincidental, especially given they were already drilling in this direction.

Ziggy dimmed his lights as they moved deeper. Crystals glowed along the path, varying in color from rich orange to pale yellow, as if sunshine was trapped in hexagonal growths. The glittering display covered the walls, dangled from the ceiling, and even sprouted in outcroppings from the springy material of the floor. A half hour of turns and switchbacks brought them close to their objective.

"Two ninety-six looks like the best we can do." Nancy called a halt to the search for another descent and consulted Ziggy's inertial navigation. "We're directly beneath the ridgeline. It's time to give this a try."

A quick search located a relatively clear section devoid of crystals. Xa set up his datapad to thump out a repeating beat, but had to tap along with a chunk of rock so that the sound penetrated the wall. Her talent couldn't make sense of the rhythm, but Xa assured them miners would recognize it as a call for help.

"So is this stuff the luxene?" Nancy ran her hand over a smooth mineral patch that glowed sea-green. The material wasn't simply growing inward. The wall itself had calcified into a crystalline structure.

"I believe so." Xa continued to tap out his message. "Coloration varies depending on purity. We're relying on the Zula to help sort and grade all that's down here."

"Anything within the bounds of the ancients' architecture should be preserved," Phasha said.

"According to the robot, we are no longer under the building." Xa swept out his free hand. "This is exactly the kind of rich vein we've been after."

"Tunnels extending from the ruins count," Tain shot back.

"Which is exactly why our agreement is so important." Nancy cut the argument short. *Now* they decided to get into the meat of contention. "We can argue the point once we're out and everyone's safe."

A low rumble shook the passage. Xa paused, tapped some more, and was rewarded with an answering series of thumps. The consortium rep launched into a surreal rhythmic conversation. Nancy finally picked up the pattern. Unlike Morse code, which spelled out individual letters, the miner's language mapped mnemonics and concepts to rhythmic snippets, making the simple language a blend of music and symbols.

"We need to move back to the last intersection," Xa said as the conversation drew to a close. "This will be messy."

They did, and it was.

Dust and a hot wave smelling of burnt flint filled the air. Drilling lasers broke into the chamber they'd vacated with the grating moans of lost souls. On the tail of that, cool wind blew in from the upper levels as negative pressure pulled most of the contaminants from the air.

A peek back into the room showed a four-foot hole to the left of Xa's drumming station. Half of a crystal formation rising from the floor had been cleanly shorn off as had those on the wall, leaving a crescent of dark crystals around the cooling opening. Indistinct voices called down the shaft.

"Get the others back to base, then send a team after Brenda." Nancy told Xa Gorsh. "And string some lights on the other side of that opening. Ziggy's batteries won't last forever."

"Where are you going?" The consortium lead stopped short as Nancy and Ziggy turned back into the ruins.

"I need to check on something. We'll be back as soon as possible."

Nancy dashed off before anyone decided to follow, leaving Xa sputtering arguments in her wake. The Packtonian wouldn't like being in charge, but seemed the best choice. Phasha and Manfort were far too enamored with the ruins. Plus, the Packtonian held more sway with the miners.

Ziggy switched his lights back on as they rose from the glowing lower levels and picked up Reemer's trail. In addition to the strong chemical markers, the thickening slime residue meant he had moved through under his own power.

Several turns later the path angled down toward a spot deep beneath the pyramid's center. Crystals grew thick here, reflecting the robot's harsh lights without producing any of their own. The jagged surface of the mineral build-up was scored and eroded as if by acid.

Dim light flickered from the walls further on, sparks of life gleaming within the broken crystals. The subdued phosphorescence bathed the area in a sickly green glow, and Nancy found her thoughts growing dark.

Gossamer threads brushed her face. She batted away what felt like cobwebs as painful memories rose unbidden. The specifics were fuzzy, no doubt thanks to the throbbing cut on her forehead. Nameless faces swirled among crushed dreams, selfishness, and cruelty.

Light burned bright up ahead, a beacon drawing her through the hazy darkness. She pushed on, the phantom webs taking shape as wispy white tissues blown across the dying crystals by a nonexistent breeze.

The billowing rectangles settled in layers along ceiling and walls, misshapen piles distorting the natural beauty and absorbing the light. The crystals beyond the dimly pulsing section shone bright, vibrant and alive as they should be. Nancy yearned to bask in that light, to break free of the suffocating thoughts looping through her mind, but her legs grew leaden. She needed to sit and rest—just for a moment.

"Are you well?" Ziggy's question was a distant murmur, though he stood by her side. Just like Reemer once had. Like others had before. Gone now. All gone. "Your metabolic rate is dropping at an alarming rate."

"The light." Her instincts told her to get to the light, even as her legs folded, and hard ground rose to meet her.

The pain of memory faded to an indistinct blur, a thick miasma wanting nothing more than to drag her down, to consume her. She floated on that sorrowful tide, watching the dying crystals drift past. Teeth bit into the back of her knees and shoulders. Two red orbs jumped into focus, looking down with concern as she passed from darkness to light. Ziggy was carrying her.

The last outcropping they passed struggled weakly, drawing the attention of more veils that fluttered down to bury it in white.

She was no geologist, but Nancy didn't think minerals typically wriggled like that. They didn't usually gasp and fart like a cowboy hopped up on baked beans either. Was there an eye beneath the gauzy layers? Her brain kicked into gear under the merrily glowing crystals as she puzzled over the writhing lump they'd passed.

"I'm fine." Nancy pushed Ziggy back toward the dead crystals. "Go help Reemer."

Moments later a sack of wet, oozing cement flopped down beside her. Bits of torn gauze hung limply from Reemer's back, the rectangles' animating force gone. Incoherent words bubbled from the catatonic Squinch. Open sores along his patchy hide spoke to the rampant mineral deficiency. Ziggy saw it too, pulled a length of fabric from an interior compartment, and helped Nancy strap Reemer into his super suit. Rolling the hundred-pound slug onto his side proved messy and exhausting, but a healthy shade of green spread from where the cape annealed to his back.

"The game's afoot!" Reemer arched upright, then slumped back to the floor.

His breathing shifted from labored gasps to steady respiration as the suit worked its magic. Nancy took advantage of the respite. Their gauzy attackers had done a number on her head. A maelstrom of images still flitted about, a storm of all that was negative and depressing in her life sitting raw on the surface. She waded through the mess, filing memories away to distance herself from the pain. Without Ziggy's help, she would have been trapped the same way Reemer had been.

"What are these things?" Nancy lifted a torn veil.

The thin substance slipped through her fingers like oily silk, weightless and crackling with static. She described her overwhelming visions while Ziggy poked at another sheet.

"They appear to be non-binary matter-energy constructs," Ziggy said. "Just as non-Newtonian fluids transcend states of matter, theory suggests the same could hold true for compounds bridging the matter-energy and mass-energy barriers. Given your symptoms, these must operate on a wavelength that interferes with conscious thought, perhaps by design."

As he spoke, the broken segments dissolved, leaving a chalky feeling on her fingers but no visible residue. *Good riddance.* Too bad there were plenty more working their way along the passage. The damned things had fed on her thoughts and the emotions evoked by the dark memories. Did they draw nutrition from the crystals too?

"Think they're natural?"

"Doubtful, given their delicate balance of existence. I've gathered what information I can. More study is needed to determine the threat to luxene production."

This could throw a major wrench into the negotiations and profit projections. The things blanketing the walls fed on the luxene like starfish devouring a reef. An isolated occurrence might not matter, but if the veils were widespread or rapidly reproduced, the consortium could find its rich luxene veins wiped out before the ore could be hauled to the surface. The darkened, sputtering minerals left behind wouldn't be fit for use in FTL reactors.

"There is one more strange correlation." Ziggy cocked his head in a very human way. "The energy signature is congruent to that of the space anomaly that disabled us."

"That seems unlikely."

"Highly unlikely," Ziggy agreed. "But the frequencies and amplitudes helping to stave off a state transition do mimic a subset of those prior readings."

"State transitions might explain how the anomaly disappeared." But it didn't account for the outrageous coincidence of running into smaller cousins here on the moon.

Damp pressure slapped across Nancy's side. She turned by instinct, right into the full-frontal embrace of undulating Squinch skirt.

"Forgive me, Mother. I didn't mean to poop in the nursery." Despite the nonsense statement, Reemer's voice was strong. So was the odor wafting from the mouths under his skirt.

"Breath mints for everyone." Nancy looked away, gulping in fresh air, her eyes streaming.

"Mother?" Reemer's eyestalks dipped low as he ran his antennae over her front.

"Okay, that's enough." She pushed him away. "Shake it off, sluggo."

Reemer blinked stupidly for a few moments as he got his bearings. "Nancy? What are you guys doing here?"

"You were kidnapped. Remember? Use those super powers of deduction."

"I *was* kidnapped." His gaze sharpened as he scanned the room. "But then I escaped. No cage can hold the inscrutable Mr. R. And to confound Mr. Big's bloodhounds, I snuck aboard the shuttle to their secret lair."

"You came down to the moon without your cape, on purpose?" Nancy avoided pointing out that he could have died, because that outcome was still a distinct possibility if he didn't explain himself.

"The bad guys were gunning for me. I *had* to go underground." He managed to sound indignant and drew himself up to his full four feet. "Plus, there was a certain female of amorous intent who wanted to—"

"I get the picture," Nancy interrupted. "We met your lady-friend. But how did you end up in the ruins?"

"I…don't know." He jerked backward like a puppet on a string. "It wants me."

Reemer's eyes went wide as he backpedaled, teetering drunkenly on his tail end. He spun away and headed down the tunnel. The giant slugs usually traveled horizontal to the ground. But Reemer stretched tall as he headed deeper into the ruins, swaying like a circus performer perched on a unicycle.

They hurried down the sloping passage, following their friend, who'd also lit up like a glow worm. At first she thought his mantle was just reflecting light. From foot to neck, green radiance pulsed in time with the crystals on the walls. But the illumination came from under his skin.

She'd never seen the Squinch move so fast. They caught up with him in a star chamber much like the one where the explosion had trapped the group, except the walls here were lined with luxene.

"What aren't you telling us?" Nancy blocked his path to the nearest glowing outcropping.

"Nothing I can think of." He tried to dodge left, but Nancy didn't let him.

"Think harder." She glared at the vertical green light showing through the center of his chest. "Like maybe you ate something interesting?"

"No, but I am hungry now that you mention it." His eyestalks curved down to look at his stomach. "Oh." Reemer hesitated, then swept back his cape and struck a pose, letting the light pour forth like a superhero emblem. "I did deprive the evildoers of their prized possession."

"Of course you did." No wonder they'd been chasing him. "And what would that be?"

"I'd have to show you, but it's uncomfortable."

"Indulge me." Nancy put steel in her voice. "I insist."

She should have known what was coming. The one constant with the Squinch was his unerring ability to repulse those around him.

Reemer ran both antennae down his front, the tactile tips pressing into his slime. She only realized what he was doing when his hide parted with a wet rip—too late to look away. From neck to skirt opened like a lanced boil, glistening slime running from the gaping wound down his front. Reemer reached inside and pulled out a glowing cylinder as long as her forearm—the source of the green light.

Nancy cleared her throat to keep from gagging. There'd been a flash of metal and something made of composite floating around in there too. She swallowed hard, focusing on the glowing item as he zipped himself back up.

"You stole a giant candlestick?" No wonder he'd been walking funny.

"I think not." Ziggy stepped in for a closer look at the dripping object. "That's a luxene core sample."

"Yeah, the thugs did call it a sample." Reemer winced as he puffed himself up. "An important one right? They took it from Ambassador Turlic's safe."

"That explains the empty case we found." Nancy took the sample, looked for something to clean it with, and ended up wiping the cylinder on her pant leg. It wasn't like her uniform could be salvaged. A zing of energy passed through her hand, and she looked to Ziggy. "Should we be worried about radiation?"

"The safety data sheets only warn against ingesting particulates."

Which, of course, they'd been doing all day already.

"It's been kind of pulling me along since I snuck off the shuttle." Reemer pointed to the glowing crystals on the wall behind Nancy. "That's where it belongs. Can't you feel it?"

The tingling energy dissipated quickly, but her ears still rang with a background hum. Whether that was from the explosion, head trauma, or the glowing core sample remained to be seen.

Nancy had done stranger things than standing there listening to a rock. She opened herself to the vibration tickling her senses, moving beyond simple hearing. The familiar buzz of her talent strove for a connection that was just out of reach. The core sample was more than just a glowing rock. But what?

"There's something interesting here, but I can't make a connection." This wasn't some random chunk the miners pulled up. "Ziggy, can you check the station records for this sample's pedigree?"

"I am still out of contact. We must get clear of the temple to reestablish a link."

31. Supply and Demand

E MMETT DID NOT find anything terribly interesting about the shuttle. But he kept digging for clues. Ziggy was counting on him to help locate the missing Squinch. Unusual as it was for humans to dock in alternate-atmosphere zones, the strategy made sense. The supplies they ran to the moon came from the other races in residence.

He personally delivered the shuttle schedules and monthly manifests to Ziggy's shipboard presence. The scant information wasn't likely to be of much help, but that didn't dim Ziggy's enthusiasm. Emmett lingered to discuss how two crime-fighting AIs might go about foiling foul deeds on a regular basis. His friend's new ability to simultaneously be moonside and on the ship was an exciting development, like making two new friends instead of one.

Emmett was used to parallel processing and multi-threaded execution, but this was something more. Ziggy's mother—another fascinating concept that bore further scrutiny—had enabled the residual ship's personality to "be" more present than technology should allow.

Emmett might even have three friends if he counted Nancy. Tracking the Squinch had been an interesting challenge. He'd been reluctant to join the hunt in person, but Ziggy made for good company. The idea of socializing with humans had never occurred to Emmet, but he'd certainly enjoyed the comradery.

Renewed resolve had him shooting out queries in search of company holdings involved with the shuttle contractor. If there were clues buried in the electronic trail, he planned to find them.

✳ ✳ ✳

If Emmett hadn't been up to his databanks in financial records, he never would have seen the transaction. One small anomaly hid among thousands of line items. Why would a human-owned company receive credits from a shell account established by their own government? Tracing the account holder through several fiduciary entities proved even more intriguing, as it led back to a source exchange owned by the Zula.

But pondering the link between ancient elders and a small company operating out of the alternate-atmosphere zone would have to wait. Emergency requisitions began to flow into central processing. Many were earmarked for personnel managers, but those coming to logistics painted an odd picture indeed.

Bedding, foodstuffs, and temporary shelters to accommodate several hundred suggested that a surge of people would soon move moonside. Which made no sense unless the powers-that-be were poised to unveil a completed mining agreement. Even more perplexing were the calls for portable shield generators, weapons, and armored escorts to protect consortium ore carriers.

Ziggy's shipboard instantiation had lost contact with his mobile unit and couldn't shed any light on the situation. *So much for onsite intel.* Emmet initialized several subroutines to monitor developments while he dove into his primary duties.

Purchase orders, emergency fabrication, and requisition fulfillment took over his main processors. Problem solving brought joy and meaning, especially when the solutions proved efficient. It was easy to get lost in the frantic rhythm until another worrisome irregularity cropped up. He only saw the encrypted message because the originator needed rescue equipment. The terse subject line said it all.

Explosion near mining enclave. Sabotage suspected.

32. If Walls Could Talk

L IGHT DRAINED FROM the core sample into the crystal fingers of a mineral formation that jutted out over the inky pool like a giant hand. Reemer had grown increasingly agitated until Nancy returned the sample to its "proper place." This outcropping looked much like the others scattered about the room, except for the intense glow as it swallowed the light.

When nothing else happened, Nancy stepped forward and lifted the dark stone cylinder. The essence that had left its tingling mark on her was gone. The call she'd felt earlier echoed from the hand before fading away.

"I have no idea what just happened." She nestled the core sample back among the jutting crystals before heading to the edge of the pool. "Do you think these all connect to the same source?"

"Quite possibly." Ziggy moved to her side, glanced into the depths, and then looked away.

The infinite illusion just didn't capture the robot's interest. As with the prior star chamber, lights danced in the depths, but these turned animated, flashing and colliding in a riotous display.

"It went home." Reemer joined her to gaze into the water.

Before she could ask what he meant, the joy of reunion hit, and her talent flared. What had laid dormant in the core sample was again part of the whole, a whole that was self-aware but rarely looked out upon the world. That larger awareness stirred deep in the water as the stars danced faster.

"I feel it," Nancy gasped.

The pool held something vast and ancient. A force too complex to readily comprehend. It noticed her, noticed them. The talent reached out, angry bees behind her eyes attempting to communicate.

"I can almost…" but words wouldn't form.

The gulf between mere human and vast intellect was too great. The presence deep in the pool sank away on a wave of regret. Nancy's hands shot out, clutching at the water, desperate to hold the tenuous contact. The presence paused.

"I am here." Nancy strained to make contact.

The connection refused to solidify. She might as well be an ant trying to grasp quantum physics.

"Are you talking to someone?" Ziggy asked.

"Perhaps it's my imagination." But it wasn't just her. Reemer gaped into the abyss too.

The robot remained immune and strained to see what was in the water, looking so comical that she snorted out a wry laugh. There really wasn't anything to see. But as the depths pulled her attention back, Nancy wondered about those who had built the temple. Those Vargans from so long ago would have left their planet, full of fear as they carved their place out on the moon. Like Ziggy, they couldn't understand how others on their world viewed life. War loomed on the horizon, deadly and without just cause. Bombs dropped, cities fell, and sorrow painted the days.

As images flashed through her mind, Nancy vaguely understood that these musings were not her own.

The planet below plunged into a nuclear winter. Life eventually rose again, strong and resilient, and civilization flourished until conflict once more swept the achievements aside. Those on the moon watched, flourished, and mourned.

Time and again civilization rose and fell. When the Vargans below once more achieved space flight, they sought to conquer the moon and gain its secrets. The people retreated into their temples to avoid confrontation. Yet the intruders did not relent until the factions of the world again fell upon themselves.

The Vargan ancestors built great underground rivers for commerce and communication, determined to hide from sight so as not to tempt future civilizations. Excavation debris formed the extensive ridgelines. The equatorial belt harnessed immense power, offering hope as they used its energy to look to the stars.

But other cultures fared little better. The elder races were young and brash back then, constantly seeking the upper hand over one another. Wars and campaigns throughout the known universe mirrored the microcosm that was doomed to repeat itself down on Vargus.

Rather than expand outward, the ancients turned to what made them unique. Spirituality and science merged at the fringes of quantum understanding, driving their knowledge to exceed mortal limitations. To escape the rising civilizations on the planet below and across the cosmos, they transcended, trading their corporeal bodies for fractal structures that would allow their race to continue in perpetuity.

But the balance was shifting. Too many eyes had turned toward the moon. Too many enemies descended. And their fall would fuel a darkness this universe had long avoided.

Nancy broke from the vision gasping and drenched in sweat, the history of the ancients a raw wound. Too much had been poured into her mind. Much was already fading. The science that had seemed so clear became a shady blur, as did the faces of those early Vargans. But she clung to the understanding of what had happened.

Tell our story.

The thought wasn't hers. They were ready to give their descendants another chance. That was why the temples had been keyed to identify DNA.

"The core sample!" Reemer hurried over to the crystals and pulled out the stone cylinder, which again burned bright. "This is how we show them."

Luxene was the key to everything. In addition to enabling FTL travel in its natural form, its unique structure also made an excellent receptor for conscious thought. The moon's rich veins had been a godsend to the ancients, a natural reservoir for their collective consciousness, a place to hide.

Now, that hidden civilization was in trouble.

* * *

"We've got to get that core sample to Phasha and Manfort," Nancy said as they hurried toward the exit. "And come up with a way to stop those psycho morphs."

Botanists excelled at naming new species. This one had come to Nancy as they'd waded back into the gauzy white thought-eaters. Even though they knew what to expect, crossing that section of tunnel had been rough. But when the flood of negative memories struck, Ziggy had simply pushed human and Squinch onward.

The psycho morphs posed a serious threat to workers and the luxene supply. Coming up with an eradication strategy was in everyone's best interest. The same couldn't be said for the information contained in the core sample.

The fate of their ancestors was in the hands of the Vargans. The Republic and Revivalists would have to jointly decide the way forward. At a minimum, they needed to preserve any luxene containing the communal intellect that spoke through the pool.

Mining costs would skyrocket. The small percentage she'd hoped to secure for the trust fund might disappear entirely. It couldn't be helped, given that the alternative was genocide.

"Not to worry, toots." Reemer used the glowing rod to tip his cowl and gave her a wink. "I'll guard this with my life."

"Good to have you back, but call me toots again and your detective shows are history."

"Calm down, doll. I'm on your side."

Voices up ahead saved the slug's life, but her murderous glare promised to beat some sensitivity into the Squinch. Work lights lined the walls as they left the glow of luxene behind and headed for the surface.

The crew had closed off the end of the rescue tunnel with a portable gate, a sensible move to keep the luxene secure. Sensors along the route no doubt announced their arrival. Xa Gorsh waited beyond the gate with a small contingent.

But these people weren't the equipment crew or even miners. A few humans were mixed in with the Argoth behind Xa. All wore desert camouflage and carried weapons, making her wonder if the T. rex invasion had reached the compound.

"Emmett's been trying to reach us." Ziggy's electronic brow furrowed as he synched with the ship. "Recent activity has him worried."

"Tell him to join the club and stand by for more fun news." Nancy waved as they approached the gate. "You're not going to believe what we found."

"Dr. Nancy Dickenson." Xa Gorsh looked like he'd bitten into rotten fruit as his skin darkened to an angry burnt sienna. "You are under arrest for sedition and corporate espionage. You and your accomplices will be detained until the current crisis is contained and formal pre-trial proceedings can be initiated."

"You've got to be kidding." Nancy gaped as a pair of guards came forward with wrist restraints for her and Ziggy. "Xa, what's this all about?"

"You have been implicated in the bombing of the Vargan ruins with intent to undermine the luxene contract you were hired to facilitate."

"That wasn't me! You were there." Her words fell on deaf ears.

"What do we do with the slug, sir?" The guard on her left pulled another set of cuffs from his utility belt, but couldn't seem to figure out where to put them.

"Another accomplice?" Xa squinted at Reemer. "Why's he glowing?"

"Ate something that didn't agree with him," Nancy said.

It wasn't much of a lie. Reemer must have sensed something bad brewing and slipped the core sample back into its hiding place. That he'd managed to do so quickly and quietly made her wonder if the massive ick-factor from earlier had been strictly necessary.

"I will accompany the prisoners to the holding area." Xa pulled a nasty looking blaster from his belt and waved them through the gate. "Inform Xi Mey that the mine is now secure. Captain Beal may send in his enforcers."

Xi Mey? Why was Xa's aide suddenly in charge?

"Aren't we heading up to Gail?" She needed to get to Captain Beal and make an appeal for sanity, but they marched right past the landing pad.

Things had changed while they were gone. Two massive shield generators fed a shimmering dome that enclosed the compound. Heavy support equipment lined the perimeter along with rows of antiaircraft weapons mounted on hoversleds. An occasional sub-atmospheric fighter roared in for a closer look before banking away, but she couldn't make out whose ships those were.

New, armored craft were parked inside the perimeter too. Their own shuttle sat off to the side, easy to identify thanks to the dinosaur-shaped dent. But the landing skids worked again, so it probably could fly.

"Things at the station are rather busy at the moment." Xa and two guards walked them into the main enclave. "You'll be under house arrest until the situation stabilizes. Don't get any ideas. Your quarters have been stripped of weapons and tools. Only my people have the new access codes."

"This is ridiculous, and you know it," Nancy spat. "I had nothing to do with that explosion."

"Xi Mey herself saw you trigger the devices," Xa assured her. "She's been quite adamant that the Vargans were in on the plot as an excuse to undermine negotiations and terminate the existing contracts. The rest of your group are similarly confined awaiting trial."

"How convenient that you weren't implicated."

"Due to the importance of luxene, an emergency council voted to institute martial law to protect galactic interests and the future of FTL." He ignored her comment and continued to brag about recent developments. "I fear the Vargans unanimously disagreed with the decision. They have filed numerous complaints which are unlikely to ever be adjudicated."

"Gee, other races claiming their moon. Can't imagine why that doesn't sit well." Nancy's glare turned speculative as their escort logged the new prisoners in with guards stationed at the entrance to their wing. Xa's condescending tone didn't match his coloration as he continued to spout information—as though for her benefit more than his own.

"Indeed. The Vargan fleets are picking fights on too many fronts. The Republic and Revivalists are both trying to defend their claim while skirmishing with each other. Fortunately, Spaceport Gail has its own resources, as does the mining consortium. Even the Zula ambassador has lent her support in the interest of protecting the luxene deposits."

Yes, Xa was definitely summarizing the situation for her benefit, which meant he had only the *appearance* of freedom. If the consortium delegate was resisting the coup, there were sure to be others.

"Talk to our shuttle pilot, Brenda Watkins." Nancy was grasping at straws as they unlocked her room. "She'll tell them I had nothing to do with the bomb."

"Ms. Watkins is ill and unresponsive." Xa's face darkened at the statement. "The poisons in her body are numerous and complex. So far, the doctors have not been able to identify an effective antidote."

An overload of exotic toxins sounded awfully familiar. "Look for Esha anti-venom," Nancy said as the guard ushered her and Ziggy into the room. "That's got to be what they used."

"Perhaps so." Xa sounded aloof, but gratitude shone in his eyes. Then his gaze shot to the corners of the ceiling. "You will be free to move about after we leave. My guards are posted at the pressure boundary to the common area. Return to your individual rooms when instructed."

"Don't we get a phone call or something?" Reemer broke his silence as he was herded to the adjoining room.

"Any messages will be vetted with the guards," Xa said. "I suggest you collaborate on your legal defense. Military tribunals tend to be swift and efficient."

33. Cell Block R

T HE CLANG OF the main doors held an unwelcome finality. But a minute later the stateroom locks clicked open, giving Nancy a look at her fellow prisoners.

Manfort paced the halls in outrage, while Phasha simply looked disgusted as he stepped into the passage to greet them. Tain Beh followed in her boss's wake with head hung low.

"What you in for?" Reemer asked Tain.

The aide lifted her head to listen to the translation before slouching down without answering.

"I can't believe they threw you all in here." Nancy wanted to throttle someone, and it wasn't any of those present.

"The Packtonians played us." Manfort slammed an open palm into the wall, leaving a dent. "None of us had anything to do with the explosion."

"Xi Mey seems to be the main culprit." Nancy had read the consortium aide all wrong.

"That woman always did show too much interest in our luxene." Phasha let out a gravelly growl. "We need to get out of here and let the world know what's happening."

"Your leaders already know." Nancy shared what Xa had told her, but cut discussions about escape short with a look to the corners of the ceiling. Their captors would be listening in—not to learn more of their conspiracy, because that didn't exist. But there was no sense sharing intel with the enemy, which made her job that much harder. "I'm afraid we're stuck here until the fleets decide who controls the moon."

"They'll use us as hostages." Manfort hadn't missed her pointed look at the hidden cameras and waited for her nod before continuing. "The spaceport and miners combined don't have the resources to prevail if the Revivalists join our fleet."

Phasha nodded, and even Tain had perked up when she'd described how the Vargans were preparing. But Nancy's mind went back to the unbridled power of Farree's ship.

"Don't discount the Zula." She got the feeling that the elder race's technology could cut through any defenses they could muster. "I'm not sure if all your ships combined can stand up to hers. Let's hope diplomacy prevails before things get put to the test."

Diplomacy, the guiding concept of her life in the department, sat sour on her tongue. Look where loyalty to the establishment had landed her. She'd trusted in the mission, the mining consortium, and Gail itself. They'd all let her down. Being labeled a criminal certainly wouldn't grow her survivor's fund, and it seemed doubtful that the promised advances in FTL would materialize under the developing authoritarian stranglehold.

Earth Force's waffling hadn't helped. Admiral Cheyung should have intervened the moment Ambassador Turlic disappeared. Now, bad actors serving their own self-interests threatened an entire species, and it shouldn't matter that the ancient Vargans happened to be encased in rock.

Captain Beal was the biggest disappointment. Stern but fair, she couldn't believe he'd back this coup if he knew the stakes. Everything pointed back to getting the word out about the consciousness contained in the luxene. To do that, the Vargans needed to put their oven-mitt hands on that core sample.

"Reemer, you don't look so good." Nancy led the sedately glowing slug over to the corner where there'd be less camera coverage.

"Really? I feel fine." The Squinch inspected his cape, which no longer clung to his mantle—a sure sign that his mineral balance had been restored.

"Oh, you're burning up." Nancy felt his forehead, then moved her palm to his chest. "Those psycho morphs might have done permanent damage."

"They *were* bad." The color drained from his face as he slapped an antenna to his forehead. "Now that you mention it, I do feel a little woozy. Squinch don't get fevers. You gotta fix me!"

"I need a second opinion." Nancy waved the Vargans closer. "Does Reemer feel warm to you, gentlemen?"

Phasha reaching out to touch the slug's forehead was the best testament yet that those teamwork exercises had paid off.

"I can't tell. He's cooler than me."

"His core temperature is the problem." Nancy guided his hand to the middle of Reemer's front, pressing the Vargan's fingertips in hard.

"Ow!" Slime erupted in response to the pressure.

"See? There *is* something wrong." She forced the fingers in deeper, earning a disgusted grunt from Phasha. But Nancy refused to let him pull away. "Reemer, just relax so we can get to the *bottom* of this and *understand* what's gotten into you."

Reemer's eyes grew wide and wild as she pushed harder. Aside from limiting the camera angles, the corner made it harder for the thrashing slug to slip away. He finally caught on and stopped struggling as a blurp of slime spurted from the small tear opening beneath the Vargan's fingers.

"Riiiight." Reemer gave her a wink and looked to the heavens, lamenting his fate with an academy-worthy bit of overacting. "Alas, the cold fingers of fate seek to pry me from this cruel world." He threw his head back and wailed, blasting them with flecks of spittle. "Do what you can for my ravaged body. I only ask that you…be gentle."

Dear lord. Nancy vowed to disconnect the entertainment library if they ever got out of this mess. Constant pressure split Reemer's hide down the middle as the Squinch relaxed muscles along his fleshy pocket.

"The slug *is* badly injured." Phasha pulled back in alarm.

"You have to feel for the problem." Nancy locked her arm around the Vargan's and forced his hand deeper, out of sight of prying eyes.

He tried to buck her off until his fingers brushed the glowing shaft hidden inside. Nancy felt the connection snap into place between core sample and Vargan. She released his arm as Phasha firmly gripped the stone. A hiss of shock escaped the Revivalist, and his eyes went out of focus.

Manfort came forward, but balked at the warning finger Nancy raised. She'd had no concept of time while staring into the pool to learn the secrets of the ancients. The montage that had flashed through her mind seemed to take forever. How much of that story now flowed from the severed stone was anyone's guess.

"That's unbelievable." Phasha let go and stepped back in under a minute.

"The slug's got a fever, doesn't he?" She needed to keep him from speaking of the vision.

"Yes, he certainly has…something." Rather than the fervent shine of unbridled belief, the Revivalist appeared thoughtful—a healthy reaction when confronted with a spiritual belief turned real. "Manfort, I'd value your opinion on this."

Phasha ceded his spot. True to his stoic nature, the Republic lead wasted no time. He pushed through his revulsion, pressed a hand in Reemer's cavity, and slipped into the communication trance without a word.

Reemer quietly zipped himself up after Manfort came back to his senses. The Squinch barely glowed now. No one said anything for a long time, though Tain Beh darted worried looks at the other Vargans.

"Hold onto your socks," Reemer said to the aide. "Your mind's about to be blown."

"The Squinch has contracted something extraordinary, but I believe he will survive. Yes, survival is paramount." Manfort turned to Phasha. "This…condition sheds new light on many things."

"Perhaps the time has come to collaborate." The Revivalist shot a glance at Reemer. "To ensure continued good health."

The only problem was that they had no one to tell and nowhere to go. Covert discussions talking around the problem at hand without divulging specifics consumed their days. Poor Tain Beh became increasingly confused with the veiled conversation, until Reemer took her aside for a session with the core sample.

Republic and Revivalist views ranging far beyond the topic of preserving living ruins underwent lengthy discussion. Nancy suspected the leap in understanding driven by their tight quarters would serve the planet well. By the third day, she was ready to kill for a datapad or—Lady help her—a vidcast or three.

Not knowing the state of the fleets was torture. A dampening field cut them off from virtually all sources and kept Ziggy isolated from his shipboard self. Their guards weren't cruel, just close-mouthed and efficient. That fact didn't stop the group from pressing for news each time meals were passed through the main doors.

The vibrations that had greeted their first night on the moon grew more intense and frequent. A clear pattern of ten hours on and two off emerged by the third day.

"It would seem that mining has ramped up to full scale," Manfort observed as the afternoon rumble resumed.

"The consortium must be in control." Phasha sounded more resigned than angry.

A buzzer overhead sounded three times. Everyone dutifully returned to their respective rooms for daily inspection. Early on they'd thought to remain in the corridor to gain an upper hand. But the guards had simply withheld meals and waited them out.

Nancy was shocked when her door opened to show Xa Gorsh accompanied by a guard with a white rectangular box clutched in his tentacles.

"I trust you are being treated well?" Xa waved the guard in.

The Argoth slid forward, set the box down, and flipped open the lid to reveal a cake—a birthday cake judging by the white frosting, green piping, and bold yellow letters that declared "Happy birthday, chum."

"He remembered!" Reemer shot forward, undeterred by the taser the retreating guard leveled. "What a guy."

"You'll forgive us for not singing." Xa turned to his man. "Inspect the other cells. I'll check this one." A soon as the guard crossed into Manfort's room, the Packtonian entered a code into the bracer he wore. "Surveillance will only be down for a moment. Have your robot download a situation report. The consortium is in control, and the Vargans squabble among themselves. Our embedded agents are your best chance. Kirsch Rainson is on Gail. Seek him out once you are free."

"That weasel from the Republic?" Reemer looked up, frosting dripping from his face.

"I find having a disagreeable associate can open unexpected doors." Xa countered.

Touché.

"How are we supposed to get out of here, let alone up to the station?"

Beeping from Xa's wrist declared their time was up.

"All seems to be in order." Xa's manner shifted to brisk efficiency. "Don't hesitate to ask if I can provide anything to make your stay less onerous."

"Access codes and a shuttle would be nice," Nancy said sweetly.

"Anything *reasonable*." He chuckled in the condescending way jailers had mastered throughout time, and Nancy gave him props for a solid performance. "Though you will be happy to hear that your pilot is much improved."

"So it was Esha venom?" Nancy asked.

With a shallow nod of acknowledgement, Xa turned to go. "Do enjoy the cake."

After the inspection, everyone gathered in her quarters. The cake drew dubious looks, not only because of the oddity but due to the smeared lettering.

"Why would Emmett think it's your birthday?" Nancy pulled Reemer away before the Squinch could cough up his digestion organ in all its grisly glory.

They knew it was from the logistics manager because chum was a term the AIs used for their sidekicks when playing superhero. That much made sense if she didn't think about it too hard.

"Well, sending cake to a robot would be silly. And I might have mentioned to Ziggy that I've always wanted a yellow-green one like this. Smells delish."

"Can we at least share?" Tain Beh bore the questioning looks admirably. "What? I can't be the only one sick of meal packets."

Nancy would rather talk about the items Xa slipped into the brief discussion, like why the Esha were involved, what network Kirsch Rainson was hooked into, and if Manfort was aware that his aide was a sleeper agent. Instead, she scoured the apartment, found a suitably stiff clothing divider, and cautiously sliced small servings from the undamaged side.

"Make mine huge," Reemer said after everyone else had a piece.

Tain dove right in, grinning around a giant mouthful. "Just like Dad used to make." The plating around his mouth curved down as he chewed. "Though, I can't quite place some of the flavors."

Manfort and Phasha nibbled at the edges of the dessert, their expressions uncertain. Nancy poked at the layers. A brown bottom resembling minced meat supported a cakey yellow sponge topped with white frosting and a gelatinous top tier. The mixed aroma of yummy confection, sardines, and something earthy wafted from the cake.

"I think Emmett tried to make something we'd all enjoy." She tried to hack off the bulk of the damage in one big chunk for Reemer, but her improvised knife refused to cut past the halfway point. "What the heck?"

A little digging exposed a corner of stiff red material supporting the upper layers. She tugged on the edge, scraping it clean with the knife as she pulled a foot-long red rectangle from their cake.

"A folder?" Ziggy went for the literal description first.

Although it was made of plexite instead of paper, a supple hinge ran down the long edge, so that she could open the old-fashioned data container.

Unbelievable. This was the one item any prisoner would kill to get—if they were stuck in a black and white gangster movie.

"It's a file." Nancy sighed.

Emmett had sent them a damned file—in a cake.

"I get it!" Snot poured from Reemer's nostrils as he doubled over laughing and pointed at the file folder. "But it's the wrong kind of file."

"I am sure this is humorous in your native language." Manfort shared a guarded look with Phasha.

"It's funny because some files cut." Nancy pantomimed cutting through jail bars with a metal file, but it was no use. Magical communication abilities or not, synonyms were tricky.

"What is in this file?" Manfort pressed.

Right. She opened the folder and held up a single sheet that read, "Trash."

"More human jokes?" The way he asked made his Republic suddenly seem a very dour place.

"I think we take this message literally. Come on." Nancy headed for the central garbage chute at the end of the wing. The pull-out bin was large enough to dispose of a body if you happened to have one lying around. She yanked it open and pounded against the thick sidewalls.

"I have inspected this equipment several times," Ziggy assured her. "Although the disposal leads outside, it remains secure, even during cleaning cycles."

Emmett wouldn't toy with them, not about something like this. Nancy studied the file, looking for a hint of hidden code or message, but it was just a folder. She threw it in, slammed the bin shut, and slapped the activation pad.

"Back to the cake. There must be more." A dull thud had her turning back. "You all heard that, right?"

Nods all around.

She slid the bin open to find it was half full of tactical gear: guns, armor, radios, you name it. Better still, the twilight sheen of false night spilled across the equipment. The back wall had fallen open.

"What do we do?" Tain shot a worried look toward the main entrance.

If they were being watched, those doors would pop open at any second. If Xa had managed to disable the cameras or distract the guards, they should take advantage of his help. Their jailers would be back soon either way.

"I think we go," Nancy said.

34. Unexpected Help

T HE HUM OF subterranean drilling masked the noise of them clamoring through the broken garbage chute. Nancy wore a helmet and tactical vest with reactive armor that would stop most disrupter blasts and low-powered kinetic weapons. Manfort assured her that the Vargan plating offered natural protection that was just as robust. Great if someone shot them in the back, but the fur down their front left them vulnerable. The same could be said for her from the waist down.

The compound was dark, but Vargus sat low on the horizon, bright enough to illuminate their destination. Halfway to the landing pad a blocky ore hauler roared into the sky, followed by two silent but deadly escort fighters. Empty trollies rolled back toward the mine entrance as the massive doors slid open to release a fresh line of carts heaped with glowing luxene.

"We can't let that leave." Phasha jabbed the wide barrel of his blaster at the ore containing the essence of his ancestors.

Manfort nodded in agreement. The Vargans crouched together, ready to go on the offensive. She understood; she really did. But announcing their presence would destroy any chance of slipping away.

"We have to get to Gail first," Nancy hissed. "Then we can deal with the luxene."

Not an optimal plan, but it was their best chance. Stubborn determination shone on those alien features. With the memories from the core sample fresh in their minds, the Vargans no longer cared about stealth.

Now they decide to work together.

The pair crept forward intent on rash action, but stopped short as sparks shot from beneath the second empty cart. The magnatrack should have switched the returning carts off to the side, but had activated too late. As the lead cart passed the outgoing shipment, it slewed sideways with a reverberating clang that derailed the fresh load of ore. Carts collided like the crashing cymbals of a deranged drummer, spilling glittering ore and blocking the mine entrance.

Shouts rose from inside as workers and armed security spilled out like angry ants. None of them exactly leapt into action. Most simply milled about surveying the wreckage. Tons of ore and twisted machinery blocked the doors and tracks. Heavy gear would be needed to clear the tangled mess and bring mining operations back online.

"Well, that was unexpectedly helpful." Nancy scratched at where the helmet rubbed her hairline. They'd take the easy win. "Shall we continue?"

Vargan shrugs lifted their plating from shoulders to tail, making the men appear to bob up and down on tiptoes. But neither had reason to argue, and they hurried toward the shuttle that had ferried them down.

At the edge of the pad, Nancy realized her mistake. A second ore carrier was waiting to load. Fortunately, they had yet to call down a fighter escort, and the crew jogged across the compound to help with the switching accident.

"So who's flying?" Tain asked as they approached the lonely, dented shuttle sitting at the edge of the field.

"Ziggy's an excellent pilot and won't need much time to figure out the controls," Nancy said.

"There is still the matter of flight clearance and access codes." The robot peeked around the rear thrusters and gave the all clear. "Although, if we can't get past the enclave's shields, I suppose docking clearance won't much matter."

"Why not leave the driving to me?" A familiar blond head poked through the open loading hatch.

"Brenda!" Nancy rushed over.

The Esha poison had taken its toll. The pilot's sturdy frame had grown wiry, and dark circles clung beneath her eyes. Their pilot shooed away her concern.

"The shuttle's access codes will get us through the shields." Benda flashed a handheld display. "A certain dashing, shiny individual arranged for one of Gail's private docks."

"Perfect. That's just down from my ship." The sound of running feet had Nancy glancing back into the courtyard. "No time like the present."

"Stop that ship!" The shout spurred them into action, and everyone piled into the shuttle.

The high-pitched whine of heavy energy weapons charging up filled the air. Their unarmed shuttle wouldn't stand a chance. Nancy fingered her gun and looked to her companions. If they had to clear out the ground defenses first—

More shouts were followed by a burst of anti-aircraft fire that lit the sky. They weren't after the shuttle. A blurred pair of magenta afterimages ripped across the ridgeline, the blasts themselves too fast to follow.

"What are they shooting at?" The target should have been backlit by the rising planet, but Nancy saw only empty sky.

"Ten o'clock." Ziggy pointed off to the left where a phalanx of small ships banked around for another run at the shield.

"Those are ours." Pride flavored Manfort's voice as six fighters swooped low and returned fire, the glittering line of projectiles vaporizing against the dome overhead.

The ground crews turned their guns to engage. The outgoing shots melted away the corner of a ballistic shield meant to protect the gunner from oblique attacks. Cursing drifted across the compound. They'd missed by a mile.

"That had to be a targeting malfunction," Ziggy said. "Safety interlocks should prevent those kinds of accidents."

The attack was largely for show. The small craft didn't have the firepower to knock out the field generators. Two more passes and stunning misses had the fighters veering away after a flyover victory lap, the universal aviation equivalent of giving the miners the middle finger.

Brenda disappeared into the cockpit and returned wearing a smile. "No casualties reported, and our clearances haven't been pulled. We'll wait for the commotion to die down and slip out as planned."

✳ ✳ ✳

Space might be a big, empty place, but there was an awful lot crammed into their immediate vicinity. They'd barely escaped the moon's gravity when the first saucer locked weapons on the shuttle. Brenda's credentials didn't impress the Revivalist pilot. The ship swooped close, forcing them toward a detainment area. Skin to skin contact wasn't something most spacefaring craft could survive.

"Hang on folks," Brenda called as she guided the shuttle into a matching maneuver.

"Link me in with the pilot." Phasha settled into the co-pilot's seat, his fingers flying across the computer interface. After some back and forth with Brenda, he called back to the others. "She'll need a minute to decrypt my personal security code."

Chaos unfolded beyond the starboard display. Sleek Republic fighters zoomed between spaceport and moon, as did slower formations of Revivalist saucers. The mining consortium's escorts varied depending on the crew's planet of origin. Most of these stood picket around the ore carriers and factory ships, though occasionally one or two would shoot off to destinations unknown.

A narrow interstellar transport with an oddly smooth hull drifted out from behind one of the ore carriers. The streamlined design marked the ship as Esha. No wonder the snakes' venom kept showing up. They were part of the consortium. Ziggy suspected that the moon's reptilian invaders came from the Esha homeworld too. *Talk about unruly passengers.* Dealing with the odd sliming event suddenly didn't seem so bad.

"Okay, we're good to go, people," Brenda called over her shoulder. "Heading back to port. Third time's a charm."

There were skirmishes out there too. Nancy watched a saucer move on a cargo ship, only to be chased away by a pair of fighters, one of which disintegrated under their quarry's energy beam. The wing of Republic fighters that responded cut the fleeing ship down before it reached the safety of its fleet.

Gail's stubby security craft were easy to spot, with their cylindrical design topped with a short-range disruptor dish. As the outer rings of the station came into view, one of those launched on an intercept course, but its port propulsor promptly fell off, sending the little ship spiraling toward the planet.

"Too many accidents," Nancy said as Ziggy returned from the cockpit.

"Station reports concur." The robot clamped into his harness. "Occupying forces are experiencing abnormally high failure rates."

From there in, docking went smoothly. Nancy braced herself for the worst as they stepped aboard Gail, but activity around the VIP docks had the slow, metered ebb and flow to which she'd grown accustomed. Brenda assured them that the area was a safe haven and mapped out several other sections being used by the loose network opposing the declaration of martial law.

Most of the resistance were Vargan, but a surprising array of other supporters showed just how unpopular Captain Beal's decision had become. The prevailing wisdom was that if the Vargans ever got their act together, the station was screwed. The people who lived and worked on Gail had no desire to be the target of a race notorious for brutal world wars.

35. Resist Stance

"**P**UT 'ER THERE, Kirschy-boy." Reemer mimicked the paw-slapping gesture that passed for a Vargan handshake, but jerked his antenna away just before contact.

Instead of gripping the slug's prehensile feeler, Kirsch Rainson's hand slapped onto the dripping end of the core sample that suddenly jutted from the Squinch's chest. Spaded fingers wrapped around the slimy object, and the Vargan went still.

Nancy would have handled that differently, but the deed was done. Despite the Republic aide risking everything, Reemer had taken an immediate dislike to Kirsch—or perhaps the opposite was true. The slug absolutely adored unsuspecting victims. They'd all discussed the need to bring Kirsch up to speed on the plight of the ancients, just not as a slimy prank.

"Hysterical." Kirsch's glare dripped disdain as he let go of the weakly pulsing rod and wiped his hand on the navigation table.

"Do you feel any different?" Nancy asked.

The light of knowing hadn't swept across the Vargan's face like it had for the others. If anything, Kirsch looked more confused than enlightened.

"Aside from a deep dislike for invertebrates?" Kirsch's mantle flared in warning as Reemer slid in for another try. "I'm not certain what you mean."

"I think the luxene is spent." Nancy turned to Manfort. "We'll have to fill him in the old-fashioned way."

The insurrectionists had gathered in Nancy's ship to plan their next move. Losing his authority to Xi Mey had left Xa downcast. He hid the outward signs well, except for a telltale yellow flicker across the thin skin beneath his eyes. The young woman who'd been his aide now had the captain's ear and called the shots for the consortium.

Nancy was surprised when Hera Mendelson showed up. The security chief had apparently been chafing under the political pressure that continued to hamstring her department.

Emmett's avatar sat atop the cleaning bot near Ziggy. Though he was decked out in full tribal regalia, a wrap-around console filled his display, obscuring the logistics manager and constantly drawing his attention from the discussion.

Ziggy seemed distracted too. The reunion with his shipboard persona had been interesting. The need to synchronize data was a given and easily accomplished when the mobile unit docked to recharge. But collaborating with Emmett and the others had subtly altered the shipboard personality they'd left behind. Surviving the cave-in had done the same for "her" Ziggy. The AI was technically one again, but small inconsistencies had Nancy worried that repeated separations might lead to personality disorders. Nothing immediately concerning, but something to watch.

Even in his diminished capacity, Xa had convinced Captain Beal to keep Kirsch on as a liaison to the Vargan fleets. The smarmy, condescending aide was perfect to fake being a traitor, and the resistance had orchestrated just enough concessions to sell the lie.

Now they needed Kirsch to see that more was at stake than any of them had imagined. This dispute was no longer a philosophical disagreement between factions or a simple case of repelling alien invaders. An entire race hung in the balance.

It was critical that Kirsch and the others understood that ancient Vargans literally lived in the glowing luxene crystals. Then they needed a plan to ensure that existence wasn't threatened. The core sample not working made the first part more difficult. Phasha and Manfort had intended to carry the core back to the fleets in hopes of gaining instant support from their respective leaders. Everything had just gotten exponentially harder.

"I can't believe Captain Beal would jump straight to martial law based on hearsay." Nancy sat between Ziggy and Emmett while the Vargans brought Kirsch up to speed.

"There was hard evidence." Emmett popped his head over the console like a prairie dog before disappearing.

She waited a good thirty seconds, but he didn't come up for air. "And?"

"And what?" The feathers of his headpiece whipped left and right as he checked his reports, again drifting away from the conversation.

"What hard evidence does Beal have?"

"The usual." Emmett looked annoyed by the interruption. "Fingerprints on detonation signal relays, purchase records for explosive compounds, intercepted messages between you and the Vargans." He frowned down at his controls and tweaked something. "Xi Mey was quite thorough."

"She'd need to hack the whole damned system to fabricate a trail like that." Cyber security combined algorithms and keys embedded in local firmware to prevent that kind of remote reconstruction. "There's no way to forge transactions without…" Without physical access to the hardware, maybe while a certain ship's captain and her AI were incapacitated. "That's why they infected Ziggy and drugged me."

"The motive fits," Ziggy agreed. "The logic of erasing my memories so they could poison you to access me always seemed circular."

"We have to get to Beal with proof it was all a setup. But how?"

"I suspect my rebuilt data files will be of no help," Ziggy said.

Reemer drifted close, held one antenna up as if about to comment, but was unable to come up with an idea.

"Sorry, what?" Emmett asked, but went right back to work without waiting for a response.

"I may be able to help." Chief Mendelson slid closer, looking acutely embarrassed judging by the way her upper tentacles kept sliding over one another. "But first, please accept my apologies. My instincts told me you and the others would never be involved in the kind of plot Xi Mey miraculously exposed.

"I'd rather hear an explanation than an apology." Nancy didn't relish dredging up the past and the suspicions from Turlic's notes, but that baggage made it difficult to trust Mendelson. "Care to fill us in on the *accident* that killed Ambassador Turlic's predecessor and why you never mentioned it?"

"So you know about that?" At Nancy's air quotes, the chief looked even more uncomfortable, but her words rang with sorry more than guilt. "I let myself be manipulated and couldn't imagine the mishap was linked to negotiations. The damned talks had barely started at that point." Her tentacles slid faster, and her voice dropped to a whisper, making Nancy strain to hear. "Uncle Basheer's death is a very private matter."

"You were related to the Argoth ambassador?" Had Nancy heard that right?

"On my second father's side. We were very close." Chief Mendelson flushed an angry green. "Current events have put things in perspective. Please let me help." Sincerity poured forth with her plea. "I can access platinum-tier cyber-breakers to compare your corrupted data with the forged evidence. Proper forensics would require a core dump from before and after your shipboard systems were hacked."

Just great. She'd had the ability to clear them all along. But that wasn't the chief's fault. They'd both been manipulated. And Nancy had left strict instructions with her ship to prevent information from being released in her absence.

"Ziggy, can you get what the chief needs?"

"Yes, Mother imaged my core systems before she rebuilt me."

"Mother?" Mendelson cocked her head.

"Don't ask." Nancy didn't feel like getting into the AI's pedigree. "I'll need to get that analysis to Beal ASAP."

Military proceedings would take too long and offered plenty of opportunity for Xi Mey to make the exonerating evidence disappear. She needed to talk to the captain one-on-one, away from prying eyes.

"They're just about done with Kirsch." Xa Gorsh had been hopping between conversations. "Your best opportunity may be tomorrow after Farree's luxene demonstration in engineering. If your data can be ready in time, I'll arrange a private meeting and sneak you in—far easier than getting you to the command bridge unseen."

"Sounds like a plan," Nancy said. "Ziggy, pull up those files and then try to figure out how much firepower that Zula ship can bring to bear if she goes all-in. Chief, bring me that analysis as soon as it's ready. Xa, I'll need your help working out a few contingencies."

Nancy didn't like putting all her eggs in one basket. She'd do her best to sway Gail's captain. But if he wasn't convinced and decided to detain her, the group would still need to move forward.

Manfort and Phasha had their work cut out for them too. Without a mind-dump from the core sample, convincing key Vargan officials to unify the fleets was going to take some fancy footwork. Brenda readily agreed to shuttle the delegates.

"So, what's the plan?" Emmett's avatar got up from his controls with much stretching and groaning.

"Seriously?" What the heck was going on with him? "We just spent a solid hour going over the details. Stop daydreaming."

"Daydreaming?" Emmett stomped around his workstation, eyes wild and voice cracking as his hockey-puck bot vibrated in agitation. "Sure, I've been daydreaming, dreaming up faulty servos and toothless cogs. Misaligned targeting computers. Doors that only close. Web-footed nanobots and ill-tempered sonic showers." He barked out a bright, brittle laugh. "Don't forget explosive bolts, bogus flight plans, and the ever-popular mistranslated coordinates—oh so useful for ill-fated rendezvous, landings, and much, much more! All for the low, low price of—wait, no—it's free. Free, free, free!"

"Um, okay." Nancy backpedaled to stand by Xa. "What's gotten into him?"

"Emmett's our secret weapon."

Nancy waited for the punchline while her robot moved in to sooth his agitated friend who now laughed and brandished the jagged club from atop his workstation.

"It's all good, buddy." Ziggy's voice was soft and reassuring. "You're doing great. Just a few more days. Team digital, remember? You got this."

"Right, team digital." Emmett climbed down and saluted with the club. "Rational heroes for wrongdoing zeroes. Thanks, old chum."

"Still workshopping that catch phrase," Ziggy whispered. "He'll be fine."

"With the Vargans squabbling among themselves, no one's done more to keep a lid on the situation than our Emmett." Xa gave a shallow bow to the Polynesian warrior. "He's worked full out, slipping little surprises into the supply chain to gum up the works—a task made infinitely more difficult since he insists on non-lethal methods. Without him, we'd have no hope of regaining control, not to mention the tons of luxene he's kept from being processed. In fact, that's why the Zula's stepping in with her own solution tomorrow."

"All those accidents were him?" Nancy thought back to the ore spill and the myriad of other mishaps big and small. No wonder the guy was stressed. She knelt by the cleaning bot, grabbed either side of his monitor, and planted a kiss on the startled avatar. "Emmett, I'm sorry for doubting you. You're my hero. Hang in there for a little while longer. We're going to make this right."

The next twenty-four hours were a blur of frantic activity and unbearable waiting. The Vargan delegates left to make their bid for peace, the security chief worked her magic on Ziggy's files, and Xa drew up plans to take back the moon in the event Captain Beal refused to cede the mining site.

The super-secret software took its sweet time digging through the shattered remains of Ziggy's data banks. After all the planning and what-if scenarios, Nancy could only wait, confined to the ship with an increasingly grumpy slug chomping at the bit to get into "the action"—as he put it.

"For the millionth time, you can't come along," Nancy said. "It'll just be Xa with me when I see the captain. Even Ziggy can't come. It isn't personal. You're both too easy to spot. We can't risk getting stopped before the meeting."

"Ain't fair." Reemer spit a wad of goo onto the deck and proceeded to paint it into a swirling mess with one antenna. "I'm the detective, and there's sleuthing to do."

"Think of it this way." Nancy huffed out a breath. "You've already blown the case wide open. Who figured out the luxene core sample was the key?"

"I did," he said reluctantly.

"And who found an ancient civilization buried on the moon?" She pressed on at his sullen nod. "And there's only one Squinch I know of that brought all the good guys together to save the day. Say it with me now. The incredible…indescribable…and inscrutable…"

"Mr. R!" Reemer crowed, his mood lightening. "Yeah, I guess I did."

"So leave a little work for the rest of us, will ya? Besides, you're part of the backup plan." She wrapped an arm around his neck and planted a friendly noogie on the top of his head. *Ah well, I needed to do laundry anyway.*

Chief Mendelson's analysis arrived an hour before the Zula's demonstration. She sent it over in a secure data container to prove its authenticity and apologized for not being there in person. Anonymous threats targeting the Zula's presentation had security scrambling. She and her people were already stretched thin, but the chief promised to break away when it came time for her to meet the captain.

Who would have made the threats remained a mystery. Untraceable delivery pointed to sophisticated methods. Kirsch assured her that no one in the resistance wanted to jeopardize a peaceful solution—yet.

36. Demon Straight

T HE MINING EXECUTIVES didn't look evil. Most were middle-aged managers who incessantly checked their datapads while waiting for the demonstration to begin. Three notable exceptions were the joint owners sitting in the front row. The woman was human, as was the man to her left. On her far side a bored male Packtonian stood behind his seat. Avarice shown on the faces of all three as they took in the glowing luxene samples arrayed on the table in front of the FTL reaction chamber.

Nancy felt sick to her stomach. The glowing crystals would be infused with Vargan consciousness. The spectators had gathered in one of the many propulsion rooms that helped smoothly accelerate the city-sized station.

In addition to providing evidence to clear her name, the chief had arranged a safe route and access to an upper control station overlooking the engine room. A trusted Argoth stood guard outside, waiting to lead them to her meeting with Captain Beal. The viewing window reflected radiation and emissions, so the people below were unable to see inside.

She'd thought for sure that Xi Mey would be front and center for the demo, but aside from some of the guards and staff scattered around the room, Kirsch was the only other person Nancy recognized. *Interesting.* Xa activated a control to let them listen in on the proceedings.

"Here goes nothing," Nancy said as Farree swept into the chamber below, followed closely by Captain Beal and Chief Mendelson.

The Zula representative glided to center stage, graceful, luminous, and framed by arching wings of energy.

"In light of recent difficulties, I will personally take charge of processing all ore products." Farree got right to the point, making it abundantly clear in her opening comments that she found the current administration incompetent. "Hopefully, demonstrating the power this new luxene offers will increase your sense of urgency and stimulate swift action to rectify the current situation." Her pointed glance didn't faze Beal as the captain handed her a glowing clump of crystals. "The Vargan moon is an anomaly bearing a special gift. This radiant luxene is unique." She held the rock aloft and ran a hand over the pulsing facets. "The trapped energy renders this useless in your engines. Our technology overcame this limitation long ago. We can safely siphon away that energy, leaving the pure material your next-generation FTL drives require." Her hand moved faster as she spoke, drawing light from the throbbing crystal. Her face shone with that power, the phantom wings flaring—a magnificent butterfly, a deadly angel.

As the transfer continued, Farree's entire body shone brightly, her eyes closed in ecstasy. Her glowing skin resembled that of Xa's race, but infinitely brighter, shifting through the spectrum too fast to assign individual colors.

The similarity wasn't lost on the broad-shouldered Packtonian sitting up front. The man leaned forward, practically salivating as his own aura blazed with greed.

The process ended as Farree folded the ore in her arms. One final throb of energy coursed into those blazing wings, leaving the luxene a dark, gleaming crystal, its inner light gone.

"This, fellow travelers, is the isomer we offer. Transformed by our technology to meet your needs." She held the darkened crystal next to the cheerily glowing luxene, its midnight black facets sinister by comparison. "Until the required modifications can be made to your primitive reactors, an antimatter priming unit can be used."

A new piece of equipment the size of a small suitcase had been mounted on the side of the reaction chamber. The metallic trapezoid was made of unfamiliar blue-gray composite. Integrated controls sat to either side of a small hatch, and viewports revealed two containment cylinders arcing with energy.

"Antimatter is dangerous technology. Our priming pump reduces the risk by using only minute quantities. In this new isomer state, luxene will stabilize the reaction at an accelerated rate, thereby producing more power. Engineers in the crowd will know it usually takes hours to prime the reaction you are about to witness."

She handed the black luxene off to station engineers who set about prepping the priming pump and reaction chamber. "With only one mine in operation, my ship can process any ore you recover. But do not let that limit your aspirations. More Zula will arrive as the operation grows. And grow it must. We are committed to bringing the gift of advancement to younger races."

The antimatter chamber flared to life, followed closely by the main reactor, an engineering miracle underpinning the charismatic words. The audience was on their feet, cheering and calling for an end to the Vargan rebellion. This lot would hide behind righteous demands for progress while lining their pockets.

Nancy imagined Farree's wings magnified a thousandfold as her ship absorbed the life force of the ancient Vargans. Regardless of the incremental advance in FTL, this was no gift. This was genocide, ripping the Vargan legacy from the fortress that had hidden them for thousands of years.

Others in the room may not have been able to see the power that flowed into Farree. But Nancy's ability told her the truth. Farree fed on the energy in the luxene, an elegant vampire draining the life force of an ancient race that should have been the Zula's peers.

A heavy knock rattled the door. Good; Nancy was more than ready to see the captain and put an end to this lunacy. But a second thud sounded more like something heavy hitting the deck outside. At her nod, Xa crept forward to check.

Danfort, the guard who'd let them in, lay sprawled across the threshold, tentacles spasming. Inky red blood dribbled from punctures in his thick neck. Nancy rushed forward, but stopped as Xi Mey stepped over the prone guard.

"I knew I smelled a rat," Xi Mey said. "Chief Mendelson was entirely too adamant when insisting the control rooms had been secured. As if my own security team wouldn't double check that bumbling fool."

A pair of sinuous black forms appeared in the doorway, flowed over Danfort, and took positions on either side of Xi Mey. The alien snakes stood five feet, with more mass coiled on the deck underneath each. Thin arms extended at neck and torso. Golden eyes with vertical pupils glittered above a wide slit of a mouth that curled all the way back to where ears should have been. Two pairs of wicked fangs would be hidden behind each false smile.

"Esha." Nancy hissed the word, drawing a laugh from the woman.

"There's a clever girl." Xi Mey didn't brandish a weapon, but the deadly snakes certainly gave her the upper hand. "I'm guessing you're the one who told this pompous windbag to find anti-venom for your pilot." She jerked a thumb at Xa.

"I've met Esha before." The stun gun in her pouch probably wouldn't work on the deaf snakes, but Xi should be susceptible to the sonic weapon. Unfortunately, Esha were lightning fast. Maybe a shootout could be avoided. "Congratulations, you caught me. Haul us in to see the captain. I'm sure he'll be impressed, considering you were also the one who framed me."

"So you figured that bit out too." Her skin glowed in delight. "There's no need to bother the captain. We can take care of this little insurrection right here. I'm sure he'll be saddened to hear that stopping the saboteurs required deadly force. But he'll get over it."

At least now they knew who tipped the station off about an attack on the demonstration. The tactic had a kind of brutal elegance.

"The council will know." Xa said.

"Oh, please. Do you really think they ever considered you to be in charge here? Playing to your insufferable ego was demeaning enough, but don't be stupid. You've been labeled disposable from day one."

Xa slipped left during the little speech, drawing the attention of the Esha. It didn't take special talent to see how things were about to go down. He'd make a run at her from the far side to give Nancy time to pull out her gun. Xi Mey saw it too.

"Fine, have it your way, old man." With a flick of her head, both snakes shot toward him.

Their speed was breathtaking, but Xa proved surprisingly agile. He darted for the door, a feint that had him reversing direction a split second later. Nancy drove a hand into her pouch, feeling for the pistol grip as Xi Mey came at her. *No time.*

She dropped and swept out with her foot, determined to take the woman off-guard. If sparring with Lobstra had taught her anything, it was to take advantage of speed and surprise. The move didn't connect, but it wasn't meant to. Xi skipped back, and Nancy rose inside her guard with a sharp upper-cut. The other woman's nose crunched under her knuckles.

The relatively light hit was a gamble. She was willing to take the counter-strike in exchange for the psychological advantage of drawing first blood. Nancy was already dancing back as Xi Mey threw an off-balance jab in retaliation. The shoulder was already fully extended; there'd be no power in the hit.

Bam!

Nancy flew backward as if kicked by a mule. *What the…?*

Xi Mey grinned, following up with a telegraphed roundhouse that Nancy blocked with her forearm. The contact threw her sideways with an electric jolt. The woman hit like a cattle prod.

"Oh, didn't you know?" Xi's natural glow was concentrated around her hands as she held them up for inspection. "Photovoltaic skin cells. I bet you thought it was just a pretty glow. Stupid humans grow wrinkled with age; we just get stronger."

Talk about an unfair advantage. Nancy dove under the next swipe, an indignant move that had her scrambling back to her feet. She reached for the pouch, but it had ripped off her belt while she'd been busy flying through the air.

Kicks were generally too cumbersome for amateurs to pull off, but Nancy needed to keep her opponent out of arms reach while she looked for her gun. It helped that Xi Mey wasn't particularly skilled.

Xa Gorsh managed to hold his own during the initial exchange, but a quick glance showed him down and holding a snake just out of striking range. The other Esha lay unmoving with a ninety-degree kink in its back. Although Xa's hands also glowed, the electricity went nowhere, as if the Esha's scales were non-conductive.

Distracted by her companion's situation, Nancy kicked out too slowly. Xi hooked her leg, and electricity zapped into her knee. Nancy howled, but managed to slam the sole of her other boot into the woman's chin.

Her right leg screamed and tingled and refused to bend enough to stand. From her vantage point on the deck, Nancy spotted the damned pouch under the lip of the control console. She crawled on hands and the working knee, wrapping her fingers around the stun gun while her opponent spit out a wad of blood, got to her feet, and charged.

One shot stopped the woman, but not the way Nancy had intended. The acoustic energy beam barely slowed Xi

Mey, but the blood curling scream that ripped through the room did the trick. The wail rose from the Esha. It slapped its upper hands over the shiny patches above each eye and dropped off Xa. Though deaf, the snakes hunted through heat and vibration. Apparently her little stun pistol hit just the right frequencies.

Note to self, no stun weapons on Packtonians.

"Trade partners!" Xa Gorsh rolled between her and Xi.

One of Reemer's spy movies would have made the maneuver look cooler. Nancy's leg still refused to cooperate, forcing her to scoot backward on her butt toward the deadly reptile. Xa did slightly better, managing to rise to his full height and block his former assistant's path.

Nancy could barely think through the screeching as she blasted the Esha into blessed silence. It went rigid with hands still clamped to its head and milky film covering both eyes. Not dead. The Esha's delicate senses were attuned to minute variations in their environment, but didn't handle extremes well at all. When overloaded, they shut off outside stimulation using mechanisms like those secondary eyelids. The thing would be comatose for quite a while.

"I'm going to enjoy frying you, old man." Xi circled, waiting for an opportunity to use her speed.

Nancy got to her feet, but the locked knee wouldn't exactly let her fight. The gun had slowed the other woman, but any shot was just as likely to hit Xa. Nancy looked frantically about for another weapon, for some way to help.

She needn't have bothered. When Xi Mey rushed in, the man simply met her head on. The glowing hits that had blasted Nancy across the room simply glanced off. But when Xa Gorsh struck back, it was Xi Mey who went flying. The fight was over in seconds with the lead negotiator standing over his erstwhile aide.

"As you told Dr. Dickenson, the power grows with age, *young woman*." Xa piled on irony as he held up a warning finger to keep his opponent from rising.

A moan from the doorway had Nancy hopping over to Danfort. The knee felt wooden, but it did bend this time. Tentacles wrapped around the hand she laid on the guard's chest as he blinked the room back into focus. Thank the Lady.

They needed to see to the guard quickly and secure the others. The zap and sizzle of electricity preceded Xa Gorsh joining her. A glance back showed that Xi Mey lay unconscious.

"Xa, does medical have more of the anti-venom you gave Brenda?" From what she knew of Esha bites, it was a miracle that he was still alive.

"Just give me a little time," Danfort rasped. "Very few poisons have a lasting effect on us. Our own venom sacs constantly filter toxins from our bloodstream."

"Recycling at its finest, but let's at least get you comfortable," Nancy said.

They hauled the Argoth over to the bulkhead, propped him up, and saw to their prisoners. The room below had emptied except for a few engineering types who stayed to monitor the reactor.

"What now?" Nancy asked as they plopped a trussed up Xi Mey down next to her Esha. "We can't afford to lose this opportunity."

"I can watch these two." Danfort offered. "The chief is on his way."

The guard wouldn't be steady on his feet for a while, but urged them to go meet Captain Beal. Stepping into the open to plead her case had been more of a gamble than Nancy was willing to admit. But now that they had the person behind the frame job and a credible witness to testify against Xi Mey, the knot of worry faded.

"Let's get to the captain," Nancy said.

Time to end this.

37. Unification

"THESE ARE SERIOUS accusations." Deep lines creased Captain Beal's brow as he flipped through the chief's data for the third time. "Security has Xi Mey in custody?"

"Along with the Esha that attacked us," Nancy said. "The chief and Officer Danfort can back up what we're saying."

Captain Beal tapped the arm of his command chair. They'd found him right where Danfort had said, in a local command room on the engineering level. The place would be crowded during space and docking detail when Gail was on the move. But at the moment, the ring of displays covering one wall were dark, as were three doorways opening onto adjoining work spaces.

Nancy had hoped Beal would leap into action based on their initial report. But the station commander had demanded a detailed account of Xi Mey's attack, Chief Mendelson's involvement, and even her poisoned tea incident. Nancy omitted one critical piece of information, the underlying source of power in the new luxene. Although she and Reemer had been the ones to discover it, that secret was the Vargan's to share when the time was right. For now, she and Xa stuck with the more tangible facts involving crimes like misleading station officials, assault, and attempted murder. To keep Emmett out of trouble, they conveniently steered clear of discussing the recent mechanical failures.

"My biggest question would be why." Beal swept his gaze from one to the other. "Your negotiations were nearing completion."

"I think Xi Mey and others took issue with allowing the Vargans to declare their ruins off limits." She looked to Xa, unsure of how much to disclose.

"Quite frankly, Captain, there is dissent among our members." Xa played it straight. "My own authority has been undercut, so I may no longer be the right person to speak for the consortium."

They were talking this to death.

"With all due respect, sir, people are dying out there," Nancy said. "Ending martial law would take a lot of innocent people out of the crosshairs and give us time to unravel this mess."

"Well said, Dr. Dickenson." A strange look crossed his fleshy face as those liquid brown eyes narrowed in concentration.

Nancy was certain he'd been about to reach for the comms panel. She gave it a few more seconds, but Captain Beal didn't raise a finger—or tentacle in his case. It was great that her talent was predicting people's actions, but no one needed a special ability that was wrong half the time.

"So you'll rescind martial law?" Nancy pressed, but he still didn't move. "Now?"

"Given your information, I would love to." Strain lines creased the captain's mouth. "But I cannot."

"Why not?" Nancy cried, unable to hold back her frustration.

"Because…" He blew out a resigned sigh, looking embarrassed. "I appear to be glued to my chair."

"For the love of—" Nancy threw her hands up—or at least she tried to. Her arms didn't respond. Neither did her legs when she attempted to shuffle back. The sensation was unlike anything she'd ever experienced. It felt as though her nervous system wasn't carrying commands to her muscles. Neither of the men so much as twitched. "Um, what's going on?"

A new presence entered the room. The radiant mist of an energy wing passed through Nancy's peripheral vision before Farree's tall, elegant frame swept into view. Her form-fitting mono-suit imitated the sparkling energy trailing the woman.

"Ceding the moon back to the Vargans is a mistake." The Zula's smile held hard edges at odds with the soft caress of her words. "Their squabbling would ultimately deprive all your allies of the luxene isomer. The greed of one should not destroy the future of all, especially when that race will soon fall upon themselves."

"Your argument would carry more weight if we weren't frozen in place." Cords in the captain's neck stood out as he attempted to face her.

"My apologies." Farree didn't so much as wave a hand, but the restraining force vanished. "I feared you were about to do something rash based on the word of this interloper."

The look she spared was more pity than anger. Nancy wasn't buying it. Her talent buzzed; each word was crafted to deceive.

"New evidence has come to light," the captain said. "Our negotiators were wrongly accused of sabotage. We've taken Xi Mey into custody for that crime and others. Martial law is no longer warranted."

"You're more worried about drawing power from the luxene than helping the younger races." As Nancy worked feeling back into her hands, she realized the men wore shocked expressions. "You were both there when she drained the energy from the luxene." And the consciousness—the very soul—of those ancient Vargans. "At the demonstration?" Still nothing. "Seriously? Can't either of you see her glowing wings?"

"Her skin does have a healthy glimmer." Xa seemed uncertain.

"As do her upper tentacles." The captain was serious, but Nancy nearly choked on his response.

How could each of them see something different when they looked at the Zula? It seemed an important question, but this wasn't the time to compare notes.

"Enough discussion." Farree acted as though they'd all just agreed upon a solution. "Things will stay as they are. Your people will repair their machines and resume luxene mining. Skip the surveys to make up for lost time. Drilling under the temples will produce the highest-grade product."

"You can't." Nancy would have said more, but those ethereal wings that only she could see flared bright and the world went dark.

* * *

Reemer slid faster and faster as he lapped the nav table. His cape actually billowed out behind him in proper superhero fashion. Maybe the private eye angle had run its course. Working with the two AIs had opened his eyes to the exciting world of super powers. While waiting for Nancy's report on her meeting with Gail's captain, they'd introduced him to a new genre of shows with everyday people turned hero by things like radioactive insect bites and chemical accidents. Capes were big with this crowd, which worked right into his wheelhouse.

"Manfort Hughes says the fleets are ready to go. They need those shields down." Ziggy turned from the comms station.

Emmett nodded in agreement. No surprise there. Emotional support and validation were a sidekick's primary responsibilities. But the heroes in the room should be the ones to decide.

"Any word from security?" Reemer figured they should get all the facts on the table.

"Chief Mendelson's people are still searching. No one has heard anything from Nancy, Xa, or the captain." Ziggy checked his notes. "Thirty-six hours is too long, and the Vargan fleets are losing patience."

"Agreed." Reemer liked that they were on the same page.

They'd tracked reports from Manfort and Phasha as the pair worked to unify their fleets for the common cause of reclaiming the moon. Talks had not gone smoothly, but logic eventually prevailed. The tenuous peace enjoyed by the combined Vargans would come crashing down if Nancy didn't make good on her promise of help. No one could pinpoint Captain Beal's exact location, but orders had been issued to double the garrison and resume mining operations at all costs. It seemed there was only one option left.

Reemer drew himself up tall to make the proclamation. A painful stich shot through his side. The core sample and other items had his hidden pocket bursting at the seams.

"Release the moon buster." He pushed through the unendurable agony, embracing the great responsibility of the superhero.

Emmett, sweet simple sidekick to greatness, nodded and pressed a button on his console.

"So it starts." Reemer bowed his head, then had another super thought. "Hey, can you bring it up on Ziggy's big screen?"

"There's really not much to see at the mo—"

"The screen!" He'd be a stern but benevolent hero. Sidekicks needed guidance.

The feathered warrior complied without another word, though he closed his eyes and looked skyward, no doubt a sign of respect from the obscure human culture he emulated.

The ship's main display lit up with an image of the moon, then zoomed in to the blackness outside Gail. This wasn't what he'd asked for, but Reemer held his tongue and waited. A flash of silver finally shot from the station as their doomsday weapon was unleashed.

The missile streaked across the starry backdrop on its way to the moon. A satellite beacon the size of a flatfish drifted by, taking up most of the screen. Their projectile passed in front of the automated relay, suddenly looking smaller—much smaller.

"Where are the cannons? The lasers?" Reemer squinted at the screen. "That little thing isn't even big enough for a thruster."

"Its low profile won't trigger the enclave's warning systems," Emmett said. "Guidance uses micro-thrust technology to home in on the impact point. Estimated detonation in forty-seven seconds."

The view shifted to a sparking image as the forward end of the tiny missile burned away in the atmosphere. The shimmering shield around the mining compound filled the scene beyond.

"Ten seconds."

The miracles of technology never ceased to amaze Reemer. Squinch would someday possess those wonders. Emmett assured him that their doomsday device would rip through the defenses blocking the Vargan fighters. Hopefully the explosion wouldn't destroy the encampment and temple. He'd only brushed the surface of the ancients hiding in the luxene, but knew they must not be harmed.

"Three, two…"

The shield raced past as the weapon headed for rocks at the base of the ridge. The blast would be epic. He braced against the navigation table.

"One!"

The image shifted to an overhead satellite feed that zoomed to the point of impact just as a puff of dust erupted where an armored conduit jutted from the rocks. The spot smoldered for a second before fizzling out.

"That's it?" To say he was underwhelmed would be putting it mildly. "You missed the stupid shield."

"We didn't want to the hit the shield, just the sensor on that exposed cable." Ziggy leapt to Emmett's defense. "Just watch."

A gentle breeze whisked away the bit of smoke. Even the cable looked to be intact. Superheroes weren't supposed to lose their temper, but this was a disaster. They'd promised to give control of the mine back to the Vargans, to protect the ruins. But everything from Nancy's meeting with the captain to this moon-busting super-weapon had failed miserably.

Deep breaths, happy thoughts. Berating his companions wouldn't help. He was about to ask for recommendations when the impossible quietly happened: the shield protecting the mining complex fell. A wide arc of the force dome near the impact site simply winked out as its generator shut down. Its neighbors followed in quick succession, the cascading failures leaving the complex wide open. The Vargan fleet swooped in.

"See?" Emmett looked entirely too smug, but perhaps he deserved to. "We just needed enough energy to trip the high-temperature shutdown."

* * *

Nancy floated in a sea of stars, the endless void of creation. Made whole by those around her. There was never any true solitude, yet she felt alone, abandoned. Too many who should have joined the adventure had turned from their roots, toward violence. Uncontrollable hunger festered in others who awaited their arrival among the stars. The people could neither stay nor go. But the strange gems that allowed them to reach into the void offered salvation in unexpected ways. So they chose a safe haven, away from the cosmos, where all were welcome.

Alas, nothing lasted forever. The time of solace was ending. The others had found them. All must rise from their contemplative existence—or perish.

The ancient enemy threatened, but another, touched by those who understood the sanctity of life and its connection to all, had also arrived. It was she who must guard the collective as it slowly rose from slumber.

Pinprick lights zipped about, flashing calls to others within the starry darkness. The time had come.

Cold metal against her back roused Nancy. The stars fled with the dream, leaving a lethargic afterglow, a reluctance to rise and face what was to come. The desire to lay dormant and let the universe play itself out might have been her own, or not. As much as she'd like to sleep, the need to take action pushed her to wakefulness and the task at hand.

"Welcome back to the land of the living." Xa sat off to the left, his mellow glow a shade pinker that the amber light at his back. "You'll find we have all the amenities: high ceiling, sturdy walls, and even comfortable seating." He slapped the metal bin beneath him. "There doesn't seem to be an entertainment lounge. Captain's off exploring alcoves for the third time in search of an exit that isn't locked."

"And the light?" Nancy fought through the fuzziness, sat up, and pointed at the yellow glow behind Xa.

"A holding bin for the first shipment of luxene. If I had to hazard a guess, Farree isn't interested in the truth about those explosions."

Right. They'd been briefing the captain, when the Zula representative showed up and…what? Cotton filled her head.

"Farree locked us in the ore hoppers?"

"To be fair, this is the work area adjacent to the actual storage bins, so at least we have food and water." Xa said. "We've been down here for half a day. Beal and I woke quickly, but couldn't rouse you. We did our best to keep you from bashing your head against anything. Do you often suffer nightmares?"

"Not usually." Visions of floating through space and struggling to wake danced at the edge of Nancy's memory. But the rest of the dream eluded her.

Standing was an adventure. Her body ached in places she didn't know possible, but stretching as she walked toward the glow helped. A locked door separated them from the adjacent room. An observation port looked out onto a tidy row of hoversleds piled high with shards of luxene. Some crystals were shattered remnants, but most had been recovered intact. Others sprouted in clusters from chunks of rock that would have been chiseled from the walls of the cave system they'd explored.

She basked in the glow with eyes closed, soaking up the radiance like sunshine. The warmth chased away an unease left by her dream and the oppressive gloom of the abandoned loading zone.

"There's got to be controls around here somewhere." Nancy turned back into the darkened room. "We need to shed some light on the situation."

Unfortunately, the control panels at both bay doors were dead, as was the one at the door they'd apparently entered through. Captain Beal rejoined them with word that the watch station below the big overhead crane included two fully stocked bunk rooms, but the communication panel there had been similarly deactivated.

The captain keyed his command override code into the panel by the double doors, but gave up in frustration. "Someone's gone to a lot of trouble to isolate this staging area right under my nose."

The luxene's glow drew them back to the observation port. Nancy took comfort in the cheery light from those ancient Vargans trapped in their gemstone prison. Time stretched into hours of fruitless searching interspersed with restless naps and half-formed plans. The following afternoon, movement in the adjacent room interrupted their planning.

38. Power Up

SHAPES DANCED IN the luxene glow, throwing long shadows across the ceiling of the loading dock as someone moved through the next room. Nancy and the men hurried over to the observation port and their unsuspecting rescuer. But the hope blossoming in Nancy's chest withered.

Farree prowled among the luxene bins, busily selecting the brightest crystals and arranging them in a neat row on the edge of one sled.

"Farree!" The captain banged on the transparent partition. "Call maintenance. We're trapped in here."

Was he insane? Xa's similarly hopeful expression had Nancy doubting her sanity. The Zula was the one who'd imprisoned them.

Farree turned a radiant smile on her audience, long fingers stroking the gem she held. The crystal pulsed, dimmed, and went dark. Farree's ethereal wings surged with the injection of power. Nancy clutched her middle as pain and loss tore an involuntary sob from her throat.

"I'm sure someone will soon come to release you." Farree dropped the dark stone and reached for the next she'd gathered. "Until then, relax and enjoy the quiet time. I will take care of the Vargan situation."

"By situation you mean the Vargans standing up for their rights and taking possession of their own moon?"

Either the Zula was simply a glutton for the power of luxene or her friends had succeeded in unifying the fleets. Nancy figured the latter drove Farree to consume more crystals.

"Antagonizing the only elder race willing to help is asking for trouble." The captain let out a massive yawn. "The Zula were here long before us and know what's best. Let Farree work in peace. She's doing us a favor by processing the luxene."

"It's not a favor; it's a power play. She locked us in here to stop you from pulling your troops back. Remember?" Nancy stifled a yawn of her own as the suddenly disinterested captain turned away. "Xa, help me out."

But the Packtonian had slid to the deck and was already snoring softly. A nap would be wonderful. She could address any lingering details with the Vargans later.

Nancy bit the inside of her cheek, the crunch and taste of blood clearing her wooly thoughts. There'd be no *later* if Farree had her way. She fought against the urge to give up as another pang of loss swept through her—another crystal drained. Farree flared with power.

"You're killing them." Nancy forced her eyes open and braced as a third chunk of luxene went dark.

"Oh, little human." The Zula spared her a condescending pout. "They were dead to us long ago. Sleep now and let me work."

Nancy locked her knees and fought to keep her eyes open as more ancient Vargan souls were snuffed out. Maybe

Farree didn't realize what she was doing. If ever there was need for Nancy's talent, this was it. She needed to wake the men and make them understand, make the Zula understand.

"Stop that!" Farree's face filled the observation port, azure eyes glittering with anger and something else— unbridled lust. The Zula knew exactly what she was doing. Killing people to gain power didn't matter. Pressure pushed against the buzz of Nancy's talent, sealing her off from images of dark avarice. Farree's delicate features grew hard as she regarded Nancy. "Stay out of my head, little human. Your stolen ability does not make you our equal. When I am less preoccupied, we will discuss how you managed to draw the attention of a race we thought lost. That line of questioning should prove interesting—painfully interesting."

Nancy woke to the gentle caress of a slobbering dog licking her face, except this one had a sickly green tongue and the fetid breath of a zombie addicted to kimchi—and it had no fur.

"Reemer, stop!" She gagged and swatted the slug's skirt away as her mind kicked into gear. These enforced naps were getting old. "How long was I out this time?"

"No idea." The Squinch pulled back, and the obnoxious odor faded—his homemade version of smelling salts, no doubt. "The call came in loud and clear less than an hour ago. It took Emmett a little time to figure out the locks down here."

"The call?" Had Farree actually helped them?

"More of a pull actually. At first, I thought it was gas." Reemer stood ramrod straight and turned to show the light pulsing from his chest. "It feels sad and mad in a vague kind of way."

So the core sample wasn't entirely spent and had sensed Farree draining the luxene. That thought had Nancy rushing to the observation port where Xa and the captain were just waking up. The Zula's row of hand-picked crystals lay dark and cold along the edge of the nearest sled, gleaming dully in the light from their brethren.

The bulk of the ore was unharmed, but the remaining crystals' inner light had shifted toward somber orange. Nancy stretched her senses. Reemer's intuition had been right, but she also sensed dread rising from the latent consciousness within the luxene.

"Emmett's still having trouble with that door," Reemer said when she tried the observation port controls.

"More of Farree's doing, I assume?" Captain Beal looked none too pleased with the situation or himself. "Why is it so hard to think straight around that woman?"

"Her fluted skirt is fetching, but I blame the glistening puss." Reemer managed to weave appreciation into his words. "Not everyone can pull off that look."

"The Zula has been messing with our minds." Nancy didn't have time to get into the many faces of Farree. "She's draining the energy from that luxene, and it isn't out of generosity. I get the feeling she's about to go nuclear on the Vargan fleet."

A deep rumble made her think that Emmett had succeeded, but it was the roller door on the far side of the ore chamber that slowly rose. The hover sleds sprang to life, pivoted, and glided toward the opening.

"She's initiated a launch sequence," Captain Beal said.

"We can't let her get the ore." Nancy shuddered at the power that would give the Zula ship. The Vargans wouldn't stand a chance. She jabbed a finger at Xa and Reemer. "You two work with Emmett and Ziggy to shut this down." A roar of thrusters sounded in the distance. They might already be too late. "Captain, can your defense drones recapture those containers before they land?"

"If we act fast." Beal was already headed for the console by the entrance. "I'll call ahead and get things moving."

"Take this." Reemer pulled the shining core sample from his chest and pushed it at her.

Her fingers closed around the warm stone and understanding dawned. The sample wasn't just drawn to the harvested luxene; it resonated and communicated with the ore. The crystals were part of a whole, individuals linked by a common intellectual frequency. The simple act of consumption had given the dying luxene a glimpse into Farree's head, a vision the ore had shared with the core sample.

The Zula was headed back to her ship and intended to wipe out the Vargans completely. Farree would leave no contenders to further complicate mining the luxene her race craved. She wouldn't stop with the fleets or moon. Powered by the ore, her ship would unleash devastation the likes of which the warring factions had never before witnessed. Once the Zula claimed the broken planet, they'd be free to administer their own mining contracts.

As Nancy had suspected since the demonstration, dark luxene was a byproduct and red-herring. The true secret to unfettered travel across hyperspace and beyond lay in the power of the harvested life-force, something that would never be shared with the younger races. The implications were chilling.

People who hadn't communed with the core sample and learned of the ancient Vargans' ascendance wouldn't understand the moral implications. How could they? No other race had ever taken up residence in minerals, which meant the Zula hadn't accidentally discovered this miraculous energy by harvesting crystals. They'd gone straight to the source. Logically, it would be just as easy—perhaps easier—for them to drain the life-force directly from other species. Fleeting impressions coming through the core sample supported that conclusion. That was the threat that had forced the consciousness into hiding so long ago. For now, the younger races seemed safe. Something about the ancient Vargans made them tastier, but tastes changed.

Nancy tamped down her panic and sprinted after the captain. There was so much she still didn't understand.

The domed command center bustled with activity. The depthless view of space took her breath away all over again, especially since battling spacecraft and wreckage filled much of the area between station and moon.

A close-up of the mining encampment showed Vargan fighters strafing the compound while Revivalist saucers disgorged ground troops. The shields were down. Emmett had come through again. The combined consortium and station forces would have been quickly overrun if not for support from Farree. The Zula ship held a low orbit, its nebula wings curling protectively over a vast chunk of the surface. Whips of energy lashed from the shifting wings to vaporize a fighter here and a troop carrier there.

The captain headed straight for his chair and sent orders out across his command network. "This is Captain Beal on Spaceport Gail. Effective immediately, I revoke martial law and formally return control of the moon to the Vargan Republic and Revivalists." He consulted the holographic projection hovering above his controls. "Battalion commanders are to commence an orderly withdraw back to the station. Avoid further engagement with Vargan forces. Specific, encrypted instructions follow."

His next transmission went to the Vargan commanders, hinted at Zula involvement, and promised an in-depth assessment of military action on both sides. The rightful owners of the moon visibly bristled, but acknowledged that immediate de-escalation was in everyone's best interest. Phasha and Manfort had done well paving the way for a rapid ceasefire.

The only holdouts were the mining consortium and Farree. The executives blustered, threatened, and claimed the station was abdicating its duty to protect private industry. The captain ignored the bullying tactic, pointing out that their forces would be vastly outnumbered and operating without proper authority. Threats of legal ramifications did as much as the physical danger to turn the tide of the brief discussion.

"Farree is the only one refusing to acknowledge the ceasefire," Captain Beal said when he broke away. "She's ignoring all communications, but must be aware of the content."

"What about the ore carriers?" Those had to be stopped at all costs.

"The first one's been playing hide and seek in the debris, but we have a bead on the second. Vienna, what's the status on recovering transport 714?"

"In progress, sir." An Argoth stationed at the inner consoles dipped her tentacles toward the inset she brought up on a nearby screen. "Contact in two minutes."

A pair of squat security drones closed on a wide-bodied cargo container. They approached to either side, dish antennas targeting the ore carrier's single thrust nozzle. There was no visible discharge, but the bursts of energy that had been intermittently lighting up the thruster stopped. With their quarry disabled, the drones latched onto the hull with short grappling arms. Judicious use of propulsion jets pushed the luxene carrier into a wide arc that would eventually bring it home.

"We've got energy spikes in the Zula cloud," the shaky old coffee-drinker from her last visit called out.

"Targets?" Beal's eyes narrowed as red warning symbols popped up across the moon's surface.

"Calculating impact points." The man's hands flew across the console, steady and sure. "Multiple strikes on picket ships, two surface targets."

"Warn the fleets," Beal ordered.

"Transmitting now. Coordinates received." Two long seconds ticked by. "Units countering."

Energy flashed under each warning symbol, lightning from the artificial nebula. A trio of fighters that had been banking hard disintegrated. Another glowed bright under its defensive shields but managed to fly on. More simultaneous events were too much to track, but the old man let loose with a litany of results, his voice loud and strong above the commotion. The enclave lost two anti-aircraft stations, the

Vargans a dozen ships equally split between Republic and Revivalists. Several ships went on the offensive, their weapons largely neutralizing the Zula attacks.

"I *will not* let that creature start a war," Beal said. "Auto-relay targeting information from the sensors. Zero latency to give them a fighting chance. And get those shields down there back online."

Farree's ship cycled through three more rounds, but Gail's advanced warning saved all but two targets.

"Sir, we've located that first cargo carrier," Vienna said. "Dispatching drones, but it's going to be close."

39. Sledding

"**T**HIS IS GOING to be tight." Reemer veered hard to the left, their scooter glancing off the bulkhead and skirting through the closing doors.

"Where did you learn to drive?" Xa Gorsh clung to Reemer's mantle to keep from being thrown off.

Reemer added a tacky compound to the secretions along his back. The Packtonian wouldn't be able to let go if he tried, which for some reason made the guy curse. This particular compound did smell like rotting fish, but safety came first. Reemer grinned at the sound of retching and pressed on.

They careened down the launch chute, chasing the last ore sled in line. Another deep rumble announced the launch of a second container. Emmett was locked out of the launch system, so stopping the last three sleds was up to them.

The maintenance scooter was built for inspections, not speed. But the sleds were carrying tons of rock and slowed further as they deployed vacuum-proof enclosures to protect their payloads. Reemer tried ramming the last one, but the blunt nose of their transport just bounced off the heavier cargo sled. He'd counted on the hover field slipping sideways, but a tow harness extending from the deck had doomed the maneuver.

"Stupid cape." Unable to free his hands, Xa kept spitting and leaning out to the side to see past the flapping material.

"Don't dis the super suit," Reemer called back to his passenger. "Use your mojo!"

Xa gawked at his translator. "What are you talking about?"

"No time." Another narrow ballistic door loomed ahead, and Reemer gunned the motor to jump in front of the sled. "Watch your right side."

A pocket of pressure swelled beneath his skirt as he took matters into his own antennae. The uncomfortable sensation grew unbearable, then released in a satisfying expulsion that left him panting.

"Sweet mother of—" Xa cut his exclamation short as the gout of mucus poured out from under Reemer's skirt, dousing the Packtonian before hitting the floor.

Extra oils made the slime super slippery. It spilled across the deck in their wake. He leaned on the accelerator, sticking to centerline so that his oily trail seeped into the tow bar slot. The sled kept coming, but slowed as the mechanism below decks met his super slime.

"That'll buy us time, but I'm low on fluids." Reemer looped around the next sled. "You've got glowy skin like the Zula. Suck up some of the luxene power and blast the next one."

"I'm not like the Zula," Xa argued around a mouthful of cape. "They're an elder race with a million years of evolution. I can't shoot lightning. I need to make contact."

A final doorway had him slewing in front so they were sandwiched between the lead sleds. Warning lights flashed red down the center of the ceiling, announcing the atmospheric barrier up ahead. Star-studded blackness loomed at the end of the tube, hurtling closer by the second. There wasn't time to do this twice. Taking out the lead sled would bottle up the launch chute.

"So jump over there and make some contact." Reemer pulled alongside the control deck of the sled about to launch.

Arms extended from overhead and slapped a thruster cone onto the rear of the sled. They only had seconds. Why wasn't Xa moving? His eyestalks swiveled around to glare at his struggling passenger.

"Maybe if I could let go?" Xa growled.

"Oh yeah." A touch of the oily mixture freed Xa's hands. "Now get in there and zap it with all you've got or we're going for a spacewalk underdressed."

Reemer steered them close, jamming his front fender tight against the sled's hull. *All or nothing.* Xa reached for the manual controls with a glowing hand. The zing of electricity shot through Reemer's back, raising bumpy flesh. Pustules ruptured, releasing mucus of unknown composition.

How embarrassing.

"It's too well insulated." Xa flattened his fingers across the controls, pressing down hard.

"Use the force!" Reemer's calm advice came out in a bubbling squeak, one eye riveted on the rapidly approaching nothingness of space.

"What the devil are you talking about?"

"The luxene." Did no one appreciate vintage cinema? "Use the luxene."

The Packtonian stretched out his free hand. The cargo deck had been enclosed along the way, but crystals shimmered beyond the observation window.

"It's too far."

The damned fool was going to fall off. Reemer dredged up more super sticky compound. With no time for finesse he simply flooded the seat, cementing both of them in place.

"I can't—" light flared inside the cargo area, and Xa's outstretched hand blazed bright. "They're helping." Energy crackled through his other hand and arced into the sled's controls, which smoked and sparked in response.

The hover field collapsed. Sled and cart slammed to the deck as sparks flew. The tow harness ripped free with a grating snap. Then the thruster fired, grinding the nose into the sidewall, but still accelerating them toward the opening. Reemer was the hood ornament for the runaway sled as it ground sideways toward the cold abyss.

The thruster cut out with a deafening pop. Rapid deceleration threatened to pitch them through the launch door, but the sled's twisted fender held fast, and they both stayed glued to their seat.

One final lurch brought them to a stop with the sled wedged sideways in the chute. Reemer risked a look, and his stomachs dropped. Space loomed a stone's throw away. The maintenance cart sat on a section of ramp extending past the inner bulkhead. The double doors hung overhead like guillotines, the one-way force-field all that stood between him and cold oblivion. But they'd done it.

A massive crash propelled him closer to the edge as the next cargo carrier in line slammed into the blockage. Reemer held his breath as death ground closer. But the momentum died quickly, leaving him giddy. Laughter bubbled from all his mouths.

"Once again the universe does its worst, but fails to thwart the inscrutable Mr.—"

Another crash, gentle but insistent. The final sled hit slipping and sliding, its over-lubricated mechanism acting as a clutch to drive the pile of wreckage forward. Reemer's eyes went wide as the deck slid past. Distant gears screeched, laboring to push the jammed carts into space.

He thrashed and heaved, jetting out oils in an attempt to unglue them. The hardened slime dissolved slowly. Reemer bunched his skirt in tight, pulling his foot back from the gapping abyss. Skin tore as he lifted himself free, moments away from dropping over the edge. The atmospheric shield brushed his left side, a tingling caress of death.

A shot echoed down the launch chute, and the pile of twisted debris stopped. Squinch and Packtonian held their breath, listening to the disconcerting sound of settling debris until all grew quiet.

Reemer's skirt burned where he'd lost skin wrenching himself free, and he wouldn't be sliming anything until after a drinking binge. He glared outside, defiant and triumphant, but resisted the urge to shout their victory into the looming void.

"See? That wasn't so hard. I knew you could blast stuff."

"I…felt them." Awe replaced Xa's shock. "The ancient Vargans leant me their power."

"Yeah, yeah, everyone's a hero." He could admit that much, but being an indestructible superhero was something else entirely. "Let's get back to the others."

The glue was mostly gone, but for some reason the back edge of his skirt stuck fast.

"I think you have a problem." Xa pointed at the end of the launch ramp where a chunk of flesh poked through the force-shield.

The crescent of hide bristled with frosty white and refused to budge when he tried to pull back. Freeze-dried wasn't a good look for him. But the mantle of greatness had been laid on his shoulders. Reemer would weather the indignity, cope with the unbearable, and *be* the superhero the universe needed. Heck, he was already so good at it that his frozen bits didn't even hurt.

* * *

Ziggy and Emmett hurried down the launch tube. A distant crash was followed by a second and a third. The floor vibrated with low growls as though they descended into the throat of some giant beast.

"Why's the floor slippery?" Emmett's bot swerved sideways before regaining traction.

"You get used to that sort of thing when traveling with the Squinch." Ziggy shrugged as the roar up ahead subsided with a series of sharp pops.

"That wasn't a launch." Emmett consulted his readouts as silence settled around them. "No decompression."

"The mollusk actually pulled it off?" Ziggy hadn't thought it possible. "Reemer really *is* super."

"Aiiieeeeeyyye!" The anguished cry echoed down the launch tube, stretching on impossibly long, a mix of ultimate suffering and flatulent moans.

"Or maybe not."

40. Remote Control

"LAUNCH FAILURE IN tunnel 407." Vienna consulted her screen. "Looks like the tube is blocked. No more luxene transports will be coming through."

Nancy breathed a sigh of relief. *Just one more left.*

"Get a clean-up crew down there," Captain Beal said. "How long to intercept on the outbound carrier?"

"Thirty seconds. Shifting to maximum magnification."

The shining hull of a silver brick jumped onto the screen. The luxene transport dwindled in size as it speared toward Farree's ship. Two interceptors raced past the point of view. The drones closed in fast and looked about to overtake the luxene. Energy flashed from the wings, and the racing drones turned to glittering dust. The luxene shipment continued on, disappearing behind the Zula ship.

The battle outside raged on, but quiet dread fell over the command center. Nancy gripped the core sample, sending up a silent prayer. She had no idea how long Farree would need to drain that much ore, or even if her ship had the capability. They'd deprived her of most of the mineral, but it was a hollow victory. The Zula would never leave in peace, a fact emphasized by her energy net lashing out to catch a squadron off-guard.

"Target queuing is offline," the old man announced. "Relays are unresponsive." He tried a few more things before slumping in his seat, again looking his age. "All we can do now is watch, Captain."

Beal had more tricks up his sleeve, but none of them restored targeting capability. Without the constant stream of information, the destruction escalated. More ships winked out of existence.

"They're sitting ducks out there." The image of a small aquatic reptile accompanied Beal's comment, but Nancy knew what he meant.

An explosion near the moon compound sent geysers of dust into the air. The shield was back in place, but couldn't take many hits like that. The ship losses were bad enough. She'd hoped people manning the compound would be off limits. But it looked as if Farree was willing to sacrifice the current operation. Acceptable loses. There was still an awful lot of moon left to exploit.

Nancy swore she felt the next strike glance off the shield. A ridiculous thought, except that the vibrations running up her arm came from the core sample. The luxene layers pulsed faster. Attacks in space sent quivers through the rod, while ground strikes made it rattle like an angry snake. The sensation resembled trying to muffle the speaker when Reemer had the volume too high on his videos.

If you can hear me, we could really use some help. Nancy directed her thought at the core sample. The rod had led Reemer to problem areas twice. Hoping for a miraculous third performance wasn't outrageous. Or was it? Resonance between luxene crystals might account for the sample sensing vibrations on the moon, but couldn't possibly track the battle unfolding in space. Yet, as time marched on and casualties mounted, that's exactly what the vibrating stone seemed to be doing.

She tried to track the chaos and correlate what came through the core sample. Surface strikes on the moon translated into heavy vibrations, while events further out caused a weaker reaction. The relative intensity matched what one might observe from a vantage point on the moon, and there was certainly plenty of untapped luxene down there.

Nancy pushed her thoughts through the core sample rather than at it. She imagined riding the natural resonance between crystals, surfing the base frequency of the luxene. The unnatural exercise felt silly.

She was about to give up when a weighty presence drew her down into inky darkness, a vast reservoir of intellect that she'd touched once before. The star pool had held surface thoughts and flashes of memory. Now, a quiet surge swelled from deeper down, as if the sleeping ancient collective slowly rose. Too slowly.

The core sample vibrated in Nancy's palm, but the conflict also played out across the dark pool surrounding her. Everything felt more poignant in the ancient chamber in her mind. The Vargan fleets, individual ships, activity in the mining camp, even the presence of Gail itself and the vast web of energy spilling from the distant Zula ship. All danced across the taut membrane of Vargan senses: sight, sound, temperature, radiation, energy, and so much more melded together through the awareness inhabiting the dark liquid that pooled beneath the ruins, ran under the ridges, and circled the moon. The watery arteries carried a lifeblood of communication, connecting thousands of luxene deposits housing millions of transcended souls.

We are here.

The answer to Nancy's unasked question resonated in her mind, anchoring her thoughts, connecting one lone human to the vast consciousness through the core sample.

A scream from Vienna drew Nancy's attention back to the command center in time to see the cracked hull of a Vargan saucer hurtling toward them. The panel of screens where it hit went dark, the source of the video feed destroyed. The software compensated quickly, filling in the blank area with overlapping views showing a debris field drifting around the shattered ring that had been struck.

Nancy had felt the ship-killing blow before opening her eyes, a distant pinprick of energy. Inputs came through a new awareness beyond the five senses, as if she'd plugged into a vast computer. The information originated at the equatorial canal, transformed from raw inputs to knowledge as it crossed luxene deposits along the connecting waterways.

A buildup of power cascaded down the fringe of the Zula web, destined to take out a reserve squadron of Vargan saucers waiting on the far side of the moon.

"Captain Beal, I have information!" She darted over to the old analyst and stuck out her hand. "Hi, I'm Nancy. What's your name?"

"Frank Kelly." He shook her hand cautiously. "But I don't think—"

"Okay, Frank, you've got a power surge building out on the fringes, right?" She waved the rod at the line of ships opposite the station.

"I see it." He nodded at his readouts.

"Can you bring up the ships in its path?"

"Yes, but the relays are out. We can't warn them."

"I need unit call-signs and command frequencies for those ships." She jabbed a finger at his console. "Now, Frank."

"That's classified!" Outrage animated the old man's face.

"What's this all about?" Captain Beal strode over.

"I can warn those ships," Nancy said. "I can warn all of them. But it'll take some fancy footwork and your authorization to access what I need, starting with the command codes for the ships being targeted."

Frank was going to argue. He looked the sort to argue. But at the captain's nod, the old man surprised her by clapping his hands like an excited toddler and diving into his controls. He spat out strings of alpha-numerics for five ships and dialed up the squadron command frequency. Nancy let the information wash over her, through her, into the core sample and the collective ancients far below. Signals raced out, and the ships in jeopardy slammed themselves into evasive maneuvers just as the Zula struck. Frank and Nancy spotted the frustrated follow-up burst forming and fired off new intercept coordinates just in time.

Numbers flowed as ship and ground station identifiers locked into place, building a communications table to direct outgoing information. Losses dwindled to nothing.

Farree must have realized Gail was responsible. A rapid series of strikes aimed directly at the station were turned away by a dozen suicide drones. Disrupters and short-band weapons attenuated the Zula attacks, but the station was still a fat target with no evasive ability. They would run out of drones under a concentrated assault.

"I think it's time to take the fight to her," Nancy said. "The Zula ship has limits. We can hit back during her recharge cycle."

Farree launched a brutal assault. Frank and Nancy threw everything they had at the incoming energy, deflecting the attack but wiping out fully half of the station's drones. Beal opened his command channel and launched into a terse exchange with the fleet commanders. They reached consensus quickly. Nancy shifted from warning to directing fleet assets.

"Watch for activity here, here, and there." She pointed out several areas on Frank's heads-up display where the consciousness below expected trouble.

Soon, every ship except those controlled by the consortium was linked to pathways in the luxene reservoir. Nancy clutched the glowing core sample and sent a wave of saucers to attack the fringes of each deadly gossamer wing. The Revivalist ships had weaker weapons but sturdy shields that overlapped enough in the close formations to survive several direct hits. They launched everything they had at the Zula ship.

Farree countered, unleashing a succession of vicious plasma strikes. The saucers took a beating, but their shields held, opening a window of opportunity while the enemy recharged. Nancy reached through the inky waters with the command to attack, launching wave after wave of Republic fighters. They dove at the alien craft on an oblique, coming in under the protection of the Revivalists' shields, firing main guns, and then banking away at maximum acceleration. Direct hits rained down on the Zula pod. The shields weakened by half based on the readings flowing through the luxene. Nancy reached for the reserve fighters. One more pass would break Farree's defenses.

"Mines!" Frank yelled just as the new wave launched. "She's deployed proximity mines."

The lead fighter picked them up on sensors and veered hard. Several points of energy lit up on Frank's display, following the flight arc. Most fell back, unable to complete the maneuver, but two accelerated like missiles. The fighter vaporized.

Nancy aborted the inbound wave. Ships scattered at maximum thrust back toward the rendezvous point. Most made it; a handful didn't. Mines along the fringes of the field went after the saucers, pounding shields and forcing a strategic withdrawal.

The moon's sensor array picked up transponder signals that kept the mines from attacking each other. Gail's computers never could have simulated the signal, but the collective consciousness quickly constructed a broadcast for their ships to use.

As the Vargans prepared another assault, unease flowed from the core sample. Something wasn't right. Nancy examined the ebb and flow of information across the ancient network below. The ships were in position with transponder signals active. All seemed in order, but a pall of dread hung over the communication pathways. The feeling didn't stem from the mysterious sensors in the great canal. Yet the sensation permeated the luxene, as if the ancients held their collective breath.

"All units, hold position." Nancy sent the command on all frequencies. "Something's wro—"

A supernova exploded across the screens. Automatic dimmers kicked in, plunging the room into darkness. Pain ripped through Nancy's skull as agonized screams poured from the luxene below, screams that only she could hear.

"Did the Zula just explode?" Vienna's quiet question wasn't directed at anyone in particular.

That was Nancy's first thought too, but the blazing energy roiled forth in tightly controlled waves too orderly for an explosion. The pressure pushing out through her ears eased. The mental shrieks settled into deep, sorrowful pangs as the ancient Vargans lamented the death of their kin.

"Not an explosion." Nancy gasped. "Farree absorbed the luxene's energy." She pointed to the brightening screen overhead. "Look."

Farree's ship shone with brilliant intensity, an elongated sun nestled within dark crimson that spread outward to reinforce the ship's butterfly wings with ropy coils of power. Greedy tendrils of energy curved toward the moon.

"Sir, readings are off the scale," Frank announced.

"Send those ships in now," Captain Beal ordered. "We need to take this thing out before it gets any stronger."

Power saturation made it hard to pick out individual spikes. The recharge time she'd come to rely upon was nonexistent as strike after strike blasted the ships moving on Farree. Targeting seemed the Zula's only limitation. She never went after more than a dozen attackers at a time.

The Vargans ignored the risks, hurling their resources into the attack despite the terror unfolding. And they died for it.

"This is suicide." Nancy felt powerless.

She continued to relay information, but the Zula's new offensive capabilities rendered most of the data useless. Those energy wings blanketed the moon in a gentle embrace as it destroyed the incoming fleets and station vehicles Captain Beal sent into the fray.

The core sample sparked and sputtered as the Zula choked off its connection to the collective mind below. Without solid intel, the Vargan commanders finally abandoned their defense of the moon and retreated to positions off Gail's outer rings.

Nancy fought through the rising static to find the hub for communicating with the luxene. But the halls felt cold and empty, as if the presence from earlier had retreated back into the depths.

"No you don't." Nancy's mental cry rang hollow across the empty cavern in her mind. *"Going back into hiding won't do you any good. Your descendants, your children, are dying out there. If you won't stand up for yourselves, stand up for them. The Zula is going to rip your glowing crystalline asses from the ground. So if there's anything at all you can do, now is the time to do it. Don't ask your children to fight your battles."*

The consciousness shifted uncomfortably, recognizing the truth in her words. The specifics remained unclear, but their history with the Zula ran deep. The collective represented the pinnacle of an entire civilization, unparalleled intellects delving the secrets of the universe. Yet they clung to anonymity, hoping to go unnoticed. *A little late for that!*

They heard that thought too. *Whoops.*

The inky black pathways raged with consternation and debate, and—eventually—resolve.

The collective rose once more, a vast wave spilling forth like expanding lava from their volcanic fortress. The starry pools and channels filled with sparkling awareness; the dark liquid turned luminous as fiery energy raced through the canal circling the moon. Power spilled forth in a flaming geyser that beat back the smothering barrier from Farree's ship.

The intensity of the counter-strike threw Nancy's perception back to the command center, shifting the battle from a visceral impression to a scene playing out on the screens overhead. Within minutes, a layer of raging energy encased the moon like the photosphere of a star.

The exchange took a lot out of Farree's ship. The nebula wings still radiated power, but shrank to their original size as they beat futilely against the fiery shield. Elation turned to worry as the Zula ship spun toward the defenders. Though smaller now, those wings could still engulf a sizable fleet— or a space station.

The approaching ship was suddenly replaced by the Zula representative. Farree sat ramrod straight in her control chair, eyes and wings blazing with power as she glared down on the room.

"Captain Beal, I have no quarrel with Spaceport Gail." Her voice was ice. "Order the Vargan fleets away. All I need from you is the luxene ore in your possession."

"Regrettably, it isn't that simple," the captain said. "You have a long list of offenses to answer for including falsifying orders, assaulting an officer, and using deadly force against units under my command."

"Not to mention attempted genocide!" Nancy said.

"Ah, yes. Dr. Dickenson." Farree pushed to her feet and strode closer. "Insignificant human, an enigma touched by the great ones yet of little value herself."

Nancy bit her tongue rather than rise to the taunt. But she wasn't above imagining Reemer dangling over the smug alien and dropping a great glob of goo on her head. What greatness was Farree talking about? Herself, probably—or maybe the ancient Vargans.

The moon still floated on the far screens, covered in its blazing shield. Nancy's heart sank. She'd been so certain the collective had been rising up to finish Farree. They'd dealt some damage, but only enough to deploy their barrier, which was just a more obvious form of hiding. Would they continue to stick their heads in the sand when the Zula came back with a fleet of her own?

Farree's promise was hollow. The Vargan luxene contained too much power. There was no way her people would abandon it. She'd most likely use the remaining ore to supercharge her weapons and break the moon's defenses. The only question would be if the Zula ship could handle the energy. They didn't dare wait to find out.

Reemer would look at the problem through his new superhero lens and say they needed to find the Zula's kryptonite. If only it was that simple. They had plenty of glowing rocks, but the luxene only increased Farree's power. As far as Nancy could tell, her biggest weakness was greed—and maybe moral ambiguity. How did you exploit those? The woman didn't even rely on Gail for supplies, so Emmett couldn't fabricate one of his ingenious mechanical failures to take out Farree's ship either.

One thing Nancy knew from the luxene collective was that Zula never gave up. Greed and pride would drive Farree until she got what she wanted—a disturbing thought that also added a useful bit of certainty to the mix. Pieces of a plan began to fall into place. There'd be a lot of moving parts, but at its core, the idea seemed straight forward.

"This might not be a popular opinion." Nancy caught the outraged glare as she turned her back on Farree to advise the captain. "If it gets rid of her, give the bitch what she wants."

"Switching sides already?" Farree's laugh of delight rang like silver bells. "You are full of surprises."

"Call it the lesser of two evils," Nancy said over her shoulder while using her talent and facial expressions that bordered on comical to convince the captain to follow her lead. "Or sacrificing the few for the many. Give us a few hours and you'll get your precious cargo."

"There's been an accident with the cargo sleds," Beal explained. "We need time to repackage the luxene. But you must agree to a ceasefire and to depart after we send your shipment over. People above my paygrade will decide how this incident impacts formal relations."

"With your failing equipment, one wonders how the younger races manage at all in deep space." Now that she had the upper hand, Farree looked more exasperated than angry. "Very well. You have three standard hours. Fail to deliver, and I'll rip the crystals from your hull."

"Don't worry, I'd rather lose a few tons of ore than my command." Captain Beal looked for Nancy's curt nod. "You'll get your precious rocks." Once the screen went dark, he turned to her. "You can't mean to give her what she wants, so what's the plan?"

"Have you ever heard of fool's gold?"

41. Fool's Gold

T HE TEAM PREPARING the luxene shipment was kept to a bare minimum. Farree might still have spies aboard, and consortium agents weren't to be trusted. Emmett supervised the construction bots and cleared the wreckage in under two hours. Captain Beal's hand-picked engineer, Verbrant, drew up designs for what Nancy envisioned and got to work modifying the least damaged cargo sled.

Final preparations took place in the launch tube. Emmett and Ziggy stood off to the side while Verbrant worked his magic. Reemer squeezed out another spoonful of super-adhesive slime and passed it to the Argoth engineer.

"How likely is this to actually work?" Nancy asked.

"The chain reaction is guaranteed once antimatter containment collapses," Ziggy said. "The weakest point in this design is the triggering mechanism. An electronic device would be more reliable."

"The Zula will scan the sled before bringing it aboard." Emmett used his war club to draw a wire-frame antimatter priming pump on the board that replaced his usual control console. "She'll be looking for any devices emitting regular pulses, such as countdown clocks. Small amounts of organic compound should go unnoticed."

"Linking the Zula tech into the sled is risky enough," Ziggy added. "Even that's only going to work because she'll expect high power readings from the luxene. We've dialed in the sled's mass and shielded the energy so that it approximates the expected load of ore."

That was the key to their deception. Emmett's team had carefully picked through the scattered ore, setting aside every bit of living crystal and filling their payload with useless, inert material. They'd painted the chunks of dark luxene isomer that Farree had drained with a luminous compound. Those mock crystals went on top of the scrap ore to sell the illusion of a full load of glowing luxene. Being chemically equivalent to "live" luxene, the drained crystals shouldn't trigger any alarms.

"It all comes down to the glue releasing fast enough." Nancy didn't particularly like depending on Squinch slime.

"Hey, I'm not a machine," Reemer complained as Verbrant slid his tray over for more. The slug dutifully plopped out another spoonful from beneath his skirt then turned to Nancy. "My formula will work just fine. They don't call me the Slime Master for nothing." He threw back his cape and struck a pose, teetering a bit thanks to the crescent of missing skirt he'd lost to the atmospheric barrier, and maybe from the pain meds.

"Who calls you that?" Ziggy's eyes narrowed.

"What?" Reemer cocked his head.

"Slime Master."

"At your service." Reemer bowed, dismissing the topic with a raised antenna and head shake that managed smug humility—his I-know-I'm-great gesture. "Others know me as Captain Slime, or sometimes Mucus-man. My people are still working out the branding."

"*What* people?" both AIs cried in unison.

"That's not important right now." Reemer pointed to the engine compartment where Verbrant applied a final coating of slime and carefully released the antimatter device. "Fear not. This special mixture degrades steadily once I apply the solvent. We can predict exactly when the bonds will fail and unleash destruction upon our foe."

"That's some mighty fine adhesive." Verbrant gave Reemer a tentacle to antenna high-five. "Let me know if you ever want to market it. There's a boatload of stress testing and certification involved, but we could make a fortune."

"I'd rather use an egg timer," Ziggy muttered.

Nancy sighed. For better or worse, their future depended on slime.

* * *

Essential personnel gathered in the command center to monitor the ore sled's journey across the void. Nancy, Ziggy, and Reemer stood behind the captain's chair. The launch went smoothly, and all readings held steady, which meant the engine modifications were holding.

Emmett had gone…elsewhere. None of them knew nor wanted to know his exact location. The logistics manager and his construction team were off preparing the real luxene for delivery moonside.

"Eighteen minutes and twenty seconds until containment failure." Ziggy had taken up the mantle of timekeeper the moment Reemer applied his solvent.

"Zula vessel, your cargo container will arrive in fifteen standard minutes, that's one-five minutes. Over." The communications officer had been transmitting in the blind with the countdown to arrival.

Farree hadn't responded to any of the transmissions, but did reorient her ship to meet the ore carrier head on. At least she knew it was coming. Three minutes wasn't much time for Farree to bring the sled aboard, but leaving a longer gap risked her discovering that the cargo wasn't the promised luxene.

"Captain, the cargo sled is accelerating," Vienna announced.

"Problems with the antimatter interface?" The captain checked his own readouts.

"No, sir. It's a tractor beam. The Zula ship's pulling the sled in ahead of schedule. Updating estimates now." She studied her console. "Sled arrives at destination in two minutes."

Damn! Farree would have a solid fifteen minutes to look things over before Reemer's adhesive dissolved. They needed to keep her busy. But how?

"Always play to the supervillain's weakness," Reemer recommended in their quick brainstorming session.

"Which one?" Nancy knew of several. "Her superiority complex, greed, disdain for life, lust for power?"

"Sure, use one of those, as long as it gets under her skin." If there was an expert on annoying people, it was the Squinch.

The problem was that for all the Zula's faults, none were likely to distract the woman when she had a big fat load of magic rocks to drain. Only one emotion strong enough to override greed came to mind.

Farree hated Nancy on a visceral level. She'd sensed it from their first meeting, and the alien's attitude in the ore chamber—the things Nancy had seen in her mind—proved it. *Why* was a question to ponder later, but something more than the simple act of being human made Nancy the perfect thorn to get under Farree's skin. The captain agreed to let her try.

"Farree, this is Dr. Nancy Dickenson. Over." No reply. "Before you leave, I need to talk to you." *Here goes nothing.* "You'll want some expert advice on handling this new luxene. It's more than just a crystal."

The nearest screen filled with Farree's scowling face. *Bingo.*

"Expert advice? From an infant upstart like you?" She'd gone full warrior angel, flaming wings and all. "Do not presume to know what I need. We discovered this power, bent it to our will, and with it have traveled to the very ends of the universe. You couldn't possibly have learned anything of import in a few short weeks."

Contempt colored her words, but it wasn't enough. Even without the talent, Nancy couldn't have missed that she'd been dismissed as unimportant. Ziggy held up five fingers, which was five minutes too many.

Judging by the racks of equipment behind her, Farree wasn't on the bridge. The angle shifted, to show luxene glowing from the open cargo area as she turned back to the sled. Nancy's eye was immediately drawn to the sparse line of glowing crystals and the trash ore showing beneath. They couldn't let Farree get a good look.

"The luxene is alive, and it hates you!" Nancy blurted out. "Don't you want to know why?"

"Arrogant and stupid." Farree spun around, eyes blazing and looking like a cat ready to pounce. "I am well acquainted with the living crystals, but you should not be." Her gaze dissected Nancy, peering into her in a way that was more than physical.

Farree's mind brushed her own, a feeling Nancy had only experienced once before. But unlike the gently coaxing contact of the Lokii people, the Zula's mind was a jagged shard honed to thrust and cut. Given half a chance, Farree would rip away any information she wanted.

Nancy filled her thoughts with nonsense and images, flipping through random memories of early days at school, the exotic landscape of planet Fred, even her first date with Jake.

Farree grew incensed. Fury radiated across the mental link. The Zula would have come right through the screen and strangled Nancy. More frustration. Direct transport capability only worked from the bridge.

Nancy's head buzzed as her talent read the alien's intent through body language, tone, and a deeper mental resonance. *Farree would simply destroy the human from afar. Gail might be a wonder of engineering for the upstart younger races, but couldn't defend itself against her ship—even depleted as it was. The assembled fleets posed a bigger problem, as did the ancient power protecting the moon. But as soon as she drained this new luxene shipment, that balance would shift.*

Nancy tried to warn the others, but a jolt sent the Zula's intent in a new direction…

Farree would go to the bridge, jump to the station herself, and haul Dr. Dickenson back. A few hours of personal attention would reveal how a human could block her thoughts and read others. More than just the souls cowering in those delicious crystals had touched this woman. A familiar presence that hadn't been seen in a very long time lingered amid the human's shifting memories. The Zula had chased the Lokii across the cosmos, feeding until the insects were extinct along with any others who could challenge Farree's people.

Another jolt and shift…

Farree would return with reinforcements, a fleet to subdue and subjugate the fledgling races that dared challenge her. She had all she needed. The Vargan moon wasn't going anywhere, nor were the cowards hidden deep in the crystalline mines. The sweet energy they'd release would make her a god. News of this discovery needed to be shared strategically, the treasure meted out to best advantage. It had been too long since her people fed on other elders. The jump-point lay just beyond the planetary orbit. She'd return in force to assure victory.

Nancy fell to the deck, clutching her temples. The talent swirled with conflicting images, things Farree was about to do, would do, might do. Ziggy held her head off the deck. The room spun, threatening to make her puke.

"What is that stench?" Farree crinkled her nose at something unrelated to what Nancy had sensed.

"Uh oh." Reemer's antennae sank low. "I forgot about that."

"Don't turn your back on me." Nancy clawed upright, desperate to keep her away from the sled. "Explain yourself!"

Farree ignored her and slid the cover off the engine compartment. The antimatter priming device sizzled and spat, sending up noxious curls of steam that made the Zula cringe and cough.

"Is that…" Nancy left her quiet question hanging.

"Two minutes." Ziggy shook his head; this wasn't the antimatter release.

"Reemer, what did you do?" Nancy whispered. Still too much time.

"The smell doesn't bother anyone underwater." The slug looked appropriately embarrassed, but the damage was done.

"What is this?" Farree scrambled to the cargo compartment, her prior inner musings forgotten. The Zula now focused on saving the luxene, absorbing its power, and thrusting the ticking antimatter bomb back at the station. The fake luxene didn't stand up under close scrutiny. "Treachery!"

The jagged mental blade speared Nancy's head, ripping past the blocking images she threw out. From painting the drained crystals to gluing together the antimatter booby trap, the entire ruse was laid bare.

"Thought we'd return your little gift." Nancy sagged in relief as the mental pressure vanished.

Farree snarled, tossed the fake luxene aside, and lunged for controls on the near wall. The sled backed out of the holding bay, its cargo moving off screen.

"Three, two, one," Ziggy called off the seconds in a metered clip.

Just before the propulsion section slipped from view, the front panel of the antimatter pump dropped off, releasing a puff of gas that had the Zula retching into the crook of her arm. A thin chunk of crystal tumbled from between the crackling containment fields within. Without dark luxene to control the reaction, energy exploded from the device. Farree spun away, her wings flaring in response as they wrapped the woman in crimson power. White filled the screen, and the display shifted to an external view of the Zula ship.

A silent explosion erupted from the central pod. The nebula wings shifted from red to yellow, pulling back tight to fan against the hull. The ship drifted with the rippling fins, stopped, and moved on like a drunken squid heading out past the moon.

"Is it over?" Vienna shrugged her upper tentacles unsure of their next steps.

"Minimal power readings," Frank said. "Our sensors won't penetrate the hull, so no status on survivors. Orders, Captain?"

"Send a squadron of recovery drones." Beal flipped controls on the arm of his chair. "Establish a containment area where the wreckage can be safely inspected."

The trajectory worried Nancy, a vague memory of something out past the moon. Ridiculous, because she'd never flown in that direction. The memory couldn't be hers, but…one of Farree's options had been to go for help.

"It's a trick!" Certainty settled over Nancy as six drones zoomed along the intercept route Frank plotted on his display. "There's a hyperspace jump-point out there. Farree's after reinforcements. Don't let her past the moon's orbit."

As if to emphasize her words, the Zula ship sprang to life and the lead drone winked out, followed quickly by the next two in formation.

"Launch all interceptors. I've already got the Vargan commanders on a secure channel." The captain's tentacles flew across his controls as another drone disappeared from the display and the last two veered wildly. He spoke into his comms panel. "Admirals, that assistance you offered is sorely needed." He had Nancy add the jump-point to Frank's plot before continuing. "We don't know how much fight is left in the Zula, but we have to stop that ship.

Transmitting the line of demarcation now. Your fastest fighters would be appreciated, but shields are advised."

Outbound saucers and fighters streamed past. Farree had given up the pretense of being disabled, but still struggled. Energy wings unfurled along her port side, leaving the ragged starboard fins to drag the ship onward.

The race to the jump-point unfolded on Frank's display. The station drones were already gone. The fighters closed fast, firing from well beyond effective range in an attempt to draw Farree into combat. She ignored them, passing over the far side of the moon and gaining velocity. Projected intercept points slipped past the moon's orbit, shifting from green to yellow to red. Farree was getting away.

Nancy rested a hand on the core sample thrust through her belt, and tried again to summon the ancient Vargans. The consciousness below stirred in acknowledgement, vaguely interested but safe and secure under their barrier. She pushed through a malaise that had again settled over the ancients, sending memories to remind them of how the Zula ship had nearly encircled their world, of the effort it had taken to beat back Farree, of the fact that they'd stopped short of finishing the job—perhaps out of mercy, perhaps for other reasons.

The collective acknowledged her thoughts, an undercurrent of pride swelling. They'd taken action to preserve their way of life and their descendants. Well-deserved slumber awaited.

A worthy feat, Nancy agreed, following the sentiment with a montage of what had transpired since: the battle, the antimatter explosion, the covert recovery of the lost luxene and its imminent return.

The damaged Zula ship came next, fleeing and disappearing into hyperspace only to return with dozens, hundreds, of Zula warships. Nancy injected the lust she'd felt within Farree, the gloating need to consume the other elder races, to become the one true power in the universe, revered and feared by all. The moon barrier broke under the weight of the enemy assault in her vision—as it surely would if Farree escaped. She showed them all that she could, a stark forecast of what was to come, neither lying nor embellishing, and ended it with one final thought: *please*.

42. Beginnings

T HE SHIELD CONTRACTED until the flaming wall hovered in a narrow belt over the moon's central canal. Just as Farree's ship approached the point of no return, the energy speared into space. The barrier reformed beyond the fleeing ship, blocking its path.

The Zula's remaining wing buffeted the moon's power, each strike registering as a massive surge on Frank's sensors. The barrier held.

This is what we will do. The thought came through the crystal rod, the most coherent sentence yet from the ancient collective.

"She can't retreat," Nancy told the captain. "The rest is up to us."

Farree fought savagely. Plasma bolts struck as the fighters caught up to their cornered quarry. The tattered energy wing that was so ineffectual against the power holding the ship in place dealt death to Vargans and station vehicles that strayed within striking distance. Allied energy bursts and missiles rained down on the Zula ship, obscuring the main hull under successive explosions. The nebula wing stopped lashing out and curled around the main ship, a protective barrier much like the one Farree had thrown around herself moments before the antimatter explosion.

The fleets redoubled their efforts and the defensive shield shattered. Energy poured into the ship until the admirals finally called a ceasefire and ordered their people back to a defensive position.

Farree's ship drifted against the starry backdrop as the energy holding it withdrew to the moon. Cracks ran along the blackened hull. The station's instruments couldn't get a reading: no light, no radiation, no energy. The Zula ship was dead.

* * *

"Good thing my super adhesive worked so well." Reemer bent to sign an autograph for the next customer in line, pausing for a photo op with the short reptile before taking its credits and handing over a tube of patent-pending Super Reemer Goop.

Mysterious tales of an alien slug from a nearby dimension who'd unleashed his super powers to save Gail's inhabitants had spread like wildfire. *Now who could have started those rumors?* Nancy snorted and scooped up one of the packages. Verbrant had neatly sidestepped most of the regulations by labeling the product as experimental with a "use at your own risk" disclaimer. The logo, a muscle-bound Squinch with an R blazoned across its chest, posed atop an eye-watering block of miniscule text. The miracle adhesive also came with a small vial of organic solvent to "undo heroic deeds." Impressive, given the battle had ended just hours ago.

"Maybe you should have mentioned the side effects." Nancy thought back to how even the powerful Zula had gagged on the solvent's stench.

"Look near the bottom edge." Reemer turned back to the next Argoth in line and pantomimed being stuck to her tentacles for a short vid.

Turning the package sideways revealed a row of fine print beneath the tubes. A long list of potential side effects included ear, nose, and throat irritation; sporadic bleeding; ocular degeneration…the list went on, ending with liver damage and possible death. A swipe strip cycled through various languages and adjusted the involved organs accordingly.

"It'll be a miracle if you two don't end up on a prison world." Nancy handed the package back to Verbrant with a shake of her head. "I need to pry Reemer away from his adoring fans for a debrief with the captain."

"Go do your hero thing." The engineer waved Reemer away and gleefully tallied up the next sale, which included a small pile of merch complete with action figures and a plush Super Reemer doll.

Reemer bowed his way toward the exit with profuse apologies and thrown kisses to his small crowd of admirers. The outer edge of the atrium was sculpted into a desert landscape with gravel paths through the arid-loving vegetation—all readily available species except for the small cactus that had been recently planted near an overhang at the door's control panel. The unexpected sight and wave of déjà vu stopped Nancy in her tracks.

"Care to explain where a Dolor pain urchin came from?" Nancy blocked Reemer's path and pointed at the juvenile plant from his homeworld. "And you might as well cover why I found one by the ruins down on the moon."

"Becky wants to learn about the people who visit planet Fred," Reemer said—as if that explained everything.

"Planting her offspring in random spots isn't going to help much."

It stung a little that Rebecca hadn't asked for *her* advice. But then again, Nancy hadn't been back to Fred in a long time. And to be fair, Reemer had been the first to see the deadly Dolor queen for what she truly was: an intelligent, caring mother looking out for the future of her species.

"Well, sure. They need to grow up a little first." Reemer bent and caressed the nubby rows that would eventually blossom into poisonous yellow spines. "Then Becky can keep an eye on them and get to see all the neat people passing through Gail."

"From halfway across the galaxy?"

"Oh, distance doesn't matter." The way Reemer cooed while smoothing the dirt out around the plant's base made Nancy think the Squinch would make a fine mother someday. "Becky can talk to her kids no matter where they go. She explained it to me once, something about vibrating in tune with tiny invisible bits that let them communicate."

"Sounds like a form of quantum entanglement."

Current networks like the one Quen had used to work on Ziggy were enormously expensive and only approximated real-time data transfers. Hyperspace relay stations cheated the laws of physics, but subspace transmissions almost always introduced latency along the data pathways. Instantaneous communication remained a theoretical possibility that would require materials with perfectly attuned quantum frequencies and sensitive apparatuses to read state transitions without changing the very thing they observed. A biological solution perfected through thousands of years of evolution would be as valuable as luxene—and a tempting target.

"No one else can know about this. Remember how much danger Rebecca was in over her nectar?" Nancy fixed the slug with her no-nonsense glare and continued at his vigorous nod. "This would be far worse than being hunted by a few mercenaries. Every spacefaring race would come after her and her kids. Your planet would get overrun."

"Never again." A rare fierceness settled over her friend, and he swore to take this bit of information to the grave.

Good. Getting the galactic races to accept the concept of sentient flora was proving hard enough. The powers that be didn't need financial incentives to look the other way while the Dolor were exploited.

Having settled the issue, they hurried through the station. Battle damage still had several rings closed and lifts offline. The brisk fifteen-minute walk got them to the meeting just in time.

"Thank you all for joining us." Captain Beal waved her and Reemer into the room. "I'd like to take roll call."

He sat at the head of the table with Xa Gorsh, Kirsch, Phasha, Chief Mendelson and a few other familiar faces. A display screen split into two panes dominated the far end of the small conference room. One of the human mining executives sat at his desk on the left, while Manfort lounged in a white recliner on the right pane. Bandages covered the Republic delegate from head to toe—not lounging; he was in a hospital bed.

Nancy took a seat, slipped the core sample from her belt, and placed the glowing rod on the table in front of the next chair over—between herself and Phasha. By now, all those present would understand that the original Vargans lived on in the glowing luxene crystals. During introductions, Nancy and Phasha made it clear that the ancients should have a say in how to proceed.

"We're going to keep this session focused on situational awareness, developing short term goals, and mapping the major milestones beyond that." Captain Beal looked none too happy. "You've all seen the damage reports. Repair crews will be working around the clock for at least two weeks to replace our lost drones and get Gail fully functional. Caring for the wounded and surviving family members are high priority, but we must ensure the moon and station are safe from attack. So I'm going to lead with the bad news first. Our salvage teams were unable to recover Farree's ship."

"How's that possible?" Manfort shot up in bed, the motion creasing his face with pain.

"We're looking into that," Beal replied. "Scans showed no signs of life in the broken Zula ship. But broadband interference blinded our sensors as the recovery team closed in. Something obviously happened during that period because the ship was simply gone when the team arrived."

"The real question is whether or not Farree called on other Zula for backup," Chief Mendelson added.

"I think that's unlikely." Nancy's brush with the alien's mind had been confusing, but one thing was certain: the Zula had been a loner. "Farree kept everything close. This new luxene was too valuable to reveal until she was in full control."

Although she didn't explain, several of those around the table knew that Nancy used more than simple intuition to reach her conclusion. After some spirited debate the majority agreed that all they could do was deploy long-range sensors to monitor the situation. The ancients below added an interesting twist by not fully dispersing their defensive shield. The roiling power hovered over the equator, a combination deep space sensor and weapon ready to protect the moon again should the need arise.

The grim accounting of casualties and damages took the better part of an hour. That the mining consortium had sat on its thumbs while the other factions got hammered became painfully obvious. Tempers flared when the consortium rep tried to blame Captain Beal for inciting Farree. Criticism rolled off the sleaze as he pivoted smoothly to propose the conglomerate take charge of the moon enclave, since their forces were largely intact and had the financial backing to push mining forward.

Thinly veiled threats of legal action and calling loans due had everyone's blood boiling. The executive signed off with a sneer, clearly expecting the group to come groveling back to take up his offer. Participating over a virtual link was probably to avoid getting pummeled when the consortium plans were revealed. Slimy—and not in the fun Squinch way.

"I can't believe you worked for that jerk," Nancy said to Xa Gorsh.

"Business and bedfellows, as your people say." Xa let out a resigned sigh. "But I fear he is right. The collective corporations have a strategic advantage. Right or wrong, mining rights were offered as collateral against their investment in start-up operations. The conflict with Farree gives them an excuse to claim default and seize control."

Talks quickly deteriorated into bedlam. While the captain urged calm, gentle pulses of interest washed from the core sample. By the way he cocked his head, Phasha felt them too. They each slipped a hand over the crystals, his wide, spaded fingers next to her slender ones. With practice, the luxene collective grew more adept at communicating. It had an interesting idea. But the proposal shouldn't come from a human.

"Captain, I think Phasha may have a solution." Nancy interrupted an argument over breach of contract to give the Revivalist the floor.

"Well, yes." The Vargan sat up straight, keeping his hand on the core sample. "Help from the consortium may not be needed to mine the luxene. We can do it ourselves. The ancients can tell us where the best deposits are." He patted the glowing crystals, hastening to add, "This would be standard luxene, not the crystals containing our ancestors. The moon has richer deposits than we'd ever imagined, many that won't require specialized equipment to access. It *would* take capital to begin, but profits should follow in short order."

A glimmer of hope, *if* they could keep the consortium from swooping in. But the Vargans already faced bankruptcy to rebuild their fleets. The Argoth and races that jointly owned the station weren't likely to extend credit to the locals either. Spaceport Gail had to move on to its next assignment once repairs were done. And the schizophrenic behavior at Earth headquarters guaranteed no help would come from that quarter.

Reemer surprised everyone by looking up from the datapad he'd been doodling on in the corner and jumping into the debate.

"I've recently undertaken my own lucrative business." The Squinch threw back his cape and approached the table, wearing the oddest expression. "I've jotted down a number that I think you'll find more than sufficient to get things started." He laid the pad screen-side down and slid it toward the captain. "Based on projections from our first day of sales, you can expect that much and more every month. The amount could even grow by several percent." He continued at the captain's strangled cough. "I know it's generous, but I won't take no for an answer. Use any excess for a luxene outreach program."

The damned slug was being altruistic, but there was only so much demand for super-smelly adhesive.

"This is very…generous." Beal snorted again, struggling to not laugh. "I'm afraid we'll need several orders of magnitude more capital to start an independent mining company. But we sincerely appreciate your generosity."

Reemer's antennae drooped, but nods from around the room helped soften the blow. He perked up quickly, really quickly.

"Okey dokey then." Reemer scooped up his datapad and headed back to his corner.

They discussed finances for a while longer, but seemed to be out of options—until salvation came from an unexpected direction.

"I find myself in search of a new venture for House Gorsh." Xa grinned at Nancy's raised eyebrows. "My recently terminated employment was actually more of a hobby. Our family's holdings are quite extensive. I'm sure we could finance what is needed with reasonable terms."

"You've got to be kidding me." Nancy didn't know whether to laugh or cry. "More negotiations?"

* * *

With a common goal of getting out from under the consortium's collective thumb, they pounded out an agreement overnight. Facilitating a motivated group proved much simpler, and Nancy earned a tidy commission on future luxene shipments for her survivors' fund.

The ancient Vargans vowed to protect the whole operation against hostile takeover. Their flashes of information also helped develop revenue projections that Xa used to persuade his accountants back home. Even plain old luxene was still a valuable commodity. But with a social status falling somewhere between crown prince and prime minister of the second largest Packtonian province, Nancy doubted Xa needed much justification to seal the deal on his end.

Nancy parted ways with a heavy heart. She'd already said her goodbyes to the captain, Vargans, and others. Emmett's avatar donned his ceremonial garb and mounted his trusty cleaning steed to see them off.

"I think I'll miss you most of all." Nancy bent to give Emmett's screen an awkward air-hug.

"That's an old movie reference, isn't it?" The logistics manager was becoming quite the film buff.

"Paraphrased but heartfelt," Nancy said. "If there was a most-valuable-player award for the past few weeks, you'd be in the running. It's been a true pleasure getting to know you. I hope we meet again soon."

"Oh, we will," Ziggy promised. "So stay on top of your game, sidekick, and keep these biologics in line. I don't want to have to clean up your mess on our next visit." Ziggy gave the cleaning bot an affectionate bump with his torso.

"Oh, the feeling's mutual, chum." Emmet grinned and clonked him back, which earned a retaliatory jab in the chest.

A flurry of pokes, prods, and one-liners flew between the two. Exactly how much affection AIs could muster remained unclear, but Nancy got the distinct feeling these two would be misting up and bawling their eyes out if not for the juvenile poking fest.

"Okay, break it up." Reemer lifted his skirt, revealing the mouths beneath in clear warning. "Don't make me pull out the big guns. You're both sidekicks in my book. Damned good ones." He said that last bit under his breath while herding Ziggy aboard.

Emmett stood vigil by the airlock as they got underway, his club still raised in salute as the ship passed beyond the moon and Ziggy secured the docking monitors.

43. Up, up, and...

T HE DREADED CALL came in less than an hour after launch. Nancy had submitted her official report two days after the battle and was surprised it had taken Admiral Cheyung so long to respond. She answered from the bridge so that Ziggy could pull up any needed information.

"Dr. Nancy Dickenson, you are a sight for sore eyes." Olaf Branson's pale features were heavy with fatigue, but his smile was genuine. Better yet, the man was back at his desk instead of transmitting from a basement bunker.

"Olaf? I figured Admiral Cheyung would want to rip me a new one himself. Or is that coming next?"

"I doubt it." He gave a rueful smile. "It's been a real rollercoaster around here. Commander Horsh is AWOL and the admiral is wrapped up in fact finding sessions. There's some pretty heavy stuff going down. Be thankful you're out in space where there's room to breathe. My head's spinning with all the changes."

"You've seen my report." She grimaced. "It hasn't been a picnic here either. The Zula made a real mess of everything. I suspect she even had a hand in Ambassador

Turlic's disappearance, but we'll never know for sure. After all the nastiness, the locals decided to set up their own corporation. I secured the usual fee for my contributions, but no long-term shares for Earth."

She hadn't even asked for those. The modest interest for herself didn't come close to the twenty-percent stake Horsh had wanted her to push. It also hadn't been her place to disclose information about the ancient Vargans. Xa and the others would have to ensure mining didn't harm the collective consciousness and didn't need outside interference. Turlic's defection was a matter for the authorities, but she suspected the missing ambassador wouldn't be resurfacing anytime soon.

Turlic's notes made it clear that he understood what Farree was up to and the complicity within Earth Force. He'd covered his tracks with dummy travel papers. By the time security started searching for the man, he was already long gone. Emmett had dug beneath the false trails and traced Turlic's route to a distant transportation hub. The ambassador could be anywhere by now, but had done his best to avoid the disaster. Nancy wished him well.

"Discussing the Zula is my main reason for calling. I read your report before it got redacted. While I personally agree with your conclusions, the official position is that Zula were not involved. The file version of your report no longer mentions the elder race or Farree in particular."

"She was pulling the strings." Could they really sweep something this big under the rug? People had died! "The Packtonians will put Xi Mey on trial for her crimes, but Farree was at the center of it all. There's got to be a load of rotten apples in the mining consortium too."

"Good, insightful thoughts best kept to yourself." He leaned in and lowered his voice. "Nancy, I'm just the messenger here and speaking as a friend. Don't spread ideas about the Zula around, or the consortium for that matter. We're in the middle of a diplomatic minefield. Cheyung and others are advocating for the Zula, saying Farree was a rogue actor provoked by Vargan instability. They've tied their careers to an elder race we hardly ever hear about, let alone encounter. Something big is brewing, so just follow my lead and keep your head down. Okay?"

"It's not like I have anyone to tell." But the idea of censoring her report—rewriting history—made her sick.

"Good. I'll do my best to keep you updated. Right now, cooler heads are prevailing, but it's hard to tell which way the wind's blowing from one day to the next. Speaking of refreshing cold, that assignment to Cauthorn is still open if you want it."

"You've got to be kidding. The poets?"

"Literature knows no bounds." He grinned now that the unpleasant discussion about her report was behind them. "Rustic setting, intellectual stimulation, good commission—you could do worse."

"No cold!" Reemer shook the injured portion of his skirt at her; perhaps an unfair comparison, but he'd already lost his pound of flesh to the icy vacuum of space.

"I'm afraid I have to decline." She wasn't ready to launch back into anything at the moment. "If things are that tangled up back home, maybe I'll take time to get the ship checked out before committing to another job. Ziggy had a hell of a scare, so it's better to be safe."

She could use the down time to mull over Olaf's news. Resting her talent for a while might even help the pesky fluctuations settle out. Even though she'd been well compensated in the end, visiting Gail had definitely tipped her into the overworked category. Heck, the boys had been pushed hard too. They all deserved a vacation.

"Not a bad plan." Olaf nodded. "Keep in touch, and I'll do the same. When in doubt, use my private line."

They exchanged a few more pleasantries on headquarters' dime before ending the call. Olaf spoke amicably enough, but the situation clearly worried him. Their diplomatic branch tended to be political by nature. During her short tenure the office had avoided internal conflicts. At least, she'd thought they had. But then again, the current turmoil may have always been there simmering under the surface.

"Well, kids, I've got some business to catch up on." After the call, Reemer scooted away from the navigation table and headed for the door. "I'll eat in my room. Please respect the do-not-disturb sign."

The slug threw the cape off to one side and swept from the bridge. *Drama queen.* Nancy hoped his "business" included deep cleaning that super suit. He only needed an occasional mineral boost, but hadn't taken it off since their time in the ruins.

"How about you?" She asked Ziggy as they watched Reemer disappear into his stateroom. "Should I have the replicators make you a matching cape and mask?"

"No, I don't have the temperament." Ziggy shook his head. "The Squinch makes a better hero *and* detective. It's amazing how easily he settles into a role. Even Emmett did well. Who would have thought logistics could be turned into a superpower?

"Well, I would have been lost without your help, so thank you."

"You are quite welcome." He drummed the tabletop in thought. "Despite the danger, I've enjoyed our travels. The harder I try to ascertain what I want, the more elusive the answer gets."

"It's easy to overthink things."

Nancy should know, seeing as she was the queen of that particular pastime. Worrying over Farree's plot consumed her waking hours. Reemer's instincts had been spot on from the very beginning. Farree had tried to kill her; Ziggy's analysis confirmed it. The deadly anomaly that had attacked her ship was under conscious control, same as the psycho morphs they'd found draining luxene beneath the temple. The horde of wispy vampires had melted away with Farree's defeat. But who could say the anomaly or worse wouldn't show up again?

Nancy had been targeted before setting foot on Gail, back when only her chain of command should have known her destination. Farree probably accessed the flight plan through Admiral Cheyung or leveraged the Lobstra consulate contacts mentioned in Turlic's journal. But why? And what if some other Zula had sent the anomaly? Not knowing what had happened to Farree's ship was bad enough. The thought of another vampiric elder wanting her dead brought icy shivers and sent her thoughts spiraling into an abyss.

"So what's next for you?" Ziggy's question pulled her from the dark. The big, red question mark flashing between his eyes looked so outrageous that she actually laughed.

The question helped Nancy focus on something other than daggers from the shadows. Securing a reliable revenue stream for the survivors' foundation had left her feeling adrift. Decisions no longer needed to be income-driven. Nancy was more or less free to do whatever she wanted, which put her in very much the same boat as her ship's digital personality.

"I still want to help people." If it was just about the money, she could team up with Reemer and cash in on Fred's natural resources. That would put her name back into circulation with the scientific community too. But the all-consuming drive to churn out botanical discoveries had shifted during her time on the Squinch homeworld. "This ability the Lokii gave me needs to be—I don't know—used? It's hard to explain, but I want to share what I have." Except the talent was currently broken and unreliable. "But now instead of helping me comprehend people, there's too much. I see what people *might* say and do instead of just understanding them."

"Like with Farree," Ziggy said. "You saw courses of action the Zula was likely to take. That seems like an extremely useful ability."

"It's mind-numbing. I need to get myself under control before we take on anything else."

"Perhaps those who provided the gift could advise you," Ziggy said. "The Lokii would make the best mentors."

"That might be something to pursue after Quen gives you a clean bill of health."

As a nomadic race, the Lokii would be difficult to track down. The telepaths were known to visit planet Fred every few years. If they'd stopped by during the recent bloom, the Squinch or Dolor might know where to start looking.

"Mother will be happy to see us." Ziggy fully supported the idea of visiting the tender.

A thorough inspection of the ship and systems would put Nancy's mind at ease. Ziggy had found a tracker planted in the navigation system—presumably around the time of the poisoned tea incident. The miniscule device didn't match Packtonian, Lobstra, or any other known technology. Nancy wanted experts to comb every inch of the ship to ensure there weren't any other nasty surprises.

The pair chatted for a while longer about hopes, dreams, and life in general. Easing up on his frantic search for meaning left the AI subdued and introspective, which wasn't necessarily a bad thing. Sometimes looking inward was the surest way to make sense of the world without.

"Incoming transmission from planet Fred," Ziggy's voice sang from the main panel, making Nancy do a double take at the mobile unit next to her. "It's a business call. They're asking for Reemer."

Mating season must be over if the workforce was back in the warehouse.

"Put it through to his cabin so we don't disturb his majesty."

Epilogue

W ITH THE CABIN door safely locked, Reemer eased open his hidden pouch and removed its contents.

"There you go." He gently sat the three little beauties into the light box by his bed. The baby cacti travelled well, but needed to dry out and absorb some sun after riding inside all day. "Don't worry, little ones. I'll find you each a nice home where you can grow big and meet lots of interesting people."

He fussed over his charges, straightening proto-spines and dabbing away bits of mucus. Gail was a hub that offered opportunity to place the plants with caring homes. Their mother, Becky, had watched events unfold through the Dolor cactus he'd planted by the ruins and wanted another down on Vargus. A nice couple with a farm outside the Republic's capital promised to take care of that.

Reemer had placed six of the little buggers so far, including one he'd given his sexy worm-woman as a bittersweet parting gift. She'd be wiggling her cute, slimy self home at the end of her current duty rotation and promised to guard the plant with her life. Becky had to approve that one to ensure her baby would be safe and grow properly in the intoxicating ammonia atmosphere.

Speaking through these cuties made for a surreal experience very different from using manmade communicators. The sensations and images that flowed between the Dolor queen and her offspring resembled those he'd felt in the starry pools on the Vargan moon, but with none of the scary confusion thanks to Becky's warm presence. Communications would continue to get stronger and clearer as the babies grew.

Reemer hummed a childhood melody as he piled sand from Fred around the base of each cactus. Hopefully the taste of home made up for being out all day. The words to the tune tickled his memory, but refused to come thanks to his personal panel deciding to beep at him.

"What now?" He scooted to the terminal.

Technology still carried a steep learning curve, but the incoming transmission source code looked familiar. It came from home, the unique prefix originating at the warehouse instead of the communication shack Nancy's people had left. He accepted the call, expecting Churl or another lead to pop up on the display. Instead, Reemer found himself staring at a truly hideous creature, his business partner.

Humans were in the running for the ugliest race, with just one mouth, sunken eyes, and knobby elbows and knees. But the guy on the screen was even more disgusting—many times over. Sharp, bony plates rose like fan coral from the crown of his elongated head to run down across wide shoulders and square back. Spikes jutted from every conceivable joint, of which there were plenty. Reemer figured the equally ugly attitude might stem from the fact that these creatures couldn't possibly hug without puncturing each other. He'd often wondered how they managed to reproduce—and why.

At least the warehouse was busy. Squinch behind Dakmar hunched low over their stations, keeping perfectly still to avoid notice. *Smart.* They didn't need any incidents.

The Champkins had showed up years back, shortly after the humans departed. They'd wooed his parents and fellow Squinch with trinkets and mirrors, but Reemer knew the aliens were bad news.

The only reason he'd entered into business with such a disagreeable race was to keep his naïve brethren from getting duped into giving away Fred's riches. Well, that and it was the fastest way to push his backwater society forward before the rest of the universe bowled them over.

In just a few short years, Reemer had gained access to technology capable of revolutionizing Squinch society. His super suit was just one example. As business boomed, he'd be able to start building a future that would someday see slugs in space—that is, slugs besides him and with their own ships and stuff. In the meantime, he'd have to deal with the riffraff.

Dakmar scowled his dastardly scowl without blinking or moving a muscle. Reemer refused to be intimidated, eyestalks straining toward the screen, giving as good as he got. Time stretched on, his eyes burning as mucus crusted over at the corners. Man, this guy was good.

"What do you want, Dakmar? I'm busy, see?"

Reemer went for gangster slang, changing the game to put his opponent on the defensive. *Check.* The guy still didn't flinch. Was he even breathing? And what was that funny symbol on the bottom of the screen?

Oh, right. A recorded message.

At least he wouldn't have to make small talk. Reemer hit play.

"One of our chambers is missing, slimeball. If you have it, bring it back. If you don't, we're coming for you."

Menacing and succinct as usual, and not even accurate. Reemer wasn't ball-shaped at all. He was more of a svelte wave of handsomeness. A few deft button-presses and swipes saved the message for future reference. It was important to keep good records.

"Just try to find me." Reemer petted his cape, the super cape of a superhero that slid sideways to expose his missing slice of skirt—a reminder to stay humble.

Still, he was his own slug now with his own ship. Correction, with Nancy's own ship. But still, Fred was a long, long way away, so a problem for another day.

He smiled at how that had rhymed and turned back to his tender little plants. Too much time with Nancy made him uncertain if the sentiment rhymed in Squinch too. Either way, the cadence nudged a memory.

He went back to humming and cooing to his charges— letting them know they were loved and soaking in the soft babble of nonsense vibrations flowing from each in return. Gurgles, burps, and gasps joined the melody as the words to Mother's song came back to him.

Shifting tides sweep to and fro,
Darkness lurking far below,
Should it find you, call out loud,
Mama's coming, strong and proud,
To bring you back to waters blue. So, darlings, have no fear,
The evil dwellers of the deep shall feel her hunting spear.

More nuzzles and a pinch of assurance had the little ones dry and ready.

"Off to sleep now, my darlings."

Reemer scooped up the plants and unlatched a side panel on his big steamer trunk to expose the clear chamber within. He deactivated the machine, lifted the lid, and carefully nestled the trio in with their sleeping siblings. Reactivating the controls stilled the telltale ripples under their skin and raised gooseflesh at the memory of how strange napping in there had felt.

Just a few days out and the three had grown noticeably bigger. Reemer tapped on the window, but nothing stirred. Even the swirling dust motes had frozen mid-flight. Good, the no-time box still worked its magic.

~

Consider sharing your thoughts!

I'd be eternally grateful if you'd share your opinion of *Spaceport Gail* or any other books on my Amazon author page at
https://amazon.com/author/steinjim
Just a sentence or two with your impressions only takes a minute and is super helpful to new authors. – Jim

… And from the depths of space, galactic heralds spread word of his deeds so that every being upon every world might know of his arrival.

About the Author

Jim Stein has a half-century of experience reading science fiction and fantasy. Don't ask him to name his favorite or even first read. There is no single answer. And honestly, who can remember back that far?

With degrees in computer science and decades in the US Navy, Jim's taken up the gauntlet of transporting readers to extraordinary realms. His speculative fiction pits protagonists with strong moral fiber against supernatural elements or quirky aliens. When not chronicling musical spellcasters in his Legends Walk series or talking slugs from his Space Slime novels, you might find him kayak fishing, tweaking old pinball machines, or getting the motorhome ready for winter in sunnier climes.

Jim lives in northwestern Pennsylvania with his wife Claudia and the memory of his muse Marley, the Greatest of Danes.

Want more?

Visit https://JimSteinBooks.com/subscribe to get a free eBook and sign up for Jim's mostly-monthly newsletter filled with writerly updates, deals, and freebies.